Behind the Private Eye

-The Private Investigator's Secrets-

Surveillance tales and techniques

by

Chris Cooper

For my wife Alison

First published 2005
Revised edition published 2006

ISBN 0-9757568-0-X

PO Box 6131 Port Macquarie NSW 2444

THANKS

Thanks to Kym Weatherley for her keen editor's eye, my wife Alison for the laborious proofreading, Michael Hessenthaler for his graphics and promotion, Ben McDonald for his binoculars photo, Giselle Mawer for detailed advice on content and format, and David Tottle for encouraging me to both start and finish this project. Thanks also to all the PI's I've worked with over the years who shared in some very strange and amusing cases!

PUBLICITY

Word of mouth is the best advertising. Who may like this book? Tell them to visit www.neomatrix.com.au/books

Found spelling errors or other mistakes in this book? Got a great PI technique to include? Want to offer a book review? Send feedback or suggestions to books@neomatrix.com.au. Contributors may be listed by name in re-print editions.

DISCLAIMER

This book contains investigative techniques. It is also designed to provide a light-hearted inside look into what goes on in the world of the PI. Some techniques described here may be regarded as controversial, but all are legal in some circumstances or some areas. The nature of investigations is so diverse that it is not possible to provide definitive answers to issues of legality in all cases. Common sense should always prevail, and the reader should take this material as a guide to augment their own knowledge and research. Remember that a PI licence confers no special powers. Each situation is different, and no responsibility can be taken for the actions of persons relying on, or encouraged by the material contained within. The reader is urged to ensure their actions are always safe, and within the laws applicable to their area. You have been warned!

This page was left intentionally blank, but with some hidden text for observant readers to find. You passed the observation test!

You are about to learn some
real PI techniques, and
read about *real* PI cases

Some names and details
have been changed
for privacy reasons

CONTENTS

PREFACE

This book was written as a training resource for anybody or organisation involved in surveillance investigations and fraud detection, in both government and private enterprise, including:

- APS – Australian Protective Service officers   www.aps.gov.au
- ASIO – Australian Security Intelligence Organisation   www.asio.gov.au
- ASIS – Australian Secret Intelligence Service   www.asis.gov.au
- Customs officers   www.customs.gov.au
- DSD – Defence Signals Directorate   www.dsd.gov.au
- Debt collectors, Mercantile agents, Process servers   www.imal.com.au
- Environmental protection officers   www.environment.nsw.gov.au
- Fisheries compliance officers (seafood industry)   www.afma.gov.au
- Independent Commission Against Corruption   www.icac.nsw.gov.au
- Immigration officers   www.immi.gov.au
- Investigative Journalists   www.alliance.org.au
- Lawyers, Solicitors (Family law, injury)   www.familylawsection.org.au
- Paparazzi photographers   www.aipp.com.au
- Parks and wildlife officers   www.nationalparks.nsw.gov.au
- Private Investigators   www.aipd.com.au & www.aipi.asn.au
- Police officers   www.afp.gov.au
- Quarantine inspectors   www.affa.gov.au

This book is not a theoretical step-by-step procedural manual, because that's not what it takes to carry out professional investigations and surveillance. The skills cannot be learned by rote. Just like the Karate professional, the best resource is a state of mind, which transcends mere knowledge and techniques. It's all about developing a sixth sense, knowing the odds and making a call; and allowing the most subtle influence to shape your behaviour. It's being in tune with your environment, seeing what others don't see, doing what others don't expect. It's lateral thinking, resourcefulness and working with the barest scrap of information, and amplifying it into meaningful, verifiable evidence.

Like some other training books, this one discusses important legal, ethical and practical aspects of surveillance and investigation work and provides 'behind the scenes' techniques. The difference is that it interweaves this discussion and practical tips with real life case studies, offering a first hand account of a how a real PI both thinks and operates – the challenges, frustrations, thrills, dangers and hard learnt lessons.

As well as being a 'good read' in its own right for anyone wanting to develop their skills in this area, the book will be of benefit to trainers of professional investigators as they can use the case studies to help their students reflect on what can and does happen in the real world. These 'warts and all' stories show the successes as well as times where things didn't quite go to plan! They also illustrate the sort of skills, techniques and resourcefulness that a professional PI needs to do their job well in what are often inherently unpredictable and complex situations.

The book addresses a deficit in training resources for many nationally recognised surveillance courses, including the Asset Security training package, several others such as fisheries compliance in the seafood industry and covert government courses relating to public safety issues. Information about supported training courses is on page 542.

I became a PI for no other reason than it seemed a good idea at the time. I never really yearned to do it, and rather 'drifted' into the industry as opposed to making a well-planned decision. Being young, I figured that being paid to sneak around spying on people seemed a good idea. It was different. My mother always dreamed I would become a stable corporate worker doing nine-to-five in an office, shuffling paperwork for a bank or some other stifling institution. My mother still dreams.

I eventually discovered the investigation industry is very different to the way it is depicted in the movies. The cases are often bland, the technology is very different from the James Bond issued gadgets, and there is an awful lot of waiting involved. It is a game of patience.

There is no room for fidgeting, no room for the ordered soul who needs to have structure in their working day. It is a game for the gambler who uses experience to better their odds. It is also a game for the chess player, considering strategy, predicting the move of your opponent. It is a psychological game full of fast driving, high-tech cameras and thinking on your feet. A game that can involve getting up at four a.m. to start a job, then spending the day dripping in sweat for hours and having to urinate into a bottle. It can be coming home at the end of a day with nothing to show for it.

It is wild and wacky, it is flexible and it is fun. It is very different, and there is no career that is quite like it in any way. It takes a certain type of personality to master the game. Anybody can do it, yet few can do it well. It's far more a talent for using your sixth sense than a skill you can learn. There is no right and wrong, and apart from some basics, no classroom or textbook can truly teach how any job should be played. It comes down to your call, in the moment. It is a game of chance, and if you're good you can beat the odds, and that's a feeling which money can't buy.

For my own business I'd written some staff training documents, and have always approved of professional development, but found very limited resources available for specialised, quality training. I had employed staff through the government's apprenticeship scheme, and sent staff on investigation training courses through Charles Sturt University, but there was never any coal-face training texts to show a surveillance investigator how to do their job.

I found most investigator training books were detached from reality, or were more at the Frank Monte[1] end of fanciful writing. Furthermore, most of these were focused on factual investigations rather than surveillance, with very little Australian content.

I was approached by a former PI, Mr David Tottle, who knew I was an experienced surveillance agent. He asked if I had any company training material, which could be used in a PI training video he was producing. After some discussion I sent him the training manual I'd written several years previously, and he soon encouraged me to publish it as a book in its own right. I was pleased with his enthusiasm, happy to share my knowledge with others, and vowed to try to raise the professional standards of investigators in Australia.

---

[1] Frank Monte is regarded as one of the industries more 'colourful' characters, known in the industry and media for operating somewhat questionably. He was exposed by an American current affairs show as being involved in an illegal bugging scam. He was also proved to have made some wild and false claims of being employed by fashion identity Gianni Versace, who was later murdered – (Sarah Crichton, 'Versace ready to go to the cleaners in a seven-figure suit' Sydney Morning Herald, 4/11/2002) and ('Versace suit set to cost 'memoir' author Monte $1m', Sydney Morning Herald, 30/4/2002). The author and associates have also been approached by persons claiming to have previously paid Mr Monte large sums of money, with no real work ever having been done. In one case this resulted in court action against Mr Monte.

PART 1

– BEFORE SURVEILLANCE –

CHAPTER 1: HISTORY OF PRIVATE INVESTIGATORS

The investigation industry is one of the oldest professions in society, spanning generations It's an industry that adapts to technological changes, and is continually evolving. Like another old profession, prostitution, the private investigation industry has often been regarded as unsavoury, evoking images of sleazy men in dimly lit rooms. Unaccountable and unprofessional people, who often worked alone selling you illegal information, and perhaps offering to 'make people disappear' as a side business. The industry has come a long way.

In the early days, the government appointed a police force to the colony, tasked with keeping law and order. People needed to defend themselves against false accusations, and although there were solicitors available, they often needed somebody to investigate matters. The lawyers were comfortable within the confines of the courtrooms or their legal tomes, but unwilling and unprepared to physically hit the streets looking for evidence, follow suspects or talk to potential witnesses. Thus the role of the investigator was born; A hired gun, investigating for a fee.

Investigators quickly found another ready market in the domestic arena, collating evidence about marital infidelity. In the early days, the law required evidence of infidelity in order to grant a divorce. No evidence meant no divorce. This resulted in investigators busting down bedroom doors to catch couples in the throes of an adulterous tryst – a sudden flash from the camera followed by a hurried escape, often while being pursued by an irate lover. This did nothing for the 'professional' image of investigators, simply reinforcing the impression of the lawless cowboy illegally gaining entry to homes and invading privacy. Fortunately the law was eventually changed during the 1970's to permit 'no fault' divorces, which effectively wiped out the majority of this unsavoury market. Admittedly there has been a slight resurgence due to the AIDS virus. Infidelity now means far more than hurt pride and lost trust, as it may in fact be fatal.

Up until 1990, with the boom in computer technology, the industry was awash with personal information being sold on a massive scale. The primary offenders were debt collectors and mercantile agents in general, who were using the information to find hiding debtors, and to locate recoverable assets. Private inquiry agents were also rampantly dealing in the trade, though to a far less extent. Despite the fact that the information was, in the majority of cases, used to assist in legal prosecutions and court approved recoveries of debts – it was illegal. The Independent Commission against Corruption (ICAC)[2] inquiry in 1992 was the biggest thing to hit the industry in decades. The ICAC investigated the unauthorised release of information from government and other databases. Many people were charged, including investigators, mercantile agents and government public servants. Numerous well-known corporations including banks and insurance companies were named as active recipients of this illegal information, using it for marketing, debt recovery and other purposes. The fallout from this inquiry is still being felt today, and the result was a rapid clean up of the industry.

The ICAC inquiry was regarded as a good thing for the industry as a whole, though there is a widely held belief that private information should be available to investigators for appropriate legal reasons. The only other governing influence on the industry has come in only recently, being the insurance companies themselves. Insurance companies have historically supplied the majority of investigation industries work, though this is changing with new legislation and other factors. Still stinging from the publicity stemming from the ICAC inquiry, and now subject to new legislation themselves, the insurers have raised the standards for their agents.

---

[2] Independent Commission Against Corruption www.icac.nsw.gov.au

Under the *General Insurance Code of Practice*[3], investigators are now legally considered representatives of the insurer. Should the agent break the law, the insurer is deemed to have done so as well, and is liable for the penalty – despite the agent being from a separate, contracted company. Insurers now require probity checks, a current investigator licence, education, work history, full insurance cover, criminal record checks and more. To be entitled to work for such high volume clients, investigators must jump through numerous hoops and prove they are reputable and ethical. Gone are the days of the 'fly-by-night' operators. These days you need to be solid and dependable, following and complying with the law in the course of doing business.

There are few industry bodies representing the industry. The oldest is the Institute of Mercantile Agents Limited (IMAL)[4], which as it's name suggests represents primarily 'Mercantile Agents'. These people handle repossessions, debt collections and legal process serving, though the IMA also represents investigators as well. In 1992 the Australian Institute of Private Detectives (AIPD)[5] was formed to represent the industry at a national level. They have prepared a draft bill which specifically caters to the industry, but the government has not yet expressed significant interest in new legislation. There is also The Australian Institute of Professional Investigators[6], which is similarly industry focused, though a little smaller and leaning slightly more towards the white-collar crime area of forensic accounting. Like many other industries with self-managed codes, like architects, it will take time to enable more formal legal recognition of the industry. The best way to achieve this would be for close cooperation between all these bodies, in order

---

[3] Insurance Council of Australia www.ica.com.au
[4] Institute of Mercantile Agents Limited www.imal.com.au
[5] Australian Institute of Private Detectives www.aipd.com.au
[6] Australian Institute of Professional Investigators www.aipi.asn.au

to provide a cohesive approach to organisational change. This is easier said than done. At least there are some forums for investigators to get together and discuss their industry or become more informed.

Government regulation of the industry has been patchy. There is no Federal Act covering the industry, and some states have been slow to implement legislation. Currently there are widely differing acts in various states covering investigators, with jurisdiction for the administration of them being held by different bodies. Some Acts refer to PI's as 'detectives', others refer to 'investigators'. Most refer to us as private inquiry agents – though this is not a term used widely in the industry. Some acts are administered by police, others by the courts, and others by various other government departments.

Generally, legislation covering private investigators is in place for the sole purpose of making agents accountable – providing the courts with a big stick to wield in the event of an investigator 'getting up to mischief'. Unfortunately the legislation often inappropriately bundles up investigators with security guards and debt collectors. It's likely that, in time, new legislation will be enacted which caters specifically to private investigation.

Contrary to popular belief, an investigators licence provides no extra powers or access to information than an ordinary citizen. The sole purpose of having a licence allows you to charge for investigative services. It is simply about accountability – do the wrong thing and you'll have your licence cancelled. As a reprimand this is ineffectual, particularly given that the vast majority of work requires no real evidence of the investigator actually possessing a valid licence. Unfortunately the law is slow to catch up with wrong doers, and few investigators have actually lost their licence. Part of the problem in the domestic market is that clients are usually unwilling to complain as it may result in their 'dirty linen' being hung out in public.

It is not a large industry, and while the government has many surveillance investigators within the police service, ASIO and other law enforcement bodies, the private sector is quite small. There are only about fifteen hundred[7] PI's really working within NSW, but there are approximately ten thousand[8] who actually hold a licence. The remainder may have left the industry, but are just as likely to enjoy the 'thrill' of being a licensed PI.

The majority of PI's are male, and yet female PI's are often less conspicuous than men, or more likely to get information out of people under pretext. Few would suspect a woman of being a sneaky PI, which is something they can use to their advantage. I encourage more females to join the industry as they bring new skills and abilities when investigating some tricky cases.

Accurate statistics are difficult to obtain in the shadowy world of private investigators, who rarely share or even compile statistics on their cases. Many working in the industry would agree however, that in the 1980's and 1990's that the majority of work was insurance based. This was due to an explosion in payouts being awarded, as well as a quickly growing industry of professional claimants draining funds from insurers through elaborate schemes and staged 'accidents'.

These fraudsters would think nothing of placing a stone in one of their shoes to ensure they limped for the benefit of anyone watching them, at least until they were awarded their payouts. In 2001 the NSW Carr government changed the law and required claimants to suffer a much larger injury proportion in order to be eligible for any compensation. Those with less than about a

---

[7] *'The Case of the Vanishing Private Eye'* by Mark Dapin Sydney Morning Herald, Good Weekend Magazine, May 29 2004, p34.
[8] *'The Role of Private Investigators & Commercial Agents in Law Enforcement'* by Tim Prenzler & Michael King, Australian Institute of Criminology, Trends & Issues in Crime & Criminal Justice No. 234, August 2002 www.aic.gov.au/publications/tandi/ti234.pdf

15% disablement were then unable to claim the large payouts and were forced to rely on a much smaller authorised scale of set payments. There has been a slight shift in the industry back to marital infidelity work, as the insurance work dries up. Life is often cyclical, so many expect the wheel will swing back in another decade or so.

According to the Federal Government's Australian Institute Of Criminology[9], insurance fraud amounts to 10% of all claims, which back in 1997 in the middle of the insurance scam heyday, was a staggering A$800 million. This is roughly $21 extra for every annual insurance premium paid by the public, just to cover the cost of this fraud. In 1999, Centrelink conducted a national tender for surveillance and investigative services, which resulted in them contracting 21 companies around Australia. In July 2000 there were 1063 cases finalised, from a total of 1446 which were originally outsourced to the private inquiry agencies. In all there was an estimated saving of over $8 million, with 747 of these cases resulting in some level of fraud or overpayment being identified. PI's were successful in saving a significant amount of money for the public purse, and they continue to achieve a cost benefit ratio of approximately one to five.[10]

Still, most of today's investigators are a new breed. The mission of getting the facts has not changed, but the playing field has. Access may be denied to many resources, such as vehicle registration records and the like, however there have been many new resources provided. Computers, the internet, mobile phones, high tech camera equipment, digital video on CD's and satellite tracking services can all be used to 'get the facts' in

---

[9] *'Insurance fraud'*, Australian Institute of Criminality, Trends & Issues in Crime & Criminal Justice, No. 66, February 1997
www.aic.gov.au/publications/tandi/ti66.pdf
[10] *'Enhanced Investigation Initiative'* Annual Report 1999-2000, Compliance Activity, Centrelink website, 2000
www.centrelink.gov.au/internet/internet.nsf/ar9900/appen9.htm

ways not even dreamed of a few years ago. The industry has come a long way from the days when we were known for our cheap shoes, bad haircuts and penchant for breaking down doors in the middle of the night. We have cleaned up our act. We now work as professionals!

Surveillance provides answers

Surveillance answers many questions. It can give peace of mind. Often people already suspect their partner is cheating, but feel they need proof for closure, to enable them to move on. Without it they feel trapped in their unhappy relationships. I rarely take on domestic work, and often counsel people that they should leave a relationship because they have lost trust in their partner. Losing trust is not remedied by evidence like a name and number, or a photo of a kiss at the door. Unfortunately, clients always seek proof, and often surveillance is the only tool that can provide these answers.

The corporate world[11] is another area in which surveillance answers questions that cannot be answered by other means. Watching and filming people commit crimes is a watertight form of evidence, which few would dispute in court. As the saying goes, the camera never lies. As the investigator, you are an unbiased observer, quietly documenting behaviour that others wouldn't normally detect. Often you may not know what you are looking for, but smallest observation could answer the needs. Surveillance is a tool, which can at times be surgical in its precision and which provides a very cost effective solution to expensive corporate problems.

---

[11] William Birnbauer, '*Companies turn to private sleuths*', The Age newspaper, 14/7/2003, www.theage.com.au

Community support

In spite of the benefits the surveillance operator can provide, they are generally not well supported by other professions or 'the system'. Insurance rorts are a common area for the investigator. Some claimants are professional defrauders, scheming hard to become a drain on society, receiving regular income from the insurance premiums paid by ordinary Australians. There are few ways to catch them, other than surveillance. Operatives must work within a tight set of restrictions that often work to protect the guilty. Society seems to accept higher insurance premiums over the simpler solution of empowering the investigation industry. Insurance companies spend thousands to discover information about a subject's undisclosed employment by using private investigators to follow them to work.

It's frustrating to know the Australian Taxation Department and several other institutions including banks usually have this information already in their electronic records, but won't release it to private investigators or even the police in many cases. PI's cannot obtain a subpoena even if the matter is before the courts, due to an extreme emphasis on our personal privacy. Even a basic search, such as identifying the listed owner of a vehicle, is not available to investigators, despite the possibility that the owner of the car is defrauding the public of thousands of dollars. If the PI is seeking an important witness in a court case where other leads have gone cold, they are denied the most useful, practical and economical means of obtaining information.

Regulatory framework

PI's have no access to information or resources that police find indispensable when investigating fraud, yet the police only have the resources to undertake the largest cases, hence the majority of fraud being investigated by PI's without adequate resources. Privacy is always an issue, but police officers already have their computer access monitored closely, and there is little reason why private investigators could not be legislated to have limited access to such databases for authorised lawful purposes. Any use could be similarly monitored with heavy penalties attached to inappropriate use. Having access to information such as vehicle registration may help solve a case quickly before the huge cost of fraud mounts.

Restricting information isn't in the Police Service's best interest. The police don't have the resources to investigate all cases themselves, yet these crimes cost the public millions. PIs needs to be properly acknowledged as significant in the process of stopping these frauds, and resourced accordingly[12]. When the public is able to make the connection between lower insurance premiums and the role of investigators, we may see a rise in support, and industry bodies are important part of the process.

In some ways, restrictions have made for better investigators. The difficulties provide a very strong pressure on agents to be clever and think laterally in solving a case. You have to work very hard to maximise the little you have to work with; to take the smallest, subtle clue and grab it, massage it into shape, then use this as a key to unlock answers and solve the case.

Legislation trends

The following is specific to New South Wales, however there is a similar situation in other Australian states. In 2005 the New South Wales legislation covering PI's was released, replacing the older 1963 Act. The new Act moves licensing to the responsibility of the New South Wales police, and tightens the responsibility of the industry in terms of accountability and

---

[12] *'Investigators want access to information', AAP,* Sydney Morning Herald, 21/8/2002
www.smh.com.au/articles/2002/08/21/1029114125431.html

training requirements. Part of the changes seem related to concerns of over-enthusiastic debt collectors, which are often 'legislatively' part of the investigation industry, despite the fact they operate in a virtually unrelated area. Following are some excerpts about industry response to the new legislation:

- Disappointing the proposed legislative review fails to heed unanimous agreement from the consulted industry stakeholders on many issues relevant to bring legislation into focus with the realities of the modern industry[13]

- It is essential for commercial interests and for the public that the Industry has the same access to information in government departments and the private commercial areas as the police have. This will assist in assuring that the commercial industry and the general public have the benefit of the ruling of the High Court of Australia so that everybody will be equal before the law as the High Court has ruled in the Kable Legislation in September 1996[14]

- Private detectives have launched a stinging attack on the NSW Government's legislation handing control of the private investigations industry to the NSW police... Mr John Bracey said the 1992 report by the Independent Commission Against Corruption stated categorically that the police should not have any role in overseeing private investigators[15]

---

[13] Institute of Mercantile Agents Limited www.imal.com.au, Review of Commercial Agents & Private Inquiry Agents bill, December 2003, (p8)
[14] The Hon. Arthur Chesterfield-Evans reciting material from the AIPD in Parliament on 21/09/2004 during debate about the recent legislation: www.parliament.nsw.gov.au
[15] *'PI fury at bill to give control to police'* The Sun Herald 15/08/2004 by Alex Mitchell
www.smh.com.au/articles/2004/08/14/1092340534700.html

CHAPTER 2: SURVEILLANCE DEFINED

The Oxford dictionary defines surveillance as *'Close observation of a person or group, especially one under suspicion'*. While technically correct, this limited definition barely touches on the real art of surveillance, as known to those experienced professionals of this unique field. Observation itself is easy, but a professional will know when should one observe, how to best observe without detection, what tools to employ, how to legally document observations and more. The surveillance professional is a multi-faceted individual who understands human behaviour, and who can anticipate the future and answer questions like *What direction will they leave...will they drive or walk?* The professional will be comfortable entering strange buildings while tailing on foot, be ready with a cover story if approached, be able to operate camera equipment in the blink of an eye, and drive like a demon, yet remain undetected, and be ready, always ready for the unexpected!

Surveillance is a game of probability, and no operative knows where they will end up, or what they may be doing. While the bankers and the accountants shuffle off to work each day, they know that they will finish at the same work address, at the same clockwork time each day. Occasionally they have to work back an hour, which can 'throw a spanner' into their otherwise ordered lives. The surveillance professional however, starts work knowing his day may finish within the first five minutes. He may arrive to find a car missing from the carport, or a For Sale sign and a vacant house.

David Bannantyne formerly ran the Australian arm of Control Risks[16], and once told me a story of the longest surveillance car follow he had ever had. In the late 1980's he was working for a

---

[16] www.crg.com

company called Websters. Surveillance was being conducted on a family man. Unbeknownst to David, the family had planned a holiday, and had planned to leave that very day. The family filled up with petrol and began driving. Fortunately David had also filled up his surveillance vehicle, as the family continued to drive and drive. After several hours it was clear they were intending on a very long drive to get to their destination. Websters then arranged for additional surveillance agents to meet the team at the NSW state border, where they booked into a hotel for the night alongside the family under surveillance.

The next morning they continued travelling, finally reaching South Australia after travelling right through Victoria. In total, the subject was followed through three Australian states, over several days, which I'm sure, must have been a record, and probably is still today. In fact this type of follow is reasonably easy with long straight roads with few choices or traffic lights, but it is still an exercise in endurance. Surveillance is often unpredictable, and you need to be ready for surprises. This in itself is what motivates many in this game. It's the thrill of the chase, the unpredictable nature, the planning, thinking on your feet and calling a fellow agent late at night to say 'Crikey mate, you would never believe where I ended up today!'

Two people can observe the same event. The untrained eye will see nothing, while the surveillance professional will observe enough to write a novel. Consider the simple scenario of watching a person walking into a house. One could document the arrival with a single line, such as '11:00am A male arrived at the address'. This does not convey much. A professional will see the same event very differently, and write: 'A male of Caucasian appearance aged approximately 35 years was observed walking from a northerly direction towards the target residence. He was approximately 5'10" tall, medium build with short, brown, curly hair. He was wearing blue jeans and a grey jumper, and was seen carrying a full shopping bag in his left *hand. He approached the address with familiarity, entering the home without knocking'*

The same event is recorded very differently. Note the mention of description, address, familiarity and direction of approach - these are important points. The item he was carrying tells us a story, and further supports our feeling he is a resident of the address as opposed to just a relative (who may enter without knocking but is unlikely to go grocery shopping for this address). The second statement provides a detailed picture of the event, which will enable a more clear understanding of (a) what is occurring, and then (b) what MAY occur next. Understanding who is associated with an address and why they are there is a big part of any investigation, and these subtle cues are often all you'll get to help put the pieces of the puzzle together.

It is easy to see something but observe nothing, and surveillance is a hard job to do well. The professional will solve the case by consistently seeing more than others would, and this is the real skill. Maximising the information gathered on a case, by exploiting every angle to its full advantage. By seeing and understanding detail, one can gather more information, as well as predict future events. Anticipation is important, because it enables the investigator to be <u>ready</u> to capture the event on film, or respond appropriately - perhaps alerting other investigators on the job, or starting the vehicle in anticipation of a follow. If you see a person walking inside a home with a slight urgency in their step, you can expect they will possibly emerge in a hurry, darting out again moments later. By noticing the ever so slight increase in the speed of their gait, you know to be on a heightened state of readiness for an imminent move.

As well as PI's, surveillance is carried out by a wide range of government departments. This is not just land-based activities either, as there are some extremely difficult and niche areas where surveillance is key. The seafood industry is one such area, where fisheries compliance officers conduct surveillance from cliff tops, from boats and helicopters. One area is the detection of illegal abalone poaching which is a multi-million dollar enterprise. These criminals often work in well organised gangs and have elaborate schemes to avoid being detected. This includes hidden compartments, infra-red goggles, helicopters, tracking equipment and undercover spies to monitor the activities of the government surveillance activities. It is not a widely known industry, but worthy of a Hollywood movie. Australian officials[17] are on the case conducting surveillance every day of the year. They do have success, and when these cases go to court it is a real eye opener. One case recently had a poacher's premises raided where it was discovered he had over $750,000 in illegal abalone on the premises at the time. These guys are no small time fishermen, and intensive surveillance is the only thing keeping these criminals in check.

The Law: Surveillance

The law does not 'prohibit' surveillance. There is no *general* right to privacy from observations. An agent sitting in a car outside a home watching others and video recording or photographing their activities is not committing an offence, even if the subject is on their own private land[18]. In fact any citizen may conduct surveillance, provided they do not charge for their services, as charging requires an investigators licence. Similarly there is no law to prohibit mobile surveillance where a subject is followed via foot, car or public transport.   There are some limited

---

[17] *'The Illegal Market in Australian Abalone'*, Rebecca Tailby & Frances Gant, Australian Institute of Criminology No. 255 April 2002 **ISBN** 0 642 24260 7
www.aic.gov.au/publications/tandi/ti225.pdf
[18] Victoria Park Racing & Recreation Grounds v. Taylor (1937) 58 CLR 497, Bathurst City Council v. Saban (1985) 2 NSWLR 704

exceptions to this, such as the NSW Workplace Surveillance Act, which prohibits an employer from conducting covert surveillance on employees without a court issued warrant.

Even when applied, these laws are designed primarily to prevent unnecessary workplace surveillance rather than hamper specific legitimate investigations where there is already clear indication of a problem. A recent example involves the company Tetra Pack, who was unimpressed about the high amount of sick days a worker was taking, and had evidence to suggest he was flouting the sick day provisions. They hired a PI to tail the worker around and observed him drinking in the pub with his mates and apparently working casually while he was supposed to be off sick. After sacking the worker, he sued them for unfair dismissal. It was later argued in court by the defence that the surveillance contravened the Workplace Surveillance Act. The Attorney General's department disagreed, stating this law was not designed to prevent the practice (surveillance), but only to regulate surveillance in the workplace.[19]

Despite this, there are always many general laws that may be applied to surveillance activities, and agents should always act professionally and not make a nuisance of themselves. Courts may find agents guilty of harassment or stalking[20], or causing public nuisance if their conduct is extreme, or unwarranted. There is so much legislation that provides courts with total discretion to find an offence committed, merely by a person being disorderly or creating a disturbance[21]. Even though their

---

[19] *'Firm kept suspicious eye on sick leave worker's health'* by Nick O'Malley, Sydney Morning Herald 14/5/2005

[20] For example the VIC Crimes Act 1958 - Sect 21a *'Stalking'* carries a penalty of up to 10 years imprisonment

[21] QLD Transport Infrastructure (Ports) Regulation 1994 - Sect 37 *'Conduct causing public nuisance'*. A person must not, in a port authority's port area, be disorderly or create a disturbance.

conduct may not be breaking any specific law, agents must ensure their surveillance activities are not disturbing the peace else they may be charged under these general clauses. Having a criminal record usually prevents an agent from having an investigators licence, so it is important to exercise caution when conducting surveillance.

Rehearsal – Preparation and predictions

Rehearsal is important in any profession, and the untrained agent will rarely practice their intended 'moves'. A good player will spend time rehearsing every possible likely scenario, to maximise the chance of success. Rehearsal is required for every step of the case, and a good agent may rehearse their conversation prior to contacting a subject under pretext. An agent may review their street directory, analysing the possible movement, the likely movement routes, the location of nearby facilities such as shops and schools. Even just marking the right page with a Post-It note can be the key to a great surveillance result versus a wasted days work.

Preparation and practice of camera techniques is important. Given the excellent opportunity of your subject appearing briefly at the door of his mistress' home, the poor operator will frantically reach for his camera, then discover he has a slight technical problem requiring a few seconds to correct. Perhaps the focus is set to the wrong distance, or the lens cap is still on. A professional will be patient and calm, camera nestled in the palm of their hand, finger lightly on the power switch and the focus set. The professional will have rehearsed the action of switching on the camera. He will have rehearsed the recording and already discovered that the daylight saving time needed adjustment, or that the tape was not cued or was missing. He will have rehearsed the physical action of lifting the camera up to take the shot, and will have discovered that he needed to move position slightly to remove the telegraph pole from blocking the shot. Mentally he has prepared for the possible actions that may occur, and his response to them. What should he do if a car leaves and he can't identify the driver? If they leave on foot, will he follow in the car? And so on.

Surveillance is often a process of waiting long hours, punctuated with brief moments of activity that can solve the case if captured properly. A common example is the transition from house to car. Nobody can tell when the event will occur as the first you will usually see, is somebody walking to their car. The process of entering the car and disappearing out of view takes just seconds. The process of swivelling into a seat or standing up from the seat of a car is often a very telling sign of the degree of back injury if the surveillance is an insurance matter. A good agent will be ready to capture this momentary event, knowing that if they waste a few seconds, then they needn't bother as the opportunity will evaporate, just as quickly as it arrived.

Surveillance is the art of gathering intelligence by observation. It need not be necessarily 'close', as persons can be observed from a remote tracking centre, watching the movement of their car from some distance away. At other times the watcher is very close indeed, standing beside the subject in a lift, quietly noting details typed on the page they are holding as they proceed to their confidential meeting. Observation does not just include where a person or vehicle went, but many more factors such as HOW did the event occur. People can 'arrive' in a multitude of ways, from various directions, walking or driving. How did they 'look'? Were they distracted or relaxed, hurried or dawdling? These are all pieces in the puzzle.

Surveillance sometimes has a clear purpose. *'See if my employee is visiting the competition at lunchtime!'* is one example. At other times the aim is to ascertain what there may be to see, with surveillance conducted because it is suspected there is something fishy going on, and more information is needed to make a better assessment of the situation.

The next time you head off to your routine job like clockwork, spare a thought for the surveillance professionals whose lives are dependant on the roll of the dice. *Will I be home tonight? Not sure, perhaps I will be driving interstate. What will I be doing today? Perhaps I will need to adopt the persona of a courier or an office worker. Perhaps I will spend the entire day in the car for nothing, or perhaps I will end up following someone to their work just moments after I arrive.* Nothing is fixed, nothing is known, and the surveillance professional must be ready for anything, which is the name of the game. Playing your cards right, so that you find out the facts with a minimum of resources, and with the odds always stacked against you. It takes a special kind of person to get it right, to get the results, and for them the lure of the game is irresistible. Nobody cares if you 'lost them at lights'. Nobody cares if you missed the great shot. Nothing matters but the evidence – did you get it on tape? Can you identify their face clearly? Did you get a follow to the work address? Were you compromised? Turning up and doing your best is not always enough, because surveillance is a tough game, and there are no prizes for second place.

The case of non-kosher meat

Key learning points

- Static surveillance and parking considerations

- Why are things seen?

- Camera techniques

I circled the block once again. Surely there was a parking spot somewhere with a view of the butcher's shop. It was almost on a corner but there didn't seem to be a position where I could see the front door and driveway at the same time. This was now my third lap. There were some good observation positions, but there was no parking allowed in these spots. No legal parking anyway. I looked enviously at the small, empty strip of road near the street corner, clearly marked 'BUS ZONE'. It had a perfect view of the butcher's shop across the road. *'How often do buses use these zones anyway?'* I wondered as I pulled into the curb. I stopped the car and sat for a moment.

Shards of early morning sunlight licked the building opposite, causing the roof to glow warmly. It was just after seven o'clock, and only the nearby newsagency was open. I stepped out to buy a Sydney Morning Herald newspaper and several bottles of drink. It looked like it was going to be a warm day. I was quite young at the time, and this was one of my first real surveillance jobs so I was still feeling quite inexperienced. Back in the car, I folded out screens to cover the rear windows, settling into the back seat of the Holden Barina to watch. I regularly borrowed this car from my girlfriend Cathy, because my motor bike had been stolen several months earlier. A fire engine red hatchback wasn't the most subtle vehicle for covert surveillance, but we often have to make do with what we have!

A guy wearing a Jewish skullcap, walked towards the shop carrying a small bag and keys. Several pages of the *Herald* newspaper went flying through the air as I scrabbled for my camera. I wasn't expecting the first worker to arrive so early, and only just got some footage of him before he disappeared inside. I kept the camera trained on the doorway for almost a minute afterwards, thinking he may step out again. I figured he might come out to place an advertising board on the footpath, adjust a window awning or carry out some other task to open up the shop. The door remained closed and I relaxed my grip, carefully lowering the camera back to the seat. I didn't get a full-face shot but did get a good side and rear profile. It didn't matter, so long as he could be identified. Had I been a paparazzi photographer taking shots of a superstar, I'd have my foot hovering near the steering wheel while holding the camera, waiting for just the right moment to step on the air horn, letting it erupt from the bonnet. I'd get a good facial shot as he turned to look, but sounding the horn would of course give my position away. I intended to stay concealed while filming any of the staff who were working at this butcher's shop.

The phone call had come two days previously. '*Chris. Hello, it's Peter calling. Listen I have a rather sensitive job, and I was hoping you could come over and discuss it. Are you available over the next couple of days?*' It sounded out of the ordinary, and I agreed without hesitation. I had been contracting to Peter's company among others, for several years but Peter rarely had 'interesting' investigations. Most were factual such as locating small debtors, serving court processes or investigating stolen cars. This was the first real 'surveillance' job he had to offer. Peter was Jewish. He looked Jewish, was heavily involved with Jewish organisations, and a large proportion of his work was supplied through his various Jewish contacts. I listened as he outlined the current situation. The Jewish High Council had very recently received a most disturbing telephone call. Because of the call, they wanted an immediate investigation launched. As Peter said himself, the very souls of their members were at stake!

The butcher's shop to be put under investigation was Jewish, selling only kosher meats. The Orthodox Jews are regarded by some as strict and conservative. Men must wear head covering (known as a Kippah), and Jews regularly attend synagogues for worship. During certain religious periods, they are not allowed to dial a telephone or turn on an electric light because this is regarded as 'work'. They are very specific as to what can and can't be eaten, when consuming food is allowed, and when one must fast. They have very strong feelings about their faith, and such rules are not regarded as just tradition, but rather God's law. My own opinion of God's law is simpler as I believe we are here to live, and love others, rather than focus on such detailed rules. Still, I have always lived in a fairly tolerant way and mused 'each to their own'

Such a strong, strict culture does have advantages such as close family ties, a supportive environment and marginally lower crime rates. As with many cultures and religions, they stick together as a community. There is a tendency to buy goods from their own, they marry their own and work for their own. They like to remain clean and pure, associating with other Jews to keep their faith strong. Unfortunately for this Bondi butchers' shop, Tony the electrician wasn't Jewish. A simple tradesman, he was tasked with installing some new high temperature warning sensors on meat fridges. He had completed an installation on the fridges at the butcher's shop several weeks previously.

It was a simple procedure, which only took a couple of hours. He wasn't Jewish himself, and knew little of their culture. He did notice the prices for meat at the Jewish butchers' were quite noticeably more expensive than those at his local butcher's in

Parramatta. *'Why would the Jews pay several dollars more per kilogram for their meat?'* he wondered. What he didn't know was that kosher meat must be very specifically prepared. The animal must be strung in a certain way, be killed by a knife slit to the throat, drained of it's blood, have special prayers said by a person 'authorised' to do so, and more. Such an elaborate procedure is time consuming, costly and labour intensive, but simply must be done to ensure the Jewish religious purity.

A couple of weeks ago, Tony had been working on the fridges of a non-Jewish, meat wholesaler in Marrickville. He was chatting sociably to the proprietor Ludwig, when a customer entered the shopfront. Ludwig's business was volume sales of meat and associated products, supplying many butchers' in the surrounding area, none of whom were Jewish. The customer ordered a large quantity of a specific cut of meat, paid in cash and left quickly in his van. *'You know, I wish there were more customers like him'* remarked Ludwig to Tony. *'An easy big order and he pays cash. Most everybody else has accounts... and you think they pay the bloody bills on time? Not likely! They want the meat in a hurry, but never hurry to pay the bill'*

Tony recognised the customer as one of the workers at the Jewish butcher's in Bondi where he had been working just recently. *'You know, I was working at that guy's shop only two weeks ago. They're all Jewish you know. They only sell to the Jews, and I tell you one thing, they're not afraid of charging the earth for their meats. My missus gets minced beef for nine dollars a kilogram, but they sell it for over fifteen dollars! I can't for the life of me figure out why though, I mean I can understand why those types like to buy from their own, but you wouldn't catch me paying such high prices, just because of religion!'* he said, adjusting the alarm panel as he spoke. Ludwig paused in thought for a moment. As far as he was aware, he'd never had a Jewish customer before, but then how would he know?

Tony said the customer was Jewish, and was a good customer. He didn't come often, but always paid cash on the spot. *'Fifteen dollars for mince... bloody highway robbery'* Ludwig said with a smirk. *'I wonder how I can get more customers like him? The market must be big, and if I can get more of that business I'd be laughing'* he said. Tony suggested he check the phone book for some sort of controlling Jewish organisation. *'You might be able to get right in there, if you try, there's plenty of 'em and they must be rolling in it, with the prices they charge!'*

Several days later, Ludwig picked up the phone. After some difficulty finding the right people to speak to, he eventually made contact with the Jewish High Council. *'Yes hello, I'm not sure you are right people to speak to, but I want to discuss being supplier to your people for meats. I sell wholesale and I think I can do good deal on price. I been in business for many year and everybody very happy with my service. I want to talk about to supply. Is this the right place to talk to?'* he asked.

Yogesh was puzzled for a moment, on the other end of the line. He'd never received a call quite like this before. *'How long have you had your kosher licence?'* he inquired.

'Kosher?' Ludwig asked. *'I don't know about the kosher licence, but I got the meat storage and d' wholesale licence. Our company has the licence for many year now from the government. I can give you names of other customers for reference an all,'* he said.

'But you have no kosher licence?' asked Yogesh with surprise.

'Yes we don't have one called 'kosher', but we happy to get one. This is why I call you in the first place. I want to know the best way to sell to Jewish people. I happy to have my factory

inspected by you to get this kosher licence if we need. My place is very clean.' he added proudly.

'I don't think you understand sir, you cannot get the kosher licence if you are not Jewish, so I'm afraid we simply cannot help you,' said Yogesh politely.

'Well, I'm glad not everybody think the same way. One of my best customer, he is Jewish butcher,' said Ludwig indignantly. There was a slight pause. 'I beg your pardon' replied Yogesh. 'Yes, that's right he is one of my best customer, and he is a Jewish butcher.' repeated Ludwig.

The phone fell silent. Ludwig waited patiently, then continued with, *'Hello, hello did you hear me?'* somewhat annoyed.

'Yes I hear you' said Yogesh. 'I hear you sir ... what did you say your name was?'

        *   *   *   *   *   *   *

Another man sauntered along the road towards the shop. I lifted the camera and began filming him as he walked. He turned suddenly, entering a private house nearby. I lowered the camera again, it was a false alarm. I continued reading my paper. My brief was to obtain ID footage of all the staff who worked at the shop, and to follow any vehicles I thought might be leaving the site to pick up meat from a wholesaler. The best result possible would be to get film of a Jewish butcher picking up meat from a non-kosher wholesaler. This would be good for the investigation, but not so good for the poor souls who later bought the unclean, non-kosher meat, and at the inflated kosher prices as well! I later found out that any Jewish customers who ate the non-kosher meat would probably be forgiven because they weren't aware of this fact. This wouldn't be the case for the terrible butcher, and possibly even other Jews in the council who had a civic duty to protect their people, and ensure the sanctity of their religion.

I watched as a government bus pulled into a stop across the road from my position. Morning commuters poured from the bus into the street. From the small crowd I noticed two men walking together, both wearing the distinctive Jewish skullcaps. This in itself was not unusual. Besides backpackers and surfers, Bondi has a large Jewish community and several synagogues. The two men began walking in the general direction of the butcher's shop, and I decided they were both built like I'd expect butchers' bodies to be, powerful and stocky, able to haul carcasses and dismember large animals single-handedly. I began filming them as they walked, alternately getting a wide-angle shot, then zooming in to capture their faces in detail.

I was feeling quite pleased with myself when suddenly a loud horn erupted from behind my car. I jumped, and the camera waved aimlessly as I strained around to look for the source of the noise. Directly behind my car I could see the lower half of a large government bus, which filled the entire rear window. I looked anxiously back at the two men as the bus let out another, longer and angrier blast from its horn. Both Jewish men and just about everybody else who happened to be nearby turned to look at the spectacle taking place. I fumbled with my camera, just managing to get some facial shots as the suspected Jewish butchers' stared directly into my car. The bus driver then gave up trying to get me to move the car, and opened the doors. Hordes of commuters poured from them, surrounding the tiny Barina, as they waited for traffic before crossing the road. Several people stared at me as I sat in the rear of the car, and I felt uncomfortable. Things were not quite going to plan. I chose not to continue filming the men as they neared the shop, because of the inquisitive crowd surrounding my car. 'Well, they saw me but *did they make a mental note about my car?'* I wondered. I was almost hoping they would not be butchers', and that they would walk right past the shop into another address. I stared intently, concertedly ignoring a young schoolboy nearby who was pulling a particularly unflattering face at me. The two men walked right up to the butcher's shop door. The first pulled open the door while the second turned around and took one more gaze at my car before entering the shop. Damn. This action answered my previous question, but I immediately had some more: *'Did they see me through the windscreen? Did they see my camera? Would any of the people nearby speak to the butchers later?'*

Half an hour later another male entered the shop, walking in too quickly for me to film. I figured I'd catch him later when he emerged for morning tea, lunch or for some other reason. The next person entering was a female, who carried a small shopping bag. I didn't film her, presuming she was just a shopper and that the butchers were now open for business. Two other buses approached the stop I was parked in, but none were as vocal as the previous driver had been. The first gave a short toot, while the next pulled alongside briefly, stared into the car with disgust before driving off. I decided the bulk of the morning traffic would have passed now, which meant I could relax slightly. My mind continually ran through the morning's events, thinking, *'Did they see the camera? Could I have parked in a better spot to get film? Would they remember the bright, fire-engine red Barina, parked illegally in the bus zone, in front of the honking government bus?'* There was little I could do now but wait.

Wait I did. It was almost two hours later when one of the workers at the butcher's emerged. I wasn't sure at first if he was just another customer who had entered without me noticing, or was actually a worker. As he approached, I recognised him, and lifted my camera to film. He glanced not once, but twice at the

39

car as he prepared to cross the road, and I again felt decidedly uncomfortable. I lowered the camera just before he actually crossed the road and buried myself in the newspaper as he approached. He walked right in front of the car but continued into the local shopping area. He returned ten minutes later with a small shopping bag, and I was relieved he didn't glance at my car once on his way back to the shop.

Once he'd entered, I figured the next period of action would occur at lunchtime when staff would come out to buy their lunch. I was wrong. I glanced up at the doorway to the shop as it burst open and two Jewish butchers' began striding out purposefully. They wore full butchers' aprons and large waterproof boots. Surrounding their waists were belts upon which hung several scabbards containing sharp knives, prods and other equipment. It looked as if they'd just killed and dissected several large beasts, and although I couldn't see any blood on their aprons, I imagined they were dripping in blood. Hair on the back of my neck rose as my heart skipped a beat. I lifted my camera and began filming their approach. They weren't wandering aimlessly while enjoying the morning sunshine. These men were on a mission. One of them stared at my car but the other seemed disinterested. I wondered if they were actually coming to approach me but dismissed such thoughts with a nervous laugh. It was still quite odd though, and I decided I wouldn't want to be walking around a shopping centre dressed in such a fashion.

There was a break in the traffic and the two men continued pacing across the road, with their sharp knives and other metal instruments clanging around their belts. They looked like knights from the dark ages, striding into battle, and I wondered if I was on the set for a Monty Python movie. It was really quite disconcerting. '...or is it Candid Camera,' I thought as I quickly placed down the camera on the seat next to me and picked up the newspaper. The knights finished crossing the road, walked straight up to my car and rapped quite forcefully on the rear window next to where I was sitting. I jumped, horrifying visions flashing through my brain of a slow and torturous death in the back of the Jewish butcher's shop. The situation was so unreal, I wondered if it was actually happening. Another sharp rap on the window, accompanied by an 'Oi! Open up in there,' alerted me to the fact that it was really happening, and worse it was happening to ME!

I noticed several passers-by looking at the two well-equipped butchers banging on the glass of my rather suspicious, darkly tinted, bright red Barina that was illegally parked. I realised to my horror, I hadn't locked the driver's door. I made a mental note to attend to this next time, that being of course if I survived this one. I had a jacket hanging up next to the rear window, but there was no question that somebody was inside the car. I removed the jacket and looked out the window. The two butchers' were standing close to the door. One of them placed a hand on the roof of the small car and stepped forward to peer into the window. As he leant forward, a sharpening steel that hung from his overloaded belt swung forward hitting my car door lightly with a metal crack. I nervously took hold of the window winder and wound the window down slightly, though not enough to allow a fist to reach through. The butchers' immediately leant forward even more, peering into the dark interior of the car.

'Yes?' I inquired gingerly, wondering what they were going to do. 'What the hell are you doing mate?' they asked accusingly.

'I... what do you mean?' I replied, trying to sound surprised. I don't think it worked.

'What's that on the seat?' he asked angrily. I looked down at the seat next to me.

'Oh that! um that's a... camera. Why ... what's the problem?' I asked, looking back through the small opening at the top of my window.

'And what the heck are you doing filming us?' he asked angrily. 'I'm not filming you. I was just ... I mean I just got this camera and I'm practising. I... we're going overseas soon and I'm just learning how to use it, that's all,' I said.

'So what are you doing here then?' asked the other butcher. 'Well I'm just waiting for my friend. He just went off to the shops to get something,' I replied, confidence still wavering in my story. 'For three hours?' he shouted indignantly.

'Well yes. He has been a bit longer than I expected. He only had a couple of things to do. Actually we also need to get some money out of the bank. Is there a Westpac bank around here somewhere?' I asked politely, trying to avoid the probing questions.

'Why are you parked in the bus zone?' he asked.

'Well there are no parking spaces around here,' I replied, looking across the road at two vacant one-hour parking spots.

'Why are you in the back seat then?' he asked, continuing the interrogation.

'Because the sun is too hot in the front seat,' I said truthfully.

'Well why don't you move into the bloody shade across the road then?' suggested the other man.

I was about to explain that my 'friend' still had the car keys with him, until I realised they were still hanging from the ignition. Another mistake I wouldn't make again. In reply to his question I simply shrugged my shoulders. The butchers' said nothing but continued to stand over the car door, looking through the small open slit in my window. More passers-by looked at them in curiosity.

The butchers' glanced around, noticing the attention they were attracting and realised there was really nothing more they could say. Hauling me bodily out of the car and dissecting me on the sidewalk was not really an option on this busy street at lunchtime. They cursed me under their breath and walked back in a huff to their butcher's shop, leaving me to heave a well-earned sigh of relief. My story did sound ridiculous, but so what? There was nothing they could do, and such denials will always cast doubt in people's minds. I contemplated driving off immediately but decided to wait another half an hour, to add credibility to my story. It would be too obvious if I drove off straight after they had approached me. I suspected they were glancing through their shop curtains from time to time, watching me. After my self-allotted half an hour had expired, I slipped into the front seat and drove away, checking my rear-view mirror as I left.

When I reviewed the footage later, I found that I'd managed to capture all of the four workers on film, with quality suitable to identify them. Unfortunately when I paused the tape to get still frames, I found that most frames were blurred with movement. I realised I should have been shooting at a faster shutter speed to get better stills, but managed to get several decent prints from the tape all the same. I notified Peter about what had happened, adding that I had managed to get ID photos of all the workers. He asked me to take the prints, as soon as I could, to Rabbi Gutnick who sat on the board of the Jewish council. Later that afternoon I visited a modest address in Bondi. I was ushered into the study room of the Rabbi's home. We sat down and discussed the job, and I showed him the photos I'd obtained. He knew most of the men and seemed pleased at the result, even though I'd been well and truly compromised.

He was quite fatherly towards me, explaining that he knew surveillance was not exactly something Peter's company did on a regular basis, and that I wasn't very experienced yet in that particular area. *'You see Chris, It is a very sensitive thing that has happened and we don't want it known outside our community until all the facts are known, and the whole thing is over. Peter is well known and trusted amongst us so he was my first choice when we discovered what was going on. I know you're not Jewish yourself Chris, but I understand you know a bit about our culture already. There are many out there who despise our people, and many who wish to destroy what we stand for. The fact that such a terrible thing as the sale of non-kosher meat to Jews, is happening from within our OWN organisation is particularly distressing,'* he said it with conviction, and I could tell he felt deeply and strongly about what he was saying.

I knew a little about the Jewish religion from my conversations with Peter, but the Rabbi went on to explain more to me about exactly what they thought and why things were the way they were. I then left his office and drove to Marrickville where I showed the surveillance photos to Ludwig, the non-Jewish meat wholesaler. He was obviously uncomfortable in dealing with me, knowing he was about to implicate one of his customers. It was difficult, especially so because he had no understanding about the Jewish culture. To him, meat was meat, and people purchased and ate meat without a second thought. He had spoken to the Rabbi at length, and had a vague understanding that it was something to do with religion, prayers and preparing meat in special ways.

He still thought it wasn't fair that he was precluded from selling to them just because he wasn't Jewish, and he even wondered about hiring a Jewish butcher, just to get a kosher licence, though the Rabbi advised that this might not be possible anyway.

Ludwig drew on his cigarette as he viewed the photographs, spread before him on the cluttered desk. *'You understand this is not easy for me. He never done the wrong thing by me,'* said Ludwig. I nodded in reply. He looked for a moment longer. *'You know what it was?'* he asked, and without waiting for a reply, *'I did checking myself and found out some things. Sometimes the customer, he always buy a special cut of meat. Sometimes everybody want the leg of lamb. We slaughter d' lambs, and we have plenty of legs. What do we do with the ribs? Now we have a hundred ribs and nobody want d' ribs. The Jewish one, he....* (He drew from his cigarette)... *he sells plenty of d' special kosher one in some cuts of d' meat. Now when all customer want is, say, forequarter cuts, he cant afford to kill lots of animal just to get d' forequarter. When suddenly supply is short for one specific cut, that's when he come to me... He didn't like it I don't think, and it is not to get d' meat cheaper. D' Jews... they have a smaller market. Not like me, you see here everything?* (I nodded) *I have a big warehouse and I have plenty animals come though. Is a bigger market and is more even. Kosher one is smaller... and then... harder to have every meat the right amount. I can understand why he is doing it, it is not because he is greedy or else he come to me more often. It only ever for d' one cut of meat, and then not every time.'* I nodded. *'Yes, I understand. It must be difficult sometimes,'* I replied.

He leant forward to his desk, staring very closely at one of the photographs. He then sat back, stubbed his cigarette out and handed me the photograph he had been looking at. *'Is him,'* he said gruffly, and began sorting through paperwork on his desk. *'I am busy man you know, I must work now,'* he said without looking me in the eye. He was in a hurry for me to leave. I gathered my photographs and slipped away from his office, realising Ludwig must feel much like a Judas, betraying his loyal customer and sending him to the slaughterhouse. He would know that those involved in the 'scam' would be in plenty of trouble when people found out. They would be shunned wherever they went by the entire Jewish community.

Several weeks later, I was driving passed the butcher's shop, and noticed it had closed down. Large sheets of white paper were stuck to the windows, preventing people from seeing inside. There wasn't any note on the door with information about why the shop had closed, merely a large cardboard sign propped against the door marked 'CLOSED'.

I learnt many things on this job. I learnt about where not to park and the importance of concealing the camera. I learnt about not leaving keys in the ignition. I learnt about supply and demand for meats. I learnt about kosher and the Jewish way of life. I learnt about the pain of those who must betray their own, and the pain of those that are betrayed by their own.

A month later I was dropping off some work to Peter. Over coffee he mentioned to me that he heard something about the butcher's shop job. I was most interested and listened intently. Peter explained that it was discovered that one of the butchers' had been collecting unemployment benefits on the sly, during the time he was working at the shop. The staff were already wary because somebody had called the shop several weeks ago, asking if that person actually worked there. They denied it, but when they saw my suspicious car near the shop, they immediately assumed it was the Social Security department checking up on welfare cheats. Little did they know the real reason for my visit! Several months later, I had to fly interstate for another investigation. After my Jewish experience on this job, I was still somewhat curious about the Jewish culture. When booking the flight I decided to request a kosher meal. Not only was it quite tasty, I was served my special meal before all the other passengers!

CHAPTER 3: WHY ARE THINGS SEEN?

An investigator aims to gather information quietly, without attracting attention. Being caught or compromised means you lose the valuable opportunity to gather adequate information, or it results in people changing their behaviour to make any such observations worthless. Occasionally being compromised by someone you are following can have some personal safety issues as well. As with everything in the PI game, there is no right and wrong, as the ideal response will constantly change with the situation around you. It's all about making a choice - choosing the best option in each situation. Being aware of why things are seen will help in considering the probability involved in each option. The human vision system is fascinating, and just because your eye can see something, it doesn't mean your brain can. The brain filters out things it does not consider important, and can be tricked by illusions.

Count the number of times the letter 'F' appears in the following sentence: *'Finished files are the result of years of scientific study combined with the experience of many years.'* Didn't find all six? Then your brain failed to see what your eyes did!

You need to try to maximise your information gathering efforts, and then maximise the capture of evidence on tape, without being detected. The following points outline what steps you can take to avoid being seen.

Seeing

A person will see or hear you, if their eyes and ears receive the sensory information. They have looked at you, or they have glanced up at hearing your car engine start, but they have only seen or heard you. This is normal, natural and to be expected. It is not preferable, but despite the angst felt by many PI novices, it is not the end of the world to be seen by others. The point to remember is: They have seen you with their eyes and heard you with their ears, but not with their brains. Relax, and look relaxed.

Noticing

A person has noticed you if they stare for longer than usual. They notice if they move slightly to get a better view of you. You have been noticed if your presence modifies their normal behaviour in any way, which could include them turning a head, or even walking right up to you, and asking why you are there or what you are doing. This is not the final stage, nor is it always a serious problem, as the clever investigator will use this to their advantage. A good example of this is in my story, The case of a favourable compromise on page 428 Rather than slink away if noticed, it may be better to stride up and directly approach them. Nothing puts people at ease as much as if you were to go and talk to them, as it will resolve the burning question that may be forming in their mind, namely why are you there and what are you doing. Sometimes people can be happy to receive an answer, any answer so they can lodge it somewhere in their brain. Even a slightly strange answer is better than an absence or of reason, as people always suspect the worst.

Awareness

The last stage is awareness. This is where the person has seen you, noticed you and has finally processed the information sufficiently in their brain to be aware of your presence. To be aware of the likely reason you are there, or that you should not be. You can be sure they are aware of your presence when they actively respond, such as closing blinds or moving conspicuously out of sight. Sometimes they become confrontational and accusatory. Sometimes they will pretend not to notice you, but will act in a way that is clear they are performing for a camera. The thieving employee will suddenly work very industriously in his normal duties, the bad back case will suddenly clutch their body in pain and the cheating spouse will suddenly adopt a cold, business like demeanour with their attractive 'lunch' partner.

One common misconception of nearly all novice PI's, is to imagine that people are aware of them. However, just because people see, does not mean they are aware. It is also important to realise there is usually not a serious issue if others, aside from the target, become aware of what you are doing. Should the store detective notice you filming surreptitiously, or a fellow passenger on a train realise you are following somebody, there is usually nothing to be concerned about. While you always work hard not to be noticed by anyone at all, the only real concern is preventing the subject from being aware of your presence. It doesn't matter how many people think you are weird or wonder what you are doing, as long as they don't have a word to your subject to warn them, you have little to worry about other than your own embarrassment. Having others warn your subject is occasionally an issue, as seen in the story *The case of stolen noodles* on page 244.

There are several factors that result in people seeing things, namely: shape, sign, shadow, surface, spacing, silhouette, and movement.

Shape

The human eye recognises shapes instinctively, which is a survival principal. The shape of a vehicle or person can be very noticeable, as are the shape of cameras. Consideration of what shapes signify can result in being seen or not seen. Consider a vehicle, which has a different look from front and rear. The human eye will always recognise the front of a car far more noticeably than the rear, and the reason is survival. Cars can be dangerous. The front of a car implies it is approaching, or may approach the person, causing harm. The rear of the car is quite different, as it means the car is departing, going away from the person and taking the possible danger with it. The human subconscious will filter these shapes automatically, and process accordingly.

In a game where every little bit helps, the choice of presenting the more aggressive shape of the front of a car (when selecting the optimum place to park for an observation) may be a bad move, despite it being far more comfortable to sit facing the right way. Even the shape of your body will broadcast a shape profile that can be read by others. The novice PI will be very conscious of his body, and anxious not to be seen. They may walk with a slight stoop, unconsciously trying to reduce the shape of their body to a smaller size, and trying hard not to be seen. While they may now be a few centimetres shorter, their shape gives away their suspicious nature.

Sign

'Sign' is the evidence left behind, which are little telltale clues which may give the game away. You may be creeping around a farmhouse without considering the footprints you are leaving. Farmers are always inspecting the ground for such things as a natural course of their business. They may be looking for animal prints, droppings or other items. Your size ten boot print may get them thinking about who is out there watching them. 'Sign' can occur in many ways. You may open a door or a gate to gain access, yet forget to close it. You may leave U-turn tyre marks on a dirt road. Forestry authorities often encourage visitors to national parks, to take only photographs and leave only footprints. A good investigator will take photographs but leave no footprints!

Shadow

People often forget their own shadow, but this can cause you to be noticed easily. Standing near the corner of a building, your shadow may fall the other side and be clearly visible. In a rural environment, you may be able to construct an elaborate hide in the bushes, but the dark shadows will look unnatural if you do not consider them beforehand.

Shadows also move, and one of the signs of a good investigator is one who is not only aware of this fact, but uses this knowledge effectively. He may park very early in the morning in direct sunlight. Hours later, as the sun moves slowly across the sky, his vehicle will eventually be covered with a pleasant shadow, thus keeping him cooler in the real heat of the day, as well as reducing the chance of visual detection around the time that activity is more likely to occur. He will be comfortable and discreet. The novice PI would have greedily parked in the middle of the large shadow very early in the day (when it is still cool), but hours later they find themselves hot and exposed in the sunlight, after having failed to consider the motion of shadows.

Surface

'Surface' can refer to a flat, clean and very shiny car. This surface reflects sunlight well, causing shiny sunspots that radiate some distance away. Any movement inside the car will result in distinctive flashes as the sun's rays are deflected. Such movement will be exaggerated by the angles, which make them glint more noticeably from a distance. A good PI will have a reasonably clean car, but will prefer to have a very slight film of grime to absorb the rays and reduce reflection. The surface of a camera lens can also be a give-away, and should be considered at all times as a possible glinting surface.

Spacing

The human eye notices spacing subconsciously. Regular spacing is noticeable, and so is non-regular spacing. If there is a line of cars parked in the street, it's advisable to blend into the existing spacing. Although there may be a slightly shadier parking space a few cars up, or perhaps a better camera angle, it may be wise to keep the same spacing to blend in. Seeing a car parked further away from the rest may alert some attention. Although there may be a legitimate reason, perhaps a car in the middle has now left. Spacing can be a visual clue to the presence of something unusual. Why didn't they park at the end of the row as one would expect? It's a small point, yet the PI is always mindful that small points can often jog the subconscious mind of their subject. Always err on the side of caution, especially when the odds of success are already stacked against you.

Silhouette

While you may feel safe and reasonably concealed, your silhouette can sometimes be a searing searchlight, bringing the attention of the world towards you. When walking along ridgelines, it is natural to walk along the very top, where the ground is flat and the going easy. The top also has a better field of view, as you can more easily see down both sides, yet nature does not often take this high road, and for a very good reason. While you may be in full camouflage dress, a silhouette is immediately distinctive and brings attention. Any movement is amplified, as the contrast against the plain background draws more attention to it. A noticeable silhouette can occur in both a country area or in the suburbs. By looking over somebody's back fence, your head may be silhouetted against the sky, yet if you take a little time to find a tiny crack within the fence, and press your eye against it, you will see just as well, and not be seen by the occupants within. A silhouette may occur when you look *around* something too.   In urban fighting, experienced soldiers will be careful looking *around* a wall, mindful that they may be silhouetted and then targeted.   Often it is best to look around the wall while lying prone on the ground, as this does not display a silhouette to the enemy.   In an urban setting with an investigator, this may draw more unwanted attention, but could also be worth considering.

Movement

Movement is a giveaway.   Nature has programmed the animal brain to detect movement easily.   It may signify a threat, or it may signify a meal.   Movement is best considered carefully, as it is one of the more important issues to be aware of when hiding from others.

Excessive movement

Too much movement is not good.   The PI will always need to have some movement, but it's important to restrict this.   On conducting a stakeout, the aim is to position yourself in a location that is optimal in a wide range of issues, such as visibility, shade, ergonomics and many more, as detailed in the section Stakeout parking considerations on page 196.   There will frequently be times you will want to move, such as to follow the shade as it moves throughout the day, or perhaps you may find the subject is doing some activity along the side of the house, and if you drive forward just two metres you will have a better view of the action.   It is not that you can't move, it's just that the movement needs to be carefully considered.   The balance of probability may favour the move as the results of evidence observed in a new position may outweigh the increased risk of detection during the move (or even after the move in your new position - *'I could swear that blue car was parked closer to the tree last time I looked!'*)

This is a common mistake of the novice PI, who will arrive and park, then decide to move a little bit to get a better view around the tree in the subject front yard. Then they will decide there is more shade on the other side. By about lunchtime, the neighbours will be wondering if the car out the front is playing a game of tic-tac-toe with itself, as it hops from place to place. The experienced surveillance professional will adopt the five P's ethos of prior preparation (see page 176), and will have researched the area fully before deciding on a parking location. He will have assessed all the issues, and will adopt his position, and then probably remain there quietly for the duration. Occasionally he will move slightly, but it is rare, given that he has put so much thought into choosing the best position to start with. Even if there is something happening around the side, he may consider it best to wait a little longer, and sure enough, the activity will move again out to the front. Patience is crucial. The impatient PI will move regularly, will be often detected, and will return with nothing.

Insufficient movement

An absence of movement can draw attention also. The human eye detects the environment, and the brain processes signals. The vast majority of signals are discarded or ignored by the brain, as it compares and evaluates what is not of interest and what should be processed further. Where a scene looks normal, people will notice little as they go about their business. Should something be out of the ordinary, it will be flagged for scrutiny, even when the brain is not aware of this process. Movement is normal, and can be occasionally used to reduce attention. A vehicle may be parked for too long in the one location. A person may be standing for too long on the street corner. That person with his bag is still sitting in the park, and has done so for three hours now!

Some level of 'normal' movement will often allay suspicion in these cases. It may be appropriate to drive away for two hours then return, as if the surveillance vehicle was on some errand, else the subject may notice it and wonder whose car it is. It might be best to move in a very overt fashion, striding decisively in a way that suggests you are a busy person and clearly not concerned by people noticing your movement. Laptops and purses are stolen frequently throughout city offices, not by the thief we *expect*, slinking around slowly looking for opportunity, but by the busy man in the suit. He is often so busy and visible that he is just not noticed by anyone. People subconsciously filter out his presence, as he does not fit their brains' alert profile of suspicious behaviour. *Hiding in plain view* is a common term used by Special Forces and other surveillance professionals, because sometimes people just can't see what's right under their noses!

Movement profiles

Movement can occur quickly or slowly, in a staggered, random fashion or in a regular clockwork motion. The human eye may recognise movement easily, but it is the unusual movement that will always draw far more attention. Every environment has a unique movement signature. A railway station has people moving in groups, arriving in a staggered formation, yet departing en-mass when a train has arrived and expels its passengers as a group. If a single passenger walks out of the railway station well after a train has gone, she can trigger the subconscious mind. Why wasn't she with the group? It is not likely to trigger conscious thought, but over time these clues cause a subject to become increasingly aware that something is not right, without quite knowing why.

Perhaps the subject may enter a department store and start shopping. This has a very different movement profile where customers browse through aisles slowly, inspecting items then moving on. To blend into this environment, the PI should follow a similar profile and browse around slowly. While they could perhaps remain quietly standing, observing the scene, their lack of browsing movement will then attract attention. Standing quietly on a train station is normal behaviour, but not in the store. Even if the subject is not looking or consciously aware of the PI on their tail, there may be others watching as well, like the store loss prevention officers. They may be working in plain clothes or observing you on camera surveillance, and you will come under notice quickly if you do not blend into the normal movement profile of the browsing shopper.

Remain too long in one location and they may approach you, question you, detect that you are filming and advise you are not permitted to do that there. Their approach to you may draw unwanted attention, or even delay you while the subject enters a lift and disappears from sight. They may see you following a young woman subject and politely ask her if she knows you, concerned that you may be stalking her. An experienced PI will be well aware of his surroundings, and will ensure his behaviour matches the movement profile so he remains quietly undetected, while continuing to gather evidence.

The case of the inquisitive cow

Key learning points

- Close target reconnaissance / covert foot movement
- Camouflage / hides / observation posts
- Working in teams / agent communications
- Contingency response / managing the unexpected

On an operation once in rural Melbourne, I was conducting a close target reconnaissance with two other investigators. All three of us were qualified Special Forces soldiers, and comfortable working covertly in the bush at night. We were all dressed in camouflage clothing, and were creeping around a remote farmhouse[22]. The aim was to assess the target, and identify the best observation positions, which could be used later that day. We had been tasked with conducting surveillance on a male occupant of this property. The area was flat with few trees and not much foliage, so movement during the day would be near on impossible without being seen.

We gingerly crept through the darkness, and got closer to the rear of the farmhouse. Not only were we trying to assess good positions, we were also trying to determine where the likely activity may be occurring. If we were to find a tractor in pieces in a shed, this may indicate expected activity, which we would then try to position ourselves to document effectively. While you cannot always predict the future accurately, it is often easy to do so by probability, if you look for sign. A worn dirt track around the side of a fence corner would indicate likely daily cattle movement, such as cows being herded for milking. A lack of dust on the toolbox next to the dismantled tractor would indicate it was used recently, and hence would be likely to be used again soon. Most people never notice these tell tale signs, yet they are all valuable clues.

There was a slight mist near the ground and it was quite cold, steam rising from our warm breath. We moved closer until we could see the rear door of the farmhouse, under a small awning. Periodically we paused to listen, which allowed our senses to be

---

[22] Entry to private land is not classed as trespass unless you are there without a lawful excuse (such as intent to steal) and you are without the consent of the owner. Consent is implied unless advised otherwise by signs or by the owner personally. See The Law: Trespass on page 273 for more details

more acute, more in tune with the environment. Pausing meant our senses weren't disturbed by the soft rustle of the wet grass underfoot as we moved. Our focus was on listening and observing rather than careful consideration about each step we took. We moved on a little further and suddenly there was a very loud and unusual noise. It sounded like an animal but we couldn't recognise it, apart from being sure it was not a dog. The sound came again, almost a muffled but very loud bleat. We turned away and took a step back towards the tree line we had approached from.

Without warning there was a bright flash of light, and then another. Instantly we were bathed in the strong light of several fluorescent lights that were mounted under the awning just in front of us. Someone inside had turned on the lights. The three of us dropped to the ground, as our military training took control of our instinctive reactions and we responded as though the lights were flares. Flares are commonly used at night in war or conflict, either with trip wires or fired into the air with tiny parachutes. They illuminate the ground and provide the enemy an easy opportunity to observe soldiers standing up. Flares will silhouette the human form, provide distinctive shadows, and often cause the untrained assailant to scurry away into the safety of nearby darkness. Moving under the light of a flare is a bad move, and the best response is to drop immediately, lie still, and then assess the situation.

The three of us were huddled together, trying to flatten ourselves into the wet grass, trying to sink in and melt away. We were close, far too close to the back door, and the bright light bathed and embraced us as we lay on the short grass just a few metres away. We had no time to think as it swung open with a thud, hitting the wall behind it. A tall man stood in this doorway, silhouetted in the light, just standing and observing the scene around him. He was calm and relaxed. Carefully looking up we could see the outline of a goat, tethered to a fence post quite close by. The goat made the same loud bleating noise, which startled us again. Our hearts were beating rapidly, nearly bursting out of our chests as our bodies prepared for flight or fight.

The man was looking straight at us, and I expected him to respond. Surely he could see us; three large men huddled on the flat grass just metres from him and bathed in the strong light. How could he possibly not see us? He stood for almost half a minute, which felt like a lifetime, and then turned away. The light switched off as quickly as it had appeared, and the door closed behind him. We stood up and began striding purposefully away, not running, but leaving as fast as we could without sounding like a stampede of elephants. The goat bleated a goodbye, but the light didn't turn on again. Breathing heavily, we soon reached the safety of the bushland behind us, whispering to each other *'He saw us didn't he? Why the f... didn't he see us?'* As we thought about the situation later, we realised what had happened. The guy's eyes must have been used to the bright light inside, so when he walked out the back, his pupils weren't quite adjusted to the slightly dimmer light in the backyard. We didn't move an inch while he had been looking at us, and perhaps our camouflage clothing protected us. He may have seen or even noticed the clump of men in his yard, but several factors had protected us from him becoming <u>aware</u> of our presence.

We moved back to the car and quietly left the area for a few hours sleep. Around five o'clock we got up and dressed in our camouflage clothing again. It was icy cold and the wind whisked our breath away as we loaded the car. Bob Lancaster[23]

---

[23] www.lancasters-global.com

drove us to the drop off point where Paul and I climbed out of the car. Paul had recently passed his SAS selection entry course, though this was his first rural PI operation. His bush skills were high, but he wasn't experienced with camera equipment. We had decided that Paul would conceal himself close to the property exit, in a small clump of bushes near the front gate. This would help in getting good identification on the occupants when they paused to open the gate, as well as to document the general activity from the front of the house.

My own position was more difficult. There seemed to be far more probability of activity around the side and rear of the house, yet there were few bushes to hide amongst. There was an old shed slightly up the hill, and although we had not checked this last night, we had decided that I should try for this in the early morning light which was just starting to shimmer over the horizon. With my pack on my back I cautiously made my way up towards the shed. I could see that it looked disused as it was missing several palings, and had a distinct lean to one side. Fortunately there was still some roof left, which would provide some shade during the day. The rear of the shed was damaged by the weather, and I walked in easily, and was pleased at my new surroundings. Although the floor wasn't level, it looked cosy and in fact ideal for a secret hiding place. Even better, the view from the shed was perfect, allowing a clear line of sight down to the house below, and the large garage behind it.

I began setting up, erecting a tripod to mount the camera. I was a few hundred metres from the house, and would require a steady camera mounting to stop the shake at the maximum lens zoom. Once I had finished settling in, I radioed to the others that I was in position and set. Next came the waiting. You can never tell how long you will need to wait for, as sometimes the farmers will come out at the crack of dawn, and sometimes they will not come out all day. It is easy to switch off and relax, but you never

60

know when the action will start. Having seen a pile of hay in the other room of my shed, I wondered if the farmer would be paying me a visit. It was likely, I mused, but fingers crossed he wouldn't come today.

The first move came several hours later, as a male was seen to walk from the house towards the rear garage. Pleased that things were finally happening, I radioed through to the others, as I began recording the scene. Soon a battered Holden spluttered out of the garage, and drove out towards the gate. I wasn't able to get a close ID shot of the person's face, as he was some distance away, and moving reasonably quickly. At least I had the movement itself on tape I thought, always thankful to get that important first footage. The only thing worse than getting nothing at all on a day of surveillance is to actually observe some brief action but fail to record it properly. Once you have those vital first few seconds, you can relax slightly, knowing you have proof you were actually there, and able to get something at least!

Like a sniper, I followed the car through my camera lens, as it lazily twisted around the dirt track along the side of the property towards the front gate. I couldn't see the gate itself, so I switched off the recording and sat back, wondering how Paul would go. Meanwhile, Paul had heard the car well before I had radioed through, and was preparing himself near the front fence. There was not much concealment for him either, he was nearly exposed, crouched in some long grass that really could have been a little thicker, and certainly longer as well. Unfamiliar with the camera, Paul held it up and braced himself as the car slowed down just metres in front of him. Paul's task was primarily to get an identification photo of any people leaving the property, including any registration numbers.

Rural surveillance in the sparse Australian countryside often means you have to sit well away, making it difficult to easily capture important fine detail. The driver swung out of the car with practiced ease, causing a distinct squeak of the door. He took a few paces up to the gate and flipped the catch, leaving it swinging open. Paul fumbled for the shot, but the guy swivelled around quickly, more familiar with his gate than Paul was with the camera. Paul cursed, though he knew he had another chance as the gate had still to be closed. The car pulled forward a few metres, and the driver got out to close the gate, his face looking away from Paul's position. The gate shut with a sharp twang, and then there was silence. Poised with expectant anticipation, Paul readied himself, as the man turned back towards the car.

SNAP, SNAP, SNAP the camera clicked loudly in quick succession, the motor drive whirring distinctively as Paul drove his finger firmly down on the shutter release. As he did so, the driver stopped and paused, looking out to the side. SNAP, SNAP, Paul fired a few more shots, with the last one being particularly blurred as the driver's head spun around in response to the unusual noise. Paul was not used to the camera at all, let alone expecting the loud noise it would make, but he remained silent, not moving an inch lest he give the game away. In reality the camera was not that loud, but in the bush setting, far away from the bustling city, any unusual noise can be heard for a long way.

The guy remained facing Paul's general direction, standing behind his open car door, just listening, obviously wondering what the hell that noise was. He heard nothing more though, so he swung back into his car and drove off. Paul drew breath again deeply, conscious of the loud beating of his heart. He knew how close he had come to compromise, for if the guy taken more than two paces in front of him he would have tripped over Paul's body pressed firmly into the slight crevice of the land opposite the gate. The indentation, which allowed water to pool during rain and encouraged the grasses to grow, had afforded him the barest of cover, and yet together with his camouflage clothing, it was just enough. I contacted Bob in the surveillance car nearby. He was several kilometres away, but was soon travelling at speed as he chased the departing Holden, armed with the registration number in case he lost the vehicle on the way to town.

It was nearly two hours before there was any further movement, but our wait was richly rewarded as the old Holden returned, together with a large removalist truck. Bob radioed through as he neared the property, though we could hear the truck labouring along the hills for miles away as it ambled towards us. None of us could believe our luck. All too often you stakeout a property and wait for hours and days and weeks with nothing happening. Here we were on day one, and there was the arrival of a removalist truck, assuring us of plenty of action to capture on film. I wondered how often it occurred that a stakeout commenced the day after the occupants moved out, which would really annoy the poor PI, though at least this was not my worry today.

As the truck arrived, another guy walked out of the house and opened the garage fully. It was a large garage, and I wondered what was inside, because it was surely larger than necessary for the old Holden. The new guy was older, about fifty or more, and I instinctively knew he was our man. It was a difficult case. He was one of the claimants from the Granville train disaster, and had made a massive claim for stress. He was not physically injured in the accident, but his stress claim alleged that he was virtually incapacitated through the horror, and couldn't work anymore. I was very young when this accident occurred, though I clearly recalled the shock of a nation mourning its dead. I knew it was sad, but I also knew we had a duty to investigate properly, and I wondered if the remote nature of his home was a factor in his difficulty resuming paid work. Still, we were only tasked with documenting his behaviour. What he chose to do that day would later be analysed in great detail by doctors, lawyers, insurers and judges. It was quite a lottery really, as he could have been sick in bed all day and we would have nothing, yet this was not the case, because today was MOVING DAY!

I zoomed in on his face, then panned out to show his full body as he spoke with the other drivers, and began directing the large truck to back up to the garage. A cattle dog raced out of the way, nearly clipped underneath the large wheels and I saw him shout out for the dog to clear off. Then he shared a joke with the others, laughing for just a few seconds that (thanks to my footage) would probably be replayed again and again. Psychological trauma is never easy to assess or discredit, though seeing him interact normally with others, laughing and even directing a truck was all good solid evidence.

The three men entered the garage, and I could hear the sound of things being moved around. The removalist driver lowered a ramp and then it started. First there was just a chair, and then a table, and then some other wooden item was loaded. All three men began emptying out the garage which seemed to be an Aladdin's cave of fine furniture, which we guessed may be part of some workshop relocation. The men took several hours to finally load and secure it all – it was a procession that just didn't stop. Clearly he was involved in manufacture or sale or something to do with furniture, and we now had several hours of evidence to show his involvement. I was glad I had packed plenty of video tape and spare batteries.

While the insurers couldn't use much of his physical activity to negate or reduce the stress claim, they could certainly make a large adjustment given his attitude, his laughter, his direction of the men's activities and generally that he was involved in the business when he had claimed he did nothing at all but sit at home all day. Without investigators on the case observing his activities, it would be very hard for the insurer to detect this via other means, as I am sure he would be quietly at home if he ever received a visit, and most home visits are usually planned and notified in advance, if they occur at all.

The laden truck groaned and squeaked as it pulled out of the property, and continued off up the road, with the Holden following it. Bob had ample warning to both, and I soon heard his car in the distance, racing madly and perhaps pointlessly to intercept the very slow moving truck. Bob only has two speeds himself, dead stop and flat out, there is little in the way of middle ground. I was glad we had a team of three, which is unusual for insurance work, though more common for large corporate jobs. Normally you were lucky to get approval for two agents, and this was exactly the job that required more than one as we really wanted to know to where that truck was delivering its load. It is quite frustrating when you only get one side of the story, so tailing the truck would give us the full picture and wrap the case up nicely.

With the truck now gone, things became quiet. The subject had returned to his house. I wondered why he did not also accompany the load, but guessed there would be others there to assist. It was a good feeling having several hours of good footage, and the rest of the afternoon to relax in the comfort of the old farm shed. I hoped there would be nothing much more to do, as the late nights and early starts always made for a tiring day, especially when watching someone or something intently. Although it may appear that not much work is being done in just watching and waiting, the heightened sense of alertness will drain as much as any hard days physical activity. Surveillance is not just using your eyes, there is constant sense of anticipation, knowing your response may be needed quickly at any time.

I decided to treat myself to a hot cup of tea. Being well away from the house, and shielded by the disused shed, I promptly set up an army stove on the dry floorboards and soon had the water quietly heating up over the flickering flame from the solid fuel tablets. It was a bit of a luxury, and it is not often that the situation lends itself to such comforts, but I felt I'd earned it though, so for the first time that day I started to relax.

CRACK, came the sound of a branch being stepped on very close to my shed, and the sound reverberated through my brain while my heart began pounding. Someone was out there. This was not good. I quietly moved to a slightly more concealed position, while I listened intently, trying to decipher the movement.

I heard another sound from a little further away. DAMN. There was definitely somebody out there, if not more than one. It was a slow moving sound, almost as if whomever out there was trying hard to <u>not</u> be heard. Moving slowly, stalking me and getting closer and closer. My eyes darted between the cracks in the boards, but I could see nothing, and yet the sounds drew slowly closer. I reached for an unfortunately undersized lump of wood nearby, and pulled it carefully nearer, preparing to defend myself against a potential assault. How did they know I was here I wondered, sure that nobody had left the house I had been watching. I wondered if perhaps it was Paul who had somehow sneaked up to my position because his radio battery was flat I wondered, though there was clearly more than one person out there by the sounds I could hear.

The hair on the back of my neck stood erect as I tried to control my heavy breathing. I was now breathing almost as fast as my heartbeat, and heavily, and the distinct noise through my nose was like a rushing ocean roar in the quiet country shed. I opened my mouth, which helped abate the noise slightly, but then I could hear another sound. Normally I find the sound of a kettle boiling extremely relaxing, and often at home I will switch it on, sometimes with no intention of making a cuppa, just for the pleasure of that warming sound. Of course now was not the right time for a kettle to be boiling, not while I was trying desperately to control my breathing and remain quiet, aware there were people outside stalking my hiding place. I glanced angrily at the offending brew, steam just starting to rising from the water as the quiet sound got louder.

Just as I was contemplating the quietest way to shut the damn thing up, two large eyes loomed up in front of me and I leapt backwards in surprise and horror, my (very) small lump of rotting wood now held poised in defence[24]. It was a good two seconds before I realised that the eyes belonged to a large cow. A wave of relief flowed over me as I saw that there was now not one but two cows ambling their way across the paddock. The cow which had inquisitively poked its head above the rotten boards and startled me was as surprised as I was, and took several steps back, the weight of its heavy body unaccustomed to such rapid movement. I decided to risk poking my head right out of the shed and have a better look, and saw that a reasonably large herd of cows was now congregating closer.

The sudden movement of the first cow was noticed by a few others, who stared quietly for a few seconds, and then they

---

[24] The client in any investigation is held liable for the conduct of the investigator, as the PI has the 'ostensible authority' of the client. Be sure you act within the law at all times, which includes trying hard to actively avoid any confrontation with the subject.

began to amble over towards me. First it was just a couple, and then a few more as the animals converged slowly. There were a few loud moos, but on the whole the herd was silent. Heart still pounding from the unexpected visitors, I decided to creep out and have a very good look around, to make sure there was nobody herding them, but the paddock was clear, so I figured I was in their paddock and they were just having an afternoon stroll.

Back inside the shed I wondered what to do. The animals weren't moving, and had now assembled into a tight pack, all staring up at me in the shed, quietly watching and waiting. 'SHOO' I hissed slightly lamely, not really wanting to make much noise myself. There was no movement in the herd. I tried again but it was no use, they were not budging. The feeling of panic was starting to return, as I realised what the scene looked like. From the house, it would look rather strange, like a giant searchlight was targeting my position. I had counted roughly thirty cows, and they were all crowded together, all facing the one direction, all pointing directly towards me.

As if on cue, the subject came out of the house at that very moment, glancing up at the herd but then continuing his business as he began packing up something on the side of the house. This was not good. I had to get rid of the cows before he came up to see what was going on. I wondered what was so interesting to them, but right now I had to think quickly. Perhaps if I threw the lump of wood at one of them, I might get them to move, though there would a problem should they decided to stampede in fright and draw more attention. I didn't need to continue thinking about this conundrum, because when I went to retrieve the lump of wood from the floor, I discovered another crisis, which would perhaps be better described as an imminent catastrophe. Compared to this, the cows were nothing. In my haste and startled leap, I'd knocked over the small stove. Normally, the stove is used directly on the ground and knocking it over usually means it would go out. The house was several hundred metres away, and I knew I could have easily packed up my stove in seconds had anyone started walking up the hill. It only takes a few quick minutes to boil a cuppa, I mean what could happen in that short time? Now things weren't so easy. The water had spilled, and the solid fuel tablets had fallen out of the stove.

The shed itself had a wooden floor, though there were large cracks in the old floorboards and I could see the ground underneath in places, covered lightly with dry hay which had fallen through over the years. The solid fuel tablet had slipped through one of these cracks, and was still burning madly in the still air underneath the floor, already having set alight some of the dry hay. The floor was not far off the ground, but there was not enough room to climb under there, even if I could find an opening. To make matters worse, the tablets were a little old and had gotten wet the last time I used them. They were now spluttering and crumbling, sending out tiny burning shards which enlarged the fire base ever more. I felt like I was dreaming a nightmare akin to The Sorcerers Apprentice, and yet there was a real chance the shed would burst into flames in seconds and could well take me with it. Among the mad thoughts at that time, I did also consider the camera footage. It was such good quality and there was so much film that it seemed a terrible shame to lose it, and I briefly thought about throwing it clear into some bushes outside the window in an attempt to save the tape if nothing else!

For a moment I stood dumbly, simply unable to comprehend the enormity of the situation, struggling to find understanding. Then I suddenly became very animated. I tried to prise my fingers through the crack, but it was not very wide. I tugged madly, trying in vain to pry the boards loose. I picked up my cup from the floor and found a tiny amount of water left which I poured through the crack. I could not direct the stream accurately to the base of the fire however, as it dripped down the cracks, annoyingly close but just not close enough. Meanwhile, the base of the fire was growing rapidly. I glanced outside and saw that my animated behaviour was suddenly even more interesting to the herd of cows, who were now jostling for a better position, crowded tightly around the front of the shed and mooing appreciation of the show. Down the hill I could see the farmer standing motionless by the house, staring up at the commotion. It would have been too far for him to have actually heard me, but I realised it was not long before he would see the smoke which was now starting to fill the room and spill out the open windows. Given another five minutes he would be watching his entire shed go up in roaring flames if I couldn't do something about it right now.

I tore at my backpack, and took an eternity to retrieve my spare water bottle. It was all the water I had left, though by now it was nearing the end of the day. I tossed the unscrewed bottle cap aside and began pouring the water through the cracks. None of the apertures were large enough to get a good solid swish of water, but there were a few. The water soon gone, I inspected the remains and found that although it was still burning, I had certainly taken the sting out of the fire's tail. Seeing a long, thin twig nearby, I poked it through the cracks and isolated the burning remains as best I could. I was also able to get a few handfuls of loose dirt which I also poured through the cracks. There was little else I could do but pray, as I watched the dying embers intently. One by one the tiny flickering flames extinguished, though it was not till the last one died that I allowed myself to draw breath freely.

I stood up a little shakily, half expecting to see the farmers face staring up at me, but he was already busying himself with other things near the house in the distance. As if the cows realised the show was now over, they ambled off slowly and soon disappeared out of sight. The shed was now very quiet and still once again, save for my pounding heart, the smell of smoke still heavy in the air. I checked through the floorboard cracks again, just to be sure, but I was safe.

I spent the next few hours slowly watching the sun slowly setting on the barren farm hillside, thinking about my ordeal. I likened it to the butterfly theory, where the flap of a butterfly wing can generate a thunderstorm on the other side of the world years later just by a chain of catalyst events, one small thing leading to another. If I wasn't startled by the cows, the burning fuel wouldn't have slipped through the cracks. If the stove was on the ground instead of a raised floor I would have been able to put it out easily in seconds. If the cows weren't congregating the farmer would have never noticed. A combination of factors and an unexpected sequence of events had made for an extraordinary day. I had no water left, but I did have some great footage on tape, and an amusing tale to tell, though all I really wanted at that point was a nice hot cuppa.

CHAPTER 4: LOCATING PEOPLE / FACTUAL INQUIRIES

There are a huge number of information sources where such personal data is stored, across both public and private sectors. Prior to 1990, the investigation industry was awash with illegally obtained information, including bank details, criminal histories, vehicle registrations, immigration records and much more. The Independent Commission against Corruption (ICAC) conducted a large inquiry into these practices, which resulted in a big overhaul of the PI industry, a large number of persons charged, and significant changes to legislation and privacy policy. The illegally obtained information was largely used by the debt collection industry, who used it to locate persons and hence recover the debt. With a huge number of debts being followed up, it was no surprise that the illegal information industry eventually came under the nose of the authorities.

Many feel strongly that investigators should be entitled to such access, even if there were more stringent controls or checks applied to it. With an often undeserved poor industry image, many may be uncomfortable knowing a private investigator was dealing in such personal data. In reality however, it is more likely that the right to use information would result in detection of insurance fraud, the recovery of bad debts or the location of important witnesses. People are often swayed by sensationalist films and books which dramatise the industry and cause people to wonder if PI's are shady characters who for an extra few grand will make your ex-wife disappear as part of their regular service. Clearly one would not want these types of people to access personal records, and this stereotype is just not accurate as the whole information industry is far more commercially mundane.

Conducting a full background check involves very in-depth research, and I've included only the very basic information here. It's a huge subject, really a minefield of sources and techniques worthy of a whole book in itself. Some sources are very obscure or even illegal to access. There are also many ways to analyse existing information to discover new links or facts. This kind of information gathering is best done by a specialist who is proficient in this area. Factual investigation has two distinct parts. One involves overt inquiries where a PI would ordinarily identify himself, conduct interviews and make little effort to conceal his interest or approach. An example of this would be a PI investigating a motor vehicle theft. Another branch of factual investigation involves more covert inquiries, where the PI treads very cautiously, ensuring his own identity and the investigation itself are not disclosed to the subject of the inquiries.

These secret investigations attempt to gather as much evidence as possible without the knowledge of the offenders, as any disclosure may spoil the evidence, or even cause the subject to flee authorities. An example of this type of covert factual inquiry may be a large fraud case. It is quite common to have many months of covert inquiries being made into fraud related matters, before the subject becomes aware. Often the first they learn of these inquiries is when they are arrested for their crime, or the investigation requires a more overt move as the next logical step. One such 'move' is known as an Anton Pillar order, which is a court sanctioned search warrant. Few people even know these exist, yet they are used as a very effective tool within some of the more interesting investigations. Provided the court is satisfied there is strong evidence against a person, they will issue an order which permits lawyers and security personnel to enter premises to search and seize items relevant to the case, such as documents, laptops or stolen goods. This action would usually only occur after months of covert factual inquiries. A recent example of this was seen with the Australian Record Industry conducting Anton Pillar raids[25] to fight music piracy. They raided the well-known internet company Sharman

---

[25] www.artslaw.com.au/LegalInformation/Copyright/04AriaRaids.asp

Networks who run the Kazaa sharing software, and seized a large number of documents and computers.

Surveillance operations require agents to be able bodied, if not perhaps slightly fitter than average to be capable of scaling fences, chasing subjects on a follow or perhaps listening or hearing things which are some distance away. These requirements usually prevent many physically disabled persons from entering the surveillance industry. Pre-surveillance inquiries and factual investigations are very specific areas however, which are suitable for a great many disabled staff. This is due to a large number of these being able to be conducted online or telephone from home. The following sections outline the basic information sources, methods, and their applications for conducting covert factual inquiries such as background checks.

Ethics on locating people

The investigator's ability to locate people is powerful, and should only be used for lawful, legitimate purposes. The vast majority of these cases relate to location of witnesses, debtors, or the subjects of surveillance investigations pertaining to fraud. These would be classed as legitimate reasons for locating a subject. Unfortunately there are some persons who engage investigators to locate people for unlawful reasons. While it does not occur often, some aggressive males for example occasionally hire a PI to locate their former partner, who may be in fear of her life. It is very important to validate the reason for any location, and to refuse any request which does not appear legitimate. A good starting point may be to ask the client if there is any violence order in place, and why the person is 'missing'. They may not be entirely truthful, but a good investigator should be competent enough to investigate their client prior to commencing work of this nature.

While it is legal to take this work provided there has been no 'actual' threat or indication of violence made by the client (*I just want to find her to talk to her...*) the repercussions may live with you forever. A Victorian PI located a person for a client, and the client later murdered them by shooting a cross bow through their head[26]. It was later discovered the deceased was a Crown witness, who was due to give evidence against the client. This unfortunate incident was devastating to the investigator who had found her, and he subsequently left the industry. Knowledge is a double edged weapon which can be used for good or evil, so be sure you properly validate any client request, and operate ethically as well as legally.

A clever ploy when you suspect problems is to ask the client what the *date* of the AVO was. If you ask '*Is there an AVO?*' the client may deny it, but asking for the 'date' seems innocuous and the client is far more likely to give you the date... which of course also means there must be one in place. This is an example of obtaining key information indirectly, by asking people clever questions that fly under their radar.

Electoral rolls

Electoral rolls are a significant investigator resource in locating persons, or obtaining general information on Australian registered voters, over the age of eighteen years. There are two types of rolls, being Federal[27] and State[28]. The Electoral roll is a publicly accessible document. Due to privacy regulations, the roll is not available on the internet. There has been much debate over privacy issues such as the harvesting of voters

---

[26] '*Private Investigators in Australia: Work, Law, Ethics and Regulation*', Tim Prenzler, School of Criminology and Criminal Justice, Griffith University, Brisbane 2000 (p41) www.aic.gov.au/crc/reports/prenzler.pdf
[27] The Australian Electoral Office www.aec.gov.au
[28] NSW State Electoral Office www.seo.nsw.gov.au

details for intrusive marketing purposes. This has unfortunately made life far more difficult for private investigators who use this resource to greatly assist their legitimate inquiries.

Rolls are available in printed format about six months after the close of elections, but these are cumbersome, quickly outdated and listed in district order. This means you may need to search through every district instead of just one state. Microfiche records are available at electoral offices, as well as libraries and even in the local office of any member of parliament, but like the printed rolls, are no longer available for purchase. Microfiche rolls are updated usually about every six months, and are listed by surname for all names in each district.

It is important to realise that any electoral roll information is often out of date, and the new records are usually only updated by the conscientious members of our society. Ironically these are rarely the persons who are being sought after by investigators. The election itself however usually results in a significant update as people advise new addresses when obtaining their paperwork. Although the material may be regarded as very outdated, it can still provides important clues for investigators, who, quite frankly, value any information at all. When there is precious little data that can be legally obtained, the rolls can provide a valuable tool to locate witnesses and debtors. The rolls are provided in surname order by state (or electoral district), and include a person's full name.

Full names

This is the first important information, as although you may have a first and last name, it is less common to have a persons middle names in full, or even be sure of the correct spelling. Verifying exact spelling is very important, particularly when investigating fraudulent activity that involves unusual or non-Anglo-Saxon names, which is common. Often a subject may have provided an Anglo-Saxon variant such as Bob, yet the electoral roll may provide their legal first name which may be something like Blanko. These are valuable clues which must be examined on their own.

Full address

The address is provided in full, and this is very important. The telephone book may have address details for subscribers, though Telstra rarely prints any unit numbers. This creates difficulty when a subject resides in a large block of flats, so the electoral roll can provide the missing detail.

Electoral division

The electoral division shows the area in which the address is situated. It allows faster analysis of roll information. If you locate your subject on the roll, you may want to discover if there are any other persons of that surname residing at the same address *(see further information below 'Same Surname Occupants' and 'Relatives at Other Addresses')*. You can search through all the persons of a given surname and check for common addresses, however this can take a very long time for common surnames. In such a case, you can use the division name from the primary subject, and then inspect the division roll only to check for common addresses, as there are far fewer names than if you were seeking all surnames in the state. Even when searching microfiche state records normally, the division field may be used to locate other common address entries slightly more efficiently. It is less information to process visually.

There is a facility for people to hide their address, by registering as a *silent voter*, which removes their address from the public roll. In these cases, the division is still listed, so there is at least one location clue to work with

Same surname occupants

Once an address has been identified or confirmed, an information searcher may elect to search through all the entries of that surname, to identify other persons of the same surname and same address. This provides full name details of other occupants at the home, which may be used to assist in identifying persons correctly. Occasionally an investigator may follow an occupant who matches the description of the subject, only to discover later he has a brother of similar age, so knowing about the brother initially will help resolve these issues. Knowing details of other occupants will always assist in pretext calls and approaches to the residence. The more information, the more pieces of the puzzle, the better you can manage the job and improve the chances of success.

Relatives at other addresses

When trying to locate a missing person, it is sometimes worthwhile contacting possible relatives at different addresses, who may be less suspicious as they are not trying to hide or evade the creditors themselves. They can often provide the subject's correct address or even work details. This is difficult with a surname like Smith as there are just too many records, however there are many surnames with a more reasonable number of entries that can be investigated. Even where there are a few pages of entries for a given surname at different addresses, one can contact these sequentially, starting with entries in the same suburb as the expected location of the subject, which will often result in success. Another point to consider is the use of middle names by your subject, as these may well be the first name for their mother or father who resides at another address, and would happily provide details of their son's workplace if asked nicely.

Neighbours

Using electronic telephone book data, you can identify the surname and initial of subscribers residing near the subject's address. By then cross referencing this with electoral records, you can get the full name of the neighbours, which can then be used in a variety of ways to assist in obtaining the information.

Reverse address

Electronic access to electoral roll data is not always easy, however there are still a few databases available such as CD ROMs and web resources. A company called Sentricx has Electoral roll information available at https://www.sentricx.info. There are a range of information broking houses that can provide access to this data (also known as the Australian Population Index), such as Australian Business Research[29]. Reverse address is a powerful tool which enables you to identify all listed occupants of an address, despite not knowing the surname. It can assist for example, with married women who may be hiding under their maiden name. This information is invaluable when approaching an unknown address. Even the smallest detail can be an information key that will unlock a case, locating a missing person or debtor, or witness.

Old address

When you locate an address for a subject that you know to be a former address, not current, it can still be used as a great clue. You may work this address to identify relatives originally residing with the subject at the time. It may be far easier to locate these relatives now, and approach them to help locate the subject's new address.

---

[29] Australian Business Research www.abr.com.au

Historical rolls

Historical rolls are available in most major libraries[30], and are a valuable tool, often overlooked. Searching historical details, you can often locate a former addresses for people. This may then help you to locate the current address, even if they are not listed in current rolls, or they now have an incorrect or silent address listed. Historical rolls will have details of any former associates or relatives who were residing with the subject at the time, including the neighbours. You can locate any persons identified in the old rolls as being 'associated' with the person of interest, and then canvas these people on the phone or on pretext to locate the subject at their new address. Often it is easy to locate a person by locating former associates as they may still be living with these people in a new address, but just not have their own details currently on the roll. A director who has fraudulently embezzled some money may not appear on the roll, however we may find his wife via historical rolls, and then locate the wife using current rolls to find the evasive director himself. These old rolls were often published with additional details such as occupations or birthdates, which may not be available in current editions. Historical rolls are also used extensively in genealogical research, in which people trace their family history.

Date of birth, occupation and sex

This data is held internally by the Electoral Commission, however it is not publicly available on the Federal rolls anymore. It is still available on state electoral rolls in New South Wales, though this may be changing with increased privacy regulations. As this data was originally accessible to the public, it may also be found by searching historical rolls which were published prior to 1990, provided the subject was on the roll at this time.

---

[30] For example the National Library of Australia
www.nla.gov.au/guides/discoverguides/electoralrolls.html

The case of conflicting interests

Key learning points

- Background factual inquiries

- Work ethics

I was contacted by Ron, a long standing family friend, who asked me if I could conduct some enquiries for him. He was planning a family reunion and wanted to look up a very old acquaintance. In fact, the last time he had seen Fiona was just over thirty years. He said the gathering was to be a surprise and asked if I could keep things quiet, as he didn't want anyone to find out until we had found her. He made a particular point of asking me not to tell his wife Lorraine, as he wanted to make it a very special surprise for her. I began to take some notes, and asked him what information he had. Thirty years was a very long time and he had so very little information about her, other than her first and last name, and the suburb she used to live in then. He didn't know the middle name and was even unsure of the spelling of her surname. He also knew her occupation, which was so obscure I hadn't even heard of it. Now extinct, her former vocation related to something like the manual setting of individual letters dies for the printing industry. I asked Ron if I could question any of his other relatives about Fiona, but he quickly reiterated that it would be best if we didn't 'spoil' the surprise.

I expressed my doubts about achieving success and advised that it was likely she was long married with a new name and occupation, and that thirty years made for a very weak information trail, particularly given that there was so little to start with! We didn't even know her middle name. Ron wasn't deterred and said that I should do my best. He said the reunion was not for some time and so there was no hurry, after all it had been thirty years already, so what was another few months.

I ran Fiona's name through every database I could, and as I expected I came up with far too many listings. Often this is the problem, finding too many people of the same name and not being able to pin them down, rather than not finding anything. None of the records seemed closely related to Camden, which was where she grew up. I began to get slightly disheartened, and, almost as an afterthought I went to the library and looked up the old electoral rolls from the 1970's. Back then there were no combined State rolls, so I had to laboriously trawl through division after division, checking each for her name, looking for the proverbial needle in the haystack. Suddenly I sat up as I read the tiny entry. Fiona Matheson, with a Camden address, and, very importantly, an obscure printing related occupation that screamed out to me 'Here I am!' I had located her, which was no mean feat, and although it was thirty years ago, it was now a solid start. There could be no question it was her, her age matched the estimate Ron had provided, her occupation was a match and her suburb and name matched. It had to be her. Now all I had to do was find her again, thirty years on!

From the electoral roll, I was now armed with her full middle name, her date of birth and more. Of most interest to me were the names of the other residents of her address. I charged over to the land titles office and conducted a title search and found that, although the property was sold long ago, there was some more information - being the names of her parents who had owned the house. Figuring that they would probably now be long dead, I could focus on the other names at this house, who would probably be her siblings.

I trawled through year after year, following each of the residents through the rolls as they moved house, got married, changed jobs and died. I was starting to form a picture. As it turned out, Fiona had apparently moved in with another man back in the early eighties, though it was clear they had not married, or that she had kept her name at least. And then she disappeared. I checked a few more years, but there was no listing. Hmmmm. I pondered for a moment, and then suddenly figured that perhaps she had finally married the guy she was sharing with. I checked this hopefully, and found that for some reason he had dropped off the rolls, but there she was! A single line entry with her new married name, listed at one of her old addresses. I had now found her back to 1984, and was closing in fast. The closer I got, the more 'electronic footprints' I discovered as her name was littered through various databases I searched. She had bought a flat in 1988, but sold it again two years later, and there seemed to be nothing since. It looked suspiciously like her 1982 marriage had failed, and she was just another divorce statistic.

After only three days of work, I finally got what I thought I would never ever achieve. An address and phone number for Fiona Matheson (now Stark), in the current telephone book. Elated, I advised Ron. He seemed strangely silent. *'So you think she is married now?'* he queried me.

'Well, hard to say. She was married in '82 to a guy called Frank, but I am fairly sure she divorced him a few years later and married a Paul. It does look like she is now Mrs Stark and living happily in Windsor, but I don't think she has any children.'

Ron was quiet, but appreciative and thanked me for my work. It was no mean feat, but I had done it. Thirty years was by far the oldest missing person case I had tackled, so to solve it in days with a bare minimum of information and through two marriages was something. I gave him the paperwork I had collated to date, and left him to contact her himself in his own time.

About a year later I heard through the grapevine that Ron had left Lorraine for another woman. It was a shame, as they were both quite close family friends, though Lorraine was slightly more so. Then I learned a little more about what had happened in that the other woman had been a very old sweetheart, who he had met over thirty years ago. Apparently they had gotten together again after all this time, she having left her second marriage about a year ago and had been again living on her own. It came as no surprise when I heard that her name was Fiona, and the elation I once felt at having cracked a difficult case become just a little sour. Had I been responsible for a broken marriage? Was Lorraine's unhappiness now a direct result of my investigative work? Should I have said no to the case, or made more enquiries first? I pondered this for some time, though in the end I figured it was not really my doing, and that Ron probably would have left Lorraine anyway after a time. It was certainly convenient for Ron that Fiona was still keen on him after all this time, as well as her being single at the time. Ron had requested that I not tell anyone about the investigation, and I needed to respect that. It was as he said, going to be a surprise, and after a twenty year marriage it was certainly that.

I thought little about the matter for almost two years, feeling just a little guilty when I met Lorraine visiting my parents home on occasions. Divorce is never easy, particularly when it's messy. Still it was really none of my business. Until one day it was.

Lorraine came to see me, asking for my help with some investigation work. I was happy to oblige, until I realised that she wanted me to do some work on her husband Ron. The divorce was slowly approaching, and Ron had been apparently hiding assets and making it difficult to resolve things amicably. Lorraine wanted me to conduct some checks to see who he was seeing at present, where he was hiding the assets and generally what he was up to. My heart sank, and I felt like I was sitting on a knife edge. I should not disclose to Lorraine about my work for Ron, but neither could I refuse the (closer) family friend Lorraine without some honest explanation. I said I would give it some thought.

After a few days Lorraine rang and pushed me to start work. I tried to dissuade her, saying that I was too busy and that it would probably not be worth it. Lorraine was not to be discouraged and pushed me harder. Surely I could help as this is exactly what I did, and who else would she turn to, with Ron having tied up her money until the case was concluded? I really had little choice, so I began 'Lorraine, *I am afraid there is something I have to tell you... there is a very good reason why I can't take this case, because it would be a conflict of interest. I honestly would take your case under any other circumstance, but you see...* (I wondered if there was any polite way to put it, but of course there wasn't) *I can't take your case because Ron is already my client*' I blurted out, then quickly added '...*but not anymore*'.

There was silence on the other end of the phone and I could hear her mind ticking over.

'*You don't mean... I mean surely you didn't... but I don't care if you did some work for him before, though he never told me about it, but this is different, this is very personal. You have no idea what he is doing to me*' she said, not quite grasping the enormity of what I was trying to tell her.

'*No Lorraine, you don't understand. I did some work for him a little while ago, some very personal work, which I can assure you would be very much a conflict of interest – and while I can't go into details, I want you to know I had no idea what he was doing at the time*'.

There was more silence, and I waited, letting my words find their home in her mind – a swirling mix of emotion and fact, blurring the line between reality and nightmare inside Lorraine's brain.

'Don't tell me you found her... Don't tell me it was YOU... you're the one who found her? I wondered how the hell he found her. For God's sakes it was over thirty years. Why did you do it Chris? Why did you find her?' she asked, obviously wishing I had never taken on Ron's case that fateful day.

'I am sorry Lorraine, I am truly sorry' I replied, not quite admitting to finding Fiona, though there was little I could do to hide the reality. *'I really never knew, but I did it and it's done, and it would honestly be a conflict of interest for me to start working for you, investigating the two of them when I already know about them as a client. I just can't do it – it would be too hard, though I can certainly recommend you some very good investigators who I work with...'* I said, trailing off.

I could tell Lorraine didn't want anyone else, but at least she could see my predicament. It was a little awkward at the time, though we have since overcome the issue and moved on. Lorraine only recently fought a very long and hard battle and succeeded in getting most of what she was entitled to when the case finally went to court, though I did not work on it, other than offering some professional advice. She knows that Ron is no longer my client, but every so often she asks me *'Are you SURE you're not following me?'* and we have a little awkward laugh.

Determine Gender by Name

Being able to determine the sex of persons is important, as it can halve the list of possible suspects, or provide other clues about where to look and what to expect. Knowing a gender means that you can target a pretext with gender specific language, which is more likely to elicit good results than if you don't appear to know the sex of the person you're seeking. In cases where the sex is not known directly, it is possible to do a language association in order to determine the likely gender. Names like Peter and Mary have obvious gender associations, but for people with non-western names it is not always easy to identify sex. Fortunately, there are clever resources available, which provide gender guessing, based on analysis of first names across the entire internet and spanning culture and languages. A good reference site is Geoff's Gender Guesser; found at http://cgi.sfu.ca/~gpeters/cgi-bin/pear/gender.php This site will quickly tell you the sex of 'Yehuda' and 'Shaindel', who are most likely to be male and female respectively. Name search references online can also give suggested nationalities for specific surnames, and other information. Next time you are wondering if the subject has bought property together with a strange named woman that could be his wife, or perhaps a man that may be his brother, gender-matching resources can fill in another tiny piece of the jigsaw puzzle for you!

Telephone Directories

These are another valuable resource used extensively by investigators. They provide contact numbers, but can also provide initials, business details, neighbours details and much more.

White Pages online

The most up to date information is always sourced from the Telstra Internet page at www.whitepages.com.au, or the yellow pages equivalent, though the yellow pages website is less user-friendly, at least as at the time of print. Having web access also enables the information to be easily exported as text, which can save time if you have several records to check.

Printed phonebooks

While they are cumbersome, it is often fast to look up these records manually, especially for investigators on the road without ready internet access. While it may not be common for many people to carry the full printed phonebook in their car, it can be a smart move for the PI who has no electronic access.

Historical phonebooks

Historical printed phonebooks are available for public viewing at some Telstra offices; with editions dating right back to a single page in the early 1800's. Where a surname and initial are already known, this historical resource can identify former address details, neighbours and other information such as business names trading at that address or phone number at the time of original printing. These old directories are also used extensively by genealogical researchers. Some of these details may require a reverse search, or the use of other information resources in combination.

Directory assistance 1224 and Vodafone 123

Often speedy access is important, particularly when a subject is active and you are filming them, or following them in the car. If they were to visit a workshop or other named or signed premises, you may want to call these premises quickly to verify the identity of the person you are following. You may confirm their identity and continue the follow, but equally likely you may find you were following their brother, and should relocate back to the home address as fast as you can, before the real subject departs. Being able to get numbers and addresses quickly can be the deciding factor in a good day or a wasted day. Remember prior preparation prevents poor performance.

While Telstra directories can provide a telephone number, you may require address details as well. This is where services such as Vodafone 123 can assist as unlike Telstra, the operators will provide full address details for you. If you just lost contact with your subject Mr Blaskowski, and you have already followed him through several suburbs, you may try to see if there are any phone entries in the current suburb with his surname, which may be a relative he is visiting. The 123 service can provide these full details to you, or even assist in navigating you to any likely address located in this manner. Remember that every second counts for a PI on the road.

Electronic phonebooks

These are an invaluable resource for investigators, and enable reverse phone and reverse address searching. Due to heavy use by intrusive direct marketing firms, there has been public outcry about privacy and Telstra has taken legal action to protect its directory data. This has made life difficult for the investigator trying to locate people for legitimate reasons. Many CD ROM directories have been forced out of business such as *Australia on Disk* and *Desktop Marketing Systems* or *DTMS*[31], but new companies like www.auslocate.com may still provide the data.

It's important to check all telephone numbers supplied, each name and each address, to see if there are any matches in the database, if available. Often a subject will claim he is not working, yet a reverse address search may result in a business name being identified, it may reveal that the subject was operating a business from home and not disclosing this to creditors. He may be working secretly in a home business yet not disclosing this employment to his insurance company as required by them.

Australian Securities Investment Commission (ASIC)

The ASIC[32] is the governing authority for all Australian companies. It holds very public details such as home address of directors, share details, financial information and a lot more. It provides date of birth information and several other useful

[31] www.mallesons.com/publications/Intellectual_Property/5927145W.htm
[32] Australian Securities & Investment Commission www.asic.gov.au

resources. It is possible to source this data directly from the ASIC, however it is often easier to use an information broker such as ABR[33] or Lawpoint[34], and these are even linked directly on the ASIC website.

Historical directorship search

This provides a list of ALL directorships held by a given name. Remember there are often date of birth inconsistencies in this information, or that people may be listed as Robert Smith and Bob Smith separately. It can often be an art form trying to identify and source the accurate data from any large database.

Each directorship or shareholding identified will be associated to a time window, as well as the home address listed for the corresponding time. Remember that home address details are often current as at the time of lodging the initial paperwork, and are less likely to be updated if there are changes thereafter.

Historical company extract

This search provides all the public details about a company. While it is possible to obtain a standard extract, the historical is always far more preferable for PI's as it contains a wealth of additional details such as former directors or addresses.

- Australian Company Number
- Current company name
- Registered state
- Registration date
- Status (registered / deregistered / under liquidation)
- Registered office
- Principal place of business
- Directors, secretaries, shareholders

---

[33] Australian Business Research www. abr. com. au
[34] Lawpoint www.lawpoint.com.au

- ○ Full name
- ○ Date and place of birth
- ○ Home address
- ○ Appointment dates
- Shares
- Charges (loans)
- Annual return lodgement
- Document lodgement

It is not always easy to read this information, but an experienced information searcher will understand many quirky details that just take a little time to understand. For example, an entry may state that a Deborah Meekings was a director of a company for a period of just one day. To the uninitiated it may look odd or even suspicious, yet an experienced investigator will immediately recognise this to be a shelf company starting director who creates companies for others. After you are experienced at this type of research, you may even notice that certain names become familiar over the years. This means that these people would have no real contact with the company or its other directors, as they are only listed for administration purposes.

Document copies

Many documents may be obtained from ASIC, containing a lot of information about a company. Annual returns are common ones, but there are many more. I once had a difficult case to solve, which involved proving that a particular person was associated with a given company. There was no record of his involvement at all in the electronic records, yet I knew there had to be a clue somewhere. I doggedly obtained all the original source documents for this company, and despite his name not appearing in the fields, I spied it in the header information for a manually processed document. It showed *LODGED BY: Paul Jackson* (handwritten by the lodging party), which is common for such documents; however it usually shows the legal company that was dealing with the administration, usually an accountant. It was clear that Mr Jackson was intimately involved with the company, given that he had lodged the incorporation paperwork personally at the ASIC office. On the strength of this tiny clue, Mr Jackson lost his lucrative position at another firm. There is no such thing as detail too small to be considered in any professionally conducted investigation

State Offices of Fair Trading

Most state Offices of Fair Trading have registers of business and association names. These registers are more likely to include a local shop or small home business, though it can include much larger businesses that have not incorporated to a company. It is possible to obtain information directly from these offices; however, it is often easier to use an online information broker. The index is often freely searchable, and shows registered names together with their status. Obtaining an extract of a business name will usually provide dates of birth and home address details, as well as the place of business address and any former addresses as well. For detailed analysis, it is preferable to obtain all the source documents from microfiche prints, as these often have handwritten entries and other minor detail that may not be included in the general electronic files (such as document lodging party name). Below is a list of 'Fair Trading' bodies (or similar entities) around Australia:

Australian Capital Territory
Office of Fair Trading www.fairtrading.act.gov.au
New South Wales
Office of Fair Trading www.fairtrading.nsw.gov.au
Northern Territory
Dept. Business, Industry, Resource Development www.dbird.nt.gov.au
Dept. of Justice, Consumer & Business Affairs www.caba.nt.gov.au

Queensland

Building Services Authority www.bsa.qld.gov.au

Office of Fair Trading www.fairtrading.qld.gov.au

South Australia

Centre for Innovation, Business, Manufacturing www.cibm.sa.gov.au

Office of Consumer & Business Affairs www.ocba.sa.gov.au

Tasmania

Consumer Affairs & Fair Trading www.consumer.tas.gov.au

Victoria

Consumer Affairs Victoria www.consumer.vic.gov.au

Western Australia

Dept. Consumer & Employment Protection www.docep.wa.gov.au

Department of Lands

Searching land information is a specialised area, which is not within the scope of this manual. The following material relates to New South Wales, however most States have similar government departments that provide this type of information. There is no national land ownership register, as each is managed by state bodies such as the NSW Department of Lands[35]. It is easy to identify any real property that is or was owned by any person. Land records show far more than just property ownership, as they hold personal associations like co-owners who must have some contact with each other. They hold signature images, financial details, indications of solicitor firms being used and much more. For commercial leases, you can obtain a copy of the lease agreement that lists intimate details of the business, such as the nature thereof, and terms and conditions.

---

[35] Department of Lands www.lands.nsw.gov.au

NSW Torrens Title Purchasers Index

This index was started in 1971, and is the 'new' system of recording land purchases. Prior to this was 'old system' land. Conversion of records took place over many decades as land was bought and sold. Some land today may still be listed under the old system, though only very few records. Old system land records can be searched if required, at the Department of Lands office directly, or via online information brokers.

The Torrens index shows all land purchases across various date ranges, and does not indicate current ownership, but rather that a parcel of land was purchased by a person at a given time. The property may have been sold since but this isn't recorded in the purchases index, as it is not a 'property owners' index. To obtain current owners details, you must search the certificate of title document.The Torrens title purchaser's index is issued in THREE date ranges as follows:

- 1971 – 1982 (searches from the start of the Torrens title system up to 1982)
- 1983 – 2006 (searches from 1983 up to 2006...being the last full year)
- 1 Jan 2006– 30 Apr 2006. (The current year's entries up to the end of last month, whatever this may be)

To search for ownership of any property, you must search against the expected purchaser's name, for the period during which they may have been able to purchase property. Clearly there is no need to search for purchases prior to a person being born, yet it is also important to consider inheritance properties, as well as property purchased in the name of an associated company, a relative or a family trust.

NSW Entries are listed in columns as below:

```
Wilson, Gavin Andrew   MENAI          T Y5673454  12/SP1654
Wilson, Gavin John     FIELD OF MAR T Y5683457  21/523452
Wilson, James Nathan   RYDE           L I43683457  436 7045
```

The columns show full name, area (not necessarily suburb though) followed by a type of dealing as a single letter then the dealing reference and finally the property reference. There are many codes and quirks in these databases. The 'T' references above indicate standard transfers (sales) of property, while the 'L' refers to a commercial lease. The entry 12/SP1654 means Lot 12 of Strata Plan 1654. The first number (12) usually means unit 12, but MAY also refer to several units together, or perhaps just a car space sold separately to the unit.

The entry 721/523452 means LOT 721, DP 523452 (Land 'portion' 721 of 'map' 523452) The entry 436 7045 means Volume 436, Folio 7045 (Volume is a sequential record number, and folio is the actual book page number) This signifies a rather old type of land reference. Further searching at the Department of Lands is required to convert this record to the standard LOT/DP style.

It's not easy to identify any records (given the complexity of the above information) for anyone who has had no previous dealings with property records. Things are improving, slowly, but it is still quite difficult to obtain the actual street address for properties listed in the purchase register. The land bodies have historically been focused on parcels of land, and have not made it easy to identify the real street address, as they only used their own numerical references. Even at the time of print, the NSW Department of Lands was offering an 'as is' street address match facility based on the Registrar General data, but this may not be correct or even current. Contacting the local council rates department will easily provide the real address details for Lot and DP references. As with other name indexes, it is advisable to search for other persons of similar surname who may have purchased the same property, as this shows an important association. The records are always obtainable if the actual property title is obtained.

There are many other obscure information sources available in the Department of Lands records such as bill of sale, vendor's index, change of names (up to 1994), Power of Attorney index and many more.

Certificate of title

This document shows the current owner of any property. It may also show any mortgage document references, or caveats. A caveat is, among other things, a form of creditor protection where the property cannot be disposed of or sold unless the caveat is removed. It is important to see who else is involved in the property, and what the nature of the ownership is, such as tenants in common, or perhaps a percentage share for each party. The title certificate also lists the transfer document reference for this purchase, so if it is not in the original owner's name, you can progressively search back through the change of ownerships. In this way you may perhaps determine the sale price for the original owners you identified in the purchaser's index.

Transfer certificate

This is the actual certificate that records the sale of the property. It is often filled out manually, and is one of the few places that have signatures publicly available. The transfer certificate may not always have the purchase price, though it usually does. If not however, it can be deduced in part by the cost of the stamp duty. Note that the signature witnesses listed on these certificates may form important clues to the case, so it is important to analyse these documents carefully.

Council records

The local council will often hold a lot of personal information on ratepayers, which may be accessible. Development approval is one area that may contain information on persons lodging such paperwork, who may in fact be different to the registered owners of the property. There are also information to be obtained from insurance certificates, details of the nominated builder, postal addresses for rate payers which may be different to the property address (such as for a rented or investment property) and more. The council will usually permit viewing of these records for free. Some records require consent of the owner or ratepayer to be accessed however, such as more detailed building plans or more personal information. Councils will often have detailed aerial photographs of properties that may be purchased, which could be a slightly cheaper or easier way to obtain these images. Aerial photographs are especially useful in rural areas, or for planning larger operations.

Insolvency and Trustee Service Australia (ITSA)

ITSA[36] provides details of bankrupt persons. A lot of detail can be provided from these searches, as bankrupts effectively lose their right to privacy. This is so that any creditors or even potential creditors may be protected from dealing with them, or may receive information to assist their actions.

It's good to obtain a full copy of the statement of affairs filed by the bankrupt. This is far more in-depth than the electronic records, and contains details such as vehicle and other property ownership, bank account details and balances, loans, associated persons, passport numbers, employment and more.

---

[36] Insolvency and Trustee Service Australia www.itsa.gov.au

Court records

Court databases are traditionally difficult and cumbersome to search effectively. While court records are usually publicly available online[37] and printed daily on noticeboards, it is more difficult to obtain historical details which would show previous convictions. There are some sources that provide historical details, and some courts do have a very limited searching facility, an example being the Supreme Court which has public access terminals. You may not be able to obtain the details of a case, but you may be able to identify that your subject was involved in certain matters. You could also acquire the details of the 'opposing' party, as in commercial cases. Once armed with this fact, the company may then sometimes provide you with information directly.

Australian Business Register (ABR)

Since the introduction of the company Australian Business Number (ABN), there has been far easier access to corporate information. The ABR[38] provides information on any business that has been registered for an ABN, and includes details on thousands of individuals who run a small business. Information about a subject's business dealings is of much assistance when conducting investigations, as it identifies what they might be doing, as well as providing a legitimate reason to 'contact' them under pretext.

The ABR register records the company name, the trading name, the suburb location of the business, the status and the dates for any changes that have been made. Historical information is also available.

---

[37] Lawlink NSW www.lawlink.nsw.gov.au
[38] Australian Business Register www.abr.business.gov.au

Credit and insurance databases

Formally known as the Credit Reference Association Australia (CRAA, or even CRL), Baycorp Advantage[39] is a company that holds details of the credit file for both individuals and companies. This can be accessed directly, or via other online information brokers such as Australian Business Research, Lawpoint or other similar companies.

Credit information is always valuable data for investigators, and although privacy legislation has restricted some of these services, there is still much that can be obtained. Detailed searches provide all the standard ASIC company extract details, together with some risk assessment details or scoring, details of judgements and other litigation that the company or its directors have faced. Credit file reports also contain drivers licence details, home address histories and other details such as employment in a non-director capacity. Where financial information is being sought on any subject, a credit search is one of the first things that should be checked.

The *Insurance Reference Service* has become part of Baycorp Advantage, and provides non-credit related personal information, such as previous claims history across a wide range of insurers. This can often hold very good intelligence on individuals, but due to privacy restrictions can only be accessed by investigators working directly on an insurance related case.

---

[39] Baycorp Advantage www.baycorpadvantage.com

Australasian Legal Information Institute (AUSLII)

AUSLII[40] is a powerful legal searching database, which can be used to gather details on case law. Some, but not all court cases are fully published and available for public record. 'Example' cases are later used by lawyers to illustrate what judges have ruled previously, and also give the legal system transparency, by showing the public what is really happening in the law. Not even half the cases are listed, however millions are listed and available for searching. Particularly when dealing with slightly more obscure surnames, as well as company or business names, it is advisable to run a search through this site. There is more often no match, however when there is a match, the information that can be gained is often invaluable material.

Web searches

Google and other web search engines, information may be often gathered using either the company name or just the name of a person. You may find a personal web site, a company web site, or media mentions of the person. It is often surprising what can be found online. Although most people will search for just names (company or personal names) to find out information about them, sometimes you can get far more information by searching for terms 'associated' with your subject separately to the name(s) themselves. For example you may search for just a phone number, usually in the quotes syntax "8250 8220" to ensure a full string match. This may bring some other reference to this number, for a website which is not connected with that name. In effect it is a type of reverse search where we look for 'other' references to an entity by using their phone, address or other information which is linked to them.

---

[40] Australasian Legal Information Institute www.austlii.edu.au

Your subject may be claiming they can't work and all your searches may result in nothing of interest. Perhaps they are telling the truth? You try one more time using only their contact details and discover that both their mobile number and home address are listed on a web page advertising casual gardening services. Of course they have not put their own name on this web page, so you couldn't have found it if you were looking for 'them' (i.e. their name) yet we have found them indirectly, and discovered they are actually working from home! You may also have a common name like "B Smith" which would be a difficult web search term which would result in a million matches. By searching for the phone number online however, we may for example find a reference to "B Smith" as finishing third in the *Randwick Runner* group's monthly surf run.

This is a casual event which lists competitors and their finishing times, and we see Mr Smith has his mobile number there as one of the contact people. This is how we were able to locate this particular web page from the million other web pages that include "B Smith". Using any other means, it may take a lot of work to discover he is involved with a running group, yet now we have a good lead on him, and his 'bad back' claim is starting to look a little shaky! It is also worth mentioning that these 'indirect' references to subjects are usually the best to use when approaching them under pretext. It would be easy to turn up at the running club one evening on the pretext of fitness, and then use this to approach the subject and engage them in a casual discussion to gather intelligence. He is far more likely to talk to a fellow runner at a meeting, than to some stranger who has knocked on his front door at home.

Other good reference websites for finding persons include www.schoolfriends.com.au which list many people, together with brief details and email contacts. Sites like www.dnsstuff.com allow you to investigate web domains or email addresses.

Trading / Tenant reference databases

These are private databases which gather personal information from a wide variety of companies. Originally for real estate agents trying to identify bad rental tenants when letting a new property, these databases have grown to include video stores and other companies which have some ongoing contact with consumers. These databases can contain information that would be difficult to obtain via other means, such as work contact details for customers, vehicle registrations, silent phone numbers which aren't published in directories and more. Locating someone who is a rental tenant can often be difficult as they are frequently transient, and are not listed on the more common property 'owner' databases, so these rental reference databases are invaluable in such cases.

Examples include: www.tenantreference.com.au, www.tica.com.au and www.rpdata.net.au

Media searches

There are several locations where you can broadly search various media organisations, and obtain details of newspaper articles, radio or TV interviews etc that may involve the subject. Detailed full text media searching is available through competent information brokers such as www.infoedge.com.au, however the web is also fast and sometimes free for a quick search if you visit newspaper sites directly. Brokers are often more experienced at searching these databases. Such articles may relate to shonky business practices that the subject was involved in, or perhaps an article stating Mr Tiajamin was injured in a shopping centre back in 1992, and lodged a claim for damages.

Map and route navigation

The aerial photography section in the NSW Department of Lands[41] has photographs of all of New South Wales, and you may view these free of charge. Similar facilities exist in all other states. Stereoscopic images are often available which enable you to view the land in three dimensions, as well as inspect the actual property you will be later observing in person. Being familiar with the property and general layout of the land can assist with more remote areas, and help you to plan the best approach or likely observation positions.

Often investigations will involve addresses of interest that are well out of the city, and require some travel. Conducting surveillance in such unfamiliar areas is difficult. Particularly so when you cannot ask too many questions about the location of an address or directions, as this may alert suspicion in the small rural communities. Having quality map and route information will ensure you are well prepared for the task ahead, which will usually be difficult enough without getting lost. There are several good national websites which have map and route navigation information freely available, such as www.whereis.com.au and www.travelmate.com.au

---

[41] Sydney Map Shop, 23 Bridge Street SYDNEY, Ph (02) 92286310

The case of the clever cheque trace

Key learning points

- Background factual inquiries
- Locating a subject

This book is primarily about surveillance. Locating missing persons, asset tracing and factual investigations are distinctly separate areas, which deserve their own textbooks. There is always some cross over however – such as trying to locate a person in order to subsequently conduct surveillance on them. One particularly clever PI once told me how he located a subject using a cheque trace. There was no current address available for his subject. An arranged medical resulted in the subject being followed to an address, yet it was known he didn't really live there as this was his brother's place. His brother always claimed that the subject was residing there, yet this was just a trick to prevent others from finding his real address. Any mail sent to the subject at the brother's address would be forwarded to him by his brother.

After exhausting all other avenues of inquiry, the clever PI wrote a cheque for fifty seven dollars made out to the subject's name. He then sent the cheque in an envelope, addressed to the subject at the dodgy address with no further explanation. The subject eventually received his cheque. Human nature is often predictable. Who would refuse free money? The recipient may have wondered where the cheque came from or why it was sent, but the desire to bank it would be there. What harm can there be in just banking a cheque? Of course this cheque was bait, an investigative expense to lure the recipient into a financial transaction with the clever PI.

The recipient deposited the cheque, and as soon as the PI noticed it had been debited from his account, he lodged a cheque trace request through his own bank, to query the transaction, as is his right under the law. The bank advised where and when the cheque was deposited. The PI discovered it only took two days to bank the cheque, meaning he was in even more frequent contact with his brother than originally thought.

The cheque trace advised the PI which bank and branch the cheque was deposited. This identified which bank they used, and what the account number was. It was assumed the cheque was deposited in a branch close to their home or work, so now the PI had a suburb to work with. The cheque trace was an electronic footprint, which he had a legal right to access as the 'other party' in the financial transaction. The PI then directed his investigative resources to this particular suburb, and by clever pretexts to some local business, he eventually identified the subject's place of work.

Being a fraud matter, one of the immediate questions was how much did the subject have in his account. While the fraud was for a reasonably large amount of money, the police had considered the fraud too small to investigate given their limited resources, which is often the case. The PI decided to continue being clever, and wrote a *second* cheque which was addressed to the subject. This time he entered a branch of the subject's own bank, though not the one which was previously used by them. The initial cheque trace provided the PI with the subject's account number, so he wrote out a deposit slip with this number, to bank his own cheque into the subject's account.

The teller naturally assumed he *was* the account holder because he was banking a cheque into the account as a normal customer would. During the course of this deposit, the PI quietly asked the teller '...*and can I have a balance on that account?*'

The teller was obliged to verify that he was actually entitled to receive information about the account. Despite this, the busy teller didn't give a second thought to this request, and provided him a printed balance slip when she returned his initial deposit slip. It showed the account as having far more funds than would be normally expected of a blue collar worker with a drinking problem, especially as it was known the subject had supposedly only recently been experiencing financial difficulties.

After the investigation had revealed his 'correct' home address, and several other clues (including his unusually large account balance), the fraud case was put to the offender who subsequently confessed under the weight of evidence against him. Often fraud by ex-employees is swept under the carpet, but fortunately this case was reported to the police who successfully laid charges. Next time you see police crime figures, remember that a portion of the solved crime figures are private fraud investigations which are almost handed to the (overworked) police on a platter!

The technique used by the PI in this case falls into the 'social engineering' category, together with pretext calls and a lot of other tools used by some investigators. As is often the case, human error is the weakest link in any security system. This particular PI effectively paid his subject to receive information about his suburb location and account balance. It was the subject's choice to bank the cheque, and as an account holder he should be aware of the implications of being the 'other party' in a financial transaction. Nigeria earns millions of dollars each year through the well known *Nigeria advance fee fraud*, and although this is fraud (as opposed to gaining information for lawful purposes such as reducing fraud), the techniques are similar.

ADVICE: The next time a stranger tries to give you money, be very careful. Always practice safe banking!

WARNING: This PI's technique may seem a deceptively simple way to locate an offender who is concealing his address, but as with any investigative technique, be sure you <u>check all applicable local laws</u> before doing anything. There is (generally) no law against posting cheques they weren't expecting to people, nor questioning your bank to determine if and how they were subsequently cashed. Despite this, laws relating to privacy as well as investigators have undergone recent changes – so exercise careful judgement at all times.

COMMENT: This investigators account of how he cracked a fraud case is but one of many resourceful methods that are sometimes employed by PI's. Ideally, legislation would provide authorised information access to PI's, provided they show reason for needing the information as part of a legitimate and lawful fraud investigation. Billions of dollars are lost to society each year as a result of fraud and bad debts, yet the PI is denied the tools required to effectively investigate these and is forced to use his wits. The police don't have the resources to take on anything but the largest cases. There is always plenty of money available to pay for investigations, though police can't work 'for a fee' and must only rely on limited government funding to operate. PI's are always available to investigate for a fee, but only the police have effective access to the information which is needed. What is wrong with this picture? Go figure! Or speak to your local Member of Parliament.

CHAPTER 5: GARBAGE SEARCHES

Garbage searches are among the 'hidden curriculum' for investigators. This means techniques that are not publicised or well documented, though they form part of work conducted by persons in any industry. This section finally documents a specialist area which is usually learned on the job over many years. It provides students necessary tools to conduct their work effectively and in a professional manner.

People laugh about PI's sifting through the garbage looking for clues. In reality few ever bother, which is perhaps unusual and unwise in an industry that needs to work every possible angle. Garbage searches are a lottery. Sometimes a dozen searches will reveal nothing more than dirty nappies and rotting food. Other times one search will reveal more information than could be gathered from months of surveillance. Searches often reveal telephone numbers, letters, payslips, bills, printed emails or receipts. This information will then assist in the investigation by providing leads to work on, such as phone numbers to ring, angles to pretext with and addresses to visit, to name a few. Criminals engaging in fraud commonly use this technique to steal the identity of victims, or obtain credit card numbers. Sometimes investigators also need to get their hands dirty to catch these crooks!

The best thing about a garbage search is that it provides different types of information, which cannot be obtained in other ways. You will never see it if you follow them, you will never glean it from talking to them. Garbage bins can be a goldmine of information that will give you strong leads to work on. Like all surveillance it is a game of chance. It's also a game for the patient, who won't be discouraged when finding nothing night after night. Pull the poker machine handle enough times, and one day it will ring up a storm. I once had a case where I searched the garbage bin of one guy for nine months straight, and while there were several months where I found nothing, the occasional gem made it all worthwhile. Although searching through rubbish when it has been placed out on the street may be a grey area legally, you are not really seeking physical documentary evidence that can be admitted in court, but information and clues. A common difficulty with investigations is knowing <u>where</u> to look, and this is where a garbage search can help. For an example of a successful garbage search, see the section *The case of stolen noodles* on page 244.

- Identify which night is garbage night. Check also that recycling goes out this night as some areas have alternate pickup dates for recycling. Ring the council for that area, or contact residents in the same street under a pretext

- Prepare a garbage search kit with latex gloves, freezer bags, garbage bags

- Attend the address around eleven o'clock on garbage night. Conduct a drive-past first, and then conduct a foot patrol. Keep the car parked out of sight of the address

- Identify a location suitable for searching the bin contents. Choose a location with some light, preferably out of sight of the subject house, at least two houses away

- Once the area is clear, put on the gloves and walk up to the bin

- Check the contents of the bin. If the bin is reasonably light, it can sometimes be carried a short distance over your back. This may reduce noise in the immediate vicinity of the subject's house, but is not always necessary if the wheels are quiet

- Wheel the bin a short distance (if required) to the search location. Lay the bin down on the ground, with the lid lying open, flat on the ground. This aids in returning the refuse into the bin after the search, as you can swing the lid up with any small items contained on it, and they are thrown into the bin opening. Also, any house numbers marked on the lid are concealed

- If there's a clearly marked street number on the bin, consider laying the bin down on this number so it is not visible, and people will not identify the address for the bin you are checking

- Pull out all the bags of refuse from the bin first. Commence searching through the individual bags

- Identify any paperwork of interest, and place into a plastic bag, or note and/or photograph if you don't intend to take the item with you. As each piece of refuse has been searched, return it to the garbage bin. Once searching is completed, clean up the area thoroughly, don't leave any signs

- Stand the bin up and move it back to the kerb, in the exact same position that you found it, then walk away

- If you have reason to suspect your searching may have been observed by a resident, don't move the bin back to the subject's kerb front directly. You may need to leave it as is and walk away. Always return it to the usual location later when you are not being observed. It is good practice to avoid any connection between the search process and the subject's address

- If approached during the search, stand your ground and provide a cover story, for example *'Yeah, I'm having a fight with Cheryl again. We walked past about an hour ago, and the bitch threw her engagement ring in this bin – I'm not sure if she did, because she's not talking to me anymore, and I can't see the ring on her finger. She better not have though, it bloody cost me an arm and a leg.'* A story with personal emotion will usually put people off questioning you, because they don't want to get involved in somebody else's domestic arguments. If they pursue it further or suggest you *'ask for permission from the owner first'*, continue in a more aggressive tone *'Yeah, well do you think I like going through this stuff? How would you feel if your girl pretended to throw out her ring! If you've got a problem with it, why don't you give me a hand here?'* Fortunately it's rare that people see or approach you while conducting a garbage search, and the entire process should only take a few minutes.

- For regular collections, consider periodically relocating the searching area to reduce suspicion

The Law: Garbage searches / Dumpster diving

While it can be a powerful investigative tool, this technique is slightly controversial, and there is some debate about the legality of conducting these searches. In principle, there is no direct legislation outlawing the practice specifically, and there does not appear to be any Australian case law to provide direction on the legal issues of this subject either. If the law doesn't define an activity as illegal (through legislation or case law), then it's not illegal.

Consider the key points:

1. Could the offence of theft apply? **YES**[43]. If you remove garbage that has not yet been placed out for collection, the garbage is still private property. <u>Never</u> remove garbage from a bin that is still located on the property[46].

2. May I legally take items I find in garbage? **YES**[43]. You may (permanently) take items from a garbage bin, provided the garbage itself has been discarded and therefore has no <u>legal owner</u>. The issue of who is the legal owner of *discarded* garbage is something that Australian courts have not yet defined. Without

adequate legislation, courts look to case law where a precedent has been set by the courts in an earlier case. You should be aware of the possibility that your actions may have you in court, where the court could set precedent and rule the activity illegal (finding you guilty). They could alternatively find the activity legal and set precedent in favour of PI's, which would then clarify the legal status.

3. Have <u>any</u> courts found this practice to be legal? **YES**[43], in the USA. This book is aimed at Australian investigators who must follow Australian laws, however some other countries have clarified the legal status of this practice. A good reference is the USA Government's *Defence Security Service* website, which has a specific paragraph[42] covering this practice. It states *'Stealing trash is not illegal. The Supreme Court ruled in 1988 that once an item is left for trash pickup, there is no expectation of privacy or continued ownership.'*

4. Is it always illegal to look through a private bin? **NO**[43]. Provided you are not trespassing, there is no specific law that prevents looking inside a bin, taking notes or photographs of information observed inside. This includes touching or moving items to examine them properly, provided you don't steal property (i.e. take an item that has a legal owner, with the intent to permanently deprive them of the item). If you are unsure of the issue of ownership, you should consider looking but not taking.

---

[42]www.dss.mil/search-dir/training/csg/security/T3method/Theft.htm
[43] This book doesn't provide specific legal advice. Each case is different. Laws change, and what is legal in one area or situation may not be legal in another. <u>Do not</u> conduct this technique if you are unsure of the legal restrictions that may apply in your case.

5. Can search warrants cover this activity? **YES**[43]. Both the Commonwealth[44] and the States[45] have legislation covering the issue of search warrants. Some law enforcement bodies and (very rarely) some private investigators do obtain warrants in order to conduct covert garbage searches. A warrant provides two key things:

   a. The court specifically *sanctions* the activity, meaning the legal status of the activity is clearly defined, AND it provides assurance the evidence gathered will be *admitted* to the court

   b. The warrant is *enforceable* at law. This means a property owner cannot refuse or prevent the search. Similarly, the local council may be directed to comply or assist as required

6. Do you need a search warrant? **NO**[43] If you can conduct a 'search' with no warrant and *without* breaking any other laws, then you don't need a warrant. Of course, no warrant also means no special powers, no guarantee of evidence being admitted and no clearly defined legal status! An example is a boy who has kicked his soccer ball into an open neighbouring property. Provided there are no warning signs erected and he has not been asked to leave, he would (in most areas) be entitled to conduct a 'search' for his ball without breaking laws of trespass or others. He doesn't require a search warrant to conduct his search. He has no special powers and must leave if asked, but the key issue is that his act of searching itself is not necessarily illegal.

---

[44] Commonwealth Crimes Act 1914 Division 2 - Search warrants
[45] Tasmania: Search Warrants Act 1997, NSW: Search Warrants Act 1985 and others

7. Will evidence be admissible? **Maybe**[43]. Any information discovered may provide *general information* to assist your investigation, and many cases are solved without ever needing to go through the judicial process. You may perhaps confront the suspect in an informal interview, and they may then admit guilt, which solves the case. This is despite the fact not all your evidence may be accepted by a court. Alternatively, it may save your investigative resources by eliminating the person as a suspect somehow. Perhaps it may lead you to other evidence which you are sure <u>is</u> admissible. If your case relies on this (garbage) information and there is a clear case of public interest, you may want to run a legal test case and possibly force the court to set a case law precedent[46] – but be aware this could go either way! The only way to be *sure* of admissibility is to obtain a warrant, though this is not easily done unless the investigation is a joint operation with a law enforcement body.

WARNING – Although there may be no specific laws to *prohibit* this practice, PI's should remember they have no more power than an ordinary citizen, and any action they take may result in legal action, depending on the circumstances. Remember laws do change, and there may be other laws which cover this activity but are not discussed here. The author is keen to make any amendments to the material contained within this book, so please advise of any corrections you feel may be warranted.

---

[46] Just prior to publication of this book the author was reliably advised that legal precedent had been set at the NSW District court level, where a judge admitted some evidence from a diary previously belonging to the occupant of a unit. The diary had been discarded into the garbage bin in the common area (i.e. still <u>on</u> the property), but found by a PI. The evidence was admitted despite strenuous objection by the opposing lawyers. The details of this case were not able to be verified in time for publication.

Blatantly conducting a garbage search loudly in the middle of the night street may result in you being charged with a general law such as disturbing the peace or harassment. Conducting these searches on your ex-girlfriends bin (i.e. without reasonable cause) may leave you open to charges of stalking or trespass. There is always a time and a place. DO NOT use this technique unless you're confident of the law as it relates to the particular circumstances of your case, and always act professionally.

Further Reading: Garbage searches

- The Art of Deception: Controlling the Human Element of Security by Kevin D. Mitnick **ISBN:** 0767906845 (Pages 156 to 159)

CHAPTER 6: PRETEXT CALLS

Like garbage searches, pretext calls are part of a 'hidden curriculum', which are techniques that are not publicised or well documented, though form a common part of work conducted by persons in any industry.

A pretext is all about pretending. The movie *Catch Me If You Can* was a perfect example of pretending to be someone you are not, in order to gain something. Rather than stealing money or committing fraud, investigators often use this technique to obtain information. You approach somebody under a pretext, and get them to give you information or do something, because they think you are someone you are not. A pretext is often described as 'social engineering'. It's a means commonly used by computer hackers and fraudsters to elicit passwords or other personal information out of people. In effect you are lying to someone, by masquerading as a courier, a former worker, or a family friend for example. There is no limit to the nature of a pretext, as it is will depend on the situation. The approach that works for a blue-collar construction worker may not work on a rich housewife.

There are two parts to any pretext: content and delivery. To be effective, you need to maximise the effect of both, as you are a real-life actor, playing a part. You need to convince your audience, and a good performance will get you valuable information instead of applause. A poor performance may spoil the job, making people suspicious and cautious, which is not good. It's important to get it right.

To start a pretext, you need to do some research and discover some key facts about what you need to know, who you need to approach, what would be the best way, the best time and so on. After doing your homework, you need to rehearse your part, working on your delivery to get it flowing smoothly, immersing yourself in the details of the part you need to play, including the choice and timing of your words. A good pretext flows, adapting and changing seamlessly according to the focus of the recipient. Rather than deliver it as a finished monologue, you need to improvise, quickly analysing every cue you receive, and modifying your material to suit. Individuals respond in different ways, and need different keys to unlock the information.

Some people are inherently suspicious. A good operator may discover this and quickly change their delivery to reduce the number of questions they ask, in order to limit any concerns. At other times a person may be only too willing to help, and you need to detect this quickly, as they could be a source of a lot of information if you realise they are comfortable talking to you. Obtaining information from people who don't know you is not an easy task, but there are several tricks. One is to make sure you give them more than you ask from them, telling them all sorts of nonsense such as how the traffic was heavy today, or how much you hate it when your mother nags you about moving that box into the garage (*you would think she would move it herself if she was so worried about it*) and so it goes on. Giving them information makes them comfortable giving you information in return, particularly if you only ask them for small details, when you are giving so much. What they don't realise is that your information is worthless to them, but theirs is gold to you! Giving red-herring information is an excellent key to opening up the information treasure chest.

Getting information wrong is another trick. If you were to ask a suspicious person for their spouses work telephone number, they would rarely oblige. Consider this approach: '*Hello, is Mary there? No? Ok, look I tried to ring her at work yesterday too, perhaps I have the number wrong. Is it still 9898 4050, or is that the old number?*' In this pretext, you have not asked for Mary's work number at all. In fact you have SUPPLIED Mary's work number to the person answering the phone, never mind that it is wrong, and you never had it in the first place. The beauty of the pretext is that you create an 'air' that suggests you were previously given the work number, and must then be authorised to have it. There now seems no harm for the unsuspecting recipient of the pretext to 'correct' your mistaken telephone number, or perhaps even give you her new number. Of course this pretext would only work properly if Mary was not at home when you rang. This is an important fact that needs to be considered when you do your background research and plan the appropriate pretext delivery time.

You need to consider what information you really need. Asking for somebody's place of work is quite intrusive, and is far less likely to be successful. Asking for somebody's work telephone number is more common, yet it also provides the real information you are seeking. It's easy to get the details from the number by looking it up or just ringing it. Asking if 'John' will be home tomorrow at four pm is quite intrusive. Advising them you have a package for John that you want to deliver around four p.m. tomorrow, which requires personal signature, will give you the same information in an indirect manner. The recipient will quickly advise you John will not be home until six p.m. (to sign), which is what you really need to know. You get this information because your FOCUS was on the signature, not John's movements. The best pretext will elicit information sideways, harvesting data in subtle, indirect ways, so the recipient of the pretext is never aware they've been so helpful.

Sometimes an open, slightly cryptic approach can work wonders. By opening a dialogue in a way that doesn't really go anywhere specific, you can think on your feet to tailor the pretext on the fly, making it up as you go along. Although you can often get off to a shaky start, you have the benefit of surprise, as your recipient is searching for connections themselves in the first few seconds of any new call with a stranger.

The Law: Pretext calls and impersonation

There are several Acts in the Australian legislation which cover the offence of impersonating a government officer, such as a police officer. There is legislation relating to providing *'False or misleading information'* to a public authority[47].

Good PI's will never do these things, and should NEVER do this. What the law doesn't prohibit is, for example, lying to a girl in the pub about your age, to perhaps encourage her to go out with you later. Similarly it doesn't necessarily prohibit PI impersonating someone who is perhaps 'interested in buying the property and wants to have a look around' or a PI who impersonates a courier with a package to deliver. An investigator often impersonates someone or uses deception to obtain *information* which may result in solving a lawful investigation.

This is distinctly different from a fraudster who uses deception to conduct their fraud and obtain financial advantage from the victim. In these cases the impersonation or deception <u>is</u> an offence, known as *'Obtaining money etc by deception'*[48]. Criminals are often deceiving in their actions, but similarly investigators often need to act in a similar manner in order to catch them out and bring them to justice.

WARNING: The law does accept cases where criminals are sometimes 'tricked' into doing something, or admitting some information that later helps proves their guilt, and many investigators will successfully use this technique to some extent in their work. Remember that a PI has no more legal authority than an ordinary citizen. This technique should be only used on

---

[47] Crimes act 1900 - sect 307b 'Providing *false or misleading information* to a <u>public authority</u>'

[48] NSW Crimes Act 1900 Sect 178ba *'Obtaining money etc by deception'*

legitimate and lawful investigations, and only to the extent required by the circumstances. Although you may not break the law while using the technique, improper or unprofessional behaviour is not acceptable, and may disadvantage your case in court. An extreme situation may have a judge not accept evidence, if they feel the pretext was overly complex or compelling that it was actually responsible for the suspect's actions. This is known as entrapment or agent provocateur, and is covered in more detail on page 498.

Project confidence

A confident approach can give the impression to any others who may be watching, that your movement is perfectly normal, despite logic telling a different story. The right movement approach can send subtle signals to others, just as the professional of the art looks for these signals themselves. Even though the layman may not consciously pick the subtle behaviour points, their primitive brain will still register 'Hey, something is wrong with this situation!' and that is not good. The surveillance professional may be able to carry themselves so well, they exude a 'nothing to see here', despite the fact they may be walking down a deserted driveway in camouflage, or perhaps striding through a secure factory facility without authorisation. Playing the part has more to do than just how you are dressed or what you say. Frank Abagnale, who inspired the movie 'Catch Me If You Can' was a professional of the art, cashing large but worthless cheques, or getting a job as an unqualified doctor while 17 years old – not just because of how he was dressed or what he said, but how he carried himself.

Restrict information about yourself

Don't supply your (dodgy) company name or contact details unless requested, or you feel it is necessary to win trust. 'Hello, I am a _courier_ and I have a delivery for Ms Chaseling' **not** 'Hello, *my name is <u>David</u> and I'm calling from <u>Austcall</u> couriers...'* Giving specifics like a personal name rather than a generic 'courier' tag makes the phone call more memorable. Personal names or similar details stick more in the mind, and can be more easily recalled later. (*'Some guy called Bob rang and he said something about a delivery'*). Specific information can also be checked back and may result in the person discovering the call is a hoax. If however the person asks for a company name, have one very ready to provide, even if it is a legitimate one, because they will never be able to verify that you are lying with any certainty – especially in larger companies. (Yes, there are four David's working here, which one did you mean?)

Two for one rule

Give <u>TWO</u> items of information for every <u>ONE</u> you get. For every question you ask such as *'What time will they be back?'* *'Do you have a mobile number for them?'* or *'Can I deliver it to them at work?'* you need to supply meaningless 'red-herring' information, such as:

- I will be in Parramatta around two p.m. today
- My wife is sick of me working such long hours
- I am unfamiliar with that area because I normally deliver the Bankstown run
- My mother-in-law is staying over at the moment and it is driving me crazy
- I really need to get to the Post Office to renew my rego because it expires tomorrow and I have a job interview in Penrith

The more irrelevant the better. Giving out more information than you ask reduces suspicion, and makes people more comfortable with you. *After all, HE told me where HE will be at two p.m., so I feel comfortable telling him what time my wife will come home today.*

Cloud the issue. Hide questions in meaningless babble. Supplying more information than necessary makes people switch off, and be totally uninterested in your call. Like listening to a salesman's pitch, they will stop listening to you, they will be unguarded, and give you whatever you need to just get you off the phone. Get them thinking *'I don't care about your mother-in-law mate'* instead of *'Why are you asking me this specific information'*.

Be vague on job details

'I think so... It is hard to read this writing (fax)'

'I have a delivery for Mr ... Ahhh ... B Chaseling I think it says here' – This suggests you have just read the (poorly completed) run sheet with delivery details, rather than exhibiting obvious familiarity with the name. Familiarity suggests you have intimate knowledge of the subject, like you may have studied a detailed report, or 'rehearsed' your spiel (unless it is obvious like Smith)

Be vague because *'I'm just the temp – I'm not really sure'* or *'It's not really my job, but* <u>Darren</u> (a specific red-herring) *has gone out to lunch and I've just been given this list to go through'*.

Obtain information via corrections

If you ask a stranger for personal information, they will often decline to provide them, or will ask a lot of questions about why you want to know. There is a chink in the armour of these natural human defences, when it comes to correction. Most people like to show they have more knowledge and are superior to others, as we all like to be 'right'. Instead of ringing and <u>asking</u> for the work number of their flatmate, it is far better to tell them a number you think it is.

Consider: *'...and I tried to call him yesterday, but I think I have the wrong number as there was no answer. Perhaps you can check I have it right – it is 8250 8220?'* You have made up a likely sounding telephone number using a suspected or local exchange prefix at least. Their flatmate will realise your number is wrong, and will usually correct you. They would not give out that work number to anyone they didn't know, but in your case, you clearly 'had' been given the work number before. In effect you obtain the information through correction, rather than asking for it in the first place. Perhaps you still have their old number? Once you are corrected, you should springboard off this exchange and encourage them to disclose more information such as *'Yes, I must have had their old number – it has been a while since I rang them. Is he still going to the gym or is he a lazy bastard? I was going to see if he wants to train together again...'*

Provide detailed red-herrings

A red herring is information that is totally irrelevant to the conversation, and is used to both distract focus, as well as make it appear that you are willing to provide them with specific details. This will make them feel more comfortable talking to you and giving answers to your questions. Be very <u>specific</u> on any red herring details – *'My mother-in-law has come down from Forbes, and is staying for two weeks'* – The specific detail supplied is FORBES and TWO WEEKS. It is meaningless, but clearly shows your willingness to give this level of detail, rather than simply asking several personal questions while remaining guarded with (all) your own information.

Be in context

A courier is always in a hurry. They often talk like they drive. In a phone call, they will probably be the first to say *'got to go, thank you and goodbye'*, rather than stringing the call out over a longer period of time, trying to continue a dialogue.

A salesman or researcher is likely to actively attempt to keep a conversation going much longer, so this is natural context for the pretext.

Believe your pretext

A good actor will adopt their role and immerse themselves into their character. A good PI will do likewise. Don't think you are a PI just 'trying' to put on a pretext, but rather believe in your character and imagine you are that character by both acting and thinking as they would. This allows better, more confident delivery.

Timing

Watch out for pregnant pauses in conversations. Keep it flowing to reduce suspicion, and to reduce the opportunity they have to ponder the reason you are asking such detail. If in doubt, talk meaningless babble or red herring information to fill gaps in conversation.

Make sure you chose your time and location to best suit your purpose. It may be best to call early in the morning, or perhaps late at night. Call their work during lunch time, or just before they rush home. Perhaps the best time is on a Friday, or the weekend. Will you call at home or work or mobile? Where do you want the subject to be when you speak to them? Do you want them away so you get their answering machine or someone else who you can ask information about them? You must control the *where* and *when* of your pretext, to maximise the chance of its success.

Remain unfamiliar

A poor question is '*What time will your WIFE come home?*' A better question is '*What time will SHE come home?*' as it is less intrusive and does not imply the caller is making assumptions about personal relationships. It is best to convey the opinion that you have absolutely no interest in anything at all, other than getting your stated business finalised quickly. Of course this can change if you detect they are likely to be comfortable discussing more personal issues, in which case you can delve in more deeply.

Appear disinterested or distracted

The less interest you show in their answers, the more likely they will feel comfortable talking to you. Engineer the conversation to appear that you only need a few answers to 'fill in the blanks' on your form. Seem as though you (personally) could not care less if they are telling the truth or not, or even what they are actually saying – provided they give you 'some' answer. You may be in a hurry to go home or to another job, and if they only give you some answer you can get on with work. The more they feel this call is just one of many, the more comfortable they will be talking to you – to 'help you out'. Don't make it sound like you are hanging on their every word and totally focused, but rather your thoughts are elsewhere on occasions.

Call out to an imaginary co-worker to '...*Turn that bloody radio down I am on the phone here!*', or take an imaginary mobile phone call during the pretext '*Hang on, me phones ringing – What? Nah look I haven't had time to get to that job, and I am on the phone right now to a customer... I will have to call you back*'. Showing you are able to be easily distracted, and that you are comfortable and relaxed in your conversation will similarly put them at ease. You may use this distraction further, to interject red herring details such as 'That was my boss on the phone – you would think he would hire more staff instead of riding us so hard! At least I get overtime 'cause I worked through last weekend'. This may win you some sympathy from them, but also the red herrings will distract them and make your conversation sound more authentic.

Empathise to build rapport

A good pretext is usually where you strike up some rapport with them, finding common ground to agree on. This puts them more at ease and they are more likely to talk freely with you. You may have done some homework to discover their interests or attitudes, which can be then used in conversation to show you share these interests or feelings. Alternatively you may detect something in whatever they either say or imply, or you may sense something in their response to your comments that will give you a lead into their brain. Find commonality in anything and don't be afraid to ask or talk about things outside of the investigation focus itself. Attempt to detect their opinions subtly before providing your own, so you can agree with them.

You may only really want to discover *if they are working and where*, but the best way to get this may be a very short talk about the sudden rainy weather or the late trains or some other topical issue which they will probably have some opinion on. You may appear disinterested or distracted when asking them investigation related questions to disguise your true focus, but may appear more interested and focused on the 'common ground' topics. They will also feel more comfortable talking about these non-personal topics first. Provided it is appropriate for the situation, you can adopt a chatty, slightly extroverted persona to talk briefly about these unrelated issues while building rapport, and then (when they are comfortable) steer conversation to elicit more specific information from them.

Personal names

Remain unfamiliar with personal names where possible, such as: *'Mr ... Chaseling or Cheeseling is it? I can't read this writing!'* Check if ethnic names have an Anglo-Saxon version. There is no point asking for Tassos Papadopoulos, if he is known to everybody as 'Tony', and the only people that would actually know his legally correct name are likely to be the authorities such as the insurance company, or their investigators! Showing unfamiliarity and disinterest conveys a comfortable feeling to the caller that you have little interest in them, and are just like many other similar calls they may receive from legitimate businesses over the years. Being able to pronounce names fluently may imply you have studied their case file well, and know more about them than they would be happy to know.

Choose word focus

'When will your <u>wife</u> be home?' versus *'When would be a good time to deliver it?'* Both sentences say the same thing, but the first implies you are actually interested when the wife will be home! The second implies (correctly) that your <u>focus</u> is in the delivery of the item. A true courier 'exudes' his true desire for fast delivery, which is evident in many ways. It is not just WHAT you say, it is HOW you say it, and importantly what FOCUS you project by the specific words you use, rather than the meaning of the words.

'I have to see her personally to deliver it' versus *'it says personal signature required here...'* The words <u>see her personally</u> are far more aggressive and intrusive than *'It* (i.e. not *me*) *says personal <u>signature</u> required'*. Personal signature obviously requires personal attendance, but this is implied, and not asked directly. A courier is only interested in the 'actual signature' for his form and does not want or even imply he wants to actually see the PERSON. Attention to such minor detail can easily make or break a case, because a poor pretext can often spoil an entire job.

'I have some <u>documents</u> to deliver' is often poor wording to use on a pretext call, because it evokes thought of insurance claim documents, court summons paperwork etc. It often quickly brings the persons memory back to such events, leaving them in a guarded, suspicious frame of mind. Why would the courier even know the contents of his delivery are documents and not

photographs or some other item? *'What documents? Perhaps I better check for investigators outside, because I now (thanks to that callers words 'documents to deliver') remember my solicitor telling me to watch out. Perhaps this phone call itself is to check up on me?'*

Use the generic 'delivery' instead of documents etc. Real couriers have no interest in the contents of deliveries. The right language will direct your focus, and this can result in a good result or an unfortunate failure, depending on how you handle the situation.

Pretext props

For doorknocks and other physical pretexts, it is often a good idea to use a prop. I occasionally use a bunch of flowers as a delivery pretext to an office location, in order to get inside and talk to workers. The staff members are usually focused on the flowers which will always be large and bright (more than my physical presence), and this is a form of disguise. (*In this case the flowers would constitute a work expense, and be charged back to the client as required.*) Of course, this does not always work as planned.

I was doing a job and my brief was to enter a Parramatta office under pretext, and obtain some specific details about the company and its operations. Our intelligence suggested there may be two or three people working in the office, probably older females. I chose a 'flowers' pretext, and walked through the tiny unmarked office door carrying my 'delivery'. In this particular case our intelligence was unfortunately wrong, and rather than a couple of middle-aged women, I was greeted by a large horde of young women! There were so many bright young girls sitting at rows of desks, and the sight of a tall, reasonably good looking male with a bunch of flowers was apparently a welcome distraction to them.

Rather than being a subtle (but realistic) pretext to gain entry to the office, on this occasion my flowers were decidedly inappropriate. I quickly drew the attention of the entire office as they were suddenly all tittering about who the flowers were for. I was nearly mobbed by a few of the more eager girls, and there was some disappointment shown when they discovered that my delivery was for another office, and I had entered the wrong one by mistake (as I then explained). If I had been given the correct intelligence to begin with, I would have chosen a more low-key prop such as a parcel for my pretext, and thus drawn less attention. Of course it was not a client problem, as they could only provide the intelligence they had. Part of the PI role is often to verify the intelligence, if there is any at all. Since the office was crowded, I could have entered with little or no props and probably wandered around for much longer as I observed the surroundings and obtained the information I needed. As it was, I was able to get the information, but not as much or as detailed as I'd hoped for because my flowers got in the way!

Pretext suggestions

Is someone home?

Ring with a computer fax tone, and then listen for the pick-up. This allows you to make numerous calls at odd hours, without arousing suspicion. (*That damn automatic fax machine is ringing again*). Make sure you remove calling station headers from your own fax, in case they have a machine to receive, else they may get your personal details from the fax header.

Stimulate movement to confirm identity

'... *So the delivery guy may have dropped it into your letter box this morning by mistake. Did you get it. No. Ok, well could you possibly check your box now while I wait, because if it is there I*

will send someone right back to get it. Sorry for the confusion...'
They will hopefully walk outside to check their mailbox for you,
while you observe them.

What sports do they play?

*'So the survey is trying to see what sporting facilities we should
bring to the area, or what would best suit the local residents.
What sports do you play?'*

When do they go shopping?

'So we're offering a free $10 shopping voucher for the (INSERT
LOCAL CENTRE). *When is the most common time you shop there,
and is this your usual shopping area?'*

Where do they work?

*'It does need to be delivered in business hours only. Will there be
someone home to receive our complimentary package? No. That
is fine, provided we have a daytime address, we can deliver
anywhere in Sydney during business hours. Personal signature
required. What address do you want it sent to?'* Don't mention
the word 'work', but focus on the *delivery*, not the address.

What car do they drive?

*'I had a car crash recently, and was given your number as a
possible witness from Alan - I think his wife recognised you?
Where were you last weekend – did you see an accident? What
car do you drive?'*

Open pretext / conversation starter

*'Hello, its Luke from Pizza Hut delivery ... I am afraid we are out
of anchovies at the moment, could I just send the pizza order
without it? What address are we sending to? Order: two large
Super Supremes (one originally with anchovies), garlic bread and
a 1.25 litre Coke'*

Open pretext

'I'm calling about the ad' / *'I'm calling about the show'*

When will they be home / verify identity

'G'day. I'm a courier with a package to deliver to... (where is it?)... Mr Subject. I'm just checking they will be there, 'cause I need a signature'

Do they live there? (Rural address)

Ring anyone at all in the town at random and just ask for them. *'Sorry, I must have the wrong number for Mr Subject. Would you have the right one for him?'* Small towns often mean someone will know of the person you are seeking.

Shopping questionnaire

Hello, I'm from Johnstone Research and we have free sample shopping hampers to give away in exchange for your answers to a few brief shopping questions.

- Do you personally do the household shopping?
- What day and time do you normally do the shopping?
- What centre do you currently shop at?
- What mode of transport do you use? (car, walk, bus)
- Is distance a factor for you? Would you travel further if there were better shops available in a new shopping centre? How far would you go?
- Is time a factor – shift workers? What is your occupation?
- Who should we address the parcel to? (and the address?)

Thank you for your time. A sample pack should be sent out within two weeks.

Further Reading: Pretexts

Pretexts are a specialist area, and *Behind the Private Eye* is one of few available which document this unique technique. The following books provide additional training in the subject:

- Pretext Book by E. Roy Slade **ISBN:** 0918487501

- The Art of Deception: Controlling the Human Element of Security by Kevin D. Mitnick **ISBN:** 0767906845

- The Art of the Steal : How to Protect Yourself and Your Business from Fraud by Frank W. Abagnale **ISBN:** 0767906845

The case of unfortunate advertising

Key learning points

- Personal information security (Agent safety)

- Pretext inquiries

I was once following a subject who had a handwritten *'For Sale'* sign in his car window, together with his mobile number. This is perhaps at the more 'extreme' end of the giving away information, because not only was he giving away his phone number (which I had already obtained anyway), he was giving away an <u>opportunity</u>. He was just asking for a pretext. I lost contact with him while following him in heavy traffic later that day, and was able to ring him on pretext about his car. He said he would be happy to show me the car, and asked when a good time would be. I explained that right now would be a good time, as I had just seen the car in the traffic and was going to stop him but he had driven off. I suggested I was not far, and perhaps he could tell me exactly where he was so that I could come right now. He said it wasn't the best time, though I persisted, saying I may not be in the area later. He soon relented, and told me he was in the local Hungry Jacks, and would be there for another twenty minutes as he had just ordered a meal.

Bingo. I said I would hurry right over, after all it was a good car... it is not often you can get a 1984 model Telstar in such a good condition, in fact some of the panels had no dents at all! Sure enough there he was when I arrived, and I got some good footage at the location as he ate with his girlfriend and then eventually left. He didn't seem concerned that the 'buyer' who had phoned him never showed up at the restaurant to check out his car. You often give away information without being aware, and that it is not just the information but opportunity you can give to others. Like many things in life, information is a double-edged sword that can be used against you, so manage what you give to others carefully. Your life may depend on it!

Phone techniques

Caller ID hiding

Caller ID is an issue to consider when making pretext calls. You can choose to hide your number by switching off the caller ID feature, through the telecommunications service provider OR register your line as a silent number, though this costs more. Alternatively you can choose to make a call with caller ID blocked just for that call. Most mobile phones have this option. Using a land line phone you can block caller ID by dialling a prefix of 1831. Blocking caller-ID means the called party can't trace your details, so in some cases this is a good safety measure to prevent them learning your identity, or calling you back to check any details you provided during the pretext. There are cases though, where it is advisable to display caller-ID, as this can make the called party feel more comfortable speaking to someone who shows their number – thus increasing the chances of success for your pretext.

Caller ID showing

For especially sensitive jobs or with a wary recipient, you may need to show caller ID to reduce suspicion. Of course there is no requirement to show a 'real' caller ID number. One alternative is to buy a cheap pre-paid sim card, and use the dodgy mobile number to ring out on. This provides your subject with a caller ID number, yet this is not your regular mobile number. If you want the person to be able to call you back, you can divert the dodgy number to your own, thus you can receive the call on your regular handset, without disclosing your own number. At any stage you can simply switch off the diversion to remove any link they have to contact you, such as if the pretext goes bad and they become suspicious, or when you don't need to offer them a contact channel anymore as the job has finished. Another approach may be to have a voicemail message on the dodgy number, which you check at intervals. The outgoing message may advise callers *'Thanks for calling Dave Dodgy from Dodgy brothers contracting – please leave your message'*. Obviously you substitute details as appropriate, but the effect is quite good. Callers will feel far more comfortable hearing a recorded message that supports the pretext – after all, if someone was playing games, why would they leave a dodgy message on their voicemail? Of course this is because it is the dodgy phone line, not the normal contact number!

This technique can also be used to elicit a contact number from someone who would ordinarily be extremely cautious about giving it out, or who may verify any caller fully before doing so. In this case you may provide them with a message such as a note on their door, letter or some other way. The message will contain some bait to get their interest (so do your homework and *target* the pretext towards them specifically just like personal advertising) together with a dodgy phone number. They will call the number, but only ever get the voicemail message as soon as they call, because you never answer it or divert it to your real contact number. The message may be structured to suggest that it is ONLY a message service, so it will never be answered by a real person, or strongly suggest this is the case. Now the subject has a baited message burning a hole in their brain, and the only way to resolve it one way or the other is to make the call and leave a contact number on the message bank. Human psychology is a funny thing, and provided the pretext is well researched and delivered, it will be hard for them to just discard the note and forget about it, without ever making that fateful call.

Another approach to providing a caller ID not directly associated with you is to make calls from a large organisation, where the caller ID number is the generic switchboard number. This provides a reputable looking landline number displaying as your caller ID, yet the called party can't return the call easily. You may have occasional access to an office line through an associate or some other work or appointment. Some city buildings have local line access with a handset near the reception or lift area, especially after hours. Use your imagination. In some cases it may be good to call from a payphone, as this information can show up as payphone and thus support some pretext you have devised. Perhaps you want to project an image of not having a mobile phone for some reason – *'I am sorry, I can't give you a mobile number as I don't have one – I'm calling from a payphone'* for example. The other party will see the 'payphone' on their caller-ID display (for most land lines), and so they have 'verified' a piece of information that you have provided them. This encourages them to believe other parts of your conversation.

Transmitting silent numbers

Where you want to show caller ID from a silent line, you can override the silent status for a single call, by dialling the prefix 1832. This will transmit your phone number regardless. This normally enables you to call a taxi or pizza and have your details retrieved automatically, while preventing your number from displaying on all normal calls. This code comes in handy in some cases, such as where you want to 'discover' the phone number of your subject. You can knock at their door and ask them under pretext if you can use their phone to make a call. Perhaps your car has broken down outside. Then you can dial your own mobile number from their phone, using the display caller ID over ride. Thus you have transmitted their silent home number to your own mobile handset! Make sure you set your mobile phone to <u>silent answer</u> first though, or they may hear your phone ring and then become suspicious about your 'need' to use their phone in the first place!

Classified ad calls

A great pretext is the advertisement. At some time in your life, you will have answered an ad, or perhaps placed an ad, and if it wasn't you, then it was someone you know. Selling a car or applying for a job; ads are everywhere and can often be used as a good psychological key. A classified ad may also set up the pretext to allow multiple callers, each inquiring about the phantom ad. This allows you to get more bites at the cherry - ideal when you need to pump more information over time, because any assistant you ask to ring the home will be regarded as just another one of those annoying calls from the ad – 'which paper did you say it was in?'. Even the fact that the opening statement, 'I'm calling about the ad', is so short, it gives nothing away, and forces the subject to fill in the gaps, providing you with some handles to work with.

Call diversions

Some tricky people have their land line permanently diverted to another location – either another land line or to their mobile phone. This makes life difficult for a PI trying to establish where the person is. If you call them at home, you expect that they are at home – though diversions confuse this logic. To get around this, you can double divert. The land line network prohibits double diversion, which is where a call is diverted to a number which is also diverted. This probably prevents diversion loops where calls get lost in the loops, or prevents the call from being routed through complicated processes. A diverted call which encounters a second diversion will therefore terminate, and cause the second line to ring, despite the fact it is diverted elsewhere.

To confirm 100% that a person is at the location attached to a land line number, you simply set up a double diversion. Divert your own office fax line to their home line. Then call your own fax line from your mobile. Your call will reach your fax line, divert to the subject's line, and then it will ring, regardless if they have a diversion in place. If the subject answers, you know they must be there, as your call can't double divert. Occasionally this does confuse people – I had a case once where the subject was especially tricky and never received calls on his line but only took voicemail messages. I used a double divert to make the handset ring, and he actually answered out of surprise. *'This phone never rings – it is supposed to be always diverted!'* he said with some confusion, and of course I was able to turn this to my advantage and together with catching him off guard I wove a good pretext and got exactly what I needed for the case.

Call back

When trying to get personal details about someone, you may be able to encourage them to call you on pretext, such as a letter posted to them, or a note left on their door. You may not have their phone number, or be sure where they are working. Rather than simply 'accept' their call as part of your pretext, you should attempt to call them back. Consider saying something like *'Hi, thanks for calling me – look I am busy on the other line but I can call you right back in five minutes. What's your number?'* This type of exchange is common, and often they will blurt out their telephone number without a second thought. Suddenly you have obtained their number, which may even be a work number if they have called during business hours, or because they want to call at work where their boss pays for the call and their time! Call back is also good because you are then paying for the call. If they had rung you on their mobile phone, then they are paying for the call, and are therefore less inclined to talk to you for a long period. When you are paying for the call though, you may find them more comfortable to talk with, and have more time to elicit information from them.

Had you approached them in a more conservative fashion such as saying you are a fraud investigator and want to know where they work, or what their phone number is, you would likely get a flat refusal or a suspicious, cagey answer. The call back technique is different though, because it is not that you are asking them for their number, but rather you are 'busy' and can't take their call. After all, they rang you. So they feel more comfortable giving you the number to just 'call them back'. Subconsciously they are thinking you will write the number on a scrap of paper and use it ONLY to call them 'right back', at which point the number will be discarded. In fact, you will be taking great interest in the call back number as it tells you so many things in any investigation. Is it their work number? Who is it registered to? What address is it registered to? (note the time and place the subject at this address on that day and time), is a business name provided (spoken) when this number is answered? Call back is just another great psychological technique, used to socially engineer people to give you the information needed to investigate the case.

Late calls

Often a telephone number is identified as being associated with an investigation, however it may not be clear who 'owns' the number. Perhaps the phone number was observed written on a document lying on the front seat of a car during a close inspection, or it may appear as an entry on the subject's phone account. We could ring this number during business hours which would connect us with a person, and we would then perhaps need to engage them in a conversation. A late call is very different though. Set an alarm and wake at three a.m. Call the number at this late hour, and it is extremely unlikely to be answered in person, and hence will often pass through to an answering machine or voicemail. This allows you to listen to the recorded message, and hence learn details like the sex of the voice on the voicemail message, the name (if spoken) of the person or company – as well as more subtle details like accent and even perhaps educational demographic. These clues can then be used later to formulate a targeted pretext call to them. A pretext to an educated (sounding) Indian male may be very different to a pretext targeted at a less educated (sounding) Australian female. Know your audience and prepare your material.

The case of not so injured testicles

Key learning points

- Pretext inquiries
- Covert camera use

I had a case where a male was claiming a large sum for a work related injury which he claimed was interfering with his sex life, due to having damaged his testicles and his lower back. In effect the largest part of the claim centred on his alleged depressed mental state as a result of the injury. This in itself was not gruesome, though all men are acutely aware of how sensitive such parts are. The result of the failure of his 'little guys' and presumably his whole system was responsible for relationship difficulties, causing him to be single, depressed, unemployable and so it went on. Proving psychological claims to be false isn't easy, because you're trying to establish court admissible evidence of a person's mental state, based on the most scant of observations or other scraps of detail.

I had nothing to go on, so I selected the ad pretext.

'Hi, I am calling about the ad.'

'Eh? What ad?'

'I just got this number to call about the ad...'

I paused hoping for something that I could use to work with, but the phone remained silent.

'Is it still for sale?' I finally inquired, trying to keep the conversation flowing, though I knew this specific detail of conversation was now limiting my pretext options slightly.

'What is selling? Oh, you mean for flat?' he replied, in a strong accent. BINGO. He'd thrown me a line.

'Yes, I am calling about the flat' (of course!)

'Why you didn't speak to agent, I thought he is to handle the selling?'

'Yes, I did, but they suggested I call you to see when would be best to come and see it, because I was hoping to do so tomorrow if that was all right?'

'Oh. Maybe I think John was going to show people, but its ok you come if you want, we be home all the day tomorrow'

Within a few seconds I had an 'in', and a very good one. I was being welcomed into his home, able to talk to him with a nice clean pretext. I also didn't miss the royal 'we' in his phraseology, which suggested he was living with someone and if this was the case, would immediately discount his claimed 'living on my own' statement in his court claim for damages.

The following day I turned up with my girlfriend Andrea. For this approach I felt it would be less intrusive to have a woman with me, and figured we could tag-team the job. When we arrived, we found a fairly run down apartment building. I guessed the flat was a rental, not for sale, and there were no signs outside either. I knocked on the door and we were let into the flat by our subject. He seemed happy to see us, though was still scratching his head over how we got his number because he had not given it to the estate agent. It was a point that was soon forgotten as we chatted amicably. He told us that the flat came furnished, and I immediately zeroed in on the bed. *'So this bed is included?'* I asked, gingerly pressing down near a corner to test the springs.

'Yes, bed is included' he replied

'I see... ahh, because Andrea kind of likes to spend a bit of time... in the bed you see, but we really hate soft mattresses and weak springs'. With any pretext it is always good to steer close to the truth if possible, as it increased believability. My statement about Andrea fitted this ethos perfectly.

Andrea feigned coyness, saying *'Chris! Do you mind!'* but it was all part of our (totally unrehearsed) show. He laughed at my comment and to our great surprise, took a little jump onto the mattress and bounced a little up and down. I was recording everything he did with my covert video camera, and was trying hard not to laugh as I thought about how the client would react on seeing the tape of our injured subject being so active on his bed. I was trying to hold my pin-hole camera steady, and aimed at our subject as much as possible to capture any movement he made. I wondered if this job could get any better, because it was going rather well so far.

'It must be working, this bed, because Anka now expecting' He said in his broken English with a coy smile. My mind suddenly stopped, as for the first time I registered what he'd actually said. I thought I must have been dreaming, and had to hear it again. 'Sorry?' I asked, my heart beating faster. He could not be serious.

'Yes, Anka is expecting child in few months, this is why we need bigger place' he continued. Andrea and I exchanged glances. BINGO!

We thanked him for his time, and left, saying we would consider the flat and perhaps contact the agent later. We now knew he worked a casual night shift. We had observed him in good spirits. We knew he was active enough to do a little jump onto the bed, and best of all, we knew he had a girlfriend... who was PREGNANT! This fact did seem to make his claims of either impotency or testicular failure a little harder to believe. This, coupled with his happy home life and, as we also discovered, casual employment, was responsible for a significant 'variation' in the final payment figure he received from the insurers.

This great pretext was responsible for identifying a fraudster who was trying to rort the system. Had we followed the more conventional approach, such as interviewing him or his girlfriend (whom we didn't even know existed), the result would have been very different. 'No, we have not sex for year now. Nothing works. You ask Anka.' would probably be the reply to such direct questioning, and if we even knew of her existence she would have readily agreed to this as well.

The pretext however comes in silently under the radar of human defences, setting up a scenario that will ultimately, but indirectly, harvest valuable information. Some lateral thinking and a degree of luck had allowed us to 'make' a good pretext opportunity. By then disguising our focus, wrapping and delivering it with precise timing, we were able to 'hit the mark'. Sometimes the best prepared pretext will fail, yet with others, the results will be phenomenal. Like so much of investigation work, there are no guarantees, it is all about probability, trying every angle to maximise the probability of success.

The case of being taken for a ride

Key learning points

- Background factual inquiries

- Pretext inquiries

- Conversation management to influence a suspect's thinking

I did another job for Control Risks that required a clever pretext approach. They had a large blue-chip client, who was being hit with an ongoing fraud involving the theft and use of a large number of paid taxi dockets known as Cabcharges. Investigations had led to identifying one specific ex-employee. Although he seemed the most likely subject, he was most unlikely to confess to the crime. Under the terms of the agreement with Cabcharge, the stolen dockets were as good as cash, and could not be 'stopped' easily like a cheque could be. It seemed the fraudster was quite comfortable with catching taxis for all manner of trips. Individually, they weren't massive amounts, but they were regular and given the number of missing dockets, there was really no end to his spending in sight.

I started doing my research, and built up a profile of him. I talked to former managers, I obtained records from government sources, I contacted referees listed on his resume and finally, I felt I almost knew him. One evening I decided to make an approach. Given my research, I felt a physical interaction was best, rather than phone contact. I turned up at his home, and not finding him there, I waited. An hour later a vehicle arrived, and I approached as he and his wife got out of the car.

'*Hello David*' I said confidently, totally unsure of his real identity, but I wanted to establish my control early. I could see I got him off guard, and was pleased I had obviously found my mark. He looked back at me with a '*Do I know you?*' look, though it was clear he had not seen me before. He did not challenge my unfounded assumption of his identity, which was as good as if he had actually told me his name.

'No, you don't know me, but I am here to talk to you about the Cabcharge issue' I replied, my comment clearly phrased as a statement, not a question. He immediately became defensive, and ushered his wife inside, then returned to talk with me. I was fairly sure his wife had no idea about this issue, which was a point we could use against him later.

'*So what is this about?*' he continued, not giving anything away at all. I could see I had my work cut out for me. We had nothing on him, other than a 'false' signature scrawl on the dockets. Not even a specific address that may provide clues. There were matching periods of his own interstate travel and the dockets use, but this wasn't enough to nail him.

I began. '*Well, we've had a large internal investigation for Boeing group, and this has resulted in a lot of smaller stuff being swept up in the inquiries. We were going to approach you about it earlier, but we didn't want it to interfere with the larger* investigation. Now that's been wrapped up with all the evidence sorted out, we can move on some of the smaller stuff, such as your Cabcharge scam'

There was a pause then he replied 'I don't know what you are talking about', though his physical demeanour suggested he was now less than composed.

'You realise it is larceny as a servant, stealing the dockets and using them. We could make things difficult for you, but I have been asked to make a suggestion. Boeing are a little sensitive with their PR, and they don't want to make a fuss; they just want to get the dockets back and the funds repaid, and they will agree to not press charges.'

'What makes you think it was me?' he asked, trying to deflect the heat as well as fish for something we may have had on him. It was time to play some cards.

'You know how big the group is David, so you can imagine the size of the investigations that we undertake, and this one involves the police, it is not just a private matter. We have everything on you. We know about all your trips to Coolangatta, about your contract work at Gilberts, and about you visiting your family last year'. I waited for this to sink in, though he weakly protested 'But that's nothing, that doesn't prove it was me, because it was not me!', though his now sunken demeanour suggested I was almost across the line.

'You are kidding right? You can't be serious!' I replied confidently. 'Of course we can prove it was you, every single one of them. We have got everything, fingerprints on dockets, handwriting analysis. We even have your face on some of the taxi videos... do you realise what I am saying? I am not asking you to help us prove you did it I am making you a generous offer. All Boeing want is their dockets back, and the funds repaid. I can't give you the exact amount right now, but I have all the details here' I said, flipping through a pile of paperwork that was well over an inch thick. The top dozen pages were photocopies of Cabcharge dockets, though the rest was some of my financial papers from preparing my personal taxation return. I figured it would be good to add them to the large pile for extra effect.

I waited while David began to fidget, visibly uncomfortable with the turn of events.

'Now, what I can do is provide you with a signed letter from Boeing, that they will agree not to prosecute you over this matter, provided you agree to repay the fraud and return the dockets. This will give you a degree of safety about it all, because we do not want publicity. And I am sure you don't want publicity either. What would your wife say if we were to let her know what you have been doing?'

I could see he was dying to know how we knew so much about him, and how could we possibly know his wife was unaware of his scam? Of course I didn't because it was another guess, but as long as he thought we did, it was all part of the show.

'And if I do, the letter will mean I never get charged ever, like… it will…' he said in a stumbling voice, all confidence drained from his smartly dressed body. I was across the line.

'…it will go away. Yes, that's right. All we seek is repayment, with no interest of course, plus the dockets back. And that even means the ones in Adelaide too' I replied. I was not sure if he had given some dockets to his mates in Adelaide as they didn't seem to be his, but I figured it was worth throwing in. He didn't dispute it, nervously looking back across his shoulder to see if his wife had come outside yet.

'So what I'll do is organise the letter, together with the amounts, and we will send it to you. Would you like it sent to your work or here at home?' I asked. It was best to offer a choice of options that each signified acceptance of the process. If I gave him an option that allowed him to say 'no' to my repayment suggestion, it would be much harder to secure the result.

'No, I would prefer you sent it to me at home' he replied. Good answer.

'Thank you, you have made a wise choice. You are lucky actually, because you nearly got swept up with the others, but we decided to let you off because your fraud was much smaller. We would never have known about you if it was not for the much larger investigation, but that is the luck of the draw I guess' I said.

I shook his hand, and I could see that he was now relieved, though still scratching his head wondering how he was caught, and what he would say to his wife. He was caught by a clever pretext that swept him up in a whirl of information. A smattering of personally identifiable details, delivered with precise timing. It was a good pretext, with both solid content and controlled delivery. It was probably the only investigative technique that could have solved this case. In the end, Boeing was fully repaid for the fraudulently used Cabcharge vouchers, and though there were no unused vouchers returned, they never had another one presented again.

CHAPTER 7: SURVEILLANCE CAMERA TECHNIQUES

This book was written to teach surveillance techniques, and not photography. Detailed discussion of appropriate lighting, aperture, shutter speeds and other technical issues is best left for photography textbooks. The following section outlines some key issues that relate to the specific use of cameras when in a surveillance operation only.

Many consider the primary tool of the surveillance agent is the video camera. The camera is valuable and used to document the situation, but it is important not to rely solely on camera evidence. Written detail for a report, such as identification of a work address or a sporting activity, may well prove far more damaging than any photographic evidence. Photographic evidence is mainly used to support the written research. The courts are often more comfortable admitting written evidence, or oral evidence and despite the effort involved by surveillance operators in gathering video, it is not always admitted in court.

As a key tool though, it's important to be familiar with it. A good soldier knows his weapon intimately, and so too a surveillance professional knows his camera. There is more to a camera than the basics of how to film. The professional knows every function, every feature and can adjust the time, set manual focus, adjust the aperture and engage recording without needing to consult the manual.

Knowing what to shoot, how to frame, when to stop and start, and what settings to adjust, become second nature. In a game where success is measured in seconds, there is no room for hesitation. Your subject may appear for a brief second to check the mail or enter a car. If you fail to be mentally and physically prepared to take the shot in the few seconds you're given, you'll miss it. Attention to detail is crucial. Even the way you place the camera down in the car is important. Just like a good soldier, the professional's weapon will be facing toward the enemy at all times, record button accessible, ready to take a shot in an instant. During times of heightened readiness, the professional's finger will rest gently on the button, the camera becoming a natural extension of his body, not a detached object requiring thought.

The camera should be prepared with charged batteries, blank tape and time/date settings correct. Considering you may be called to give evidence later, your reputation may hinge on these actions which could be ruined by a stupid mistake. *'So if your video tape is displaying the wrong time* (perhaps a daylight saving oversight) *how can we believe anything you say, it's clear you're incompetent and you're trying to present evidence that is patently false'*... and so it goes on.

- Check your equipment prior to going to a job
- Ensure batteries are fully charged and always carry plenty of spares
- Use a different tape for every job, and ensure the tape is correct for that job
- Ensure tape is correctly cued. Be careful to not record over previous footage when reviewing video on the job. Ensure the tape is at the <u>end</u> of previous footage. Use the camera *end tape search* feature if possible
- Consider recording two seconds of a black screen on arrival, to separate jobs and days – else use the date or scene management features correctly
- Use a sports setting or other high shutter speed if possible. This provides clearer still images, though you may require good light for this to be effective
- Keep a camera very handy to get a quick shot, ideally on the seat next to you

- Keep the camera facing the correct way, lens towards the subject, with the on / standby switch uppermost to enable fast activation

- Consider resting a hand on the standby switch for fastest response. Cameras take a few seconds to start recording once turned on, so keep close to the switch. A few seconds fumbling for the switch may miss the action

- Look for movement flags to get camera ready for action. If movement is suspected, switch to standby and raise camera ready. Movement flags could be <u>sounds</u>, such as a door or gate closing, engine starting, voices, dog suddenly barking. It could be <u>visual</u>, such as blinds or windows closed, lights switched on or off. Shadows or reflections can also provide advance warning of movement

- Brace your body against the vehicle, or a wall or window. Always try to secure the camera as still as possible when filming. Amateur footage is all over the place - shaky video that makes viewers seasick. This is because they don't brace their body effectively, are not aware of how important it is to maintain a steady shot. They may also be hyperventilating or over excited. Stay calm, but brace for a rock steady shot. This technique is where you hold the camera against a solid part of the vehicle. Common brace positions are against the headrest, on the shoulder of the seat in front, or even through the headrest. You can also brace on a raised knee, against the side of the car, on the dashboard or steering wheel. Windscreens aren't tinted, so it's best to brace away from this unless you have a long range shot

- Learn how to use any complex edit search feature to accurately position the edit points. This provides far more professional footage by cleanly removing any unwanted footage from the end of the last scene

- Don't film through mirrors. Although this may sound like a clever technique, it rarely works well. External mirrors are dirty, and the glass is not designed to the same tolerance of camera lenses. Expect poor, fuzzy results. You will also encounter problems later in court with aggressive barristers suggesting that you filmed in a mirror to make his bad right arm look like it was healthy because it is actually his left arm – due to the mirror reversing or inverting the shot. This can be easily seen if there is any text such as street signs in the video, because the text is then reversed

Camera types

Very small cameras (Mini-DV) are good for close in shots, foot follows, shopping centre visits and train follows. They often don't have long range optical lenses, so are less suited for long range work, but are often small enough to fit discreetly in a pocket. Larger format cameras have long optical zoom lenses such as 30x, and are great for long-range work such as vehicle mounted and continuous recording. Ideally it is best to carry two digital cameras on any job, which allows both flexibility and backup in case of equipment failure. Having two cameras also means you can do video editing on the road. You can review footage on one camera while report writing, yet have the other ready to shoot any unexpected action that may occur while reviewing the other one. Two cameras provide a backup in case one of them fails. Consider taping up the camera with black electrical tape, which reduces shine from the camera, making it more covert. Cover every part of the exterior that is silver or white. Cover the front lens markings (focal length) with black tape or permanent marker.

Pinhole cameras

Another important PI camera is the pinhole, which is a camera mounted covertly in some housing like a mobile phone or other accessory, or even sewn into a jacket or bag. There are no limits to the locations for mounting a pinhole camera, but it is often easier to have it in something mobile, so it can be carried and aimed more easily, or left in position. Some pinholes have a wire to connect with the main camera, which is perhaps carried separately in a bum bag or other location. More advanced pinhole cameras can transmit wirelessly to a remote receiver, however the range of these is often limited, and the picture quality sometimes disrupted. A wired pinhole camera is far better for quality, but perhaps slightly more restricted in applications.

The pinhole camera is designed to allow close up video evidence gathering, such as undercover work including trap purchases[49], but also for recording a good ID shot close up. These cameras are often used for a door knock, where a traditional camera would not be suitable. After over fifteen years as a surveillance agent, my belief is that a good PI should have a good camera, but that there is not a lot of difference in models. Provided the camera is small with a good optical zoom range, the selection of camera is not nearly as important as how you use it. A good workman can often create a masterpiece with poor tools anyway, so the key aim of this book is to teach you how to conduct surveillance – not which camera to buy. Personal preference is perhaps important, and with new camera models coming out every other month, any comparison in a textbook of specific models or brands would be quickly outdated.

---

[49] A trap purchase is where an undercover agent purchases an item (such as counterfeit product) from an offender, in order to gain further evidence

Wireless cameras

These are perhaps an 'exciting' type of technology, yet good results don't always follow. Wireless cameras give flexibility to be discreetly placed in a variety of situations. They may be left in situ, recording and transmitting activity elsewhere. There is no end to the possible location of these cameras in every day items, such as dummy mobile phones, dummy ball point pens and many more. A good manufacture of these items is Swann Communications at www.swann.com.au, and their products can be purchased all over Australia. www.ozspy.com.au and www.spyshop.com.au also retail a wide variety of covert investigation equipment.

Disadvantages

- They often have high power needs, meaning large batteries or the possibility they will run flat

- The transmission range is usually very short, as often required by the Australian Communication Authority depending on the frequency used. Most devices will not exceed 100 metres, and may even struggle to achieve this with thick walls degrading the signal. Using large receiving antennas though, the range can be increased

- Wireless devices often work poorly when used in a mobile environment. While you may have the smallest wireless device which transmits a clear picture, you may find that movement such as walking closely behind a subject may result in very poor quality video. The weak signal may show interference with white noise static or flickering

- Wireless devices usually need a dedicated receiver, which is additional bulk, and another item needing battery power

Wireless cameras are useful in some situations, though if it is possible, you should strongly consider a wired approach which is less hassle and bulk, and provides better quality images.

What to film

Depending on the stage an investigation is at, you should concentrate on filming slightly different things to ensure good quality evidence in your final report.

On arrival

- Scene shots of the address and detail shots of any vehicles
- Detail shots of any signs or registration numbers
- Get ID footage of the subject as a priority, and <u>later</u> go for full body shot.
- Stay close, but do not cut off their feet or hands. Give them room to move, else they will keep walking out of the frame. Capture their full body, with a small amount of space around them for context and to accommodate their movement.
- Occasionally zoom in for close detail on facial features to get a better ID.
- Occasionally zoom in on areas such as injured limbs, like a close up of the right ankle, or on documents the subject may be reading.
- Occasionally zoom right out for context, showing them situated in the general area.

Generally

- If you lose contact with your subject on a follow, record a still shot of the street sign showing last point of contact with the subject, then record two seconds of black screen as a visual separator. This documents the location and time automatically.

- When filming documents such as those spied inside a parked car, go as close up as possible with correct focus. Use a fast shutter speed or sports setting on the camera to more accurately get a still image. Record several seconds of the detail in question. Pan slowly with occasional pauses to capture all the details, and then pull back slightly to record the full document. One of the most common mistakes is to record too quickly, and get a blurred, unusable image. Relax and do it slowly and cautiously.

- Use the camera for recording audio. If the subject is talking in a public place and you can overhear, you are legally permitted to record their voice. Consider leaving a recording camera in a bag near their table. Record verbal operator notes if necessary, so just talk while recording and read out street signs, registration numbers or other details.

- Don't be aggressive in your filming stance. Be relaxed and natural. Holding a camera to your eye or directly in front of you is psychologically aggressive and attracts attention. Hold it at waist level and use the flip screen to frame the shot, which also keeps you face down, reducing your facial exposure. Alternatively hold the camera to one side while using the screen. Only use the eyepiece while in the car, or for a long shot while some distance from the subject. Squinting into an eyepiece advertises to others that you are filming. If possible, make it look like you are simply using the camera to review footage, while you watch the screen.

- When filming through a chain wire fence or through a rainy window, the camera will struggle to retain focus on the subject, and may alternate a change in focus to the closer object. This looks terrible so the simple solution is to set the focus to manual or infinity. This can also occur when filming across a busy road and traffic constantly passes across the lens, disrupting the shot. As well as fixing the focus to manual, you may also consider fixing the exposure as well, particularly if you are shooting into a dark garage and white vans keep streaking across the shot which will constantly confuse the camera's auto-exposure.

Tripods

- Use for continuous recording, or for long distance shots, particularly in rural areas.

- If you suddenly see activity, consider recording it for a short time while braced against the car. If it continues, take a short time out to set up the tripod properly. The resulting steady shot is often worth the loss of a few seconds of activity.

- When panning on tripods, consider moving the actual legs of the tripod instead of the head. This can often reduce unnecessary movement and enable finer pan adjustments left or right. A small movement of an extended tripod leg translates as an even smaller movement in the actual camera, so the shot remains steady.

- A tiny tabletop tripod is very effective for use in a café, on the rear parcel shelf of vehicles, or even on the ground. Small and light, it enables the camera to be left in position unattended for continuous recording situations.

Running bags

When following a subject, it's often difficult to maintain contact when they change transport. Following a subject in a car may be expected, but what if they park and continue on foot, the transition from road to footpath can cause difficulties to the unprepared. The professional is ready for this and has his 'running' bag packed.

Always carry a running bag and keep it ready with a video camera, spare battery and tape, a mobile phone, pen and paper and a baseball cap for a quick change of looks. Also consider a PI licence badge or wallet in case of needing to impress someone to get assistance or information. It is also good practice to have some coins for bus and train fares, so you are not delayed or conspicuous when seeking change for fares or meters. These are some key items that will allow him to carry on with the job seamlessly, like spare tape and batteries and a baseball cap. You never really know where you are going or how long you will be, as the subject could board a train to go anywhere. A running bag also allows you to discreetly carry the camera. The best types are shoulder strap models, which enable you to hold the camera inside the bag itself while walking. In this way your finger is ready to activate 'record'. You can also easily make some adjustments easily from within the bag itself prior to pulling it out to take a shot. The bag shouldn't contain anything else, particularly anything that is bulky, may rattle, or may obstruct the camera being taken out quickly. The last thing you need is to spill things on the ground and attract attention or to waste valuable time.

Shiny PI badges

There are several schools of thoughts on the use of shiny PI badges. Some consider it tacky, only used by those who want to inflate their authority, or have a 'frustrated cop' mentality. Others including myself have used these 'tacky' and entirely worthless badges to great effect in getting assistance from the public. A real PI usually has no legal authority at all, and the poor licensing identification means few would recognise a real badge anyway. It is particularly good for impressing people you may want to formally interview. Shiny metal conveys authority, and can be used with a confident, assertive personality to get results. It is also entirely legal. There is no law against showing such badges, provided of course you never impersonate a policeman or other government authority, or imply or state you have legal powers which you don't have. A good PI is only interested in results, and would be comfortable using all manner of techniques to achieve their aim, even where it may be considered embarrassing! A good source of PI badges is www.signal-one.com.au under the heading 'badges', though they can also be sourced from many locations over the internet.

CHAPTER 8: SURVEILLANCE VEHICLES

When choosing a surveillance vehicle, there are many factors to consider, including the type of surveillance work you are doing. A four wheel drive is good for country areas, a sedan is good for city areas, a tinted car is good for static locations and a non-tinted car is best for follows. The style and model is really a matter of personal preference. In general they should be low profile colours, non-descript styles and mechanically sound with fast acceleration. During follows high acceleration is far more important than high speed, so zippy hatchbacks are often good. There is no golden rule. Occasionally a very visible vehicle can be good, especially when you have a suspicious claimant that is looking for a nondescript tinted vehicle. They may never look twice at the bright red sports car, or aging yellow Datsun following them!

Vehicle inventory

There are several basic things which should be carried on any surveillance operation. The following is a list of the standard items that should normally be found in the car:

- Plenty of petrol
- Job documentation including: operator run sheet, claimant medical reports, accident reports and any other information relating to the current case
- Video camera
- Digital still camera
- Spare batteries for all items, and spare blank video tape. Ensure both tapes and batteries have plenty of capacity, and far more than you expect to use. Running out of either is poor form, and a waste of an opportunity which may not arise again.

- A tripod suitable for in-car use
- Mobile phone
- Car charger (for phone, cameras and other items)
- Power inverter which converts 12v to 240v, and allows use of 240v chargers
- Note paper, laptop computer or organiser, voice recorder
- Urine bottle (an old apple juice container, or other wide necked bottle)
- Iced water (at least 50% more than likely to be required, at least three litres at any time)
- Some food snacks or meals
- Two way radios (if required)
- A second video camera (if required)
- Map of surveillance area (Include a compass for rural locations)
- Various changes of clothes, including beach / hot casual and more formal for clubs / restaurants

Vehicle selection

A surveillance vehicle is like an office. It is used for extended periods, and should be well set up. Poorly arranged and badly set up vehicles will result in poor results and an uncomfortable working environment.

Engine

Engine in good condition, reasonably powerful for quick follows. High acceleration is far more important than top speed. An automatic is preferable, as this enables you to talk on a radio, or operate a camera quickly while driving (be careful!)

Tyres

Mobile surveillance usually necessitates slightly more aggressive driving as the surveillance agent must maintain contact with a vehicle that is probably travelling an unknown route, and must also jockey for position while trying to remain inconspicuous. Standard tyres are not appropriate for this more difficult driving style. Wider tyres can easily be fitted to most cars, and this increases the surface area of road contact. This provides a lot more safety to the driver with reduced stopping distances, and also means less tell-tale tyre squeal on executing a tight U-turn, or suddenly taking a tight turn while following an unpredictable subject.

Style

A four-wheel drive vehicle is likely to be higher than normal sedans, and this is an advantage when trying to see over a sea of other cars in a crowded car park, or over a tall side fence into a rear yard etc. A 4x4 is versatile and can drive over gutters or median strips if required to get into a good location for a quick shot, or to maintain contact with the subject on a tricky follow. Being larger than most sedans, the 4x4 is a good, comfortable vehicle to work from for longer periods of time. A 4x4 vehicle is often required in rural locations. A small, hatchback sedan is a particularly good follow car, being discreet and zippy. These are not as comfortable for longer periods, but are great on fuel consumption. They are often very quick vehicles, as they are small and light. The turning circle is also very good in small cars, which is quite important when on a follow, as quick U-turns are often required to get into position or maintain contact. A station wagon gives more room, particularly for sleeping if conducting a very early morning rural start. As with a 4x4, any larger vehicle is always slightly more noticeable.

LPG fuel tank

Having a dual fuel vehicle is a good idea for any professional investigator. Apart from the fact that LPG is usually less than half the price of petrol, having dual fuel tanks means you can increase your fuel range. A PI can never be sure where they will end up, and when following a subject for long distances, it is far preferable not to have to refuel, and it is certainly poor form to run out. Having double tanks affords you peace of mind.

Colour

Very common, dull colours are good. Lighter colours are cooler as they reflect heat. White is fine, though is a little bright, especially during night surveillance, and it contrasts poorly with dark tints which makes it more memorable. The best colours are silver / metallic, dark greens, blues, greys or anything common.

Vehicle security

Alarms

Alarms are important as the vehicle often contains expensive equipment like cameras and laptops, which are not always able to be removed. Sometimes items must be left in the vehicle during quick foot pursuits or refuelling at short notice. Ensure the alarm doesn't sound audibly when arming or disarming as this draws attention to the vehicle. A simple light flash is all that is required.

Ignition kill switch

This is a secondary theft feature that requires drivers to activate a hidden switch prior to starting the vehicle with keys. Surveillance subjects may become aggressive and out of malice try to obtain the keys by assaulting the PI in order to steal or damage the surveillance vehicle. It is a good security feature regardless, for occasions such as should your keys fly out of your pocket on jumping out of the car to commence a foot follow for example. In some cases, the car not starting as soon as you turn the key can be used as part of a pretext, suggesting the vehicle has broken down. This may allow the vehicle to remain in a difficult location with less suspicion, or perhaps encourage a subject to allow the PI into their home to use the phone or conduct a conversation to elicit information.

Central locking

Central locking is a must for any surveillance vehicle. This facility reduces the time to get into or to lock a vehicle, and every second counts when on a follow, particularly when starting or ending the vehicle component. Taking five extra seconds to manually lock a door may result in losing contact as they enter the crowded shopping centre. Central locking is required for speed and security.

Vehicle cooling techniques

Sunroof

A sunroof is often the best way to ventilate vehicles, without side windows visibly down. Be aware of nearby units or balconies that may have a view into your vehicle. Consider placing a spring shade screen across the open sunroof to reduce light entry, while still permitting hot air to escape. A sunroof can also be used to observe high balconies, or if necessary, used to get height for a quick shot, for instance over the top of a fence.

Roof vents (Muller vent)

These provide ventilation and allow the hot stale air to escape. Ventilation can be increased by fitting small 12v cooling fans inside the cabin of the surveillance vehicle, thus providing continual air flow without having any windows open. Many caravan accessory outlets stock dedicated vents and extractor fans. Some surveillance agents even cut ventilation ports in the floor of the vehicle so venting can be achieved without the distinctive vents on the roof.

Inflatable mattress

Thermally insulated self-inflating mattresses are particularly good to block out light, visibility and more importantly, <u>heat</u>. The mattresses can inflate to wedge into windows, but can be quickly removed when required. Thin inflatable mattresses covering the vehicle windows provide excellent insulation against the sun, as well as making the windows look totally black underneath the tinting. On overnight operations, the mattresses have a dual purpose and can be used conventionally. When not required, they can be deflated and stored in a small space.

Second skin roof

In some very hot climates cars have a double roof, or drivers fit a large thin board to the roof racks which almost fully covers the vehicle. This effectively keeps the car in the shade at all times, as heat is reflected by the (white) board and does not directly hit the metal roof. Hot air can move easily through the gap between metal roof and board. This technique can look very natural on a work van, but perhaps less so for a small sedan.

Air-conditioning

Air-conditioning is important for operator comfort; a cool working environment reduces operator fatigue and enhances alertness. It is also important for equipment. Video cameras and other electrical equipment are quite sensitive to heat and especially humidity. Video cameras may not work under these conditions, flashing 'DEW' (or similar) if too humid. This is to protect the video heads from any damaging moisture. Another issue is visibility. High humidity can quickly mist windows and reduce visibility, especially during rain or early mornings. Misty windows result in difficulty observing and poor quality video, as well as possibly alerting people to the fact that there is somebody in the car breathing heavily!

Thermal mass cooling systems

These are an excellent idea, though used more commonly in the USA than the Australian investigation industry. A thermal mass such as bags of ice or water is prepared prior to surveillance. When conducting covert surveillance, the vehicle is cooled by way of a pump recirculating the air inside the vehicle through a radiator. This cools the cabin of the vehicle by transferring the heat to the thermal mass (ice). It allows cooling without noisy engines or consuming a lot of battery power. Being a closed system though, the cooling only lasts as long as the thermal mass is colder than the ambient temperature. Commercial covert cooling systems are available from specialist PI shops such as www.teleradio.com.sg/dvcs.htm, though the technology is basic and some PI's prefer to build their own systems. There is DIY information about this subject on the web as well.

Vehicle camouflage

Weather shields

These allow windows to be cracked open to provide ventilation, but conceal the opening from view. They also provide cover when filming in the rain, and allow the camera to film directly through a crack rather than through a soaking wet, misty window.

Tinted windows

Tinted windows enable you to remain concealed within the vehicle. Ensure metal film is used as this is better quality, reflects more heat and is more durable to resist scratches (although avoiding scratches altogether is best!). To clean, use soft rag and soapy water.

For best results, apply a 35% film over all windows, then add a second layer film over the top, but leave a thin strip on the top of the rear window (aligned with a demister wire), and two small camera ports on the left and right hand sides (top of side windows). This provides very good heat and light protection, as well as visual concealment inside the vehicle. By having most of the windows with double tint, the light entering the vehicle is drastically reduced and for most situations, no extra level of concealment is required over these windows. Tinting reduces the light entering the camera lens. Filming through tint (especially double tint) does degrade the image, but during the day this is not a major problem. Under low light situations such as dawn and dusk, night operations or dark locations such as basement car parks, it is necessary to use the camera ports with the lighter tints. By shooting through the small sections, which have only single 35% tint, a far better image is obtained. Some surveillance vehicles have 20% all over, but this is not good enough for the bulk of the windows, as well as being too dark to shoot under low light conditions.

As an alternative, white tint, or *'Perforated Window Graphic Film'* is readily available from www.3m.com and screen-printing shops. Sign writers often prepare stickers that have many perforations for buses. The inside of the sticker is black so occupants can see out easily, however the outside has printed advertising on it and people can't see in. Some government departments such as police surveillance or response groups use a white 'tint' outside to make a van look like a refrigerated van which has all white windows. A casual glance at the van leads you to think it is filled with refrigerant insulating foam, as there is no distinctive dark tint – yet inside there is a response or surveillance team of officers who can see out from every window easily! This approach is good for general observation, but the perforations make for very poor video or camera shots as they cases images to be fuzzy, as well as lower the lighting etc. One alternative is to make a removable flap of the graphic film, so you can film directly through a small section of clear glass if you are careful. White tint also helps reflect more heat than black tint. Of course it is only appropriate for a white van as it would not look right on a car.

Window SOX

These are elastic mesh covers which act like removable window tinting, and are easily found via web searches, K-mart or in baby shops. They offer several benefits to investigators:

- Windows can be fully open without appearing conspicuous
- They prevent insect and dust entry
- They make existing tinting darker, and can be used to subtlety change the appearance of the vehicle

Windscreen covers

To quickly erect screens, flexible twist-shades are good. Covering a windscreen with shades makes it less aggressive, and looks more natural when a car is parked for some time in the one place. The screens reduce light entry into the vehicle. Often a gap in the side of the screen, or if one screen is lowered slightly, will enable good visibility out the crack. These can also be used to completely block out light and visibility on side or rear windows.

Markings

Remove all markings from the vehicle such as stickers, signage, and dealer markings on numberplate surround. The more generic and less unique the vehicle is, the better. In some cases it may be appropriate to add sign markings, to dress the vehicle for use as a pretext such as a road survey vehicle. In these cases ensure that the signage can be easily removed later.

Vehicle administration

Power

A power inverter plugs into the cigarette socket, and converts 12v DC into 240v AC. This can power battery chargers, laptops and the like. For periods of an hour or less, there should be no requirement to actually run the engine. For longer periods it is best to run the engine or else the battery may run flat. A 300 watt model is good, and it should include the following protections: low/high voltage cut out, overload/temp cut out, short circuit / reverse polarity protection, and soft start (reduces damaging spikes during ignition start). While inverters are good, it is even better to have a direct 12v charging system to run a laptop, as this is more energy efficient than converting to 240v and back down again. This also reduces the heat generated in the process, which is an issue for hot surveillance vehicles

Water

It is important to have more water than you think you will need, as static surveillance is very hot work, and even air conditioning removes a lot of moisture. Take a frozen 1.25 litre bottle of water, together with at least two litres of plain cold water. Collapsible fridges are good to keep drinks cool. Collapsible water bladders with drinking tubes are excellent. These allow easy drinking without spills, and can be used without taking your eyes off your target

Waste

A two-litre apple juice container is a good receptacle for urine. Find a secure location to store the bottle upright, but within easy reach.

Mirrors

Suction style rear view mirrors can be affixed to the interior of the windscreen, and assist in observing blind spots. As they can be angled out wider than existing side mirrors, they permit circumspect side observations, while you can remain comfortably seated, facing forward in such situations as watching a vehicle in a car park or a doorway.

Spot mirrors

These only cost a few dollars from service stations or auto parts shops. They are very good for situational awareness on investigations. Conducting a vehicle follow is never easy, and requires a higher degree of awareness for safety. These mirrors assist in road visibility while driving, allowing quick lane changes during a follow by easily showing blind spots. During static surveillance they help pick up on any movement around the vehicle (such as suspicious neighbours), providing enough warning to conceal your camera.

Seat covers

Dark seat covers assist in reducing the light reflected through the vehicle. Leather seats are good in hot conditions, especially when sliding in and out of seats quickly on a follow. Seats should have lever recline levers, instead of rotating wheels. Lever adjustments are much faster to raise and lower seats, which is important when moving from the back seats to the front seats. Rotating wheels are too slow to be adjusted quickly. Leather seats are an advantage for comfort, wear, heat, cleaning up spilt coffee or sweat. Repeated sliding into or out of the front seat can result in worn upholstery. Leather slides slightly better, enabling easier movement from back to front. When you are sitting in a car seat for hours every day, the extra cost of leather is well worth the benefits.

Sun-visor pouch

These provide low cost, easy storage of notepads, pens, sunglasses and the like. A surveillance vehicle is a professional vehicle, which, to enable full focus on the task of observations and recording, should be as convenient as possible to operate. Efficient storage allows efficient work.

Rear seat desk

This is a low cost storage item that attaches to the rear side of the front seat headrest. It stores pens, spare tapes and headsets, then folds down to provide an in-car desk for easy operation of laptop, or writing observation notes.

In-car navigation

This is electronic road directory navigation by voice or LCD maps, often using GPS for positioning. These units are very effective for investigators. They reduce time and energy on navigation, and enable better focus on the job. They allow you to get to jobs faster, via a shorter or better route. You will also be able to return quickly to the subject's home if contact is lost, despite being unfamiliar with the area. The moving map can also act as vehicle radar, showing you the road ahead while following a subject. This allows you to close up when there are several side street options ahead, even if you are out of sight of their vehicle at the time. When it is clear there are no side streets up ahead, the following distance can be increased to reduce your exposure. Should the subject enter a dead end road, this is easily identified by looking at the screen, and you can hang well back, perhaps leaving several minutes before going in to check which house number the vehicle is parked outside. Occasionally during a follow in heavy traffic, the navigation screen will show alternate route options, enabling you to leap frog the congested traffic by taking a parallel or alternate route as shown on the screen.

Tracking

This is where a vehicle movement is tracked electronically, either as a full remote system or as just a covert logging device that can be accessed later on the vehicle's return. Tracking is effective for monitoring locations and timings, such as when verifying work activity submitted by surveillance operators themselves. Electronic records are more accurate than manual records, and harder to fudge. It even provides good general security for the surveillance vehicle which often has expensive equipment inside, in case it is stolen or broken into. It assists with the allocation of investigator resources where there are several PI's being tracked by a central office. If tracking shows another agent is nearby they may be easily utilised to assist on the follow or difficult job, when operating in a two-up situation. It also shows the route history when an agent can't recall the route taken, or where a subject paused briefly at an address that was not able to be documented with a street name at the time.

Personal waste management

Long-term vehicle surveillance requires appropriate waste management. Unlike most other occupations, conducting surveillance in a vehicle means you are not able to leave the vehicle when nature calls, nor are you able to move the vehicle away to visit the toilet and then return, as any movement will always attract unwanted attention. Leaving the scene is not advisable, as the tendency is that this will always be the exact time that the subject leaves their home, so that on your return you will spend hours watching a vacant house without knowing they have just left! A hot vehicle means that you require plenty of fluids to keep your body hydrated, but always consider the end result. Coffee and donuts often feature in movies with tired cops on a long stakeout, yet perhaps an alternative drink would be preferable as coffee is a diuretic and promotes more frequent urination. These considerations are just part of our required working environment, and any guide book on PI's would be remiss in not covering this point in some detail.

The choice of urine bottle is important. It should have a very secure screw lid, and have a wide enough opening to enable easy use. Soft drink bottles have a relatively narrow neck, which render them far more difficult to use safely, as the urine stream must be aimed far more carefully into a narrow hole. A wide neck allows more flexibility and less concentration on the task, as it can act as a physical guide, allowing the investigator to continue observing the scene during the process. While there may have been nothing happening on the stakeout for hours, things always seem to get complicated when you start urinating. Vehicles will always move, people will exit buildings and things generally happen, so it is worthwhile considering mounting a camera securely on a tripod prior to starting, just in case. It's a dilemma considering the importance of capturing the surveillance footage versus the need to finish what you started. Stopping mid-stream is never satisfactory.

The common two-litre milk bottle is <u>not</u> advisable. While it has a wide neck, the screw threads on these types of bottles are not secure enough for the surveillance vehicle. This is because it may be trodden on, or bounce around during an aggressive follow. The plastic bottle itself is also not as strong as juice containers, and I can think of nothing worse than a urine spill inside the vehicle. An ideal bottle to use is a two-litre apple juice bottle, which has the required wide neck with secure thread, is quite strong, and has a capacity suitable for a full days use by most people! The apple juice bottle is also a form of camouflage and allows you to empty the contents more comfortably in the gutter without being concerned about others looking at you.

It is preferable to keep doors closed at all times to remain undetected, so most PI's elect to retain the urine bottle within the confines of the vehicle until the conclusion of the job. Some do prefer to discreetly empty the bottle into the gutter or grass. Occasionally emptying urine bottles during operations enables you to use them for longer. Perhaps there will be times that you fill it up more than usual, or even occasions where you would prefer not to have a full bottle kicking around the car. Some PI's have specially modified vehicles that have a urine disposal point where a bottle may be emptied through a tube or hole in the floor of the vehicle, which removes the disposal issue, at least for fluids. It goes without saying on team jobs that all PI's 'bring their own', because nobody likes to share a smelly wee bottle.

Female investigators can have problems with urination on long-term surveillance, as even a wide mouth apple juice bottle is just not adequate to allow comfortable relieving. Female PI's sometimes carry a mini prosthetic penis, which is a medical device specifically designed to allow women to pee like a man. These are non-invasive products which are held against the woman's body and enable her to direct the urine stream with a high degree of accuracy. This can then be easily aimed into a more standard urine bottle for secure disposal later on. The slightly cupped end is designed specifically to capture drips near the end of the stream, resulting in a pleasant and hygienic (or so I'm told!) experience with little fuss. One of the better web sites for these slightly unusual, but inexpensive medical products is www.travelmateinfo.com.

There is the issue of solid waste within the context of surveillance vehicles. I'm happy to say I've never gone quite that far, though an associate, Brendan, once advised me he used Tupperware. Considering surveillance is often spending hours in a hot car, the prospect of lingering toilet smells within the tight confines is not appealing, and best avoided. I have also heard of portable potties being used occasionally, usually with a larger vehicle such as a van. The best solution is to manage your personal ablutions appropriately, so that there is no solid waste on the job. Go easy on curry the night before a long stakeout. In the unfortunate case where a number two is required, I suggest relocating the car, despite the greater possibility of being noticed due to the movement. Sometimes moving the surveillance car just once is enough to compromise your position, but the movement can also be used to benefit the job in some circumstances. See section Insufficient movement on page 54.

PART 2

– DOING SURVEILLANCE –

CHAPTER 9: SURVEILLANCE PREPARATION

Prior preparation prevents poor performance is a common phrase drummed into every army recruit. In many ways the surveillance investigator has to prepare for a battle of sorts – a battle of wits, a battle of the unknown and unexpected. Often, the job will throw you a curly problem that will cause the unprepared to fail, so it is best to prepare an investigative plan before starting work. There is nothing quite like following your subject in a car for a long time, realising they were prepared for their long journey, then realising you will run out of fuel before they next stop. There is nothing like watching your subject enter a secure corporate building dressed in their suit, while you are forced to remain outside in your conspicuous shorts and t-shirt. If only you had brought an appropriate change of clothes, you could have done a sneaky walk-in with them, and tailed them right to their office. Similarly, you don't want to find yourself in a suit on a building site. Your corporate dress will draw unwanted attention from hefty workers in singlets, eying you warily as a possible safety inspector or company manager.

Preparation takes many forms, and choice of attire is but one issue to consider. There is also mental preparation, physical preparation, information preparation as well as equipment considerations. The surveillance professional is always ready with a full tank of fuel and the right change of clothes. He has coins ready to throw into toll booth turnstiles, and the batteries charged in his camcorder. He is rested knowing he may be facing a very long day. He has done his homework and already knows a lot about the job before he arrives. He carries food and water, some props for effect... a child's toy on the front seat to allay suspicion... a road survey sign... a hard hat or glasses.

The professional adopts the mind of his target. He knows where they will go, and anticipates what they will do. Rather than be surprised, he is ready, and in tune with his environment. As the subject drives into the beach car park on a sunny day, the surveillance professional will casually reach over to retrieve his beach towel, also ready for a day on the beach. The professional was prepared, playing the odds to win.

Pre-Surveillance inquiries (Urban)

Effective surveillance preparation will always involve conducting inquiries and checks prior to commencement, answering questions such as does the claimant actually live at the address? Who else may reside there, particularly if they may be confused with the claimant? Is the claimant operating a business, or attending a regular workplace? What is the general daily routine and best days and times to conduct surveillance?

- Collect all information from client, and study the brief.
- Obtain a road map image of the address from www.whereis.com.au or other sources, for reference. This often shows the precise house number location along the road, as well as checking the road name is correct. Including map pictures in reports for the client is good as they add colour and interest as well as forming a reference clearly showing the subject's local movements near their home.
- Conduct a telephone directory search of the <u>name</u> to get the current phone listings.
- Conduct a <u>reverse phone number</u> search[50] on <u>any</u> numbers supplied for the subject, across business and residential directories. This may provide details such as businesses associated to that property, or names of other

---

[50] Telstra finally won a protracted legal battle to assert copyright over phonebook data used in reverse search software. Companies which dealt with these have been forced out of business (such as Oz on Disk, and Desktop Marketing Systems)

persons residing at the property. The more information you can obtain on the subject and the address, the easier it is to manage the job.

- Conduct a phone directory search of the surrounding properties, across both business and residential directories[50]. This provides details which may assist in a more general nature, such if you need to contact neighbours on a pretext, or to make an assessment of the area with regards to identifying the best location to park.
- Conduct an Electoral roll[51] search to obtain occupant name details for the address.
- Check what night is garbage night (if appropriate – contact neighbours or council).
- Check Land Titles office details for property ownership (if appropriate).
- Conduct a pretext call if appropriate.

Departure checklist

- Check video camera operational and settings correct for time, zoom and focus.
- Are all batteries fully charged and sufficient blank video tape available?
- Ensure video tape in camera is correctly cued (don't record over other jobs).
- Check vehicle inventory to ensure you have all items.

---

[51] The Australian Electoral Office www.aec.gov.au

CHAPTER 10: COMMENCING SURVEILLANCE

Starting a new surveillance job means you need to become familiar with your operating environment. You need to be very sure you identify the correct location to start with. This is not always as easy as you may imagine and it wouldn't be the first time a surveillance operator has spent an entire day watching the wrong house. Even for the professional it can occasionally happen. With poor numbering, especially on rural properties, it can be difficult to get it right. Because of the possibility of compromising the job, you can't always 'ask' the neighbours for fear of alerting your subject - knocking directly on their door by mistake!

It is very important to bracket the address. When looking for number seven for example, it is not enough to identify numbers three then five and think it must be next door, because there may be a 7A, or it may miss a number with the address being 7-9 but marked only 9. It may even be just wrong, which took me a day to discover once *'Yes, that's our old letterbox, we really should change the number now we have moved, especially since it is so close to the right number, and next door doesn't have one... we were just using it for the mailman as there was no box when we got here...'* Great. Thanks. With any 'normal' occupation, like a tradesman for example, identifying the correct address is so simple it bears little conscious thought. You just ask someone nearby, either for the number, or perhaps their name... or you can contact the person themselves for directions. This simple point becomes a tactical exercise for the surveillance professional as he tries to accurately identify the address without resorting to something that may spoil the job. He cannot always take a very simple, yet direct approach like knocking on doors.

Once you have correctly identified the address, it is time to familiarise yourself with the 'movement matrix' that is associated with this address. Each point in space is situated on a network of movement which constrains it to 'probable' sequences. The movement matrix includes connections with all networks - rail, bus routes, walking tracks. To really know your subject, you must pick movement trails, predicting their progress through each network, or even where they are likely to change networks.

In being familiar with all the movement networks a subject may use, you can start to determine their probable movements. What is the likely route they will take? Would they walk to the station, or perhaps drive since it is too far to walk and the station parking area is good? Is there a bus route nearby? Where is the stop? What is the optimal route to the closest shopping area? What are the access points to the local school? Is there a back access gate that leads to the park at the rear?

When starting surveillance, an amateur will simply find the address, and then sit there waiting to be 'shown' the way by the subject when they later drive off. The professional will have done their homework. They not only *know* all the 'ways', but have physically rehearsed them. During the chase, the professional will know where to drop back and where to close up, to maintain discreet contact with the moving subject. The amateur will struggle, each twist and turn in the road a new surprise. They may be unprepared that the subject is *likely* to park shortly because *this is the back of the station parking area.* Rounding a corner to find the subject has vanished at a tee-intersection, the amateur will take a chance with 50/50 odds and take a left turn. The professional however, is playing a stacked deck. They know the odds from their physical rehearsals and study of the movement matrix. The professional turns right, and will shortly regain contact with their prey not too far up ahead, and so the chase (for them at least) continues. The professional chose the 'right' way, not by chance, but by calculated probability. They are not just lucky. They are a professional.

Surveillance on arrival – First time

There are several points that should be considered on the very first day of surveillance. You must verify that you are really at the right address, and generally familiarise yourself with the area – identifying the movement matrix and determining the probability of various routes that a subject may take. This also involves determining all the possible observation positions, together with assessing the strengths and weaknesses of each. Sometimes a position may be ideal for watching, but very poor for starting a follow, so consideration must be given to what is best at the time.

- Start the job earlier than you may decide would be normal. An extra hour on the first day of the job is rarely wasted even if nothing happens during this time. Far better to spend an hour than to waste the entire day if perhaps your subject leaves home slightly earlier than you decided to arrive. The subject may be a shift worker starting at seven a.m., which means he may be leaving just after six a.m. If you decided to arrive on day one at six thirty a.m., you will waste the entire morning not knowing they have already left.

- ACCURATELY identify the correct address. Be very sure - mistakes are poor form.

- Check numbering either side of the real address, don't rely on expecting number 42 to be next in sequence after numbers 38 and 40, so look for the 42 AND the adjoining 44 to be sure.

- Be aware of 'lettered' numbering such as 1 and 1a addresses. A glance at a partially obscured letterbox may show 42, yet it may in fact be 42a.

- Be aware of address ranges like 42-48, such as for commercial buildings or apartments.

- Know where to look for street numbers – not all places are obvious.
- Check for numbers on road name signs, as some have address ranges in small print.
- Check for numbers printed on curbs and gutters outside homes.
- Check for numbers printed on the roads in your street directory.
- Check for numbers on front doors.
- Check for numbers on front fences.
- Check for numbers on letterboxes.
- Check for numbers on any addressed mail found sticking out of letterboxes. The postman will usually know which house is which, so the mail can provide numbering very easily. As it may arouse suspicion if you are seen by others, this is a last resort check, though can be a very good resource to use. Consider checking address detail on mail for neighbouring properties as well if required. Remember that opening other peoples mail is a federal offence, as is removing the mail from the property, though merely *inspecting* the address or names printed on mail that protrudes from a letterbox (or that which is lying nearby such as in common areas), is not against the law.
- Check for numbers on garbage associated with an address. Mail, statements and other printed matter containing address detail will often be readily accessible. There is benefit in conducting a full garbage search for other reasons as detailed on page 108, however often a quick check of a recycling bin or rubbish lying nearby may give you the clues you need to identify the address number.
- Check for properties that do not have a street frontage, other than a driveway. Such properties are common in

Australia and known as a 'battleaxe block', after the shape they leave on a map, where the axe 'handle' is the driveway and the property is the blade. These can often lead to confusion as the letterbox or number may be visible on the street frontage, and may lead you to wrongly assume the house adjoining the driveway is the correct one. This is particularly so when the house on the street has poor or missing numbering, or when the battleaxe property and the front property have very similar numbers, such as a letter suffix like 42 and 42a.

- Conduct a drive past (see below).
- Conduct a foot patrol.
- Describe address fully and accurately (see below).
- Note the distance in kilometres from your office.
- Identify and describe the observation positions (OPs).

Surveillance on arrival – Generally

- Always arrive at least one hour prior to the first expected or predicted subject activity. Where activity is known to occur at a specific time, you should arrive at least **half an hour** prior to this event time. Unlike other occupations your entire workday may be wasted if you miss your subject departing because you were just a little late. Be early to ensure you are well prepared and ready, as a professional investigator.
- Conduct a drive past.
- Conduct a foot patrol (if appropriate, as this allows better observation).
- Describe any vehicles that are parked on site or parked directly outside the property. Include the order of cars, for example: '...*Ford Laser behind Ford Falcon*'.
- Describe garbage bin location (if required).
- Observe position of windows and doors.

- Enter and park at a suitable observation position.
- Shut down vehicle (see page 199).
- Lock all doors.
- Remove ignition keys, or conceal from view - hang a cap to obscure keys for example.
- Crack your window open for ventilation.
- Ensure all screens or curtains up.
- Have the camera record black screen for two seconds (a clean break from the last footage to make later dubbing or review easier, as well as to document your arrival time electronically on the tape).
- Have the camera record a few seconds of the target house. This is a scene shot, to document the start time and job location.
- Wait for action to occur.

Surveillance drive-past reconnaissance

This is where you drive the car past the area you wish to observe. The purpose of the drive past is to allow you to quickly visualise and assess the area, without drawing attention. In effect the movement itself is the concealing factor. People are comfortable with cars that MOVE on roads, yet they will notice cars STOPPED on roads.

- Prepare for the drive past well away from target house, not 'just down the road'.
- Organise your vehicle neatly, allow ready access to equipment and files.
- Prepare the camera. Ensure tape is ready and cued, battery power ok, focus *fixed on infinite*, time/date correct, fast shutter speed selected.
- Consider recording the drive past with a camera held against the window. Fast shutter speed selection ensures steady still frames. A wide angle field of view

184

allows non-monitored filming, but consider zooming quickly to capture items of interest while driving, such as vehicle registration numbers which allow off-site analysis of detail later.

- Commence drive past of property.
- Travel slightly slower than usual, but not noticeably so. The aim is to provide movement concealed visibility, not to draw attention due to slow speed.
- Continually assess area for key detail, such as:
  - Persons on site
  - Vehicles on site
  - Registration numbers
  - Buildings and access points (driveway and gates)
  - Signage (indicates occupation – plumber etc)
  - Location of good observation positions (OPs)
- Consider propping (brief dead stop) to capture any item of particular interest if warranted. Remember that response to vehicle sound is different in rural environments, so while a vehicle may appear concealed, the sound of slowing and starting may giveaway your presence.
- If action is occurring during a drive-past, consider stopping briefly to get a few seconds of video documentation if possible, and *then* move on if required. The action may not occur again, and the video footage can be invaluable later, so this is a priority. It may not be *generally* possible to pause so close to the front of a property without attracting attention, but if this occurs only briefly and then the vehicle moves on, it is not uncommon behaviour provided it's not repeated, and you don't remain there too long.
- Consider zeroing odometer on passing the property, to enable better identification at other times, like later at

night. Reference the distance to known points such as closest intersection.

- Once past the target property, continue smoothly at the same speed. Do not speed up suddenly after passing the property, as the engine noise will convey your behaviour or interest in this property much louder than your vehicle appearance. Continue well past, then prop or turn off and wait for a period to allow your 'movement ripples' to subside and persons to forget they saw or heard you.

- Be cautious executing a U-turn on dirt roads as this generates attention. Be aware of signalling that you are leaving. Conducting three drive-pasts in a day to check for activity may result in a worn u-turn area near the property, and this is likely to draw attention of locals as unusual vehicle behaviour in the area. When doing a drive past, you can't turn around until you are not only out of sight but out of sound. Farmers have keen hearing and will easily pick the sound of the U-turn from some distance away. Consider varying the precise location of your U-turn to spread out the tyre marks if appropriate.

- If possible return via another route to avoid further exposure. Only conduct another drive-past again if you feel the benefit in observation outweighs the increased risk in detection.

- If there is no alternate route possible, return via the same route past the property, but ensure there is sufficient time. In rural settings, consider you may be one of only five vehicles that use this road, or one of five that use it this afternoon, so any movement may attract attention. Consider a much faster return trip so engine noise is different on the second journey and provides less time to observe vehicle.

- Consider using a taxi. For a ten-dollar fare you have access to a 'different' vehicle, which can drive past without raising suspicion. This way you are protecting the exposure of the surveillance vehicle, and enabling property visibility even after an earlier compromise.

Surveillance photographs

While a lot of surveillance involves video, this is a difficult medium to work with in some situations. It requires equipment to view and the video itself is often difficult to reference easily, especially if the footage is several minutes long. Having good quality photographs included in the report will always look professional, as well as assist those reviewing the case. With any case there are three basic shots that should be included:

1. Good ID shot of the subject – front and profile
2. Good shot of subject's home and work – front and rear
3. Good shot of subject's vehicle

These establish the case and clarify that you were following the right person, and watching the right house. It provides some context when later discussing the case, as it enables visualisation of the subject and their home. Sometimes the picture of an address may be used to prompt others when you are questioning the behaviour of the subject. Seeing a large lawn they may be more inclined to delve into who normally mows the lawn for example, because any picture tells a story.

After the surveillance video has been taken, good investigators will go through this and obtain still images of various scenes to be included in reports later. The aim is to provide a storyboard of images that depict and reference the video. It enables others to assess the quality of evidence without having to sit through the video, or make their own notes.

When capturing storyboard images, attention should be directed at detail such as identification of persons, vehicles and signage, as well as the actions depicted. If the case is corporate theft, the images should be captured that best show the subject holding the stolen items as he lowers them into his vehicle. For injury cases, the aim is to capture the furthest extent of movement, so if a subject raises his arms above his head, the photograph should depict the maximum extension. If a subject bends over, the photo should be captured when he is fully bent over.

Doctors and others can examine these images and determine angles and make other assessments easily by reviewing a static photo of their maximum travel or movement extent, yet this can be difficult when looking at a moving video. Rather than having busy doctors pausing rewinding video to see activity, the static images provide hard copy references to the material contained on the video. This enables the professionals to skip boring bits and move directly to sections of relevant interest. They may even analyse the exact angles of body movement observed in the static images, which is difficult to do with moving video. Angles of movement can show the range of normal movement exhibited by the subject, and static images highlight these brief but important occurrences that may be missed when viewing the full motion video.

CHAPTER 11: STATIC SURVEILLANCE (STAKEOUTS)

Deciding where to park is often a crucial issue to the job. The most subtle variance in parking may result in being 'sprung', or perhaps missing a good shot due to an inconveniently located telegraph pole. A good agent will case the site first, and then when ready, he will pull into position quietly and stop, not moving lest it draw attention. In a difficult situation you may have somebody else park and get out, leaving you there, as this can allay suspicion. This can help where the nosey neighbour may become suspicious, when, as they stare at the arriving car, they realise that there is no-one exiting. Because of this issue, jobs near schools can be killers due to the public concern over paedophiles. Not being able to move means you need to get it right first time and nothing is as obvious as a car that keeps 'moving' a little here and a little there!

While you are waiting on a stakeout, check and recheck all your equipment, your documents, your position. Mentally rehearse all the possible scenarios that may occur during the course of your surveillance, including which direction may they go? What will you say if approached by a neighbour? If approached by the subject? Clean the surveillance vehicle of unnecessary rubbish such as food wrappers or empty drink bottles. The car is a very small office and any clutter will encourage poor results. Maintain a good 'watch and listen' on your target property.

Only then if you have done everything else possible, can you think about relaxing. Switch to radio 2RPH on 1179AM which is a good PI station. It is designed for blind people, and their presenters read every newspaper over the air. It's better than reading a printed version, as you can then keep your eyes on the job and listen to the entire paper being read. Apart from being free, it is also very accessible, especially when some surveillance jobs start at four a.m. and the paper shops are not open for hours to come!

Loitering pretexts

Today's climate of terrorism, paedophiles and thieves means people are more wary of strangers. A PI is often approached by people inquiring about what they are doing, and why are they hanging around. It is important to be ready for these exchanges rather than being caught off guard. If approached, some possible loitering excuses may be *'I'm waiting for my mate to get here from Bathurst, but I forgot to get our work site address, and I'm an hour early as well. I'm waiting for his call, but he is out of phone range now* (due to loss of phone signal on the drive from Bathurst). *We're working around here – I think it is this street but I can't remember the number... I'm parked here because this particular spot has good radio / phone reception and I am waiting on a call from my base...'*

Another loitering pretext may be *'I live nearby but the floor-sanding contractors are in to sand our floors. It is making such a racket I can't think straight, so I figured I would get out of the house for a few hours and work on my laptop in the car...* (followed by some detailed red-herrings like...) *they told me it would only take two hours but they are only half finished. Still, the floor should look great when it's done. My missus was complaining the baby sick was too hard to clean out of the carpet'.* One of the best loitering pretexts is the very personal *'I am having 'issues' with my girlfriend'* which usually encourages people to leave you alone for a little longer.

Of course the best answer to give is one that is targeted to your audience and to the suburb, to the specific person who has approached you (check their dress and language etc.). Think laterally and be creative, there are no wrong answers, and often a crazy sounding answer can be the most believable as it actually gives them something to think about, rather than have their brains *wondering* about why you are there. Some people are simply satisfied with a tick in the box answer, like a henpecked husband *'Look Mildred, I really don't know! I asked him like you wanted me to, and he just told me he was doing a noise survey, so I left him again. You go and ask him if it means so much to you!'*

Depending on the person who has approached you, and their likely connection to the target, the best loitering excuse is the truth. When asked what you are doing here by a suspicious resident, you can look them directly in the eye and say *'I'm a private investigator, and I'm doing surveillance'*. This response doesn't give them much to work with, and will often stop them in their tracks. They may suspect you are a PI and not want you around, but having you admit that you actually ARE a PI is unexpected.

Often these types of people think that you will move on once 'discovered', however your disarming comment is basically telling them you have no intention of moving and care so little about them knowing you are there – that you are prepared to tell them what you are doing. There are many cases where it may be a very good idea to be honest in this way as it may reduce concern or further unwanted attention (including a visit by police), and other times people are sometimes prepared to help you in some way.

When in a city building, loitering props may include a mobile phone which you use to make it sound like you are having a long conversation, or even a baby doll disguised as a real baby. (see: The case of the mistaken itinerary on page 372) There's no limit to the imagination for a good pretext prop.

Response to a compromise

A surveillance investigator who claims they have never been compromised by a subject is either lying, they have done very little surveillance, or they are so cautious that they simply never get results. Being seen and subsequently approached by a subject is fairly common for a PI, who is often working alone. There is only so much you can do to prevent being seen, and the more time you spend follow someone, the greater the odds are that they will detect you. Provided you didn't do anything inappropriate to draw attention to yourself, there is no shame in being compromised as it is part of a PI's life.

The aim of surveillance is to gather information, and a PI will attempt to remain concealed as this usually enables them to get the best information, and does not affect the behaviour of their unwitting subject. There are some cases where the 'value' of a particular action taken by the PI may be greater than the need to prevent compromise. Consider the old school PI's who used to burst in on cheating lovers, to take flash photos of the illicit activity. This action clearly compromised the PI and made it very clear that photo's were being taken of their sex act, but of course this was as expected by the PI. In this case the 'value' of the incriminating photos exceeded the need to prevent compromise. This 'bursting in on lovers' activity doesn't occur much in today's society, but the philosophy remains that getting the desired 'result' is almost always more important than preventing a compromise.

Sometimes you can watch someone for months or follow them for hundreds of kilometres without detection. Other people are so aware of their surroundings that they may approach your vehicle even before you have finished parking nearby for the very first time. As with many things in surveillance, there is no 'right' answer as to what to do in any case, as it is highly situation dependant. Soldiers are taught to patrol through the bush with a constant expectation of a surprise attack, hence they continually assess the situation and mentally rehearse their response options as the environment changes. A good PI is always ready for compromise and similarly rehearses their options at all stages of the operation.

Response considerations

1. What is the level of awareness (of the person) to your presence, and what have they seen? Just because they notice you doesn't mean they know why you're there. They may think you are lost and come to help you out, or they could be coming up to ask you for directions themselves. Relax!

2. What is the disposition of the person? Are they likely to be aggressive? Are they likely to believe a story you tell them?

3. How close to the subject is the person? If you are compromised by a neighbour several houses away, you may not be concerned at all as they will not be likely to communicate with your subject. If you are compromised by a close associate, family member of the subject or the subject themselves, you need to be more cautious.

4. What stage is the investigation at? In the initial stages it may be best to take greater steps to prevent compromise, yet this may not be necessary in later stages. Consider the case where you have finally identified a subject working on a building site, but you have not got very good video of them due to visual obstructions. If the investigation is at a late stage and the allocated surveillance time is nearly up, you may consider going right into the site and taking considerable risk of compromise in order to get very good images of the subject working.

Response options

1. Provide a pretext, such as a loitering pretext (see page 190). Some people will literally believe anything, and may just want 'an' answer, and will leave you alone if you give them a reasonable pretext. The aim here is to prevent them from thinking you are a PI.

2. Be too busy to respond. On seeing them approach your car, have a mobile phone to your ear. Acknowledge their presence with a distracted wave, but carry on your conversation. It could be a very important business call, or perhaps a very personal call. Seeing you on the phone may at least partially answer their query as to why you are there – because you are on a long emotional phone call. The more 'personal' the call, the less likely they are to intrude and question you. Consider '...I told you not to leave my number in your phone, Julie you know what he's like... so what did he say? But he doesn't know does he, did he see us? Well leave the lazy f...wit... haven't I told you...' A clever and creative PI may string the important call out for long enough that they get bored and eventually go away without even speaking to you, or the highly personal nature of the call may send them scurrying off almost as quickly as they had initially approached you. The fact you are so disinterested in their presence (due to your 'call') puts them immediately at ease – at least to a degree, as they feel you have more important things to worry about and can't be watching them or else you would have rapidly finished the call to deal with the situation differently.

3. Refuse to tell them why you are there. This arouses suspicion, but *may* be appropriate, especially if you have already provided them a pretext which they don't believe,

and they continue to push you for the 'real' reason. There is no law which requires you to tell a private person what you are doing in a public location, no matter how suspicious your actions.

4. Question them back. In some cases you can switch the situation around and demand they tell you why they are approaching you. Putting them on the back foot can sometimes make them stop questioning you. It would not be the first time that my aggressive response has led to them apologising and making some reference to '*I just wanted to check... you can't be too careful these days...*' People expect the behaviour of suspicious people to be evasive if questioned, so your confident response and willingness to engage in a dialogue does not fit their expected suspicious profile – even if you still don't tell them what you are doing.

5. An example of this is detailed in The case of the Belmore Bomber on page 206.

6. Admit you are a PI but switch their focus. If you are watching them for a bad-back injury matter, you may suggest or imply you are trying to catch them out on infidelity (or the reverse). A comment like: '*What do you mean? Ya worried ya missus is checkin up on ya?*' may cause them to rethink the situation. Perhaps you are a PI, but NOT for the reason they were expecting. I had a case once where my subject approached me almost aggressively, but after I explained I was actually trying to catch out his *neighbour* for *social security fraud* he was only too willing to help me, and gave some quite detailed information. It seemed he was not on the best of terms with his neighbour, and was happy to 'stick it to him'. I thanked him profusely, and almost as an afterthought, I said '*Look, you wouldn't mind if I perhaps call you tomorrow to check a few things?*' and then asked for his

work number which he readily gave me. Of course all I was trying to do was find out where HE was working, so clever management of the compromise led directly to solving the case. An even better example of this technique is described in The case of a favourable compromise on page 428.

7. Leave without talking to them. Simply drive off or walk away. This is not the preferred option, but is sometimes appropriate where the person is very aggressive and you want to avoid confrontation, or where you are absolutely sure no other response technique would work in that situation.

8. Admit you are a PI. In some rare cases it may be appropriate to be truthful with the person who has compromised you, without going into specific details. One example would be where you are approached by a police officer, which is not uncommon. In this case you should identify yourself (as is required by most legislation), and <u>probably</u> also advise who you are conducting surveillance on. There is generally no reason to go into further details such as the name of the client, or specific reasons for surveillance.

Stakeout parking considerations

There are many factors to consider when parking, and it is an issue which requires a lot of planning. For example: Which way to face? Where is the shade? What is the likely direction of departure? The surveillance professional will carefully consider and execute parking with a high degree of precision, resulting in him greatly increasing his odds and stacking the deck in his favour.

Visibility

Ensure the parked position has reasonable visibility of the action you want to record. Traditionally a position is taken on the opposite side of the road to the subject's house, located at least three houses away but preferably more. Often a good angle can be gained from a more unusual location. Have a good look. Can you observe the home through a gap in the trees further up? Can you sit in another street entirely? Can you park in the driveway of a vacant house nearby? The best location for visibility is not always the first, look carefully. The parked location should provide a view of what you need to see, but if there is unlikely to be much action at the address, consider parking further away. In some cases it is best to park out of sight of the subject's address, and simply wait for their vehicle to drive past for a very discreet start to the follow.

Departure direction

Attempt to park on the OPPOSITE side of the road to the likely departure point of the subject. If the subject drives past the surveillance vehicle on departure, it increases your vehicle exposure to him. Best that he drives away without ever seeing you near his home, as he is likely to see the vehicle plenty of other times.

Response

Ensure the position permits a rapid response to any movement from the address you are watching. The best position to watch an address from may be two streets away, but this may mean you will not be fast enough to follow them. You need to be close enough to the action, with a clear exit path. Ensure that your position will not be parked in, and will not require a slow three point turn. Preferably face the vehicle in the likely direction of departure to enable a fast response.

Concealment

Find a position that conceals. Hide the surveillance vehicle under a low hanging tree by the side of the road. Park behind other vehicles. Park so you can see the subject's vehicle in the driveway, but are not actually visible to the home. Try to ensure that you are parked in a position where something is actually obscuring visibility of your vehicle from the windows of the home.

Attention

Ensure the position won't attract too much attention from the subject or neighbours. Choose to be outside a quiet home instead of a busy one with several cars and toys on the lawn. Park near an older person's home. Try to position yourself exactly between two houses, so that you are not directly outside either. Each home will assume you are visiting the other. Park next to larger trees or bushes - even if they provide no shade, they obscure visibility of the car making it less conspicuous and hence attracting less attention. Park with the REAR of the vehicle facing the address to attract less attention from the subject. The front of a vehicle signals 'possible danger', and naturally attracts more attention than the 'safer' rear. Balance this with the ergonomic considerations (see below). Rear facing if you need to conceal the car more, front facing if this is less of an issue.

Concentration

Find a location which does not require too much concentration to observe the subject's address. Parking three blocks away is very covert, but requires a lot more concentration to observe any movement. Parking directly opposite requires little concentration, but is not covert. Find a good balance. Night surveillance requires more concentration, so a closer position is preferable, particularly given that the darkness hides the surveillance vehicle. Parking in a busy location or street requires more concentration than parking in a quieter location, so you need to balance concealment with concentration.

Distance

Park as far away as possible, while still being able to see, record video and become aware of movement at the address. Parking some distance away permits the use of the engine and air conditioner if necessary, where the noise will not attract unwanted attention.

Shade

Sitting for long periods in a car is hot work and finding a shady spot is far preferable to an exposed one. A shady location provides a more discreet position, attracting less attention. Shade moves. Use a compass or road directory to calculate north. Then calculate where the shade will be during the day. In Australia, the sun rises in the north east, and sets in the south west. Park so you will be in the shade for the next few hours and consider moving halfway through the day if necessary.

Ergonomics

Park so you can easily watch the address without strain if possible. This reduces fatigue, and aids concentration. Park with seats facing towards to the address if appropriate. Remember that a car may draw slightly more attention if it is facing the house, so you may need to compromise on one of these issues.

Shut down the vehicle

While parked in a static location, ensure you 'shut down the vehicle' with:

- All doors locked

- Keys out of ignition, or <u>concealed</u> from view (Hang a 'cap' to obscure keys)
- Window / skylight cracked open for ventilation
- All screens, covers or curtains up
- Reduce unnecessary movement inside the vehicle that results in reflected sunlight glinting and flashing across the street as the car shakes when you move within.
- Be quiet. No loud phone calls or radio chatter

The case of waterside violence

Key learning points

- Agent safety

- Conducting static surveillance

One of the many surveillance jobs I worked on was the stevedoring company 'Patrick's' dispute with the Maritime Union Australia (MUA) over waterfront reform. Our mission was to obtain video and other evidence of the Unions which showed them either breaking the law or otherwise obstructing the company's legitimate operations. The dispute went on for a very long time, and unsurprisingly we found evidence of some people on the picket line doing the wrong thing.

With unions enforcing somewhat restrictive work practices, management felt they were impeding their ability to conduct an efficient business. For weeks I worked the Patricks site, spending hours in the tall cranes with a zoom lens on my video camera, and wearing a balaclava to conceal my identity. The media and the unions[52] hyped up the balaclava security-guard angle, trying to make management appear as bullies, where balaclavas

---

[52] Maritime Union Australia. *'War on the Waterfront'* www.mua.org.au/war

were somehow offensive or an aggressive gesture designed to strike fear into opponents, like war paint. The reality was totally the reverse. Not only where there no security staff (at least at my Sydney site) wearing balaclavas, but only a handful of PI's.

It was a high profile case with lots of emotion, and we needed balaclavas to protect our identities from the angry hordes who would scream out obscenities towards us every day, and threatening comments 'You're f...ing dead meat. We are going to torch your car and break your legs... we're going to put your face on the internet with your home address and you'll wake up to a brick through your window every night...Jump you f...wit. Kill yourself and save us the all the trouble'.

Down below the unions had a few guys who had their own camera lenses trained on us, just waiting for us to remove the balaclava for even just a second to capture our identity. It was hard to remember to keep it on for so many hours when the natural subconscious reaction is to remove it briefly to have a drink or cough etc. Even at night the rabble didn't let up – they made a lot of noise to ensure we didn't get much sleep. When up the cranes at night on observation duty, there was always someone below with a laser pointer trained on our heads trying to burn our eyes out.

The balaclavas were protection for camera operators, viewed as management spies by the aggressive workers. This was despite the fact that the only directive to the PI's was to capture 'evidence of violence' occurring at the picket lines. Later court action[53] revealed the terror felt by some workers who were trying to travel through these areas.

---

[53] Vaughan v Patrick Stevedores [2001] NSWSC 1126 (10/12/2001) '...lined with people who shouted abuse and threw projectiles at the bus. Whenever the bus stopped it was shaken.

There were aggressive scenes which we captured on tape and played out in court each day. Here we were just doing our job and wearing balaclavas to protect our identity from the angry hordes openly threatening to kill us, and yet the newspapers reported the 'management bully' aspect – as if the three or four PI's in balaclavas with video cameras were somehow threatening to the two hundred odd beefy waterfront workers manning the picket lines. None of the PI's really cared much about the dispute issues. Don't believe everything you read in the press. Although we were never correctly identified as PI's instead of security guards, it goes to show how PI's can get a bad reputation for just doing their job.

When to conduct surveillance

As with parking, reporting and everything else, detail is everything. The success of a case can hang on the most subtle of details, and timing is no different. After researching the behaviour and nature of their prey, the surveillance professional will carefully consider the best timed approach to ensure success. Weekday, weekend, day, and night – everyone has a routine. The faster you pick the routine, the faster you can hone in on the sweet spots. It is an expensive exercise watching someone for hours when they do nothing, and the professional will avoid these periods, often picking them by instinct. *'I won't do them today, I will do that job again tomorrow'* is something they may say, yet ask them why this is the case and there is no answer. A mix of instinct and experience will guide the professional to success.

Men jumped on the roof and began hitting the bus with baseball bats... Mr Vaughan was terrified'

Choosing a day

- **GARBAGE DAY**. For a first day, consider starting the day *after* garbage day for the subject's address. When a subject drags their garbage bin in from the street after pick up, this is an ideal time to obtain good ID footage, as well as record them doing something physical. Check with the council earlier for their garbage collection days.

- **WEEKEND / PUBLIC HOLIDAY / WEEKDAY.** Consider all the factors in the case. In an injury case, you want to catch them working. If it is suspected that a subject is working, then focus on weekdays. A younger subject may have a part-time job on Saturdays or Thursday nights so focus on those times. If the subject is not working, you could cover weekends when they may link up with other people who are usually working (and hence unavailable) during the week. Sport is often a weekend activity, and a good opportunity for surveillance.

- **DIFFERENT DAYS.** People have routines. Always attempt to cover several different days of the week for each job. If you do three days surveillance on a job, and each day is a Monday, you are not covering a subject's routine effectively. Preferably do two different weekdays and one weekend period on each job, which will broadly cover their weekly routine. This may lead to requests for further surveillance, if perhaps you discover them conducting some activity on a particular day. More hours may be authorised to cover this particular day of the week again. If you only cover the same day each week, your chances of covering their busy day are one in seven. Do three days, and your chances of finding their regular busy day are three in seven.

Choosing a time

Assess the age, occupation, nationality, address, demographics and other issues. It's no fun wondering if your subject has already left for the day finding you are wasting your time, or the client's money. Start a job at least two hours_prior to the first expected movement at the address for any new surveillance job. Start a job at least one hour prior to the first expected movement when doing it on a subsequent occasion. Starting times include:

5:00am	Concreters, builders, shift workers, rural locations, address far from city subject address located some distance from city (may drive for an hour or more to get to work)
6:30am	Standard start time for most jobs
7:30am	Weekend start time
8:00am	Subject known to not be working
7:45am-9:15am	Movement HIGHLY likely. Be ready!
11:00am	Subject known to remain at home, night workers who rise late
1:30pm	Afternoon standard start time. Preferably prior to mail delivery, in order to cover subject collecting the mail from the letterbox
2:30pm-4:00pm	Movement likely for mothers with small children
5:00pm-6:30pm	Movement likely for workers returning home
6:30pm-8:00pm	Good outdoor lighting (dusk/dark) for seeing into windows of homes to identify occupants before they close the blinds

Morning or afternoon starts

Start in the mornings for all new jobs, except for home units. Afternoon starts for addresses that are a home unit, so you can identify the subject when they pick up their mail from the letterbox. Late afternoon start for rural jobs. Observe the layout of the area just before last light, so you can formulate your position for the next morning, and possibly be there to do a night reconnaissance.

When to finish surveillance

For a morning, stop as soon as you discover the subject is not home and at other times consider waiting for their return. People often have items to unload on their return, such as shopping and child seats, and they will check mailboxes. Do not routinely stop surveillance on an address just because the subject is not home, use the opportunity to be well set up to capture their arrival home.

If you have followed the subject to a possible work location, consider stopping two hours after their arrival, unless you can actually observe them at work. Consider that they may go out for lunch. It is a waste to continue surveillance all day with little prospect of success during this time. Use the time to work another job if possible, and return to cover the departure from the workplace for this job later in that afternoon.

If you lose contact when they leave home, consider the duration of time they are going to be away for. Look at their dress and demeanour. Perhaps they will return after an hour, perhaps they are going to drop off a passenger or pick up milk and then return in thirty minutes. Consider waiting one hour for a possible early return home, unless you feel the subject will be gone for most of the day. Don't finish immediately after the subject returns home. Consider waiting for an hour, as they may get changed and then go out somewhere else.

Poor weather

Consider the weather. If it is too hot, it will be uncomfortable in the surveillance vehicle, but the subject is more likely to be active. In rain or poor weather, it is more difficult to observe through rainy windows and the subject is less likely to be active outside. Despite this, people are more likely to <u>run</u> to avoid bad weather (run to and from a car or shelter), and the weather itself helps conceal your presence. The best weather condition for surveillance is usually overcast, which affords you some shade.

The case of the Belmore Bomber

Key learning points

- Long term surveillance

- Managing neighbours during static surveillance

- Foot and mobile surveillance

The investigation industry is small and specialised, particularly in the area of surveillance. Over time most PI's will get to know or even work with many others. Usually a PI works alone, but every now and then a larger job arises whereby several will work in a team, which is more common in corporate surveillance jobs. I first met Ben McDonald[54], a fellow PI on a rural surveillance job. At the time we were both still keen and enthused about PI work, and we soon hit off a friendship as colleagues. Ben and I worked a lot of jobs together and every one had its share of laughs, danger, fast driving and intrigue. While you spend a great many hours patiently waiting for something to happen, it would be rare to encounter a job that didn't have something worthy of dinner party conversation.

---

[54] www.omegaline.com.au

Probably the longest running corporate investigation I have ever done was operation 'Belmore', which I did with Ben and several other PI's. I have not heard of any other job before or since which has had such blanket coverage in terms of man hours doing round the clock surveillance. It all started with one quiet employee, who had been working for a very large and well known employer for many years. Some changes in the workplace were made, and this worker decided he didn't approve – so much so, that he decided to take his grievances to the boss – not just his boss, or even his boss' boss but in fact the big boss of the whole show, who is still a household name today. The worker's grievances were a little rambling, but they were specific enough to cause great concern, and were squarely targeted at Mr Big Boss and his family. Nobody really knew much about the quiet worker, which (apart from his general weirdness) caused even more concern – the fear of the unknown. All too often we hear in the media and elsewhere, that it is the quiet ones you have to watch – and watch we did.

Mr Big Boss decided he wanted to know what this guy did, and where he went every minute of the day. He wanted him watched around the clock. He wanted plenty of warning should he ever approach the family home, or buy a truck load of fertiliser or do anything that may suggest he was going to go 'postal' (to coin a phrase after the quiet American postman of a few years ago, who decided one day to kill all his co-workers in a shooting blood bath). For the first few weeks Mr Postal was still going to his usual work at the Global Monolith Company, which made surveillance a little easier, as their own workers kept an eye on him during the day. We had routine and took him to work each day, and took him home again in the evening like clockwork – always off in the distance quietly watching him and quietly following him and documenting his every move. In fact it seemed his movements were just so routine, so clockwork that it unnerved Mr Big Boss and his team, who were convinced his clockwork nature was just the public face of a man who harboured a ticking time bomb inside him – tick, tock, tick, tock. Nobody wanted to be too close when he finally exploded.

There was much consternation when he actually resigned, in a scrawling letter personally addressed to Mr Big Boss – filled with some emotive words, implied suggestions and colourful language. It didn't seem he wanted to resign as his job was everything, but since the workplace restructure it was just 'not the same'. Some argued he was like *Rainman* who was quirky and harmless, and merely resented any form of change to his world – rather than doing anything about it. Others argued he was cold and calculating and knew exactly what he was doing. The mere fact that work was his entire world appeared a real worry. He didn't socialise with others much, and didn't seem to have outside interests.

Big Boss and his big team were not impressed at the fact he gave a full three weeks notice when he had resigned. In fact they quickly offered to pay him out in full (and more) if he wanted – and he was free to leave on the spot. Mr Postal didn't take long to consider the carefully worded offer from the Global Monolith HR department; however he chose to reject it. He decided to continue coming to work each day for the next three weeks, despite the fact he didn't actually need to. This unexpected behaviour caused even more consternation, and encouraged the speculation that he didn't have anything to live for apart from his job. Nobody really knew what would happen when he didn't have it anymore, and although his life seemed monotonously routine, we all knew he was a very unknown quantity.

It was a very long three weeks for the management team, who waited with baited breath – emergency numbers on Post-it notes stuck to every key desk, consultants drawing up conflict resolution strategies and security beefed up on every level. Each day we would take him to work, and each afternoon we would take him home again – all from the safety of our tinted vehicles as we discreetly followed behind him. Eventually it was the last day. There had been no further correspondence from Mr Postal, and he had been performing his duties at work as usual – but at lunchtime he approached the main office and demanded to see Mr Big Boss. This caused an immediate ripple, which turned into a tidal wave as phones rang hot and strange men suddenly appeared at the office with him – also 'waiting to see someone' or other – subtle bulges under their suits.

The designated HR consultant had been briefed about this possible scenario, and was quickly there to explain the situation, to sympathise with him about the workplace restructure and the fact that Mr Big Boss was not available at the moment, but if he was – would have certainly been there to speak with him in person. *'You know how these business meetings are – in fact he is not even here at present. He is away on... business'*. Mr Postal was no small framed man and he was decidedly unimpressed, but eventually left the office quietly and later went home after he finished work, taking his tired old work bag with him. We always wondered what was carried in that bag each day. Security had quickly checked his now vacant locker, and in fact the entire section in which he had been working. Hearing these surreal details reminded me of a scene in the movie *Monsters Inc*, where management suspect there is a child in the scare factory and teams of response droids are dispatched to inspect and 'clean' the area. After many years of quite ordinary work, Mr Postal had become a square peg in a round hole and management were worried.

The fact that nothing much 'happened' on his last day did nothing to quell the fear and suspicion. In fact it was just too easy, too uneventful, and it seemed he was playing with us, toying with us and lulling everyone into a false sense of calm, right up until the day he was going to go postal. It was frequently noted that he was now free of his workplace and had the time to concoct and scheme and plot his time of carnage. *Perhaps he was meeting with some unsavoury associate right now?* They would wonder, but of course the surveillance team would be ever ready to report that he was still at home alone, and had not met with anyone of interest. Mr Postal didn't get a new job, and nor did he go to any interviews. With little social life and no gambling or drinking problems he had little to spend his money on, so after twenty years at the same place he probably didn't really need another job.

The Global Monolith Company had already paid him a full and rather fat redundancy even though he had actually resigned, which probably didn't encourage him to look for work ever again. No doubt it was discussed at length when they decided to pay him such a fat redundancy, though I personally felt this was perhaps the wrong approach. While many 'normal' people might be grateful for such a generous offer and possibly withdraw their grievances – Mr Postal clearly had a very different value system, and the offer of cash could well be viewed with contempt by him. I figured he could well have been happier by being offered some menial position that was 'created' especially for him.

With the full resources of the Global Monolith Company at his disposal, Big Boss didn't seem worried about the impressive cost of our surveillance. Now that Postal wasn't working, we had two PI's assigned to him at any one time, right around the clock, working twelve hour shifts. He didn't go out much for the first week or so, and then one Tuesday he was followed to a local shop where he picked up a new computer system. This did surprise some, as he was not viewed as particularly intelligent and nobody would have ever guessed he had IT ability or even the inclination. It was just another unpleasant surprise to management, and each new turn of unexpected events did little to encourage them to terminate the intensive surveillance. Some of Mr Postal's written scrawls seemed uncomfortably close to the American Unabomber's manifest. Given the Unabomber had only recently been arrested amid intensive publicity, the case was very fresh in people's minds. Few villains achieved such global notoriety that even Microsoft Word included their tag name in the software's internal dictionary as the Unabomber did. Big Boss clearly felt that Postal was in the same category as the Unabomber, and didn't want him achieving the same notoriety at his expense – and so our intensive surveillance continued.

It is difficult conducting such long term surveillance without getting caught. The mere fact that he spent so much time at home meant our surveillance team was also parked in a static location for just as long a period. Fortunately we were able to watch his house from a few vantage points, and had one good location which was quite some distance away. Initially we were quite discreet, but within the first two weeks the local residents had become aware of our presence, and now that almost three months had elapsed – our presence was something of a talking point. Every single day there were two agents waiting in a car in the same place. At seven a.m. and seven p.m. the agents would change shifts like clockwork. While many may find the idea of spending an entire day sitting in a car quite absurd, the fact that we had been there for so long was doubly so. It was pointless trying to conceal ourselves given our blanket presence, so we had to accept the local interest and just try to minimise our exposure as best as we could.

Mr Postal owned an aging dark purple Statesman which looked as if it had been painted by a group of inebriated school children. The car was parked under his carport and was still registered, though nobody ever saw him use it which was just another weird quirk to muse the hours away. He did start it every week or so, but it would just run for a quarter hour blowing a lot of smoke, and then he would turn it off again.

Postal always walked, or caught a train or bus, which made the follows a little interesting. A foot follow on public transport requires a great deal more skill than a vehicle follow. A PI may have a lot of tools in his car such as cameras and chargers, laptops and phones, maps and wee bottles, change for toll gates, spare clothes for a disguise and just so many other things. Take the surveillance car away from a PI and he must work that much harder. He must physically carry everything he needs, yet still look inconspicuous and blend into his surroundings. Without the comfortable camouflage of his car he is naked and exposed. He has limited options and must act quickly or the target will suddenly board a bus, and leave him standing on the footpath watching the job drive away.

We never knew where we were going because Postal was never predictable. He would catch three trains and a bus to get somewhere, though there was often a much more direct route. He would travel right across Sydney to visit some obscure specialty bookshop. He once carried a large (empty) glass aquarium on public transport from Hornsby back to his home in Belmore, despite there being plenty of shops closer to home. Once he travelled to Newcastle on an overnight trip, travelling up by train and walking almost three kilometres to a quiet motel where he met two Croatian friends. This caught our agents a little by surprise as they had not planned their dayshift to be extended. The trains back to Sydney had stopped by the evening, so they were forced to stay overnight and wait for the morning crew to travel up first thing in the morning. Despite these surprise outings though, Postal spent most of his time at home, largely on his computer. The glare of his computer monitor would bathe his front porch in a bluish haze, often until the early hours of the morning. Very occasionally he would go for a walk after he finished on the computer which was a little surreal as we tailed behind through the quiet streets. He never walked briskly, but always with purpose – though it was a purpose we seldom understood.

For every aspect about Postal that was weird and unpredictable, the other residents in his home suburb of Belmore were the complete opposite. It seemed every 'other' resident in Belmore had a clockwork routine of banal normality, and this would often be a talking point as we sat in the car waiting for Postal go walkabout. After so many months we knew each character in the street quite intimately, knew what car they drove, what time they left for work, how often they would mow the lawn and what they did on the weekends. We didn't have the real names for these characters, but after months of studying them, we had named them after their own individual traits and appearance.

Father Christmas was an easy one. He was a rotund man about fifty years old, who lived in the house we were parked outside. His large belly and wiry, slightly unkempt beard made naming him easy. Initially, Father Christmas was a little concerned about our presence, glancing a few times as he left one day, though it was at least a week and a half before he had actually realised we were even there. It is quite surprising how much of our world we just don't see as we go about our lives. Even after he noticed us, it actually took a few days for him to fully accept our presence. One day he had a closer look and realised there was someone inside it, so he quickly looked away in a rather obvious attempt to pretend he didn't realise there was anyone inside. He could have been more discreet as he peered through a wide crack in his curtains later that day!

Father Christmas didn't work, and seemed to spend a lot of time in his garden, or sitting on his porch reading the paper, or watching the sun go down with a quiet cup of tea. The following day he decided on a different tack, and came out almost boldly, approaching the car in a very obvious manner and staring intently, not so much to see anything, but more in an attempt to say '*I know you are in there, and I am making it obvious that I know, so whatever you are up to, you better go away now*'. He walked inside and returned again later than afternoon to repeat the process, clearly surprised that we were still parked there.

It was not until the following day that he walked right up to the car and pressed his face to the glass in an uncertain, stilted manner – clearly trying to assert his authority as 'owner of the house', which was perhaps supposed to give him some control over who parked outside it. Seeing me inside, he pulled away quickly and took a step back as if stung by a bee. Although we had been there for two weeks by this stage, I was sensing the job was going to go on a whole lot longer, and figured we should possibly say hello.

I wound down the window and said '*Hello!*' in the friendliest voice I could muster. At first there was no response, and then he gruffly said '*Hello*' back to me, quickly followed by '*You can't park here you know, this is a private street*'. I answered '*Why?*' which seemed to annoy him a little as he was clearly unprepared for this response. '*Well, you can't. This is my house and this is a private street, so you can't just park here*' he said, his voice gathering confidence towards the end of his sentence. I let the words hang there for a moment, as if to illustrate the illogical statement he had made. '*I am sorry, but I think this is actually a public street, and I think that means we are allowed to park here'* I replied politely. *'Yes, you can park here, but you can't just stay in the car...'* his voice trailed off as he realised his argument lacked the weight of law and was more a statement about accepted behaviour rather than allowable behaviour.

He stood there for a moment, looking at me through the now open car window. I hoped I was less aggressive showing my face than remaining encased in the tinted shell of my car. *'Well, what are you doing?'* he asked, to which I replied cryptically *'Well, we are just parking here for a little while'*, which didn't really answer his question. He snorted and walked off inside without further comment, but was out again about half an hour later. Obviously he had been on the phone to somebody, and seemed more confident again. He walked up to my window and rapped on it. I began winding it down when he blurted out *'I know. I know what you are doing. You are a private investigator.'* He stood there with arms folded, as if he had finally solved a mystery and now that he had exposed us we would have no choice but to move on. I looked back at him and paused, then replied *'Yes, that's right'*. There was not a lot I could have said after being there for two weeks already, so I figured it would be best to be honest.

Father Christmas looked unsettled at this response, apparently figuring we would either deny it or drive off, but not happily agree with him. *'Well, who are you watching?'* he asked after a long pause. *'Well, I can't tell you that because we are not allowed to disclose details of the case'* I replied. Another pause. *'But you've been seen already. We know who you are now!'* he said, clearly not sure why we hadn't felt encouraged to move on after being 'discovered'. *'Well, that's alright. Obviously we're not watching you then are we!'* I said with a laugh. He didn't share the humour, but instead began looking at all the houses in the

215

street. It was a long street and we could have been watching any one of them, and though I could tell he was itching to know which one it was, he refrained from asking again. It was clear that we weren't going to tell him.

Over time we slowly built up a rapport with Father Christmas. The first few months were a little awkward as each day he would step out and check to see if we were there, with a look of surprise on each occasion. He even came out at some odd times during the night as well, once at about three a.m. to have a quiet smoke and see if we were really still there outside his house. After about three months he had become familiar with our routine, and knew we usually changed shifts at seven a.m. and seven p.m. He almost forgot we were there at all, apart from when other residents in the street queried him about the strange car outside his house. Eventually he began to have a quiet chat every now and then, and was even pleased to have us there. On one hand it was slightly disconcerting, but on the other he was indirectly receiving near round the clock security for his home due to our constant presence, though as for exactly what type of security it was he wasn't sure.

Father Christmas's nearest neighbour was a single mother with a young teenage schoolboy. The mother was a very ordinary looking woman who was on the plump side of slightly plump. She wasn't quite obese, but together with her rather bland facial features and drab clothing, she wouldn't turn many heads. Some of the others would occasionally make some unkind remark about the reason for her being single, but I am sure she had a lovely personality somewhere – it was just not showing very strongly. She made a point of ignoring our presence and seemed quite disinterested in the world other than going to work and coming home to make dinner.

Some people are like that. As for her son, it was very clear he needed a strong father figure in his life, and wasn't developing well. We had nicknamed him 'Water boy' given that he was often seen wearing his favourite Balmain Tigers football jersey, but would probably not quite make the team due to his undersized frame. He seemed to have a poor general behaviour and wasn't particularly bright. We rarely saw any of his friends come for a visit, and the most activity he ever seemed to display was throwing a ball around in the street, though he wasn't particularly successful. He would also call out witty remarks about the weirdos parked nearby - 'Must be pretty smelly in that car by now – youse haven't even opened the windows to let the farts out!' he would call out to no one in particular.

He seemed pleased to have someone to talk to, even if we didn't talk back. Every day he would come home from school at the same time, and each day he would then put on a rugby jersey and throw his ball around, or sit with Father Christmas on the front fence and talk about last nights footy. He was mad on football, and clearly looked up to the big men who played the big game. No doubt he saw them in his subconscious as a collective group of father figures, and probably yearned to play professionally one day. He would have only been about fifteen years old, but it was clear he hadn't been blessed with a solid footballer's body and would be lucky to make Water boy, which is how we came by his nickname. Still, at least he had a dream, even if it was unattainable.

I often wondered how much we have to thank our parents for, not only for our genes, but also our nurturing and upbringing. Seeing his mother's single life and her son's unruly behaviour, there did appear to be a connection. Water boy was always wandering around aimlessly with a snarl on his face as if he was annoyed at the world for his lack of father and general lot in life.

He seemed to have good reason to feel this way. I almost felt like befriending him - showing some interest and enthusiasm for his life to stimulate his development, though this did not fit with my role as an investigator and could have caused problems along the line. After he started kicking his ball in a way that encouraged it to hit our car, I felt less inclined to be so compassionate, though I did smile when he would retrieve the ball and quickly run inside again after any such impact.

'The old man' was another Belmore character, who carried a walking stick and would amble up the street in his own good time at least once each weekday – except for Thursdays. He had a routine, but we could never pick the time exactly. Usually it was the morning and he would walk so slowly that it was a wonder he managed to get anywhere. It seemed his whole life entailed shuffling around and it would take him about ten minutes to walk up the road. Still, he never seemed particularly annoyed when he walked, and given his age I figured it was probably comforting to him that he could walk at all. My own three year old daughter was already complaining if I tried to help her, as she wanted to do everything herself, and I figured this need for independence remains with us until the end.

No doubt he would not last long after he was unable to do the walk, because then there would not be a lot left for him in life. Once The Old Man was shuffling past a driveway so slowly that he was almost hit by a reversing car, who then tooted angrily at his slow nature. The Old Man just shuffled on without missing a beat, clearly unconcerned about the car – though I did wonder if he even noticed it was there. I liked the old guy and nearly felt compelled to run up to the car and have a go at the driver to give the old man a break – but I guessed it would be taking things too far, to take on a private street police role.

There were two 'hotties' in the street, being women that drew a certain level of interest from the largely male PI crew manning the job. One was 'Yummy mummy' who had a very tight bottom and always wore tight fitting clothes. She would walk past in the morning and again in the evening, always with her young daughter by her side. We often took bets to see when she would round the corner each day, and once I managed to win about five days in a row. We knew she lived by herself as one of the guys had tailed her home several weeks ago out of sheer boredom.

'Sporty Spice' lived several houses away from our position, and drove a red sports car. A little older, she still looked good and had a great figure. She would usually wear short skirts and would flick her long blonde hair every so often. She knew we were there, as did a lot of residents in the street over time, and I often wondered if she played up to the fact we were always watching her. After hours and hours of monotony, it was always exciting to see Sporty Spice come home from work and take the bins in or water her garden – bending to pull out the weeds on occasions. Fortunately we were always armed with long range lenses, so we rarely missed the action. When working a weekend shift, one of the hot topics of conversation was 'who had Sporty Spice taken home last night'.

We clocked a string of males connected with Sporty over the months, some lasting just an evening, while others sometimes stayed there for a week. We always knew when she was pulling a sickie as she would sleep in on a weekday when she had a guy over, then would often head off to the beach for several hours to work on her tan. She must have been almost forty, so when she turned up once with what looked to be a teenage boy, our PI crew almost cheered in appreciation. She had done very well that night and we had to laugh as this young kid was seen washing her car the following morning with some degree of enthusiasm. He didn't last long, just like the others – though it seemed more of a way of life for her than a problem. She was clearly assertive enough to make her life choices as she pleased.

Occasionally on a Friday and usually just after lunch, the guy down the road would park his work truck outside his house and unload a large number of beer cartons. He would carry them into the house with his equally shady looking mate, then drive the truck off again. The following weekend we would see his other mate come and collect most of the cartons again, loading them into the boot of his old Falcon. It just seemed to be another standard clockwork routine for our Belmore family and we wondered how many other frauds were taking place right underneath peoples eyes. If you saw it once you would think nothing of it, but after practically living in the street for months we were well aware of what was going on around us.

Postal had very little contact with his neighbours, which was probably just as well given that most of the street knew our PI team was there. He was a loner, and only occasionally did he greet any of the other characters that regularly appeared as they went about their life. He did spend a lot of time at home, so he had less opportunity to make such occasional acquaintances. Although the street knew we were there, they didn't know exactly WHY we were there, or who we were watching. This did seem to raise some degree of speculation, and Father Christmas was clearly proud of the fact that the weirdos were parked outside HIS house, and that he even (occasionally) spoke to them briefly – not that we ever told him much though. On more than one occasion a fellow neighbour was seen scurrying past our car and into his house for some whispered conversation and peering back at the suspicious car full of men which had been parked there since about March.

'Chubby' was another Belmore 'personality' worthy of dissection and endless discussion by our under-worked PI team. Chubby worked as a Chubb guard on the trains and had a physique to match. He worked a rotating shift which we had long ago worked out. We knew he was on morning shift when he would walk up the street around six a.m., and when he was on afternoon shift we would see him around two p.m. Postal often travelled by train, and we had seen Chubby at work on the trains on a few occasions, though he never seemed to see us or Postal on his travels. In fact he never seemed to see anything at all as he ambled around with his equally unobservant partner. It was perhaps an unkind observation, and his disinterested appearance may not necessarily mean he was incapable at his job, though it certainly did not inspire confidence. Chubby was always in his own world, and every day he would walk up the hill with a faltering stride, carrying his duffle bag.

He would walk a few paces, then stop and mutter something to himself, and then he would walk on a little further then mutter some more. He looked slightly tipsy but this seemed to be his general demeanour rather than the result of excess. He would occasionally look around suspiciously though he never seemed to look further than his own head when he did so. On about three occasions he did his weird pause and mutter right next to the surveillance car. On the third time Ben wound down his window and said hello which gave poor Chubby a right start and sent him scurrying off faster than we had ever seen him. Over the next few weeks he seemed to have forgotten this exchange and ignored us, though he did once have a muttering pause next to the car and suddenly realised where he was standing. He jumped and scurried off in a startled manner despite nothing in particular happening.

Chubby's life seemed to be one big surreal daydream though we could well be guilty of the same ourselves. After months of sitting in a car day and night, our own lives had taken on a surreal daydream existence as well, and the difference between sane and crazy was starting to blur. We were living in a Belmore 'Groundhog Day', a day that had no beginning and no end. All the Belmore personalities would come and go like clockwork, and we knew each and every routine. It was a guessing game about which car was going to leave next, who was going to come home next and would Yummy Mummy be wearing the tight tights again. Day after day we struggled to find the differences, to prove to ourselves that we were not in an infinite loop of existence.

Fortunately there were some surprises to punctuate our repetitive existence, like the day the young couple had the big fight and she moved out, though she was back a few days later. It wasn't the first time they had argued, though we did feel for the guy as it seemed clear to us she was the unreasonable one. The police came to visit the old couple in the house across the road, but they only stayed for a few minutes. No doubt they were politely inquiring on the whereabouts of the couple's son. We knew he wasn't there as they had kicked him out last year after they discovered their shed was full of stolen equipment. Father Christmas had mentioned the story to us once late one evening. The son was a bad apple and only occasionally visited.

We were there to witness the reunion once and it was clear he 'forgot' to call ahead, just turning up at the front door one day. Father and son had stood there silently for such a long time, looking at each other, then there was a big hug and they went back inside. He didn't stay the night though. Chubby once came by at around eleven o'clock when we knew he was on morning shift. He was dressed in shorts and a tee shirt and seemed the happiest I had seen in weeks. We figured he was taking a sick day and wondered what he would do with his life. Much later that evening the night shift crew got the fright of their lives as he suddenly stumbled into the car in a drunken swagger, bouncing off with a thud then careering on down the street towards his home. He had got his revenge for the earlier incident, though it seemed to be accidental and at any rate he was clearly incapable of recognising the irony in his stumble.

There was another young couple living several doors down, and we watched with some excitement as her belly slowly increased in girth, they came home with a new cot, a stroller, and several other baby items. We didn't actually notice when she went into hospital, but one day she just wasn't there. About a week later she returned and there was much excitement and the whole street was buzzing. It was nice to see, though it was also annoying as there were just so many cars in the street for a few days that it was hard to watch Postal's house easily. Soon though, life got back to normal again. Much later on, and shortly before our job actually finished, we witnessed an ambulance taking away the old lady who lived on the corner. It was difficult to see if there was a sheet covering her body as they wheeled her in, so we weren't quite sure if she had actually died. We never saw her return to our street and although we knew she may have just gone to a nursing home, we rather fancied the thought that we had now witnessed not only a birth but also a death in the street. By then it was confirmed. Our lives were going round in circles.

Every few days Postal would go on a trip. We had so much warning that his departure was always a lazy affair. Postal would always come out to check his mail box, and then a few minutes later he would check it again, just to be sure. You could set your watch by it, knowing he would be out again within five minutes of the second post box inspection. This odd behaviour was just another factor which had led to his rather apt nickname. And then Postal would walk to Belmore station in a direct but not quite brisk manner. Our PI team would swing into action, dropping one agent at the station ahead of him, or occasionally both tailing behind on foot. It would depend on where we thought he was going. Sometimes it was best to have both agents on foot, but if it was a Wednesday afternoon we knew he was likely to go to the Croatian club so we would have one PI tail him on the trains while the other drove directly there with the car. It was exactly like 'The Truman Show' in real life. Postal was being watched around the clock and had his every move documented, videoed and analysed in detail – yet he was apparently oblivious to it all.

You do see some odd sights when you spend your life quietly watching others. A fellow PI, Michael Rumore,[55] has been in the industry for many years, and has plenty of stories to tell. One wall of his office is plastered with surveillance photos and news articles depicting the most unusual cases. One photo is of three youths just innocently walking up the road. I asked Michael what the significance of this photo was, and he laughed, saying that one of his agents had been conducting surveillance, and saw these characters knock on a door. After receiving no answer, they went around the back of the house and soon returned to the front with their large duffle bags looking decidedly heavier than before. The three youths then visited the next house, and again emerged from the rear yard with a little more in their bags.

Michael's agent decided to record some video of their third break and enter, and followed them up the road as they struggled with their heavy haul. Michael pointed out another photo on the wall where the trio was being 'questioned' by

---

[55] www.rumore.com.au

police who were clearly interested in why they were carrying half a dozen video recorders and other items in their bags. Chalk one up for the 'solved crime' statistics thanks to private investigators, who never seem to be properly valued by our community. When you are on surveillance, you never know what you are going to see sometimes.

We had been on the case for about six months, when suddenly it seemed Groundhog Day was finally going to end. He had left home much earlier than he did usually, and began walking in an unusual direction. We had been tailing him slowly (by car) for almost an hour when we began to realise he was beginning to approach his old workplace. It seemed crazy for him to walk such a distance when he would normally catch a train, but we began to realise he was actually walking to work. We made a preliminary call to the client. *'Hi, yes look... we are not sure, but it seems (Postal) is walking towards the building. Yes his old work... no, from home, he has walked from home... I know it is miles away... yes, he is carrying his old blue bag... no I have no idea. We never know... Yes I see... at the corner of Belmore road... we will. Bye!'*

Hearts thumping we continued the follow, noting that Postal was walking decidedly faster than he usually did. While the last six months had been uneventful, we may have been lulled into a false sense of security and now something was going to happen. It was such a long walk and we could see beads of perspiration glistening in the morning sunlight as he strode along. The entire experience felt rather surreal as he steadily continued towards his old workplace. We felt like we were on a runaway train, knowing it was going to crash and knowing we were unable to get off. All we could do was follow, watch, and wonder what would happen next. It was, on one hand very good, in that after half a year of intensive surveillance, we were finally able to provide early warning that Postal was on his way, and the client seemed both pleased and quite alarmed.

After several frantic phone calls he was now just a block away, and we were now in constant phone contact with one of the client's representatives, talking to them about Postal in detail, each and every step he took, describing his demeanour, the size of his bag and so on. Hearing a screech I spun around and saw a dark blue Falcon narrowly miss a pedestrian as it rounded a corner at some speed. There were two men in suits inside the car straining to look for Postal who was now up ahead, I guessed they must have been part of the (over) eager response team. Postal didn't even turn around at the tyre screech, so he had either not heard it, or perhaps had other things on his mind. He was now only a hundred metres from the front door of the building and despite his flushed face now dripping with perspiration, his pace hadn't slowed but rather increased as if he was now on the home stretch. Not having had direct contact with the client myself, I was unsure how they were going to respond. We were just the surveillance team, and we had been waiting and watching for Postal to go psycho for six months now, so that we could provide early warning for the client. What happened after that was not our responsibility, other than to record any activity on video for later prosecutions. Ben was in the passenger seat with his camera focused on Postal as he strode along, while I tried to position the car for the best shot.

Closer and closer he strode and I saw two uniformed guards step from the doorway and adopt a defensive stance as he approached. I think the guards were expecting some kind of escalating exchange, where they would 'deny' him entrance to the building verbally, and only get physical after some level of conversation. True to his form, Postal was as unpredictable as ever and simply barged right through the two guards as if they were nothing more than an apparition. It was clear that at least one of the guards had not braced himself for such an unexpectedly direct approach, as he was sent flying down the short flight of steps, nearly performing a complete somersault. His two way radio followed and clattered to the ground, splintering into pieces as his colleague grabbed Postal by the arm. The guard was a large framed man, but so was Postal, who merely shrugged off his grasp and barged on into the foyer, maintaining the very same pace he had done on his approach to the building. He didn't look ruffled by this exchange, and in fact worryingly he didn't seem to have registered that it even occurred. It was as if he was some creature from a *Terminator* movie that just couldn't be stopped.

Inside, two men in suits came from a side area and tackled Postal as he attempted to climb the stairs. We could just see the suits though the glass doors as they struggled to push him to the ground, but he wouldn't go down and seemed to have inhuman strength. The suits struggled to hold him, grasping at his sweaty arms and legs as he just fended off without a word. By now the bigger guard had a firm hold on the blue bag and was holding it as best he could, while Postal strained to climb the office stairs – while capably fending off two the men in suits. It was only when the younger guard had scrambled back up into the building that Postal finally went down with a bloodcurdling shout. By now there were four of them pinning him to the floor, and he still put up a worthy struggle.

Watching the surveillance video later was enough to give you motion sickness, as Ben had been laughing so hard while he recorded the scene and the camera was bouncing around. Of course we could well have been blown up at any moment if Postal had explosives in his bag, and I wondered if the larger guard realised this when he had been yanking on it so violently to stop Postal climbing the stairs. The front doors closed automatically, and it became difficult to see inside. It was clear the team inside had managed to contain Postal, and the client liaison officer I had been briefing suggested we stay outside. Knowing this person was probably just up the stairs along with most of the management, it came as no surprise he sounded just a little flustered. Obviously they had not anticipated he would actually enter the building, but nobody could really predict Postal's actions.

We waited there for almost an hour until the police turned up - a young constable and an older officer, who looked like he had seen it all and was now ready to retire. They both entered the building and we waited another twenty minutes. Eventually we saw Postal walking from the building carrying his blue bag. He looked flushed, with his hair now ruffled as if he had just been through a wild storm, but he walked off. I tried ringing the client liaison back, but the line was engaged. We moved off to tail Postal home again, and I saw the guards and men in suits peering from the doorway at his departing form. The police drove off shortly afterwards, leaving us to slowly follow Postal as he walked and walked and walked. Who knows why he didn't catch a train. It was well after lunchtime that he arrived home, and we didn't see him come out again till the next day.

Curiosity had been killing us as we wanted to know what had happened inside the building. What had the police said and what was in the suspicious blue bag? Much later that day we got a very terse report of the events, namely that Postal had stated he wanted to see Big Boss, and that the police had advised him he was not entitled to enter private property and that he should leave quietly. There had been some debate on the issue, but at no time did Postal say why he wanted to see Big Boss, or what he was carrying in his blue bag. In fact, much to the dismay of the client, the police had ordered that Postal's bag not be searched, and that he was free to go. Apparently there was no legal right to conduct the search, and although Postal had roughly pushed past the guards, they had not actually told him not to come in, and he had not actually been violent to them as such.

There was apparently some legal debate about whether he was trespassing or not, and he had not made a verbal threat so he had broken no law. The only thing which could have been vaguely pinned on him was the damage to the two way radio, which had clearly been destroyed, The client however, had quickly decided not to push for damages over this – and even if they had it was not altogether clear if the guard had just dropped it himself after being 'accidentally' bumped by Postal on entry to the building. This guard had moved towards Postal at the last minute when he realised Postal was going to just barge in, so it could also have been argued that the guard was at least partially responsible. It had taken nearly an hour for police to arrive on the scene, by which time I guess they would have found an allegedly disgruntled ex-employee who had 'just' wanted to see management - pinned to the floor by four security men. No doubt Postal had calmed somewhat during this long wait and the scene would have looked like a clear case of over-reaction.

I sensed that there had been some discussion between Postal and one of the client representatives during that long hour, and strangely the client seemed far less concerned about the event that we would have expected. Although we continued to maintain surveillance on Postal after the event, the client seemed suddenly less interested, and by a week afterwards was not even calling for the daily briefings on his movements. The entire situation was certainly some validation of our extensive surveillance, as we had been able to provide early warning of

Postal's approach to Big Boss. Given that there were four security men waiting for his arrival and still he had almost managed to climb the stairs to the office area – we wondered what would have happened if there was no such early warning provided by us. And still there was the mystery of the blue bag, which now would never be solved. It was immensely frustrating, though it did provide for lively discussion and speculation as we whiled away the hours on the job.

We had expected the client would be even more anxious to cover Postal's activity and yet now they were almost disinterested. There was much debate among our PI crew about what had transpired during the hour long wait for the police that day. Had Postal explained his grievances in a way that gave understanding and allowed the client to better cater to them. Had the security men made some threat to Postal which they knew he would respond to. Did Postal have some blackmail information about Big Boss or his company, and perhaps the client had chosen to finally give in to Postal's demands – whatever they were. It was a fascinating topic, and intensely maddening to not have the facts, but that is all too common for investigations. You can work hard to put the jigsaw pieces together, but all too often there are some pieces missing and you just have to live with the half completed puzzle.

Much later we heard from another Belmore identity that Postal was writing 'The History of Belmore' – a personal account of his own suburb. This would explain his late nights on the computer, but it seemed so out of character it was barely believable, and who would bother to write such a piece? All the information pointed to him being nearly illiterate, and there was much surprise when he had bought the computer in the first place. Although we had never seen him do any research, talk to local identities or visit the Belmore 'sights', this eccentric history project was perhaps strange enough to be believable for the unpredictable Postal.

About three months after the security event, we got word that the job was finishing. There was no explanation from the client whatsoever. It had just stopped. It was the strangest feeling to wake up the next morning knowing we didn't have to go to Belmore again for another shift. It had been nine months of continuous round the clock surveillance with two agents on together. Our PI team had built a life around this job and it was almost disconcerting to know it had finished. Despite the fact that it may sound weird to 'want' to still be parked in that quiet Belmore Street, there was an incredible desire to know how the story ends. We had been living a 'Trueman' style reality show, and now the season had ended. No more would we watch our favourite characters go about their lives. No more would we be able to hypothesise about the unpredictable Postal, or analyse the behaviour of Chubby. No more would we be able to play guessing games about who would be next seen in the street, no more would we be able to comment on Yummy Mummy's tight pants or Sporty Spice's overnight acquaintances. I wondered how the neighbours and residents would react, as one of the biggest things in the recent history of Belmore had now finished and they would wake up and wonder if it had all been a dream. It was over.

We had followed him for such a long time and yet he had never caught us, which I figured was due to luck, skill and Postal being more preoccupied in his own world – wherever that was. We did the sums and discovered that the total cost of the surveillance job was about that of a small, three bedroom house in Belmore. It was an incredible expense. What was the real issue between Postal and Big Boss? I wondered some more. Had Postal been so weird as to subtly 'encourage' Big Boss to mount the extended surveillance job. Had he known all along that we were following him but he kept it stringing along just to make Big Boss pay out the big bucks. Perhaps he was playing some psychological game – here we thought he was having a very odd life and yet he was in fact having a ball at the expense of Big Boss' sleepless nights. I wondered. It was just strange enough to be true.

Although I have not heard anything about the job since, I occasionally drive through Belmore when I am in the area. The case finished several years ago now, but still I get a certain thrill in seeing some of my favourite characters wandering about their lives. I saw Yummy Mummy had a new baby, though I was fairly sure she was still living alone. Water boy had certainly grown and filled out a lot, but was still a little undersized. I have never seen Santa Claus or the Old Man again and wondered if they had passed away. Given half a chance I probably would have attended their funerals as the characters of Belmore had grown on me over our nine month reality experience. I took photos of all our favourite characters at the time. Years later my wife saw them, exclaiming – *'Honey that's so funny – they're all EXACTLY as you told me they were!'*

CHAPTER 12: IDENTIFYING PEOPLE

A key part of surveillance is knowing what or who you are watching. What many people take for granted, the surveillance professional has to fight for. The bank worker knows the identity of the people he deals with, because of the stringent documentation being presented to him. The tradesman knows who he's dealing with because is given an address and the name of the client before he starts working for them. Even with occupations that have very little customer contact such as a cashier in the supermarket, you at least get a good look at the customer's face! The surveillance professional has none of these things. In the 'cloak and dagger' world of the PI, being direct is not an option. The ultimate test of your skill in identification is in court, where you may be on the stand, biting your fingernails as the video tape plays. There is always a chance they will loudly proclaim *'Hey, that's not me, that's my brother!'* - a situation every PI dreads.

There is just no way to be sure, so, how to begin? If you THINK you have the right person, you start on them, follow them and try to get their name at the earliest opportunity. Occasionally you need to whittle down possible subjects in a family household, where several people match your description. Identifying an exact person in a particular ethnic community is difficult, and in my personal experience it seemed that many of these communities are disproportionately represented in insurance fraud, which doesn't help. These communities can often be very close-knit, and extracting information can be difficult. You are trying to identify Mr Xi-Wang Chin, who is known simply as 'Bob'... now where do you go with that?!

Like all surveillance, identification is somewhat based on chance. There is very little opportunity to prove the identity of a subject completely, and it is often difficult to be sure at all. It is best to source at least two separate ways of determining identity, as two fragments of possibility will always be stronger than the pieces on their own. Hearing a first name and later seeing the full name on an envelope addressed to the property would constitute two pieces. In effect the surveillance professional uses a form of the Federal Government's 'one hundred point identity check' (often used for verifying new bank accounts or driver's licences), and each piece of information has a value. Knowing you are seeking a male at that address and finding a male could be worth ten points. Having him fit a physical description may be worth twenty points. A first name may be thirty points. Matching his vehicle registration may be worth seventy points, and so on. Without the ability to see photo identity documents, the surveillance professional can only rely on piecing together the jigsaw of possibility.

The following is a list of a few points to get you started, though the only limit to these approaches is your own imagination, and the more novel and targeted the approach, the better. The surveillance professional must have a vivid imagination, and can see the best technique for the situation. What works in one situation will fail in another and vice versa. As ever it is a game of chance, so the professional must always know how to stack the deck in his favour.

Identification techniques

Ring the subject's mobile while actually watching for them to answer the phone. If the subject lifts the phone to their ear when you ring, there is a good chance the call was initiated by you, and hence you can link a face to a voice, and to a conversation you have with them. Hearing a *'Hello Robert speaking'* would be nice if you were looking for Robert. It would not be an absolute ID, but it just adds to the probability factor that you have the right guy.

When you have followed a subject to a place that has a public address system, you can have them paged. I have seen some strange looks as a booming voice comes over the PA system in the local RSL *'Mr John Hicks, telephone call for Mr John Hicks...'* Human curiosity leads Mr Hicks to the telephone despite the fact he hasn't told anyone he was even going to the RSL. Perhaps it is not for him, but there is only one way to find out. It is quite satisfying to see the recognition in their face as their name is called, then they go to the phone. Often the best approach is to hang up before they get there and keep them scratching their head, though you could also use the opportunity to engage them in an extended pretext.

Walk up and ask with the wrong name. *'Hello, look I am sure I know you from somewhere! I have forgotten your name. It's... It's John isn't it?'* (blank look with a negative response) *'Oh, sorry, what is your name?'* The subject will rarely refuse, as the approach is quite direct, and suggests you are trying to remember them from somewhere. They may be keen to 'put you right' with their real name, to allay any embarrassment you both may feel about forgetting one another, and speed the process of recognition (if any). Even after they have given you their name, you can continue if the situation allows. *'That's funny, I am sure*

I know you... do you work at the steelworks. No. Where do you work then?'

Often the most direct approach is the best. I have had people ask me *'How the hell did you get this information so quickly?'* Quite simply, ask them. Of course you need to know precisely how to ask, because there is a right and wrong way, and the right way uses a psychological key to maximise your chance of success. No guarantees, but it will always give better odds than *'Excuse me, are you Mr John Sempelton?'* which has very low odds of success, and will have them shooting back 'WHO WANTS TO KNOW?!'

Check the mail. Often just looking at the address on the front of an envelope is sufficient to ensure you have the right person. It is one of the few pieces that show a surname as well, but be wary of maiden names or even old mail addressed to a former tenant who left before the subject moved in. This can be helpful though, as it could be used as a great, clean pretext. After clearing mail from their box bearing the former tenant's name, they will be unlikely to question someone else asking about this particular name. They will happily advise that the person doesn't live there anymore, and will then have mentally passed you as making a legitimate inquiry. Now you are under their psychological defences, and can springboard from this to continue the conversation with them.

Vehicle registration checks are now more difficult. Privacy laws dictate that you cannot receive information about a vehicle owner. There is however the facility to CHECK the ownership details of any car with some states, as this is required for a purchase confirmation. By providing the name details to the NSW RTA or other state body, they will usually either confirm or deny that the vehicle is registered in the name you supply. This is not always a preferable approach, especially given that a vehicle may be registered in any person's name, but can be a good 'last resort' approach. Seeing a car in the driveway and knowing it is registered to the same name you are seeking has got to be worth at least sixty points!

Consider asking a neighbour. Wait till the subject is out, then say to them. *'I was looking for John, but he isn't home. Does he still live there? Ok, it was actually my girlfriend that knows him and we are not sure she got the right John. Is he tall with red hair? No? What does he look like / what car does he drive'.* Not the best approach as it may have them later asking John if 'that guy' got in touch, but it can still obtain good results.

Arrange a delivery to them and get them to sign for it. *'Thanks mate, there you go. Now can you sign here? And write your first name here... thanks.'*

The case of a wandering pot plant

Key learning points

- Follow techniques
- Identification of subject

On one case I did for a fellow PI called Joanne, we were trying to locate a female who had skipped off with a sizeable amount of money from her now ex-partner. She had gone into hiding, and was not directly contactable. She had set up an intermediate contact, being a male who worked in a city building. Any inquiries, such as organising the divorce papers, were to be passed through him, He was not a solicitor, and it was clear he was not going to give up the details on Tracey's new location. In fact he would do nothing other than pass on messages and correspondence. We didn't even know who he was as all we had was a first name, John, and his mobile phone number, which made it difficult to further identify him. Joanne Rowell is a clever

237

PI, and she decided the best approach to both identify him and try and locate Tracey was to deliver Tracey a large pot plant from a 'former friend'.

The plant contained a slightly cryptic note 'Tracey, sorry I have not been in touch for so long, but I was overseas. I will give you my new address when I settle in again. Hope you like the plant, SC'. We delivered the plant by a standard courier to John, and then waited outside the building. The plant was quite bulky, and clearly needed watering regularly else it would die. While John could have kept the plant in the office for days or even weeks, we figured he would probably arrange for it to be delivered to Tracey fairly quickly. Late that afternoon, we spied a man coming out of the building, carrying our distinctive pot plant. It had to be John, so the plant had successfully identified our first unknown person. John struggled slightly as he carried a briefcase in one hand, and the bulky plant in the other. We had figured he would catch a train, but suddenly realised he was walking into a small car park. This made life interesting, as it was now peak hour and traffic was packed. Knowing this could be our only shot, we had to follow that plant!

John took off and headed south across the Harbour Bridge. Traffic was bumper to bumper and although we had two cars in pursuit, it wasn't easy. As time ticked by, John and the plant continued south, and then still south until finally he reached Bundeena, a very southern Sydney suburb. I had been watching my in-car navigation screen and realised he had finally entered a road that had no ready exit without back tracking, so it was clear he was about to arrive at a destination. We had been tailing him for almost an hour, so it was with some relief that I realised this, and decided to give him just a little room to move. I let him drive just out of sight for a moment, given that I had been behind him for so long, and the roads were now very quiet.

I quickly sped up again but he had disappeared. I sped up more but still I couldn't locate him. In a panic I travelled at high speed to the end of the road but nothing. I cursed. We knew he had to be somewhere along this road as I had lost sight of him for less than ten seconds. Unfortunately all the houses were leafy estates with longer driveways and hills to obscure visibility. We looked for almost an hour, but were not able to relocate the car. I was very disappointed, but at least we had managed to identify the mystery John, and were now fairly sure which road he lived in. I rang Joanne and told her the news. She was disappointed, but accepted that was the nature of investigations and we still had a few leads. One was the dealer strip on the number plate – which I gave to her and suggested she follow up on it. I then drove back home dejected that we had followed so long without a solid result.

Several days later Joanne rang me to say that she had managed to extract the home address from the dealer under a pretext, and had confirmed it was a house in the street that I had nominated. It was not easy to pretext this information, however she had been able to supply the road name which I had given her, which had made the dealer think she already had the right address, so it was then an easy step to get him to repeat the address with the actual house number. Furthermore, she had done some more digging and discovered that Tracey was now in a relationship with John, and was living at this address. The client was very impressed, and was then able to effect some legal action against Tracey to recover some of his former assets. It was a difficult case but we had solved it with the help of a pot plant worth $4.95. While police and intelligence agencies have a wide range of tools and laws to enable them to gather information easily – a good PI has his wits, and using some lateral thinking you can often achieve the most amazing results. Use your imagination!

CHAPTER 13: FOLLOWING BY FOOT

For some lazy PI's, their vehicle is their castle. They loathe escaping the safety and comfort of the castle walls. Rather than get out, they prefer to drive everywhere, and if a subject is followed to the train station, this is where 'contact was lost'. Heaven forbid they have to actually get out of the car!

The surveillance professional has a different opinion, and will view the vehicle as a tool that will only be used where necessary to get the best result. Knowing a foot follow can bring far better results, he will often welcome such an opportunity, pleased to be able to escape the sweaty confines of the hot car and to stretch cramped legs. A foot follow will always give far more opportunity than any vehicle follow, as you are able to observe their whole person (as opposed to just the rear of their head in the car). You can often see them for a far longer duration, observe how they move and use the opportunities provided by the increased activity when on foot.

There is nothing particularly special about a foot follow, and there are few trade secrets to learn. Few PI's have a newspaper with a peep-hole cut in the middle, or use any fancy props or tricks, it is primarily about feeling and positioning. After making an assessment about a hundred aspects of the situation, the professional will position himself just right. He will have assessed the movement matrix, he will close up when the subject approaches a crossing between networks, such as a building entrance, or a train station. He will drop back if there is some inquisitive behaviour seen in the subject or their associates. He will close up tightly if a good ID is required or some evidence of walking, but drop well back if the focus of the job is to simply identify where they go. Sometimes a mobile phone can be a great prop to use, as it allows you to wander aimlessly or loiter while conducting your important call. It also suggests you are less aware of your surroundings, and are therefore less threatening to those you are watching. Subconsciously they will feel you are too engrossed in your call to be watching their movements.

In the manner of the real estate catch-phrase, it is all about location, location, location. The professional constantly assesses and adjusts his position to best suit his surrounds. He will time his movement to best conceal himself, while allowing good opportunity to observe and document. He will close up or drop back, swap sides, sit at the bus shelter, or slide into a shop with a view through the windows.

While in an area that can be readily seen by the subject, your movement needs to be very casual, relaxed and nonchalant. Your eyes may wander, you may feign interest in the surrounds, and above all, act 'normal'. Hurriedly ducking behind telegraph poles is generally poor form and very obvious. The professional slides around with practiced ease, appearing to others as if he is familiar with his route, and already has a focus in his mind. That focus is <u>not</u> staring at the subject, OR <u>refusing</u> to stare at the subject OR walking like a robot OR walking like a pimply kid who was seen too many 007 movies and does the telegraph pole dance. The key is to relax. It's a proverbial 'walk in the park', but unless you feel this right down to your bones, your behaviour may emit 'subtle' signs that scream 'look at me!' In the immortal words of Obi Wan Kenobi, 'use the Force!'

A foot follow often provides good opportunity to get a clear shot of your target, so remember that getting to the destination is only half the battle. If you are any good, you will have some good evidence of your stroll. At intervals you may stop and take a shot for several seconds, to capture their gait, their general body movements and appearance. Such shots also provide good evidence of the walk being undertaken. It is easy for the defence counsel to refute that the defendant walked far if there is only a few seconds of video. It is harder to deny when there is regular

241

clips showing the walk in stages, with surrounding areas to show context, such as the actual streets or route being taken. Our society will rarely comment loudly if you are seen with a camera, so the concern of being spotted by others nearby must be weighed up by the quality of results you obtain. In many cases it is best to be very open about the use of your camera, which allows for better and clearer shots. Often the fact that you are so open about your actions will allay suspicion, as it is clear you don't care who sees you. The amateur may display unnatural behaviour trying to focus their camera hidden in the bag, and will end up with a poor shot, and provoke others nearby to wonder if they have a bomb in the bag. It's best to relax and be casual. There is of course always an appropriate time and place, so use your judgement.

It is surprisingly easy to walk right behind someone and film continuously, using a flip screen held at waist level. With practice to keep the camera steady, the entire walk can be documented very clearly, including stairs, shopping etc. This does not apply to all cases, but the professional knows when is best. He may elect to get closer towards the end of the job, or when he has picked the subject as being particularly inattentive to their surrounds.

It can also be a good time for a pretext, as you may be able to engage the subject naturally in conversation. *'Got the time?'* *'Know when the next bus comes?'* *'Do you know where the newsagent is?'* These are all conversation starters that can (for the professional) soon lead to their subject's name, occupation and what they had for breakfast. This is because on foot they are exposed and approachable. Try knocking on the driver's window during a vehicle follow to get that information out of them. Good luck.

Foot follows often require you to run. You simply can't do effective surveillance on foot if you are not prepared to break into a run when required. While constantly monitoring your position and follow distance, you often need to close up, and this is best done quickly. Provided you will not be seen, the aim is to run as fast as you can, to close up quickly. You can't get a good clear shot while constantly moving, but if you prop, take a shot, run to a new position when safe, then prop and take another shot, you will have some good tape, rock steady and in focus, because you have bought time while running. There is a time to be casual, and there is a time to hot foot it, such as when they turn a corner. A running bag is imperative, to allow ready access to camera and other gear.

Scoping for a taxi is not a bad idea, as this can be used as a mobile platform, offering a covert and steady place to shoot from, with a driver who can move you into position quickly. Your cab may travel past the walking subject, then pause as you document them walking towards you, getting a good ID and good evidence of their gait. Without the taxi to leapfrog you past them, it is difficult to get the front on view, so surveillance video is often just their back walking away all the time. A professional will engineer the situation to cover multiple angles to best document the situation.

On conducting a foot follow:

- Change your appearance if possible as soon as you leave the vehicle. Take a cap off or put one on – the opposite of your 'vehicle' appearance.
- Keep your distance correctly.
- Travel on opposite sides of the road if possible, at forty-five degrees to the subject's rear.
- Use window reflections to monitor the subject while not looking directly at them.
- Use shops or gardens to stop and take quick video of the subject walking along.

- Consider entering shops or other businesses and record the subject through the windows (be more careful using banks as this may alarm their security).
- Consider actually walking directly and closely behind the subject when in reasonably crowded shopping areas, while recording video from a hand held camera. Use flip screen (wide angle), but don't continually stare at camera, simply walk along, occasionally glancing at the screen to ensure framing is correct.
- Close up quickly (run!) as soon as they enter a building or shopping centre.
- Close up quickly (run!) as soon as they turn a corner or disappear from view.
- Consider hiring a taxi (see working with taxis on page 310).

The case of stolen noodles

Key learning points

- Contingency response / managing the unexpected

- Static surveillance / managing neighbours

An associate, Bob, rang to ask whether I was interested in going to Queensland on a job, and it sounded like fun, so I accepted. Our task was to investigate a male who was involved in a rather nasty accident some years previously. We had to ascertain whether he was currently working or not (he claimed he wasn't), general details about his character, background and physical ability. There was a lot riding on this case, and a friend of his, also involved in the accident, had recently been awarded over three million dollars by the courts. The story commences in 1992.

Bob, his girlfriend Julie and I, were cramped in the surveillance van as we began the long drive from Sydney to Queensland.

Some twelve hours later we arrived, exhausted, at our hotel in Tweed Heads. It was the best available, a spacious apartment with great views of the water. It was now about ten p.m. on a Saturday night. We decided to simply dump our gear and do a night time CTR (close target reconnaissance) of our subject's unit. Fortunately the address was just a few kilometres from our hotel, and we soon arrived in the area. Almost as an afterthought, Julie carried with her an empty champagne bottle to assist in a possible cover story for us, being three friends out on the town for a big night out.

The block of flats was very dark and we struggled to see the numbers, looking to find unit eight. There were push-button timer switches near every flat, which would have lit up the whole area for a few minutes. Since we were unwilling to draw attention to our presence, we continued stumbling about in the dark. Eventually we worked out the odd numbering system and realised that unit eight was on the second floor above unit seven. We began climbing up the stairs.

Halfway up we heard a door closing and before we could move, we saw the dark figure of our surveillance subject leaving his flat and descending the stairs. The three of us stood there in the darkness, incredulous that we'd driven all day to get here, and 'BANG' out he walked as soon as we got there. We had but a second to contemplate our possible misfortune, as the subject quickly trotted down the stairs, and promptly ran into us on the dark landing. 'Oops ... sorry...' he said, a little startled, and took a step back. 'No worries mate, have a good night mate (hic)... can't see a bloody thing in this dark...' we slurred as we continued up the stairs to the third floor, Julie flashing the champagne bottle conspicuously as we passed.

We continued up to the third floor, and began walking along the landing, cursing ourselves and cursing our luck. Had we blown it?

Did our cover story hold? Did he see our faces? We were relieved to see our man continuing to walk up the street without so much as a backward glance. It would have been too dark for him to identify our faces anyway. I left Bob and Julie, beginning to tail him on foot. He wasn't moving fast, and it was relatively easy in the darkness. A block down the road I realised my mobile phone was still in my car.

I was annoyed at my lack of preparation, and should have expected the unexpected because I was well aware that is the nature of the industry! I was further disheartened to realise that my car keys were still in my pocket. No 'comms' (communication), and no vehicle backup. Bob couldn't use the car without my keys. Great! Who would have expected that things would have turned out as they had, but in this game, you have to be ready for anything.

I spied a phone box up ahead. I thankfully remembered that I had a phone card in my wallet. We were moving at an average walking pace, in a straight line, and we were the only people around. I sped up, and quietly closed the gap between us. I hopped into the phone box, opening the door quietly because the target was still walking only a few metres away, and dialled Bob's mobile phone. He and Julie were standing next to my car, a few blocks behind now. I explained as clearly and quickly as I could, how to break into and start my van. I was glad it was an old model, and this could be done without too much trouble. I left the phone booth and ran to catch up. We had gone over a kilometre now, and seemed to be heading for the centre of town.

Another five minutes plodding the quiet streets. I spied yet another phone booth, this time down a cross street I was passing. Emboldened by my previous success, I decided to leave my tail yet again to make another phone call. I ran down the cross street, jumped into the booth, and dialled. Bob, by this stage was mobile and cruising through the area. I blurted out my location and direction of travel, before running from the phone booth, leaving the handset swinging. I sped back to pick up the tail, and stared intently up the deserted road, but couldn't see him. I continued running as quietly as I could, and kept an eye out for Bob and Julie in the van. I must have misjudged his speed, or I was very fast on the phone, because I soon found myself about to run into the subject for the second time that night. He was walking slowly through a car park situated at the end of the main road. I stopped dead, almost sure he'd heard me, and leant back against a nearby bush. He didn't turn around. I spun around however, as the lights of an approaching car shone upon me. It was Bob and Julie in the van. There was no vehicle access from the end of the road to the car park, as it served only the nearby shopping centre on the other side of the road. Bob drove off, hoping to find a way around, and I continued on foot. We were leaving the residential area, and entering the centre of town. I could now see our hotel just a few blocks away, towering above the skyline.

Closer and closer we got. I was eyeing off another phone booth, and looking around for Bob, as the subject actually approached our hotel! I smiled, thinking we could have stayed at the hotel, and picked up the tail as he cruised past, when to my utter disbelief, he entered a pub directly beneath our own hotel! Three people drive for twelve hours, book into a hotel and go to visit the surveillance address. They bump into the subject leaving at ten p.m. at night, and then follow him on foot for a full three kilometres back to the very hotel they're staying at! I assumed that the situation could not get any stranger, but I was wrong! I went to the phone booth near the entrance to the pub, but didn't need to ring as I spied my van rapidly approaching. I flagged it down and explained that I had the subject inside the pub beneath our hotel. They were as incredulous as I was. We parked the van diagonally opposite the pub door, and Julie went in to check it out. She returned shortly with a confirmed ID of our man, drinking at a table with some male friends. We assumed he would be there for some time, so we returned to our room, and began sorting the gear out. We all altered our appearance, I put on a long-haired wig, Julie put her long hair up in a bun and we all changed shirts and jackets.

We returned to the pub, which was (thankfully) reasonably crowded, and bought a drink. We all got a good look at our man's face, and, when appropriate, moved our party to a position almost right behind him. He barely spoke a word, and when he did, it was difficult to hear him over the live band that was playing. We eventually decided to call it a night, and walked out and up the stairs to our hotel room at around eleven-thirty to get some sleep.

Around two o'clock I woke up, feeling restless. The band was still going strong and I could hear the noise of the revellers spilling out into the street, three stories below. I walked from my bed to the open balcony, smelling the salty sea breeze wafting through the balmy night air. It was such a pretty sight: the waves breaking on the sandy beach, palm trees swaying softly. It was a pity that the noisy pub below spoiled the scene. I looked down at the four or five people that were drinking on the footpath outside. The hairs on the back of my neck began to prickle. I stood on the balcony in my boxer shorts, looking down at our subject talking to another male. The subject. That's right... there he is. 'There he is!' I began to yell. 'THERE HE IS!' I was yelling almost loud enough for them to hear me below as I frantically began grabbing my camera gear, trying to rouse the others. Bob soon stumbled out from his room, rubbing his eyes, wrapped only in a hotel towel, saying, 'Calm down Chris, you're having a bloody nightmare.' He stood there dumbly, watching my frenzied actions, as I tried to explain. *'No really... I mean it... he's down there... outside balcony.'* I was standing on the little hotel balcony in my underwear, with camera rolling, and I was quickly adjusting the focus onto the target down below. Bob wasted no time, and was soon rushing for his own gear.

I wasn't aware of it at the time, but later perusal of the footage taken revealed our subject being handed a plastic bag of what appeared to be white powder. It was handed over in an almost surreptitious manner. We will never know for certain, but it very much appeared that we had just filmed our subject taking part in a drug deal. Why else would white powder in small plastic bags be changing hands outside a pub at two o'clock in the morning? After the transaction, the two males went back into the pub. We waited there almost an hour, until three a.m., when we got some more action. He came out of the pub with the same male and they were both drinking (something he's claimed under affidavit to court that he never does), and talking. They crossed the road and entered a very poorly lit, deserted car park. There we lost sight of them. We decided, since we were still both rather scantily clad, to remain there and await his return. We were both well awake by now, and were soon happily chatting over a cup of tea, about various funny jobs that we'd done.

He returned some time later, and again we filmed him while we sat on the white plastic outdoor chairs. I decided, since it was all happening, that I would get dressed and go downstairs to set up the van. I ended up getting more film from the van and tailed him a short distance to a parked car. He spoke briefly to the driver who had been sitting in the dark for some time, before returning once again to the pub. Exhausted, I decided to call it a night. It was now four o'clock, and we had to be up at six. I flopped into bed.

By six thirty we were on site after completing an early morning close target reconnaissance. Things look different in daylight, and this job looked tricky. We couldn't observe his door from the road, instead choosing to watch the entrance of the entire block of flats, hoping to recognise our man when he left the general area. We did this on the Sunday, but I felt that there had to be a better way. We really wanted visual of his front door.

The next morning, I decided to approach an adjoining property, to politely request permission to hide in their backyard for an extended period. A very conservative looking woman answered the first house I approached. She began listening politely to my friendly spiel, but soon appeared quite agitated, quickly refusing me, and bolting the door when I left. You get that sometimes!

I walked around the block, and knocked on the door of a well-kept house on another street, whose backyard was next to the end of our units. The door was answered by a quieter version of the woman from the movie *Mrs Doubtfire*, who listened with mild interest to my request. '*Um ... I'll have to ask my husband, dear ... I won't be a moment.*' Well, at least the door hadn't been closed in my face yet. A friendly old man appeared at the door, followed by his wife. He seemed quite interested and listened to my proposal. When he heard that I was in the Army, his friendly disposition became even friendlier, and his smile broke into an almost cheesy grin. '*Army? Why, I was in the Navy for years, based at... and we... and then I...*' He seemed pleased as punch that he was being given the chance to be a part of a real OPERATION. I think he fancied himself a bit like the husband/wife teams harbouring escapees during the resistance movement in the Second World War. Whatever he thought, the deal was clinched, and I was soon being shown through to their back yard.

They obviously had far too much time on their hands, as the garden was immaculate. It was almost a little too good. There was precious little lawn left. It was all paths, rockeries and organised patches of well-tended flowers and vegetables growing happily. Where was I to site my observation post. I looked forlornly for a large bushy spot full of weeds and overgrown. Nothing. Oh well, you can't have everything. I set up on a concrete pathway. The site was great, but not well camouflaged. There was good visual of the subject's door across the back fence, and washing lines and common areas as well. Luckily a large tree near the fence had branches hanging down which concealed the Doubtfire's backyard.

Some time later, the old man quietly approached and offered me a small garden seat. I accepted thankfully. Some time later again, the old lady came around. She whispered from a short distance away, *'Is it OK to give you this?'* I looked over and saw she had a cup of tea ready. *'I didn't know if you took sugar, but I put one in anyway. If you don't take sugar, I can always make you another one!'* I wasted no time in accepting her offering, and (quietly) thanked her. I was no more than twenty metres from our man's front door, but the fact that I was over the fence gave me a psychological advantage. People are less likely to notice things over their back fence because that is not in their 'world'. They will usually never go there themselves, and hence the mind filters out stimuli from that area. I could have been in a more inconspicuous spot further away, but if I was actually on his property, in <u>his</u> space, his subconscious mind may have noticed me more readily.

I began to wonder why we started the job so early this morning when we knew that the target was out drinking until at least four o'clock (underneath our own hotel!). He wasn't going to be getting up awfully early this fine, sunny Monday morning. He was going to sleep in till late afternoon, like any sensible soul. I was becoming a little bored by around midday, when lunch arrived.

251

The lady had brought me a tray with a plate of sandwiches, a can of fizzy drink and a few biscuits. Bob rang a short time later, wanting to know if I wanted some lunch dropped off. I explained that I didn't need one, and was being well supplied by my friendly hosts. I could handle this! The novelty of the whole situation kept me amused for a good few hours, until finally we decided to finish up. It was stinking hot, and we were both ready for a swim at the beach, Bob especially so, as he'd been sitting in a car sauna with the windows up, baking in the sun for about ten hours now!

We returned to the job early on Tuesday morning, and I simply walked down the drive and took up my position again. My chair had been packed up, but I found it folded near the garage. I had failed to mention that I was intending on spending the entire week hiding in their backyard, as I thought it might scare them off. I thought it best to take it one day at a time.

The first happening of the day was around eight, when the old lady came out to water her garden. She spent a considerable period of time watering each and every plant, and it was almost painful waiting for her to notice me. Eventually she did, and I gave her my best smile. She was initially mildly startled, obviously not used to strange men hiding in her garden, but she kept her composure, and returned a nervous smile back. She slowly continued watering all the way up to just a few metres away from my position, then leant forward slightly as if this would make her voice carry further without her actually having to physically get any closer.

'*How is it going?*' she whispered, barely above the gentle spraying of the hose.

'*Good thanks*' I whispered back, thinking that at this time our subject would still be in deep sleep (probably drug induced), and would not have woken up yet, even if his hot water system had exploded. I didn't want to spoil things for her though.

'OK' she whispered back, and began watering away, back to the house again, at a slightly faster pace. She returned shortly with a plate of buttered toast and a cup of tea. The woman was a godsend. I finished my food, and went back to the waiting. A large part of an investigators life is waiting. Just watching, and waiting. You have to be prepared to wait for hours, and it is not unusual to come home, after waiting for the entire day, with no action whatsoever. You get used to it after a while and end up doing a lot of thinking. It is good for your imagination, or simply as stress relief, if you can use the time in a mentally constructively way.

It wasn't until late afternoon that we got our first real action. The subject emerged from his flat and walked down the stairs to a garage below. He returned some time later. That's all we got for day three, but at least we got a good photograph of his face for ID. We called it quits and returned for a nice meal at a restaurant overlooking the water.

The Doubtfires' had obviously got the idea by Wednesday, as the little seat was waiting for me at my regular spot. Breakfast arrived on time, and all was going well. Suddenly, there was ACTION! The subject left mid-morning, and began walking towards the road. I notified Bob through the two-way radio, and he called back to confirm he now had him on visual leaving the front of the address. I grabbed the gear, placing it into my running bag, took a quick look around the garden for the old folk, then ran through the azalea patch and scaled the garden fence. I was hoping I didn't leave any tell tale footprints, but, well... the chase was on. You have to do what you have to do.

I let him go for a bit, allowing a fair distance between us. He wasn't walking quickly, and neither should he be. After all, this was sunny Queensland and there's no rush when you are on welfare. We followed him to a large supermarket. He disappeared inside and I ran to close up. I couldn't find him at first, but I moved through the store, checking the aisles one by one. At the end of the last aisle was an arcade that led into the general shopping complex. He wasn't in the arcade. Had he seen me following him. Did he wait until he got inside and then run out of sight?

I decided to check the supermarket again. I moved through, checking each aisle as I passed it. I checked the rear of the shop. I fumbled in my bag as I walked down the corridor, trying to locate the off switch on my two-way radio. The radio was currently bleating *'Bravo Charlie. Do you read me?'* a little too loud for comfort, and was in competition with the price checks being called through the quiet supermarket. *'Can you read me... CAN YOU READ...?'* Silence. I had managed to locate the off switch in my overflowing bag of goodies. (Phew!)

I reached the end of my aisle and there he was! I quickly turned up another aisle, without making eye contact. He was talking with a store employee by the meat and deli section, which is why I didn't see him before. They were chatting between aisles. I tried to make my exit from the store as fast as I could, but was hampered by the diligent shop assistant who had been observing my progress up and down the aisles with my bag under my arm.

'Hang ON mate. I'll just check your bag' he demanded. I opened my running bag to reveal a mobile phone, two-way radio, tripod, video camera, 35mm camera and a mass of wires jammed inside. He pondered for a moment, looking at the odd selection, and then let me go, visibly unable to comprehend what the hell was going on. I left the shop, and began searching

for a section between the outside window advertising, so I could film down the aisles. I wasn't well concealed but decided to bank on the psychology of people inside being only concerned with the space inside the shop. They could see me through the painted lettering on the window if they looked, but hopefully they would only look around within the store. No sooner had I brought my camera up and rolling then he began walking up the aisle. I continued to film as he walked towards me, and to my amazement he put two small packets of noodles up under his long white tee shirt, and wedged them into the elastic of his shorts. First a drug deal, then shoplifting, all on film... this bloke was going for a hat-trick!

I watched as he sailed by the same assistant who had questioned me earlier, smiling at the thought that he'd failed miserably, while I actually had video evidence of a real store theft! I let him go for a bit, then continued the tail as he left the car park and headed back home. There were three guys hanging around a hotted-up sedan in the car park, who had been watching me acting strangely in the area. They obviously had little to do in their lives other than hang out at the shopping centre car park and spin tales about their cars, or drinking stamina. When I began tailing the target home, they watched me, finally realised what I was doing, then sped off. They were obviously not friends of our subject because they didn't acknowledge his presence when he had passed them previously. Once they realised I was following him however, they unhelpfully decided to catch up with him in their car and have a quiet word to him. I was actually filming from some distance away, as the car approached him. I even got film of him removing the stolen packets of noodles from his shorts to carry in his hand. As I watched, the driver called to the subject. He approached the car, and knelt down to hear what the driver had to say. Obviously the conversation went something like this 'Hey mate ...

255

did you know that some bloke from the supermarket was following you?' 'No ...sh** ... Thanks mate ... sh**!'

I continued filming as the car sped off, and the subject began to walk very quickly. He was soon running and walking alternately. He was looking behind him constantly, and was not a happy young man. Luckily he still hadn't spied me and I kept out of sight quite some distance away. I noted that he no longer had any packets of noodles in his hands. I switched my two-way radio back on, and called Bob, who was really quite exasperated by now, not knowing what was going on. I briefly explained the situation to him, and which direction the subject was currently going.

Either there was some interference, or the security personnel for the local RSL were using the same radio channel, because as I ran past the front of the club we both heard:

'Security Base ... this is Zero One'

'Base over ... go ahead Pete...'

'Yeah ... are those blokes working for our club?'

'Nah ... I don't think so ... said something about a subject heading south ... Dunno ... sounds really weird!'

I smiled, thinking about our radio transmissions passing like ships in the night. I wondered how long they would be speculating in their own little world. *'Remember the time that we had those blokes on the air, talking about following somebody. I'm still sure it was the cops' 'Look Roger, we've been through this a thousand times. If it was the cops, they would be on a different channel''* They never would solve the mystery.

Bob must have been very close by, because a few seconds later I saw him cruise past me to catch up with our man. The main road was quite straight, and there were no real problems in following him, especially when he was more than likely returning home. When he could no longer see me, I began running myself. I ran as fast as I could go towards the main road. I ran past it and saw the target removing his t-shirt, still walking quite quickly. I could see Bob driving the van past him at the very time I scurried across the end of the road. He would be off to occupy a position near the flats I mused, in order to get film of the subject returning home. The 'offender' was still running a bit, and then walking. I saw he was now bare-chested, carrying his tee shirt in his hand as I lost sight of him. I guessed he was trying to change his appearance.

He was constantly glancing furtively behind, and it would be nigh on impossible for me to follow effectively along the same road. My main aim was to get to the Doubtfire OP before he arrived to his unit, and get a shot of him returning home. Running if possible. There was a road running parallel to the main road a short distance down, and I made for it as fast as I could, my running bag held firmly under one arm. I was now sweating profusely.

I turned into the parallel road and continued my furious pace. There was still some distance to go to get home and though he had a head start on me, I was confident I would make it... just. He was obviously not very fit, because he kept slipping from a run, back into a fast walk. I passed a number of cross roads as I ran. Sure enough, just before reaching the Doubtfires' house, and passing the last crossroad joining our two roads, I looked across to see the target running almost alongside me. He was a mere fifty metres from me on the main road, and I was on the road parallel to his. I watched him throw yet another glance behind him. Luckily for me, this glance was over his left shoulder. Had he looked over his right shoulder, he would have seen me flat out, probably red in the face, dripping in sweat carrying a heavy bag. But he didn't. I almost wished that he did, just to see the look on his face!

As I came down the driveway of the Doubtfires' still going like a locomotive, my wish to see a startled face was fulfilled. Unfortunately, this was through seeing the startled look on the lovely old lady's face, as I steamrolled past her, into her backyard. I grabbed my gear, and rapidly got things rolling. I even had just enough time to put the camera hastily on a tripod, as our man came into view. He came running towards the flats, then stopped to check both up and down the road.

Little did he know, Bob was filming him from directly across the road in the van, and I was filming him from just outside his front door through the fence in the Doubtfire's back yard. We watched him quickly scurry into his flat. He would probably be having a rather scarce meal tonight. He obviously thought we had followed him due to his shoplifting, removed his shirt to change his appearance and, sadly, would have dumped the evidence (the noodles, his dinner) on the way home.

Mrs Doubtfire ventured over to me again, some hours later, saying, 'That's funny, I thought you were still here in the garden and then you came running down the driveway. I didn't see you leave!'

What a gem I thought as I said, 'yes', looking guiltily at her azalea patch for damaged plants or footprints. Luckily, there was neither. Later that day we observed him taking his garbage bin out, and other residents took their bins out over the course of the evening. After Bob and Julie and I finished another fabulous dinner, we cruised past and picked up a number of rubbish-filled plastic bags from our subject's Otto bin. We drove off and took the garbage back to the hotel to sort through. It wasn't too bad. Sometimes we find bins with dead rodents, really wet, dripping and decaying vegetable matter, or soggy sanitary napkins. This one was not too bad. It appeared that our man had just done a big clean up and we got a few good finds. There were a number of discarded letters addressed to him, namely: a few demands from creditors, two from his real estate agent saying he will be evicted from his flat imminently for non payment of rent and a couple of personal letters. There was also a letter from Social Security including his reference file number, advising him of impending changes to the welfare system, and other information. Probably the best discovery was the employee copy of a taxation group certificate. It indicated he had worked four months in the last financial year, and detailed exactly how much was paid. Pretty solid evidence, and a little contradictory to his statement to the court that he hadn't worked at all. It was an excellent garbage find, but I couldn't help thinking it was a shame to get so much on one case when on others, sometimes, you can't get a thing. It is just our friend 'probability' having more fun with our jobs and keeping us on our toes!

The next morning we were back at work in the Doubtfire's backyard. It was around ten o'clock, which wasn't long after I'd finished the morning toast and tea Mrs Doubtfire had brought. The subject walked from his flat and down the road again. I notified Bob, and waited until he got out of sight before trampling through the garden mouthing 'sorry' to the azaleas, and jumping the Doubtfires' back fence again. We followed him a block or so to a public phone booth, where he made a call. Obviously he thought that his home phone was bugged, and was making a dodgy call. I knew that his home phone was still working, as I had called him earlier in the day to check he was still home and to ensure he was up and awake. It's kind of like a wake up call. If you think somebody is still asleep inside, you can ring just once or twice to wake him or her up. They will then usually get out of bed and on with their day after being disturbed by the phone. This means that you can get on with your day, observing what they do with theirs. Otherwise you are both wasting your time. Life is too short to sleep in forever!

He returned home from the phone booth, but left again soon afterwards. I was grateful the Doubtfires' were not about, as I was feeling guilty about wading through their well-kept garden all the time, and wondered if they were purposely keeping clear of me. We followed our man to the local shops. He returned home carrying a large number of cardboard boxes under his arm. He had obviously decided that it was time to clear out of his flat. He was probably going to do a runner before the real estate people evicted him. We didn't get much more during the day, but he did visit his garage once, with one or two of the empty boxes. We decided that we would come back at night to check what was inside.

That night we went to Jupiter's Casino. We were picked up by a limo from our hotel, and chauffeured to the casino with champagne, courtesy of Bob. Bob was out to impress Julie, and to generally have a great time. And that we did. Neither of us won much from the tables, but at least I didn't lose any. We returned to the hotel by limo again, and decided to have a quick look in the target's garage, changing from our suits into some 'sneaky peek' night clothes. We figured he would be clearing out pretty soon, and wanted to know what was inside the garage. We tiptoed past the units in the dark. At least we were more familiar with the building layout this time. We got to the door, and Bob whispered, 'OK, you stay here as lookout, I'll have a peek inside.' Unfortunately the garage was merely one short flight of stairs below unit eight, so we were very close. Bob slipped inside, and began rummaging around. A few moments later, the target walked straight out his door, and began descending the stairs. He didn't spend time locking his door or even closing it properly, just barging straight out and letting the screen door bang loudly behind him. I was right underneath him as he descended the stairs, and I felt that he would have heard me call to Bob however quietly I did so. I thought for sure that Bob had heard the door above him banging and was on his way out. I darted around the corner and hid, expecting Bob to be hot on my heels.

Tricky as the situation was, I'd failed in my duty as a lookout. Bob hadn't heard the door because he was bent right over with his head buried inside a large box, and was looking through the contents with a torch. The target must have heard Bob, and walked straight up to the garage door and uttered a line we mimicked for years later *'Is anybody in there?'* Bob pulled his head out from the box, a large torch and papers in hand and stared at the subject. There was an uneasy half-second as both men stood looking at each other in the dim light. *'Sorry mate... must have the wrong garage'* Bob said gruffly, as he pushed past him. He walked briskly away, then started running as he passed me around the corner concealed in a dark alcove. I ran too, and we both breathlessly met up further down the road. We returned to the hotel, laughing our heads off and had some difficulty explaining the tale to Julie.

Eventually it came time to return to Sydney. We both knew that the subject was going to do a runner, and leave his flat with a dozen cardboard boxes of his things, either tomorrow or the next day. Unfortunately though, it's not cheap paying for two investigators for a week interstate, with expenses such as the hotel bills and thus, we had come to the end of the budget. It was annoying because we were going to miss filming the move, and also miss getting his new address. I was also annoyed that he was going to clear out owing more people money, such as the real estate agent and the other creditors whose demanding letters we had found discarded in his garbage. We detested the thought he was going to get away with these things. At least though, we would have saved our client a considerable sum of money as a result of our investigation, and that eased our annoyance somewhat.

When we decided to call it quits and finish up, I felt I simply had to get a photo of the Doubtfires' for my memoirs. I already had a photo of me on my little seat, with a cup of tea and toast in their backyard, but felt that I should really get a photo of the three of us together. I gave them a large box of chocolates, which I had bought previously, and they were overjoyed. I felt like I was their surrogate son. They were so happy that I began to feel guilty about how little time I spent with my own grandparents. When I asked for a photo of the three of us together they were even happier and Mrs Doubtfire rushed off to fix her hair. I had to tell her she looked fine and not to worry. I wanted a photo that reminded me of them as they were. I set up a tripod in their living room and got a quick photo of us on the camera's self timer. Their joy was obvious and I could tell that I had made their week. Bob was round a moment later, knocking at the Doubtfires' front door just as I started to dismantle the tripod.

Earlier, when we decided over the radio to finish the job then and there, I had told him I needed a few minutes to get the photo and give them the chocolates. As soon as we decide to finish a job though, Bob tends to go into a 'Let's get out of here!' mode, and begins to stress if he is delayed even for a minute after that point, despite the fact that we may have been waiting there for hours. Anyway, we bade the Doubtfires' goodbye, thanking them profusely, before returning to the hotel. We packed up, and began the journey back to Sydney. We edited the videos and finished the report. I placed the receipt for the Doubtfires' box of chocolates into my tax file, under the 'Agent Expenses and

Informer Payments' section, and closed the chapter on another story in my book.

The conclusion of the job was that the client was pleased with our investigation and happy with the video footage. We contacted the subject's real estate agent a few days later as part of the follow up investigation, and we were told that the subject had cleared out, owing rent. He had moved out the day after we had left and the agent held little hope of recovering his money. I wished I'd had more time to watch him. To stay on him until he moved out, get a new address for him, and contact all the creditors to provide them with new details. I could inform Social Security, give the video of him shoplifting to the supermarket, ring the police about the drugs, and so on... but you have to draw the line somewhere. Besides, both Bob and I have our own business to attend to, and time is precious. You have to do what you have to do. Bob still reminds me about this job from time to time, and I'm sure we'll both never forget it. It was amazing, exciting, and a hell of a lot of fun. It's great to be able to integrate a good job with a good holiday.

'You know you let me down as my lookout that time... If I'd been in Northern Ireland...' Then one of us imitates the hesitant phrase; 'Is anybody in there?' and we both crack up in fits of laughter!

CHAPTER 14: FOLLOWING BY VEHICLE

The transition between two addresses or even a change in the *type* of transport is a vulnerable time for a subject, providing the surveillance professional with a good opportunity to observe. A man's home is his castle, and often people will remain safely behind their walls for hours, out of the camera's reach...

With few clues about the impending departure of a subject, it can often catch the hunter unawares when the person darts out and away into the traffic. If there is a garage door for example, to slow their departure, it is far easier as there'll be a warning sign that movement is imminent. The departure must be acted on very quickly as the loss of five precious seconds can easily result in losing contact with the subject, and wasting a days work. Little things such as keeping keys in the ignition (where possible) become so important to the professional... detail, detail, detail.

After successfully negotiating the departure transition, the bulk of the follow is easier, provided there is not heavy traffic. While the amateur may consider the follow literally 'just a follow', the professional is seeking opportunity to document the subject's behaviour while in their vehicle. Wedging a small camcorder adjacent to the sunshade will allow ready filming of the subject in front, even while both cars are in motion. A camcorder flip screen allows you to view the scene, while the vehicle itself braces the camera to keep it steady. This way you can capture and document each nuance of activity, each head flick, each lean across to check the directory. Subtle clues can be detected on a replay, such as the familiarity they displayed when passing an address they visit at other times. The mere documentation of their driving may be sufficient to discount claims they cannot sit for more than fifteen minutes, cannot drive more than ten kilometres, or perhaps are too depressed to go out in public. For an infidelity case, it is very common to observe a kiss inside the vehicle before a passenger alights, and this behaviour is exactly what should be documented on video. Seeing a person driving normally may not be exciting, but to the medical professionals, this behaviour can be very telling. As always there is not much to go on, so you have to do what you can, and should always try to keep the camera rolling.

The route will tell a story about where you are going and any departure from a main road must indicate that a potential destination is approaching. The transition to the destination is difficult to cover well, and the professional watches for this with keen attention. The subtle head flick that says *'I want to park now, where is a parking space?'* is one key, though there are others. A slight hesitation, a blinker flick but then cancelled quickly. When the subject begins to park, the professional must be ready to do likewise. Although taking the lead from the subject, the professional must be faster to park, and ready to document their exit from the vehicle cleanly.

In cases where there is no parking at all, a professional may sometimes just prop in the middle of the road for a few seconds and capture the video of the subject exiting the car. For an injury case this is a key action, getting up from a seat and swivelling around. It is also a good opportunity to get a good ID shot as the face emerges from the doorway. As the subject walks off, the professional must be very ready to follow. This is not the time to pack a bag of tricks, as the subject will quickly disappear and success depends on a few crucial seconds. Often people time their arrival to match a train or ferry or some other activity, which means you have to be very ready or you will be watching helplessly as they sail away!

Although foot follows are not difficult for the experienced operator they can be difficult to professional for those starting out. It sounds easy to follow someone discreetly on foot, but there is a real art to judging distance. Too far back and they will turn a corner and disappear. Too close and you become exposed. Unfortunately there is no rule of thumb. It's managed purely by instinct and tempered by experience.

As previously detailed, foot follows are a crucial skill to professional. It's an excellent opportunity to document the subject on video, where you may capture them bending to pick up something they've dropped, swivelling around to change direction, chatting to a stranger or more. It is not just about moving from one location to another, this is a prime opportunity to document the situation well.

Vehicle departures

Commencing a follow when your subject moves is often known as a 'take away', and is often the most difficult part of a follow. You must first be alert enough to be aware of the impending departure as well as being quick enough to commence a follow before you lose contact with them.

Record video of the subject climbing into their vehicle, if possible. Consider continuing to record the subject as they reverse out or drive off – they may spin their heads around to check for traffic, or twist their torso to retrieve seatbelts. This action may be significant in contradicting supposed neck or back injuries.

If you get advance warning that the subject is about to depart by vehicle, consider quickly relocating the surveillance vehicle (a preliminary move). You may be able to reduce exposure of the surveillance vehicle to the subject if it is moved slightly further out of sight when they actually depart. If they are likely to take a moment to depart (perhaps the subject is fully in the vehicle, but waiting for a passenger to enter), consider moving the surveillance vehicle out of sight to a nearby cross road. Then commence the follow as the vehicle drives past the intersection, not from your static observation point.

If you have not actually recorded the subject entering the vehicle or driving out of the address, try to get a quick video shot of the follow. Record a quick three seconds of the subject's vehicle driving, soon after their departure. This will log the accurate departure time in video evidence, as well as show the client you have successfully identified the subject's departure and have commenced a follow. If you lose them and have no video at all, others may wonder if you were there at all. If you have been unable to previously identify the full registration number (perhaps when a vehicle is exiting a closed garage), the follow is a good time to do so on video, as you may lose contact later.

During a vehicle follow

Maintaining a follow is the easiest part. Be cautious about recording a subject through the windscreen as you drive, as it is very easy for the subject to observe this through their rear mirrors. As mentioned earlier, you can easily wedge the camera next to the lowered sun-visor, which allows you to discreetly record activity in the car ahead, however do not overuse technique too much or use with an observant target, especially when parked close behind them.

When approaching traffic lights, be sure to close up the gap quickly, else you may encounter a red light while they continue on. Use an alternate lane to close up if possible.

It is not advisable for investigators to run red lights while conducting a follow, as it is dangerous and against the law. Missing a set of lights does not always result in lost contact, as you can sometimes make up time and relocate them further down the road. The trick is to better anticipate the traffic conditions, and to prepare your driving behaviour to reduce this possibility as much as you can.

Keep a reasonable distance from the subject. Try to remain in visual contact but keep as far back as possible, without limiting your options. Try to feed a 'sandwich' car (also known as *one for cover*) in between you and the subject, in order to reduce the exposure of the surveillance vehicle. Try to make sure any sandwich vehicle is likely to be reasonably quick off the mark, rather than an old bomb being driven by an elderly person for example!

Be well aware of all traffic both ahead and behind. Anticipate the subject's likely intentions. If they are in the right lane, perhaps they are turning right soon. Do not use turn indicators if possible. They are designed to attract attention, which is not good in a follow. Use them only if a vehicle travelling closely behind you may run up the rear of you, or may honk in annoyance of your unadvertised turn, attracting even more attention to you. Drive smoothly. Do not attract attention by making sudden movements, turns or braking heavily. The bonnet dips under heavy braking, and is quite noticeable.

Consider getting scene shots of major road signs. This will show that the follow did actually go as far as stated, and may assist in identifying the route later. Lower your hands on the steering wheel slightly. This means your hands are not visible in the target's rear view mirror, and is effective in reducing detection. Psychologically, seeing hands reinforces the fact there is a 'person' in the drivers seat. Seeing hands may cause the target to take more note of you, or try to see a face, in order to see who 'owns' the hands.

Reduce your facial exposure. Wear sunglasses or a baseball cap. Lower sun visors to reduce light, increase shadow and actually obstruct visibility. Consider scratching your face / eyes / nose at lights (or when right behind the subject in traffic), or performing some other similar absent-minded activity that will partially obscure your face with your hands for short periods of time. This activity also makes you look less aware of your surroundings, and hence less likely to be a surveillance agent. If the target watches you pick your nose (for example), they will assume you are not aware that you are being watched. This puts them at ease, thinking they have the upper hand. It also obscures your face from their view. You will have also provided them with a focus point. As they observe your unpleasant personal habit, their attention is captured so they are less likely to focus on the possibility that you may be following them. It also shows them that your own focus is on your nose, rather than who is around you, and this further allays suspicion. They may think: *Surely you can't be interested in me if you feel comfortable enough to grab a quick nose pick, so you must not even be aware I am watching you!* Of course it goes without saying that any behaviour should be moderate, as any more than a subtle attempt at a nose pick can result in drawing too much attention, and this spoils the psychological ploy to allay their suspicion.

Vehicle arrivals

Another difficult part of any follow is when the subject vehicle arrives at their destination, which is known as the 'put-down' or 'drop-off'. Get ready with the camera as soon as you believe the subject may be likely to stop. Indications may include leaving a major road and proceeding through quieter streets, or slowing down to look at street numbers. Consider switching your camera to standby, to assist in capturing video of the subject climbing out of the vehicle. Get your running bag ready, so you can grab it and run if necessary, as soon as the subject goes on foot. Successfully capturing a subject climbing <u>out</u> of their vehicle is the sign of a good investigator. Capturing the 'getting

IN' is easier, however the climbing out is often better to gather for evidence, showing the subject exerting more effort than simply sitting down into the driver's seat with the <u>aid</u> of gravity instead of working against it. Keep the camera ready. As soon as they stop, bring the camera up and get the shot. You may need to pause your vehicle in an unusual location to do so, like in the middle of the street, and then move it as soon as you have the 'getting out' shot.

Be ready for the subject to adopt another means of transport as soon as they get out of the car. They may go on foot but they may be picked up by another vehicle, or catch a bus for example. Park the surveillance vehicle securely in a suitable location with the doors locked. It is easy to forget basics in the heat of a follow. Ensure there is no information visible through the windows that may indicate the nature of the job, the actual subject's details or expensive equipment. Grab the running bag and GO! Continue following the subject on foot.

Lost contact response

We all lose contact with a subject at some stage, either by accident, by a bad call, or perhaps by an intentional backing off to reduce exposure. Losing contact with a subject while on a follow is not always a major problem, it is a simple fact in the game of chance. The aim is to minimise lost contacts, and maximise any benefit when they do occur.

Sometimes a lost contact can be a good thing, as when you later reacquire contact with them, you will have had very little exposure while en route. Given a few known addresses, you can simply check them in sequence to see if the car is there. If so, you can be sure they will not be suspicious. Lost contact may well provide a needed toilet break. You may need a leg stretch, a lunch stop or even just some fresh air. Given some thought, people are creatures of habit and can sometimes be found through an accurate assessment of their likely behaviour. A forty year old male departing home at ten a.m. on a Saturday may well be found in the local hardware store, for example.

Rather than try and doggedly stay with the subject at all times, a lost contact means you can return to the home address and set up ready for a good arrival shot – well framed, no obstructions, good parking location, camera focused and on a tripod. People have to come home eventually, and the return home event may be associated with unloading shopping or other items. If you try to follow them all the way including right back to home, you are unlikely to be positioned in the best location to capture this activity cleanly and smoothly, or may draw attention when moving into location. Few people will be worried about a suspicious car when they are returning home, especially with shopping on their mind. People are often focused on their task and will mindlessly unload their items, despite the fact you are parked directly opposite.

This location may draw some suspicion, but it can be perfect for the precious few moments while the activity is occurring. By the time they start to relax from their immediate arrival tasks, and tune back into their surroundings, the professional has melted away undetected with his precious footage. Lost contact is where you have lost sight of the vehicle for at least a few minutes. Make a quick assessment of the direction of travel, and continue in the same direction for a few more minutes. Assess the likely destination of the claimant, based on their departure time, the way they are dressed and if others are in the vehicle, for example.

Check likely or known destinations such as shopping strips, railway car parks and shopping centre car parks for short term parking. Conduct a floor by floor systematic search if appropriate, though consider the claimant is unlikely to continue driving past any vacant bays. Only search up to where there are plenty of vacant parking spaces, unless there is cheaper early bird all-day parking on some upper levels.

CHAPTER 15: WORKING IN SECURE AREAS

Surveillance is rarely static, and you are frequently on the move. Often the only opportunity you have to observe people is while they are in motion, or in the transition from home to car and back. When they arrive at a location, you want to know exactly what they are doing inside. What is their purpose there? Simply documenting the fact they entered an address does not convey much detail. The professional needs to write a good story, and this means you often need to go in to get the goods on what is happening.

Some agents are wary of getting too close, and prefer not to follow into a building. Others may wait for some time outside, then venture in quietly and try to 'find' their subject buried within the building. Others will barrel right in with the subject, standing next to them in the lift and walking them to their office. There is no right or wrong, as each case is so very different. So many factors are involved, from the demeanour of the subject, the type of industry, the ethos and security in the building and much more. It is a game. Get too close and you will be compromised ('sprung' or 'burnt'). Stay too far away and you get nothing. Somewhere in between is a narrow line, a knife edge between success and failure, and the professional can see and feel this line, always pushing dangerously close to the edge.

There are many ways to gain entrance to a secure area, ranging from simply asking to get let in, right up to an elaborate pretext. Each case is different. It's not always necessary to gain access at all, because it depends on the focus of your inquiries. Rather than trying very hard to get into an area to see where someone is working, a simple telephone call may provide all this and more from the safety of your office. It is about working smarter, not harder. Knowing what you really need, not what you think you want. If access is required, knowing your environment intimately and planning your options is imperative. How many seconds does it take before the garage door closes when a car exits? What is the level of security awareness of the guard on the door?

Lateral thinking is a key part of the surveillance professional's tool kit, and this must often be applied to gaining access to secure areas. It can open up a world of possibility if you think beyond the matrix that most of us live in. If a job was to require gaining access to a highly secure area, many people would take one look at the job and say it couldn't be done. The professional however, will consider their options carefully, do their research and come up with a novel solution. *'...and now that I know when the manager will be away, I will seal myself up in a large box marked with Westinghouse fridge labels, and have myself courier delivered to this manager on a day when he will be away. This will get me right past all the security checks, quite possibly delivering me directly to the office I need to get to, despite some head scratching over why John needs a new fridge!'* Don't laugh! It's an age old solution that worked well for the Greeks in Troy. This may be somewhat extreme, but the message is to think outside the box - or inside as the case may be!

The Law: Trespass

Merely entering private property doesn't always constitute the offence of trespassing, despite this being a commonly held belief. Like many State's legislation, the NSW Inclosed[56] Lands Protection Act 1901 Section 4 dictates that you are guilty of 'Unlawful entry on inclosed lands' if you enter private property without lawful excuse and without the consent of the owner. If you are conducting inquiries on a property in relation to lawful investigation, you will have a 'lawful excuse'. Unfortunately this phrase is not defined in the legislation, but laws relating to

---

[56] The official legislative spelling is Inclosed, not Enclosed!

investigator licences clearly recognise the right of a PI to conduct surveillance as a lawful activity.

Provided there are no locked gates or signs such as *'Do not enter'* or *'No Trespassing'*, and the owner or occupier has not told you to leave, then you are not specifically 'without the consent of the owner'. An entrant upon land for some lawful purpose (such as delivering a parcel addressed to an occupant) is assumed to have consent unless notified to the contrary by the occupier[57]. In addition, <u>both</u> conditions have to be met to constitute a trespass offence in any case.

A PI doesn't often need to enter private property, but in some circumstances this will assist in solving a case, provided it can be done legally. This type of legislation was designed primarily to protect property owners from theft or damage. It is not designed (for example) to prevent an investigator from discreetly walking down an unobstructed, unmarked private driveway to perhaps photograph some items in the rear yard which may be suspected of being stolen. Many people enter private property each day either by accident, because they want to knock on the front door to sell something, or perhaps because they are looking for their lost dog. None of these people will be guilty of trespass because they have a lawful excuse.

It is important to know your local laws, and remember that laws also change over time. What may be legal in one State or time may not be legal in another. In Victoria for example, the Private Agents Act 1966 - Sect 27 has a specific offence titled *'Unlawful entry'* which prohibits agents from entering private land without 'lawful authority', although this phrase is again not defined in the legislation (but is stronger than the NSW legislation which is

---

[57] Robson v. Hallett [1976] 2 QB 939
Also: Halliday v. Nevill (1984) 155 CLR 1 Criminal Law - Trespass - Magistrates Courts (Vict.) – As discussed in a High Court judgement

just lawful <u>excuse</u>). This section places even more onus on you to ensure your actions are appropriate for the circumstances. This very specific clause highlights the fact that entering private land does not always constitute an offence under any other legislation. Some over-zealous debt collectors or PI's probably once pushed this issue a little too far which resulted in this clause.

Queensland and Victoria also prohibit a person entering a dwelling house without consent[58], and while this is (surprisingly) not actually an offence in other states, the courts will often take a dim view of this behaviour and may consider it a 'breach of the peace', or class it as harassment. Queensland legislation prohibits being found in a 'house or yard' without lawful excuse, and also states it is an offence to enter with consent if the consent has been obtained by 'deceit, fraudulent trick or device, or false and misleading representations as to the reason for entry'.[59]

A court may use its discretion to find you guilty of this offence if it feels your actions were inappropriate. Yet if you had reasonable cause to suspect there could be a stolen backhoe on the property, a court may accept this.

There is a clear difference between entry to private land such as a yard, garden or shed, and entry to a private dwelling. While technically this may be legal in some circumstances with very good reason, it will usually be viewed poorly by the courts. In a case in South Australia (Poznanski v. Stosic), an investigator entered an unlocked dwelling house to search for evidence, but the courts rejected this defence saying he did not have a satisfactory legal excuse[60].

---

[58] s.48A Invasion of Privacy Act 1971 (Qld), s.27 Private Agents Act 1966 (Vic)
[59] s.48A(1A) Invasion of Privacy Act 1971 (Qld)

A very good reference to issues relating to trespass (and private investigators in general) may be found in the section *'Interfering with property'* from a Report to the Criminology Research Council[60]. This is an extremely informative report which every PI should read.

Always act professionally, always observe 'No Entry' signs or locked gates, and always leave immediately or identify yourself if asked. Know and respect the law, but don't be afraid to do your job. A timid PI will never get all the evidence. Be assertive (within the law), and catch those offenders!

The case of long airport delays

Key learning points

- Managing secure areas

Sometimes getting out of a building is as difficult as getting in, and I have found my car locked in secure car parks more times than I can remember, waiting for an opportunity to escape as another car opens the garage door. A common ploy also used by many thieves is to tailgate authorised staff through security doors. As any security consultant will tell you, the human factor is always the weakest security link in the chain and it doesn't matter how expensive or elaborate the security features on the doors are, it will rarely stop a person from tailgating.

Recently I gained access to a very secure staff parking area at an airport, after following a worker off a plane and all the way to his car past two security access areas. The worker soon left,

---

[60] *'Private Investigators in Australia Work, Law, Ethics and Regulation'* (Page 16) by Tim Prenzler, School of Criminology & Criminal Justice Griffith University, Brisbane 13/07/2001 www.aic.gov.au/crc/reports/prenzler.pdf

leaving me inside the restricted area. With the garage door now securely shut I soon gave up waiting for someone to open it, and chose to use the fire escape. This being right after some terrorist scares, the airport workers were tense and observant. I finally emerged from the fire stairs, not to open air, but to a highly secure area in an Air-Express sorting room, full of international cargo bound for planes. This was not the easiest area to exit from quietly, and a screaming buzzer sounded as I walked nonchalantly from the internal fire door. This didn't help conceal my escape.

I walked briskly but didn't run, as staff began to call. 'Hey. Hey YOU! Hey stop that guy!' and I almost made it. Just seconds before I was going to break into a run, thinking I had managed to sail right past the guard on the gate (whose focus was on people entering, not leaving), I could see I had better stop before I was wrestled to the ground in a serious incident! Credit to them for catching me, they were scratching their heads. 'You know this is a highly secure area. How did you get in here?' they asked.

My explanation that I had come in via the fire stairs was not believed, as it was countered by the car park being a secure airport facility which required card access. We had a stand off. At this point I stopped arguing with them, and threw it back at them.

'Well, how do you suggest I got in here?' I asked, which they really couldn't answer. They asked for some identification and let me go. I was amazed that they didn't ask to see inside the bulky backpack I was carrying... full of cameras, two way radios, my laptop ... just as well they didn't look, or I might have been there all night as a terrorist suspect!

CHAPTER 16: WORKING IN BUILDINGS

Getting inside many modern units often requires using electronic security intercoms or common keys. The following methods are some of the ways investigators use to get into the common areas of buildings, in order to mark the front door of a unit, check for vehicles parked in a secure car park or other investigative tasks.

Warning: These techniques are NOT methods to 'break in' to private property, but rather clever and lawful (in most situations) ways to take advantage of security loopholes or use social engineering to gain access to <u>common areas</u>, but ONLY for the purpose of a legitimate, lawful investigation. Although these 'common sense' techniques may not appear to break any laws, there may be general or privacy laws which prevent this activity in your area, and laws do change over time. One example is Queensland legislation which states it is an offence to gain consent to enter property by false and misleading representations as to the reason for entry'.[61] Do not use these techniques without appropriate legal advice or knowledge.

Gain secure access – Mobile phone method

Remain close to the door, but *on your mobile phone*, which gives you a good excuse for hanging around. You may need to pantomime a twenty minute call. It appears you either have a key, or are about to be buzzed up by an actual occupant, but are just 'finishing your call'. Appear absent minded when approached by an exiting person, but perhaps become slightly more animated: *'NO, I TOLD you I wasn't going to pick you up... Well what gave you that impression?'*

---

[61] s.48A(1A) Invasion of Privacy Act 1971 (Qld)

You are too busy with your call to be engaging with the resident opening the door, or to answer their questions. When someone is having an argument on a phone, normal protocol is to leave him or her alone. Use this to your advantage. When they pass through the door, just lightly 'catch' the door perhaps with your foot, but continue your call. This off-handed approach sometimes looks more natural. Continue the argument until the resident has left the vicinity. If you were to immediately enter the building as they exited, this looks suspicious and may elicit an *'Are you alright?'* response. By delaying your *actual* entry, it appears you are not particularly desperate to enter the building, but have just casually kept the door from closing for convenience, thus saving you from getting out your own key or buzzing up, because you are *just about to finish your call.*

Gain secure access – Buzzing method

Buzz other units on pretext with a delivery. Take an envelope addressed to a fictional person. Buzz the highest unit number possible. This means they are usually further from the actual entrance door, and it is less likely they will come to the door to accept the delivery rather than buzzing you up. Claim you have a courier delivery and thus gain entrance. Ensure you visit this particular unit. 'Discover' the addressee error when speaking with this occupant and decide to go back and check with the radio in your car (or some other excuse), and walk away, but you may not then need to leave the secure area itself. Consider using this opportunity of talking to the resident you initially buzzed, to gather further information. *'On the job sheet in my car I thought it said Unit five, but it is marked here Unit four. Do you know the people who live in Unit five? Perhaps this is for them? Do you know when they normally get home?'*

Gain secure access – Propped stick method

Prop a stick of reasonable thickness, but short length (about ten centimetres) against the opening of the door. With luck and good placement, it is possible to sit some way off the door, watching a resident open the door and depart, the stick falls across the door jamb, the door swings closed and catches on the stick, remaining open. A hanging stick can do the same thing but is harder to engineer. Hang a stick dangling down a short distance near the top of the door, close to the opening section. The door can open, but then the stick end drags across the top of the door and falls down between the door and jamb, thus obstructing it when it tries to close.

Gain secure access – Obstruction method

Place a significant obstruction, like a large garbage bin right at the doorway entrance. When a resident exits, they will be delayed at the obstruction. You can use this delay to assist your entry – the extra seconds enable you to time a 'natural' approach to the doorway, entering as the other person pauses in the doorway momentarily. Use the obstruction to assist by saying 'SORRY – I was just helping John clean up some of his garbage. Can you hold the door open while I wheel the bin into the lobby area?' or perhaps raising your eyes (implying it is not your bin), acknowledging that some people are so inconsiderate!

Gain secure access – Walk in method

Commence in the afternoon when residents are getting home, and thus walking into the building. Time an approach to walk in with them. It will be best to walk slightly *in front* of them rather than behind. Following behind is slightly more aggressive. Walk right up to the door, and then fumble for keys or feign pressing a buzzer while the real resident approaches you from behind. Suddenly 'notice' the resident, as if you were not previously aware of their presence, and then walk in with them. You may wish to 'catch the door' and delay your entry slightly. Otherwise they may watch you enter the building, but see that you did not actually knock on an internal door or open it with a key, meaning your actions are suspicious. Use your mobile phone to assist. You are too busy on the call to notice the resident nearby, and cannot be engaged in conversation or questioned, because you are obviously 'busy'.

Gain secure access – Key method

Some common area entrances are keyed to accept electricity authority master (skeleton) keys, and some investigators have been known to acquire these. Communal entrance locks are traditionally keyed very loosely, and often have several master key systems (estate agents, cleaners etc.), which significantly reduce their security, and increase the chance that any key will fit. Most people simply don't think to try keys when they find a lock as they assume the lock is secure. Never assume. Be aware of the laws and exercise caution if you choose to use this technique, as the court may use it's discretion to assert that a locked door implies lack of consent to enter, even if you have a key that will open it easily. If the court <u>also</u> determines you did not have a lawful excuse then you are liable to a charge of trespass. Every situation is different. Working on a large fraud matter the court may consider your activities lawful and accept the evidence gathered in this way. When working on a domestic matter without reasonable suspicion of something occurring (sometimes known as a fishing expedition), the court may rule against you.

Gain secure access – Beam break method

Most electronic garage doors use a beam break mechanism to detect if a vehicle is obstructing the doorway. The sensor is a laser-type light shone and reflected across the driveway, under the roller door. By simply obstructing this beam, the door will not close. It will <u>open</u> when requested however, so if you want to get the surveillance vehicle inside the car park, you can obstruct the sensor with something, and then wait. When the next vehicle goes either in or out, it will OPEN the door, but your obstruction will stop it CLOSING again, hence it remains open.

This provides you ample time to move the surveillance vehicle into the car park. Be aware that once in and the door closed, you are stuck until someone else opens the door. Try not to leave the door open indefinitely as this attracts attention from residents. To obstruct, try not to use masking tape as this easily arouses suspicions. Use something innocuous such as a cardboard box, or a plastic chip packet that has 'accidentally' become stuck around the sensor or reflector. Perhaps it was the wind!

Gain secure access – Lift jockey method

Buildings with secure lift access often poses a dilemma for investigators, who may want to determine where an apartment is situated on a floor (to aid external observations) or to perhaps mark the doorway to detect subsequent movement. Depending on the size of the building and frequency of movement, it is sometimes possible to enter the lift at the ground floor and remain patiently in the lift for someone to access it on the floor you require. This technique may have you riding the lift for some time, though it is worth considering. Using this technique at lunchtime (or around five p.m.) in a secure city building, you will usually gain access to the required floor within half an hour.

Working in city buildings

A city building is a network. Movement can occur through corridors, up stairs, down lifts and out doors. A surveillance professional will quickly assess the movement matrix, which includes the building complex. A subject may enter the building from the road network, and then leave via a footpath network. Each network has its own characteristics and probability, and the professional will assess each to determine the 'likely' movement the subject will take. Accurately predicting movement is half the battle won, as it greatly increases the odds of success.

All too easily the amateur will think the subject will exit via the same door they entered, but the professional knows better and will case each possible exit, be familiar with the building complex, and may choose another exit to 'sit off' and wait for the subject to reappear. Anyone who has received a medical examination in the large medical offices on Elizabeth Street, Sydney, would be aware that there is a duplicate 'back' entrance in Castlereagh Street. For the single surveillance agent, this poses something of a dilemma, as it is difficult for one person to cover both exits at the same time.

Depending on the case, the agent may elect to cover the front entrance on arrival (a safe bet), but perhaps the rear on departure, especially if the office in question is closer to the rear elevators, which will lead to a rear exit. If the subject has been there before however, they are quite likely to enter via the rear as it is perhaps closer to the station. These subtle details are analysed by the professional to maximise their odds, because there is nothing quite like that sinking feeling as you watch the hours go by with no movement, and slowly realise you made a bad call. It happens to the best of us, but it happens less to the professional who is stacking the odds in his favour.

When a subject enters a large city building:

- Identify if there is a *lift indicator* in the foyer, showing each floor.

- If there IS a floor indicator, consider not entering the lift with the subject, but closely observe the lift indicator. Note every floor the lift stops at, on its upward journey. Check the services index board in the foyer (if present) and identify what businesses are located on the floor(s) visited by the lift.

- Take a scene shot of the services board and/or at least two seconds of video of the board showing the business details listed for the floor of interest. Ensure good focus and a steady shot to enable the specific details to be later recorded in notes when reviewing the footage. This includes names, phone numbers, floor numbers and so on.

- Wait for the lift to fully return to your level, and ensure that the subject is not still inside. People occasionally make mistakes regarding the correct floor, and sometimes return to check the services index board in the foyer before returning up again.

- Catch the lift up to the subject's floor, or all floors that the lift stopped at on its upward journey. At the floor(s), conduct a quick inspection.

- If there is a lone receptionist and limited or no waiting areas, either remain in the lift or ask her for dummy directions and then depart.

- If it is possible to actually wander around the floor, do so. Ensure you walk in a confident, assertive manner. Consider perusing some 'paperwork' as you walk or conduct a dummy mobile phone conversation, in order to look busy and unapproachable. These items can assist you to stay there for some time.

- If you can locate the subject on the actual floor inside a suite or office, note the signage on the doorway/window. Take a scene shot if possible.
- If you cannot locate the subject, consider calling their mobile phone for a brief few rings, this may assist you to locate them when you hear the ring sound nearby.
- If there is NO floor indicator, or there are several other people waiting to enter the lift, consider physically accompanying the subject inside the lift.
- Wait for the subject to press their destination floor button.
- If necessary, press a floor button ABOVE the floor selected by the subject.
- Travel in the lift with the subject to their floor.
- When the subject exits, quickly observe the entrance foyer. Check if there is actually some form of waiting room, is there several offices on this floor? Is there a single receptionist ready to observe and greet any persons exiting the lift? Which way does the subject walk? Are they familiar with the location? Then remain in the lift and continue up.
- Unless there are multiple exits or other reasons, don't wait on the same floor as the subject. Remain in the vicinity of the entrance foyer and await their exit.
- If it is necessary to observe or wait on the subject's floor, consider waiting five minutes to allow them to settle, and *then* return to their floor and commence waiting
- Identify ALL exits. Check:
    o Main entrance
    o Rear / side entrance(s)
    o Mid floor corridors or arcades to adjacent buildings
    o Basement car park
    o Fire doors

CHAPTER 17: WORKING IN APARTMENTS

Home units have many people crammed into the one building. The common areas will often give subtle clues to the type of residents. Are they upper class people who will be nosey and security conscious, or is there a run-down feel where nobody cares who is there or what they are doing? Key points to note for these buildings are access points: front, rear, side, and this should include pedestrian and vehicle entrances. The letterbox area, door security and garbage location are other key issues to assess.

It is not always easy identifying the exact unit number, or where this is situated within the building. Once you can pick the balcony of the correct apartment, you immediately have greater access to information, such as ascertaining if they are home or not - or you could document activity seen on the balcony. The difficulty of identifying a resident in an apartment building necessitates preparation. It is often wise to do a door knock, or perhaps start in the afternoon and watch for the mail to be collected, so you can observe who collects from the box number you are watching. Anticipating when they will emerge is not always easy, but a warning bug is often a useful device allowing you to hear their exit from the safety of your car out the front, while reading the paper. Marking the door is often important, as this gives a good indication of the general movement, especially if you are worried that you missed their departure while you ducked into the nearby takeaway for ten minutes to get lunch or go to the toilet. Doors can be easily marked with a matchstick or preferably a small twig, propped at an angle which will be disturbed if the door is opened.

Communal garbage areas make it easy to sift through the garbage during the daylight hours. You will rarely attract any attention by doing this. It is so brazen you will never be suspected. It is not always easy to sift through a dozen bins worth of rubbish, but when the opportunity presents it is often worth it. A lazy operator will turn up their nose and claim they are paid to watch the subject, not search garbage. The professional will always take the opportunity to harvest good information, and it will regularly pay off. This keeps the professional's success rate well above average. It makes sense - why struggle to follow a subject in heavy traffic in an effort to get a work address, when you may find their employers name listed on paperwork sitting in the open garbage bins outside? It is all about working smarter, not harder.

Identifying unit numbers

What _unit number_ is the subject in?

To find out which particular unit a subject is residing in, follow the suggestions below:

- Check the electoral roll records – unlike telephone directories, these show actual unit numbers
- They may own the unit - check the *Strata Plan* number on the Lands Department records – this is normally the unit number, e.g. Michael Jones owns '**6/SP34241**'. This usually means he owns unit six (sometimes this refers to other areas such as a separate parking space etc.).
- Do they have a publicly listed telephone number?
- Contact a company which uses caller ID, (e.g. pizza or taxi companies) hiding your caller-ID, and then supply *their* listed telephone number, asking for 'delivery'. If that telephone number has called for delivery or collection previously, the exact address will be listed on the company database, and may be obtained from the telephone operator via pretext.

- Do you have details for the likely subscriber? Contact Telstra on 132 200. The exact unit number may be obtained from the telephone operator.
- Contact the subject directly through a pretext, asking to confirm their unit number (*see the separate pretext section* on page 178).

Identify unit – elimination method

- Conduct background checks (see page 72).
- Obtain all listed telephone numbers for the block of units via phone directory CD's.
- Examine the addressee names on any mail observed for any unit (see page 290).
- Obtain all electoral roll listings at this address. Either reverse search the electoral roll, or look up each surname discovered from the phone or mail searches above.
- Match the lists to identify which telephone lines go to which unit. This may not identify which unit the subject resides in, but will certainly identify which ones they DON'T reside in. By a process of elimination, the correct unit number can often be obtained, or at least reduce possible choices.

Identify unit – estimation method

- Check the mailboxes to see the highest number shown. Assume this is the number of units in the block (be aware some larger units have two separate mailbox areas).
- Count the floors in the building.
- Divide the number of units by the floor to determine the number of units per floor.
- Units are often numbered from ground upwards, starting from one, so count up to determine which floor the subject unit is likely to be located on. You may also

count down to determine another possibility if numbering is reversed.

- Where you can see one or more units to determine their location, you can estimate the position of the subject unit within the building.

Identify unit – phone ringing method

- If the area is quiet, you are likely to be able to actually hear phones ringing inside the units. While standing close to the unit doors or inside common areas, briefly ring each phone number to identify which unit the sound is coming from. If the subject's phone is not being answered, simply ring this one several times, while quickly moving through the building, and listening for the ringing sound.

- If you do not wish to actually ring the subject's phone, you can often eliminate other units by ringing numbers you have listed for other residents, and identifying which connection is for which unit. See the elimination method above. This approach will assist in identifying phone connections to particular units even if there is no Electoral Roll listing or other information showing the unit number.

Identify unit – light method

- Stake out the units at night when all units have their lights off, then call the subject.

- Use a pretext that you are calling from another country, and are unaware of time zones, or use a fax machine tone to call. As it is a mindless computer ringing, not a human sound, it enables you to call several times in succession if required (without suspicion), until they answer.

- Identify which unit light goes on, presumably in response to your call.

- Calling at this time may also reveal the outgoing message on answering machines, when the phone is normally answered in person at other times.

- People are often more psychologically vulnerable when they have just been woken, and may have their guard down. Calling at this time may result in them telling information they may have normally have not disclosed. *'Hmmm – what? No I just woke up. Yes – call me at work in about 6 hours that would be good. The number? It is 8250 8220'*

Identify unit – mail method

- Commence surveillance of the address at about one p.m. on a weekday

- On arrival, check to see if the mail has been delivered to the unit letterboxes.

- When mail is present, check the addressee details of any mail sighted. If the subject's name is listed on any mail, their correct unit number will probably be printed on the envelope as well.

- If you cannot identify any mail *addressed to the subject*, make a note of details for mail addressed to other unit residents, and use this information to assist location by elimination.

- Flag the mailboxes. Ensure there is something physically sticking out of each letterbox, which will act as a flag. This can be existing mail already waiting there, or may be a brochure or sales flyer you have brought, or 'borrowed' from a pile at the local real estate agent office, pizza shop or similar local business.

- Stake out the letterboxes, and watch mail be collected by the unit residents.

- Flags identify if mail was collected (when you blinked), and by which unit. It can be difficult to identify *exactly which* box a person checks as it happens very quickly. It is far easier if you can see the flag sticking out of the boxes – and when one box is cleared, this is the box now missing the 'flag'.

- Observe each resident, and attempt to match up the supplied description of the subject. Video any resident that looks like a possible match, so if they are the right one, you will have an image to study later.

The Law: Mail

It is important to know the law in this area. Touching, reading, documenting or even photographing the 'addressee' or other details shown <u>on</u> any item of mail observed is not an offence. Removing mail from the property or opening any item of mail <u>is</u> a Commonwealth offence[62].

Identify unit – note method

- Place a clear note on the unit front door, asking for the subject to call you.
- Be sure to just use their first name. Include a convenient tear off section on the note, containing your telephone number.
- Sign off using very common initials (AH) instead of a full name, as this will keep them guessing; there are then more name possibilities they must consider, and more likelihood they will decide they think they know the

---

[62] Commonwealth Postal Services Act 1975 no. 54, 1975 - sect 93 *'Tampering with the mail'*

author. Reading a vague horoscope in a newspaper for example, one naturally aligns one's brain to facts which match in their own life, and this PI technique makes use of the same phenomena (*'Perhaps the note was from Andrew?'*).

- Stake out the front door and observe who tears off your telephone number.

- There is no requirement to include your correct telephone number, but it may assist in checking facts – *'Sorry who is calling? I am not sure I know you... what is your LAST name?'* Sample text from such a note: *'Julie! I have managed to lose your telephone number – can you give me a call? 8250 8220 – Just wanting to finally return that stuff - AH'*

- On receiving the bemused call from the claimant, say you don't know what it was for (be vague) but you remember something about Alison (your girlfriend) saying she had lost her address book and needed to return some stuff. *'I'll get Alison to give you a call when she gets back. What number can she get you on? ... She mentioned she'd lost the unit number but thought it might have been unit 4 is this right? ... Perhaps she can give you a call at work tomorrow, because she is likely to be back quite late tonight...'*

- Progress through information piece by piece throughout the call, sprinkling red herrings as you go. Get one piece, chat some more (red herring) then ask for the next piece. Supply a suggested *'unit #4?'*, so the subject will either agree this is correct, or provide the correct unit number. Providing a wrong guess suggests you must have once been trusted with the information, so reminding you is OK! Asking outright for *'What is your unit number?'* is very intrusive, and much less likely to get a good response. Be sure to always supply <u>more</u>

information than you ask for – all red herrings – and the more specific the better. Examples: *'Yes, we've had several late nights this week … we went and saw Enormous Horns at the Sandringham last night, Alison seems keen on the drummer, but I don't see what she sees in him!'* OR *'She has managed to lock her phone by typing in the wrong PIN a few times. What a DRAG! I told her to keep it in a safe place, but she didn't listen.'* It may seem odd to say this to a stranger, but it works very well. Many people chat to strangers like this. Neither sentence gives any important or true information and may even bore the caller. This is good. Keep their mind occupied on the drummer from Enormous Horns instead of why you want their work telephone number.

Identify unit – garbage clues

- Search through the refuse during the middle of the day, looking for addressed mail to the subject with a unit number marked on it. Any garbage at all may have the association between name and unit number, such as a discarded electricity bill or other paperwork.

Identify unit – real estate clues

- Ask the real estate agent for confirmation. Find the local managing agent by asking other residents, as one agent often manages a whole block of units.
- Check for communal noticeboards, body corporate telephone numbers.

Identify unit – early warning device

- Secrete a small early warning device near the door of the unit in question, then monitor this outside the building.
- When you hear the noise of the door opening through the device, standby to observe or follow the next person that

exits the doorway. They would have just walked out of the unit you are trying to monitor.

Identify unit – call-out method

- Contact the subject by phone on pretext. *'Hello, is that Mr Smith? It's Brian from Express Couriers. We had a delivery addressed to you, but our guy on that run is still very new (John had an accident last week, and his van will be off the road for at least another two weeks!) It says on his sheet he left the envelope in your letterbox, but it looks like there may have been a mix-up with another delivery he's made. Could you possibly check your letterbox to see if your delivery is there, because if it's not – I will need to call him back to sort out the mess – I do apologise for any inconvenience'* This pretext can often draw out the occupant in order to 'check' his letterbox, which will allow you to match a face to the unit number.

- Be sure to stress the urgency of his checking the letterbox right now *'I really need to sort this out quickly, in case there has been a mistaken delivery – I'll wait on the phone until you get back if you like – I just need to sort it out for you.*

- Consider making a real delivery. A recent magazine inside a plain brown envelope addressed to them is sufficient to allay most suspicion. The 'actual' delivery of the item can also be accompanied by a telephone call, advising delivery has now been completed, eliciting another letterbox walk on video, or more discussion with the occupant.

Surveillance on units

- Are the car space bays marked? Can you identify the subject's vehicle by the corresponding unit number painted on the ground?
- What exactly is inside their garage? Bicycles? 'Work' related materials?
- What can you see underneath the door crack?
- What can you hear through the door?
- Where is their balcony? Is there any washing hanging out on the balcony? Can you see into the units?
- Can you hide in the stairwell space underneath the bottom set of stairs? This is good to keep you close to the action if you do not already have the ID of the resident, and are regularly monitoring a door flag to determine who is who. They may just walk to a car in the car park, or empty their bin internally, but you may miss this activity if you are outside.
- Can you observe the units from the stairwell of an adjoining unit building? This would mean you'd have height, to assist in looking onto balconies or into units. It also keeps you off the street, out of the car and away from the subject's premises.
- Where is the garbage area?
- Is there a communal laundry? Communal drying area?
- Is there a communal toilet (for your own use!)?
- Can you gain access to the electricity/utility room using master keys? (Perhaps you can observe discreetly through the door / window.)
- Where are the electricity / gas meters located? Monitor the readings to identify if someone is inside. When do they rise? Often it is possible to be given advance warning of an imminent departure – approximately one hour after you note the gas meter ticking over – they are having a morning shower prior to their departure. Units

often permit regular monitoring as few people question strangers in common areas, thinking they must be associated with another unit. Perhaps the flat is vacant – this is readily evident if the electricity meter reading does not change overnight, and this clue alone could save you a wasted morning of surveillance.

- Flag the actual unit door or garage door, with a small stick, against the door close to the opening side, propped up at an angle of forty five degrees. When the door is opened, the stick will fall. Check this flag at intervals to identify movement through the doorway.

- Can you set up continuous loop recording of the entrance door or letterboxes? This is good when you have not yet got good ID footage. Check the internal door flag (stick) after each person exits. When the flag is finally disturbed, you will actually have footage recorded of the subject. This verifies your presence on the job to the client and may eventually help to prove a 'going to work' routine to the court by demonstrating regular departure time and dress standards. It will also permit you to take some time to study the ID video, instead of trying to remember a brief glimpse you may have had.

- Mark the letterboxes if possible with mail or brochures. This provides additional safety, alerting you to the fact that an occupant of your unit passed by when you blinked, because the 'flag' has suddenly been removed.

- Units are often unsociable locations where most people don't know each other that well, and there are a relatively high number of strange visitors at various times. Use this to your advantage, and stay close. It may be possible to park in the visitor spaces. Look for these often marked 'V', 'V1', 'V2' or just 'Visitor'. Sometimes it is good to park right inside the car park and comfortably watch for their car to depart.

CHAPTER 18: WORKING IN CAR PARKS

Documenting the loading or unloading vehicles, and good, close-up documentation of a subject climbing into their car is important. Be ready to prop and record them climbing out of their car, then find a permanent parking space. Ideally, the parked location will allow you to observe the subject's car, so you can remain in location in your vehicle while they load up their car with shopping. If your current position is not ideal, move the vehicle to a better position later.

- A good spot has visibility of the driver's door and boot.

- A good spot is one that enables an easy follow out of the centre. Stay well clear of obstructions such as bollards, kerbs or other cars to allow easy exit if necessary.

- A good spot is often *close* to the subject's vehicle because car parks are full of strange cars, and people will rarely take notice of their surroundings. Remaining close will result in better footage, and shots of the subject loading shopping into a car is *significant* footage that should be recorded as effectively as possible. Remaining further away means there is a high likelihood that another car will park obscuring your line of visibility – thus obstructing your camera shot.

- Consider taking steps to keep your line of visibility clear. One good method is to lay a shopping trolley on its side in any space you wish. Usually this means that other cars are much less likely to park there, as they would have to physically move the trolley or other obstruction you place there, before parking.

- If possible, set up a continuous loop-recording of the subject's vehicle using a tripod in your surveillance vehicle, then return to the subject. If you lose contact with them, you may still end up getting the footage of them returning to or loading their vehicle using your static mounted camera. Alternatively, you may be able to follow them from the shops and record them loading or entering their car from another angle, effectively having two separate camera angles recorded. Why limit yourself to a single camera? The more bases you have covered, the less likely that magic moment will be missed.

- If unsure about which vehicle the subject will depart in (perhaps you spot check their workplace and discover ten cars in the office car park) – consider recording ALL vehicles, including accurate number plate shots, by walking around the car park casually filming number plates. When the subject later departs you will already have a good image of the vehicle and the plate number, without even knowing which one it is. Video allows you to capture a large number very quickly, without looking suspicious or taking too long by writing plate numbers down manually.

- Consider approaching the driver of any vehicle that may be intending to park in a position that obstructs your line of visibility. A short explanation such as *'Sorry, we are conducting a surveillance operation here at present. Would you mind parking just out of THIS particular area?'...* perhaps followed by a cryptic *'...just in case.'* Show a shiny metal investigators badge[63] for added authority, and be sure to mention 'the royal *we*' to imply there is a full team working, rather than just you as an individual. Notifying strangers of your surveillance operation is unlikely to spoil the job, and is quite likely to enable you to get much better footage. As always, each situation is different, and you need to make your own assessment.

---

[63] See Shiny PI badges on page 158

CHAPTER 19: WORKING IN TRAINS

It's all about the stairs. Railway stations are an excellent environment for the prepared surveillance agent, and there are almost always stairs involved, which leads to good footage on many injury cases. Following a subject through the milieu, the amateur could find themselves unprepared for the transition to the railway network. Having coins or small notes ready is vitally important. You need to transit smoothly, or else you may lose contact, or draw attention to yourself by trying to hurry through a barrier without paying.

Knowing the station layout is important, as it is often a good location for a clean ID shot while the subject patiently waits for the train. A good vantage point is often the station stairs, or even the opposite platform. Use the crowds to your advantage and get really close. It is difficult to get footage of a subject ascending stairs if there are too many people in between, so often the best plan is to 'tailgate' them just metres behind. People are usually more focused on the stairs, not who is behind them.

People make phone calls in trains, they talk to their associates, and they read work related paperwork. This warrants getting very close to your prey as the information gathered can often be exceptional. The trick is to pick the odds and assess the value of such proximity. Sometimes it is safer to remain well out of sight and wait for them to exit the carriage, while at other times you should be sitting right behind them.

The action of getting up from a seat is a good indicator of the level of back injury, so you should aim to capture this on video. It is often good to start recording continuously well before they disembark. Although this may 'waste' tape while they sit there motionless, continuous recording will capture the full movement of them eventually standing up from their seat and walking off.

Unless they have some items that will provide advance warning of their movement (an unfolded newspaper on their lap, a jacket on the seat next to them), there is never enough reaction time to start the camera rolling, so it's best to be rolling in advance. Besides, the professional will have several hours of tape and battery available to him, so there are no worries about recording tape while there is nothing happening. Continuous recording will almost always capture the stand up action. Once again, it is all about improving the odds.

Key things to aim for here are good documentation of *ascending and descending* the large railway stairs. On arriving at a railway station during a follow:

- Get close to the subject *immediately*, and record them as they ascend and descend the large staircases. Recording a subject ascending a large set of stairs is particularly good, highlighting the true nature of any leg injuries. Be sure to get the shot right, get closer than usual if required. Be bold!

- If not possible to observe from a distance in front, walk *directly behind them no more than 5 metres away*, ascending and descending the stairs with the subject. Remember it is normal to walk closely to others in this environment. Hold the camera slightly in front of you, and attempt to keep it as still or smooth as possible. Use the flip-out screen to ensure the shot is framed properly.

- If possible, remain close behind the subject in order to listen to which station they want to go to when they purchase a ticket. If you didn't quite hear them, simply ask the attendant for *'Same ticket as them'* or *'Which station did the last person buy a ticket to? I forgot to ask them where we are going!'*

- If you lose contact with the subject at the ticket booth, simply continue through to the platform without a ticket. Ideally you would have purchased a weekly ticket prior to the job to prevent this problem but it is difficult to cover every eventuality on a surveillance operation. Regardless, you can purchase one later, jump the barrier or show the guards your shiny PI badge[64] and explain that you are following a 'suspect'. Don't mention 'claimant' as suspect sounds more exciting, while claimant is more of a legal term. Using the word 'claimant' may result in them being less inclined to assist, or result in them taking more time to process you. Consider having a five-dollar note in your hand, and just thrust it into their hands for the ticket if there is any problem. Even if they request you to wait for 'security', explain you simply have to continue the follow or else you will lose contact with your suspect. Move away from them quickly, refusing to enter into a dialogue unless they attempt to physically restrain you. Be assertive, because there are usually only seconds to spare. Only the most narrow-minded guard will spoil your follow under these circumstances!

- On arrival at the platform, immediately move well away from the subject.
- Note which platform they are waiting on (make a note as it is easy to forget later) and where on the platform. The stairs at railways stations are staggered to better distribute crowds else the train would always be crowded near the stairs. Clever or regular commuters anticipate this and will often move to a particular spot which assists them alighting at the other end. Observing this can highlight familiarity with trains, or help identify regular commuters, and can also help predict which station they may get off. Everything happens for a reason.

---

[64] See Shiny PI badges on page 158

- Identify the destination of the trains on this platform. Check the indicator board or quickly ask the guard. Consider a quick video location shot of the destination indicator board.

- Consider going back to the ticket booth, and purchasing a ticket before the train arrives (if you have not done so already), to avoid any potential delays at your destination station.

- If you don't already have good ID footage of the subject, consider using this opportunity to get some while the subject is static. Consider even walking across to another platform entirely, to shoot across the railway tracks as the subject sits waiting on the opposite platform.

- Consider setting up a continuous recording of the subject sitting there waiting, in order to capture them *standing up* when the train arrives. This action is more important to get than the initial 'sitting down', but far harder to actually achieve, due to very short reaction times and lack of movement warnings.

- Wait out of sight, preferably on the <u>opposite</u> side of the platform to them (for example, as if you are intending to catch a train going in the other direction). There is no need to maintain continuous eye contact of the subject while they are just waiting on the platform, especially since they are likely to spend time looking around while they wait, causing you unnecessary exposure. Ensure you visually cover the railway stairs or exit point, just in case they decide they are actually on the wrong platform, or change their mind and walk out again.

- While waiting for a train to arrive, casually check that your subject is still waiting. They may be doing something of interest that is worth recording, or may have met up with an associate. It is easiest to get good identification footage of associates while they are static.

- When any train approaches, move in to observe either the subject or at least the train doors to see if they intend to board the train.

- Wait until the train actually departs before moving back, just in case the subject suddenly realises it is their train and makes a quick dash for it.

- If the subject clearly intends to board the train, make a final destination board check, and attempt to record them actually walking onto the train.

- There is no requirement to enter the *same train doorway* as the subject. Consider boarding another carriage.

- If you choose to enter the same carriage doorway, consider keeping a camera recording right behind them. This will record them boarding the train, ascending or descending the internal train stairs, as well as sitting down.

- When the train is moving, use the interconnecting carriage doorways to move closer to the subject's position.

- If the subject is sitting in the carriage entrance foyer, consider remaining in the adjoining carriage, observing the subject through the carriage windows near the internal door at the end.

- If the subject is sitting in either the upper or lower deck sections of the carriage, use the opposite deck to move around them if required (instead of walking right past them), so you end up located BEHIND the subject, in the carriage entrance foyer.

- If possible, set up a continuous recording of the subject in order to capture the movement when they later *get up out of their seat*. This movement is difficult to capture, as there is little warning of them doing so - they normally just stand up quickly, before you can react. Recording exactly how a subject moves when they stand up is often more important in assessing their alleged injuries, than getting them just passively sitting down.

- Continuous recording may also show the subject ascending or descending the small internal stairs *while the train is in motion*. This is a significant action worth recording, and is unlikely to be repeated elsewhere. Be bold!

- To record continuously on trains, consider using the floor, possibly with a prop to adjust lens angles, or sit the camera on your lap or bag. Consider bracing against the internal glass or walls. Deploying a tiny tripod may also be appropriate.

- Do not be overly concerned about attracting attention from other passengers. Be as discreet as possible, but remember the other passengers are strangers, who are unlikely to either know or approach your subject even if they become aware of what you are doing (unless perhaps you are filming a pretty young girl!). Your footage of the subject leaping briskly out of their seat may well be the evidence the court needs. It is often worth the small risk that you will be 'discovered', or the 'embarrassment' at fellow passengers staring at you wondering *'What the hell is that guy up to?'* while attempting to get the shot.

- If the subject is reading documents, or speaking on their mobile phone – consider approaching or sitting right behind them, to listen to their conversation (recording it is legally possible, as it is clearly in a public place, so use the video camera to do it), or to view the material they are reading. A quick glance at their documents may well solve the case, when weeks of surveillance may have never revealed that information. They may be reading study materials for a course they are doing, a schedule or timetable, work roster or company documents. Discovering this information may well assist your case, and is likely to produce a far more professional report. If possible, get a quick recording of the documents close up. Ensure you have a fast shutter speed, and consider manual focus. Only consider this if the subject appears engrossed in their work, and you consider them unlikely to look around quickly. It is often best to get an image of the documents for later analysis, than trying to actually read over their shoulder.

- When the train approaches a stop at which the subject is likely to disembark, consider commencing a continuous recording if you have not already done so. Likely destinations include major city stations, the closest station to a known appointment or the subject's home or work.

- Consider remaining in the train (near the door) as the subject finally walks off, and record them *from inside* the train for a few seconds. This is an easy position from which to get a quick shot, and one that also clearly shows you successfully followed the subject to a final destination station, and did not lose them. Cover your back.

- Move quickly to get coverage of the subject either ascending or descending the railway stairs. This is always priority in injury cases.

- Consider getting a quick location shot. Two seconds of video showing the station name, which will be painted on a nearby seat or sign will suffice. Only attempt this if you are confident of not losing contact with the subject in the train crowd exiting the station. A location shot shows professionalism and clearly identifies in evidence exactly where you are at that time. Additionally, the relatively 'still life' location shot may provide a welcome relief from an otherwise sickeningly jerky video and it provides a neat visual cue or index in an otherwise 'disjointed' video tape. It clearly paints a video storyboard of what is going on and where (it also adds a precious two seconds to the total videotape time!).

- Once out of the station and following on foot, be ready for the claimant to adopt another form of transport. They may quickly board a bus, a taxi or be picked up by a waiting car.

- Consider hiring a nearby taxi, and use it to assist your follow from this point.

CHAPTER 20: WORKING IN BUSES

Bus travel requires a higher degree of contact with the driver than does a train. They are also a more confined space, which can make for challenging times. I followed a woman onto the bus once in my early days as a PI, and when the driver asked me where I was going, I said to him *'I'm not sure. Where are YOU going?'* This wasn't the right response, as he replied *'No you tell ME where you are going, and I will tell you how much it is'*. This painful banter continued for a few rounds, and he did not seem to understand that I really didn't care where he was going, I just needed to get on his damn bus, and if he would just give me a ticket, any ticket, we could both be on our way! If we had stood there arguing for a moment longer, I could sense that the subject would look over at us with interest, wondering who on earth was that idiot that didn't know where he was going. I learnt my lesson that time, and from then on when asked by the driver where I am going, I will be ready with my answer: *'ALL THE WAY!'*

- If the subject boards a bus, consider following the bus by vehicle.

- Position your vehicle behind the bus, and stay close. The subject will not be aware of your presence unless they are sitting on the back seat and should chance to look behind them.

- Get a location shot of the rear of the bus. Record two seconds of the number plate and the bus route number. This marks the boarding time in evidence, and helps you remember exactly which bus it is, because it is easy to lose contact in traffic and buses can all look the same. Besides, location shots make your video longer and provide a nice storyboard effect, which aids understanding and adds to your professional finished product.

- At any stops, hang back slightly, and stay close to the kerb side. This will assist you in seeing the passengers getting out of the bus.
- If you are not already recording the exiting passengers stepping off the bus at each stop (just in case), consider doing so, especially a likely destination such as the closest stop to the subject's home, the end of the route or a major stop.

Alternatively, consider boarding the bus with the subject.

- Have loose change ready to give to the driver for the fare to speed up the process.
- Listen carefully for which destination stop the subject asks for when they purchase their ticket from the driver.
- Consider saying '*same destination please*' quietly to the driver after they have just served the subject, then study the printed ticket for clues as to where you are going.
- Ask for a fare to the destination marked on the front of the bus, or if this is unclear, simply ask '*What is your last stop on this route?*'
- If possible, set up a continuous recording of the subject in order to capture the movement when they later *get up out of their seat*. This movement is normally difficult to capture, as there is little warning of them doing so. Recording exactly how a subject moves when they stand up is often more important in assessing their alleged injuries, than recording them just passively 'sitting down'.
- Do not be too concerned about attracting attention from other passengers, as it is likely they will not notice you, and even if they do, they will probably not care. Even then it would be unusual for them to actually do something about it. It is perfectly normal for a PI to look strange to others on occasions, provided you do not draw attention from your subject.

- Delay your exit from the bus for as long as possible to provide some separation from the subject as they walk off.
- Consider filming the subject exiting the bus, and then through the windows before you get off quickly. Use the bus as a concealed location to shoot video from in the few seconds before it actually departs again.
- If you are following a bus by vehicle and it is approaching the city or some other busy location where parking may be difficult, consider boarding the bus at the next stop. Ensure you are reasonably sure of the route the bus will take and that it is likely to continue down this main road for some time. Ensure that you know exactly which bus it is, both number plate AND route destination number. Overtake the bus and drive quickly up the road to a position near a stop the bus is likely to pass. Quickly park the vehicle and run to the stop, flag the bus down and board it. Boarding the bus while the subject has already been on it for some time is good to allay suspicion.

CHAPTER 21: WORKING IN TAXIS

As a professional PI, I have jumped into cabs and said *'follow that car'* on more than one occasion. Cab drivers will often be happy to assist, but it is not good to be too dramatic, lest they think you are a crazed madman who will wreak havoc with their cab, or jump out without paying. Not all will be keen to join in a car chase with an unknown passenger, so it is best to pick your driver carefully if you have the time. Some will revel in the excitement, and be only too happy to help, though all will appreciate seeing cash being waved around early on, as this makes them worry less that you will leap out unannounced because you are 'on secret business' (Yeah right!).

Sometimes there is really no need to inform the driver at all. I have, on occasion, just casually asked the driver *'Hi, look I am travelling with that car up ahead, so they know the way, just stay with them'*, and it worked. Luckily the driver was most pleasant and chatty, and never asked why I was taking a cab and not travelling in the other car. They make an ideal impromptu surveillance vehicle. A taxi is easy, commonplace and comes with a driver to assist you. What more could you want? A good example of the use of taxis is found in the story 'The case of the undercover taxi driver' below.

Taxis can be an effective tool for the surveillance operator:

- A taxi provides good cover and is cost effective.

- A taxi provides a good base to record video from discreetly (for short periods).

- A taxi can 'leapfrog' a walking subject, driving right past, and then pausing *in front* of them as they walk. This permits you to get a nice and clean front ID shot. Don't have tunnel vision and only follow behind your subject, as few people will be concerned about being followed from in front.

- A taxi can easily conduct a vehicle follow.

The case of the undercover taxi driver

Key learning points

- Contingency management / managing the unexpected

- Hiding in plain view

- Foot follow techniques

- Effective use of a taxi as a surveillance tool

It was a simple enough case. We had an unidentified female that was getting up to some corporate mischief, and we were informed that she was to be meeting our client's representative Tom, for lunch. We already had a rough description of the girl he was meeting, and he had indicated that she was likely to be working for a legal firm somewhere in the city. I was expecting them to finish up at about one thirty p.m., and hoped it would be an easy job following her back a short distance to the city on foot. I wandered down to Circular Quay, together with my partner, Alison.

The restaurant was inside the overseas passenger terminal building, which is quite exposed. There were multiple exits on both sides of the building, together with doorways that led to adjoining areas. It could have been difficult to manage alone, and I was glad Alison was with me. I thought it was perhaps best to take a table inside, because the large windows allowed patrons inside to have a clear view of the outside areas, and it would look far less suspicious to be relaxing inside at a table. Hanging around outside could allow us to be further out of sight, but we would not have fit the movement profile for this area, and would soon look slightly out of place. I conducted a walk through the restaurant, and spied the pair in a cosy booth. I've met Tom on several occasions, so he certainly knew what I looked like, and I saw him glance up at me as I walked past his table. Having located them I felt far more relaxed, knowing not only where they were but what she, the target, looked like.

I returned to collect Alison who was waiting outside, and we both walked in and asked for a table to have a coffee. It was quite a large restaurant, though there were few people inside. I wasn't really concerned where we sat, as my surveillance subject was sitting in a booth and would not have a good view around her anyway. The female maître d looked less than impressed at our request for coffees alone, as if we had perhaps mistaken her fine restaurant for a cheap café. She bustled off in front of us, as if to say she was busier than us and had things to do, so we should be grateful we were even getting a table at all!

We approached the booth where our couple were eating their lunch, but I assumed we were being led to the spare tables closer to the window, where we would be out of their line of vision. Suddenly without warning, the maître d stopped and began preparing a table. Being a fine restaurant, there was a lot of 'stuff' on the table such as three sets of cutlery, appetiser plates, lunch plates and so on. Her movements were clipped, and it was clear she did not appreciate having to clear a table for the couple that 'only' wanted a coffee.

I was pondering the atmosphere she was creating, and wondered if she was subconsciously trying to send us a message that while she would serve us, we were not welcome, at least if we were only wanting coffee alone. I quickly realised that the table she was preparing was right next to the booth where Tom and the mystery woman were dining. Our table could not have been any closer if we had tried, and given that the booth was quite enclosed around them, it would probably be that our table was about the *only* thing the couple could see as they had their lunch.

I had to make a split second decision. I could have politely asked for another table, but the maître d was already halfway through her table clearing and, together with her 'helpful' attitude, I could see myself debating the issue with her right next to the couple, who would undoubtedly notice this annoying exchange. My other alternative was to make a conscious choice to 'hide in plain view', and sit at that table, despite it being directly under the noses of the couple I was hiding from. Alison is a smart girl, and glanced at me quickly, knowing I had to make a quick call on this unexpected situation. I nodded slightly, indicating I was happy with our choice of seats, so she promptly sat down with a smile, looking relaxed and facing away from them. I sat down opposite her, and immediately saw that the couple were themselves noticing our arrival. Tom made no real eye contact with me, but I was sure he had seen me because there was really no way he could have missed me, sitting where I was. We both ordered our coffees while we perused the large dessert menus, trying to imply that we might order more shortly.

I used Alison's body to shield myself from them slightly, so I presented a slightly obscured form to them, though they could still clearly see me. One of the tasks was to get a photograph of the mystery woman, which would normally have been quite difficult, considering she was virtually concealed within the high walls of the snug booth. My position directly opposite her gave me ample opportunity to get the shot, and after carefully picking my timing, I discreetly got a very good identification shot of her sitting there. I showed Alison the photo on the digital camera screen, knowing she would not have seen the target very well earlier in her brief glance. Alison studied the photo, and then we began quietly chat while studying the dessert menu.

I could see they were getting ready to finish up soon, and I wished we hadn't ordered our coffees already. It reduced our flexibility as we might not be able to leave quickly and quietly, if we were to attend to our bill or evade the staff without paying. Checking the menu I could see the coffees were nearly five dollars each, which was to be expected I guessed. I knew I only had a fifty dollar note in my wallet, so I could not even leave a ten dollar note on the table easily. I scolded myself for not being as prepared as I should have been. A good PI will always carry small notes for exactly such occasions, as you never know when you need to leave a café or jump out of a taxi quickly to chase your subject. There is rarely time to get change when every second counts.

I looked around, but the staff seemed very busy doing nothing, and there was certainly no sign of our coffees. It did seem like a nice place for a leisurely meal for those who could afford it, but like the steep prices, the speed of service reflected the fact it was not a fast café or takeaway, so not the best choice for people in a hurry. I smiled, wondering what the maître d would say if I called her over to ask for our coffees in takeaway cups. I thought better of it.

Tom and the mystery girl stood up, after settling their account, and I watched them slowly walk away. Alison and I briefly pondered our situation, both coming to the same conclusion. The coffee was just too slow to arrive. We stood up confidently, as if we'd just finished a scrumptious lunch, and sauntered out of the restaurant, unnoticed by any of the staff. I almost wished I had been there to see the look on her face when she realised the 'coffee couple' had done a runner (unless perhaps this was exactly what she was trying to achieve)... but of course we had work to do.

Tom walked the woman towards the city, but she soon separated from him, and walked up towards the Rocks. I could see Tom, and wondered why he looked so flustered. I could see him turning around, and then looking back at the woman as if he felt compelled to see where she was going. I watched him pull out his mobile phone, and was not surprised to then hear my own ringing.

'Where the hell are you? You lost her, why weren't you here, I told you what time we would finish lunch!' he barked, in a very unimpressed tone of voice. By now the mystery woman was approaching George Street. I replied in a quiet, dead pan manner 'Tom, relax. She is walking up the hill to the corner now'. There was silence on the phone, and I could see Tom swivelling around some more, looking intently at everyone he could see. He would have realised I was on the job as soon as I'd said that, because that was exactly what she was doing.

After a pause, he said in a remarkably calmer voice 'Oh, that's you with the mobile phone to your ear is it?'

'Yes' I replied, '...so just leave it with me now'. I could tell he was busting to follow her himself just in case, but he left me to it.

I had to laugh to myself, realising that Tom hadn't seen me, even though I had been sitting virtually next to him for almost twenty minutes. Especially since he would have probably been looking for me as well! I figured he must have had a mental image of me hiding suspiciously behind a telegraph pole, trying hard not to be seen. Being so close and right under his nose, he simply failed to recognise me, despite the fact that he had looked at me as I sat down. This was a perfect example of people seeing but not observing. My behaviour was so expected, 'just another couple sitting down for lunch', that his brain filtered out this information entirely.

Alison followed up on the woman's side of the street while I followed on the other side, diagonally opposite and behind the subject. This gave us the flexibility to respond to changes in direction, as well as separating us so she would not associate us visually as a couple quite so easily. Up on George Street, I could see the woman standing on a corner. Tom had said she would be likely to walk back to a city office not far away, but nothing was ever certain. She was looking around, and I wondered if she was checking to make sure she wasn't followed. My mind raced with possibilities, and I suddenly realised what the likely scenario was. She was looking for a taxi. DAMN. This wasn't in the script! The plan was that she would walk back to a city office! Nobody had warned me about her taking a taxi! I envisioned myself chasing her cab on foot through the congested city streets, which is a technique I have employed once before, though it's certainly not ideal. As if on cue, a taxi drove past her, but it wasn't going her way. I nearly fell over the curb trying to hail it, and was soon asking the driver to do a U-turn and go back into the city.

George Street is a busy thoroughfare and no sooner had we turned around than I could see her getting into her own taxi. My mind was too busy to register the fact that I'd made a successful decision in pre-empting the taxi, as I was trying to find Alison. There was a little traffic, and I had to make another quick choice. I could push the driver to stick close to the other taxi, or I could stop to collect Alison. Not wanting to leave my partner behind, I asked the driver to pull over. Alison hadn't seen me get into my taxi, and was striding purposefully after the departing taxi, but then glanced around as we pulled into the curb. She walked up to the taxi without comment, as if she had been waiting for it all along, and soon we were racing after the mystery woman again.

There were now a few cars in between us, and I wondered if we would lose her. The taxi in front pulled through a very orange light and I held my breath for a second, but our driver pushed his way through the intersection and remained close behind. Our procession wound its way through the busy city and we eventually found ourselves in Paddington. As soon as we started to enter the back streets, I realised we were about to arrive. We had some flexibility with two agents in the cab, and I asked Alison to remain with the taxi when we stopped, so she could then be dropped off slightly ahead. I would jump out as soon as we eventually did stop, which would leave us with an agent either side of the arrival address. This technique would physically separate us so we would be less recognisable as 'the coffee couple' they noticed earlier, but would also provide a better opportunity to manage the job. If one of us had difficulty observing in our location, the other would likely have a better one.

The woman's taxi began slowing as it approached a modern apartment building, and I asked the driver of our cab to stop quickly. I jumped out and ran off while Alison remained in our cab, which then passed the other cab which had now stopped. Alison asked her driver to stop a short distance further, and we both watched expectantly, now either side of the mystery woman's taxi. Eventually the woman left and walked straight into the apartment building. BINGO, we had finally and successfully followed her to a home address. The mystery woman's vacant taxi turned around to go back into the city, so I flagged it down, as Alison approached me. I asked the driver to pause briefly outside the apartments so I could take a photograph, and then we drove back to the city. Although I tried to gently prompt the driver about his last fare, he said little more than he had picked her up from the Rocks. Had he been more forthcoming it would not have been the first time I got some good information from cab driver. Being naturally talkative, they are just as likely to sprout off something like their last fare was a girl who worked at Westpac bank and lived in Potts Point, or some other equally useful snippet, but this was not now the case. Tom rang and was equally pleased with the address we had obtained, and asked me to email the photos through. I would love to have seen the look on his face when he saw the photos. Although he initially thought I was not even around at the time, the photos proved I was not only there but virtually sitting at his own table!

Several days later, I was asked to run the job again. Tom was scheduled to meet the same woman again in a hotel for lunch, and expected they would finish around one thirty p.m. I visited the ATM to withdraw some spare cash. I was not quite sure how much I would need for the job, especially with taxis involved, and I know it is always good to have small notes for flexibility. I walked out to a taxi rank and surveyed the waiting drivers. The one at the start of the rank looked just a little timid, and I thought it best to let him run. A moment later he was off with a fare elsewhere, and this allowed the taxi queue to move up. I was happy with the look of the next driver in line, and hopped into his cab. As we drove, I sounded him out, first answering his standard question of what work I did with a non-standard answer, being that I was an investigator, and was going to follow a mystery woman at one thirty p.m. He took the bait, and expressed more and more interest in what I was doing. Gauging his response, I began to feel comfortable that he was the man for the job. By the time I had arrived back at the hotel, a plan had been agreed on that I would be his trainee driver, and that we would engineer her hailing *his* cab on leaving the restaurant.

The driver, Branco, seemed more and more excited at the plan, and he intently studied the ID photograph of the woman I showed him on my digital camera. He had parked his cab directly outside the hotel and was ready to take the mystery fare. Branco walked inside to go to the toilet, but I then saw him talking to the staff at the front desk. Right at this time I got a call from Tom that his meeting had finished, and that she was on her way down. I motioned madly to Branco who saw me, but Branco obviously didn't share my sense of urgency.

Over the years I have lost some great opportunities for want of just a few seconds. It is difficult to convey how crucial split second timing is in surveillance. Blink and you lose them, blink and you miss that great photo, blink and they run a red light, blink and... the mystery woman decides to take another cab. Nobody cares how many hours you have already been waiting, because the game always seems to hinge on how you handle what invariably happens in the blink of an eye. Another vacant cab pulled up behind us.

Branco began walking back to the cab, looking pleased with himself. I felt helpless as I watched him amble towards me, the mystery woman now following just a few steps behind him, out of the hotel door. I watched the scene in slow motion, powerless to do anything about it. I couldn't communicate with Branco as the woman would see and hear anything I said to him. I didn't want to draw any attention to my presence in the cab either, lest she decide to take the other one, thinking I was a passenger and that my cab was occupied. Branco walked up to my window and before he spoke I was able to whisper quietly '*Right behind you in the scarf*', just as the woman reached for the rear door of the cab. Branco turned around as the woman then saw me seated in the front seat.

'*Oh, sorry*' she said, and turned to get into the cab directly behind us.

Branco immediately recognised her, and called her back. '*It is my trainee driver. I'm showing him the city.*' he said, and I held my breath for a second, pleased to hear the door open behind me as she got into the cab. Branco hurried around to the driver's side and got in a little officiously, as he started his meter and drove away from the hotel.

'*Where you goin?*' he asked.

She replied '*Just to the city thanks, to Martin Place*'. Branco drove quickly through an orange light, then said to me '*Now, you have to watch the lights, you can't do that too much or else you have no licence left*'. I nodded in agreement. Branco then proceeded to give me some instruction on the city streets as a commentary. At first it was a flurry of comments and I began to worry he would continue the ruse for too long or appear forced, but then he cleverly switched his banter from instructing me, to finding out more about the mystery woman.

'*So where do you work?*' he asked.

'*In a bank*' she replied, rather vaguely. He pressed further, his conversation gently probing from a variety of angles. I thought she may clam up, but he was able to prise more and more information out of her. I was not convinced she was telling the absolute truth, but I could tell there was enough substance to verify she was telling enough of a truth for the information to be valuable. In fact there was little reason for her to lie. She was talking to a taxi driver, one in a million cruising the anonymous streets. She didn't know him and he didn't know her, and they would never see each other again. What she didn't know was that the trainee driver in the front seat was getting to know her far more than she could ever imagine.

The cab neared Martin Place, and she motioned for it to stop. Branco switched off the meter and she handed him a ten dollar note. She told him to keep the change, then got out of the cab and walked off into the anonymous crowd. I waited a moment, then smiled at Branco and said thank you, though I could see he was also thanking me, for brightening up his day with a real life mystery where he got to play a starring role. He knew he had done well, doing nothing more than his job, but with a real purpose in mind.

The woman moved briskly and I followed quite close behind, wary of losing her in the fast moving crowd. She walked with purpose up to a large bank building, opened the door with familiarity and disappeared inside. I looked around to see if Branco was still there for a knowing wink, but he was long gone in the bustling city traffic. I was pleased at the result, and mused over the events that had just transpired. An investigator has neither special powers nor many special gadgets as seen in the movies, and yet he has the whole world at his disposal. An observant mind and a clever, lateral thinking approach to problems goes a long way. *There is always more than one way to skin a cat.* My unique method of following her resulted in her paying for my own taxi fare, as well as being able to be a fly on the wall, listening to her talk about her life! I would bet the mystery woman would barely register I'd been her silent travelling companion for that journey. She had seen but not observed me, and had probably already forgotten I was a little part of her life. I was so close under her nose and yet she had not seen me hiding in plain view.

♦

CHAPTER 22: WORKING IN SHOPPING CENTRES

Shopping centres are great, with open air movement, crowds to hide among, and of course shops that stimulate activity as people browse, move, and interact with others. It's not easy following a shopper in a crowded centre, and one must maintain good concentration as people have a tendency to melt into the crowd.

For an injury case, you need to document the process of bending or reaching to collect goods, and the carrying of the shopping bags back to the car. Often it is wise to plan ahead and perhaps leave them shopping while you reposition the surveillance vehicle to better cover the actual loading process.

The aim of the job is to maximise the quality of the video evidence. It is often better to get ten seconds of close-up video of them loading their vehicle, than it is getting thirty minutes of them ambling around the store. Consider the focus of the job. What is the client's ultimate aim, and how can this best be achieved. A case of 'psychological distress' may have the person claiming they are not comfortable with crowds, in which case the aim is to get a lot of video exposure of them in the crowds, including arranging the backdrop to maximise the crowd visible on the screen. A lot of close-up shots in this case will not be useful, as it does not accurately show the evidence you need to provide.

Use windows and look through, don't watch them directly. Remember browsing shoppers often glance around so you may need to maintain your distance. It is easy to film people through windows while they are inside the shop, and depending upon the type of shop you may not want to venture inside with them. Find a line and stay close but don't cross it.

If it is an injury compensation case, one key issue to aim for is good documentation of the subject bending using their upper body as well as their lower back. It is also good to document the fact that they are self-sufficient and can perform normal domestic duties such as shopping.

The car park is an easy location to film. Be ready to stop and record the subject climbing out of their vehicle. THEN find a permanent parking space if you haven't already done so. Ideally, the parked location will be suitable to *observe* the subject's car, so you can remain on location safely in your vehicle while they load up their car with shopping. If your current position is not ideal, consider moving the surveillance vehicle later.

- Be FAST in following the subject into the shopping centre as they are often busy, crowded places and it is easy to lose contact.
- Follow the subject through the centre. Maintain close attention due to crowds, but try to keep some distance, especially if they are browsing and looking around.
- Utilise any seats, small tables or cafes as a location to prop and record footage. Place camera on a seat for example, and use the screen to frame the shot, rather than 'aggressively' or more noticeably using the eyepiece.
- If the subject appears to be in one place for a little while (in a queue or having just entered a large shop, OR you lose contact altogether), consider quickly returning to the surveillance vehicle and repositioning it to a better location near their own car.
- Be wary of security guards and cameras. Try to act naturally, relaxed and fit in discreetly with the environment. Consider purchasing a small item such as a drink. Get a shopping bag and carry it around with you. Browse shops yourself, instead of maintaining an aggressive steely-eyed 'stare' at the subject.

- Use window glass to monitor reflections thus facing away from the subject, which allows you to watch them far less obtrusively.
- Physically enter other shops and monitor the subject through your shop's windows.
- If you can easily see the subject inside a shop, consider filming them through the window into the shop. They are unlikely to see you, as their vision is largely focused inside the shop confines, which limits their awareness.

Trolley cam

When entering a supermarket, consider using 'TROLLEY CAM':

- Get a shopping trolley, preferably one with an advertising sign fixed to the front, which assists in concealing cameras.
- Place a few items inside the trolley, particularly a case of soft drink cans, cereal boxes or similar *flat* objects lying on their sides – near the front of the trolley.
- Place the video camera on the box, close to the front of the trolley. Preferably use a covert housing such as a fitted bag, or use covert camera that films through a pin-hole.
- Keep the lens close to the wire bars, and roughly *in between them,* else they may obscure the image.
- Fold out the screen so the image is easily seen.
- Pull back the zoom so it is on almost wide angle.
- If you cannot see or use the screen – ensure you manually set the focus to three metres or similar, otherwise you may find the auto-focus mechanism decides to focus only on the bars in front of the trolley, hence the subject will be out of focus.
- Start recording.

- Consider occasionally looking down at the screen to ensure the camera is operating correctly, and the shot is framed precisely.
- Consider using a small item to temporarily cover the small display screen – enabling you to easily check it discreetly without disturbing the camera, while concealing it when it is not being used.
- Consider using small items to assist in angling the camera correctly, using them to raise the front of the camera if required.
- Approach the subject, wheeling your trolley towards them.
- Progressively select small items from the shelves, placing them into the trolley to maintain your shopping cover.
- Don't make eye contact with them, but continually look at the shelves as if seeking items or comparing prices.
- As they move, move with them, keeping the camera pointed at them at all times.
- Monitor the camera regularly:
  o Is the focus still correct?
  o Is the shot still framed correctly?
  o Is the battery flat or have you run out of tape?
- If possible, leave the trolley and walk away from the subject slightly, reducing or limiting your personal exposure. The 'trolley-cam' can continue to record them without you. Continue moving the trolley when the subject has gone out of the shot.
- Perhaps the most important shot to get is the checkout shot. Be sure to be ready for this. On approaching the checkout, make sure you have a clear shot of them unloading all their goods from the trolley on to the counter.
- After they have finished loading all their goods at the checkout, do not wait for them to pay as this is your cue

to relocate. Wheel your trolley out of sight, and then walk out of the store. If stopped by staff or security, your excuse may be *'I forgot my wallet. I'm just going to get it from the car'*. Show them your bag if necessary.

- Once you have used 'trolley cam', do not attempt to continue following the subject to other shops, as you will probably have had too much exposure by then. Return to the surveillance vehicle and await the subject's return. Use the time to prepare the situation in order to get the best possible video evidence of them loading their shopping into the car.

- Consider terminating surveillance of the subject as soon as they have finished loading their car, then rush back to their home to arrive there just *before* they do. This will enable you to set up and be ready for their arrival, enabling a clear shot of them returning home, as well as unloading the shopping. If you actually follow them home, you may be identified by the subject (*'he was right behind me in the shops'*), you may lose the subject, you may miss some of the unloading action or you may be observed arriving at the location by the subject who is out of their vehicle, and possibly more aware of their surroundings. Being ready and waiting for their imminent arrival from the shops means you are not forced to jostle for a good parking position outside their house when you should be capturing the action of their arrival and unload. Good PI's always think about how to get the best result, while novice PI's often feel they must stick to their subject like glue. Giving your subject a little room to run is a very good idea, and allows you to both better prepare for future activity as well as get you out of their subconscious vision.

The case of bad table service

Key learning points

- Follow techniques

- Service of legal documents under difficult circumstances

I received a call from an associate at Pinkertons[65]. They had an urgent task, but all their usual surveillance operators were busy. The job sounded simple enough, to serve court documents on a guy called John. Of course nothing in this line of work is simple, and I soon discovered why they needed a specialist, as opposed to using a standard process server. The subject was a very difficult customer, who had a long history of violence and intimidation. He was very difficult to serve and I could see that the job wouldn't be easy. To add to the potential drama, the judge required the documents to be served within twenty four hours, as legal wrangling had held off the 'possible' allowable window to the last minute. If we couldn't serve him within twenty four hours, he was not required to attend the case which was due to be heard in a week's time. The clock was ticking.

He had previously been under surveillance for other issues, and we had his address. My instructions were to proceed directly to the lawyer to collect the documents, then go and serve him at the earliest opportunity. Not only were there documents to serve upon him but some video evidence as well, and if we did not serve these now, there would be insufficient time to admit them into evidence due to court peculiarities. I attended the lawyer's office and collected the material. While I was there, I was shown some surveillance video, and again advised that this was a slippery character who would not be impressed about being served, and had wriggled out of previous action based on denial

---

65 www.ci-pinkerton.com

of correct service issues. This was the kind of guy that would look you in the eye and state he was only the 'brother' of the guy you needed, or some other story which left you with nowhere to go.

Armed with the documents I proceeded out towards the site where Andrew was waiting. He was the PI currently watching the subject. He was an experienced agent, and I was comforted to hear the subject's car was still in the driveway, which meant he was home. This was half the battle won already.

I was reasonably close when I got another call, as Andrew quietly advised me 'Sorry mate, the job's gone mobile. He is in the blue Commodore heading south along...' and the chase was on. I wasn't quite close enough to be of support on the follow, but with updates from Andrew, I knew I was close behind. He had left with his family, which made him a little more vulnerable, though I knew not to take any chances. Andrew soon advised that the car was entering the Westfield shopping centre car park in Miranda, which made me relieved, knowing that we had him virtually cornered. In the small confines of the car park, he could not escape service easily, and if lost we could always sit on his car and await his return. The bounds of the car park meant we were both cornered in a sense, though at least we had the upper hand with the element of surprise. Cornering an angry wild animal isn't always healthy.

Tyres squealing, I raced around and around the narrow car park ramps, until I finally located his car, parked where Andrew had advised. I found a space close by and jumped out. I noted that I had ready visibility of his car from mine in case we had to wait him out, though I was hoping we could serve him inside among the crowds rather than in the dark car park. Glancing around I couldn't see him, so I briskly strode to his car and had a quick look inside for any information. All I saw was an envelope with his name on in sitting in the passenger footwell, which at least further confirmed his identity. I left the car and hurried inside.

Andrew had him well tagged, and I soon linked up with him inside the centre. He was a sitting duck there with his wife and children, ambling around the centre slowly window shopping. I could also see though, that he was street savvy and rough, with frequent backward glances to scan for predators. He was a coiled spring, and his face showed a lifetime of anger, almost out of place in the family environment, and barely registering his young daughter tugging on his jacket.

We used height to our advantage, following the group from a level above. A group moves slower, like any pack of animals, so in a sense they are easy prey, though that also means more pairs of eyes searching for danger. In this case however there was only one pair, as the others were occupied by the trappings of Western life, beaming from the brightly lit store windows. We stalked them slowly and carefully, biding our time while we waited for just the right moment to pounce. Often you cannot pick the time, and are forced to grab the precious seconds as someone darts in or out of a doorway. Today, the luck of the dice was on our side.

Our good fortune soon increased further when the group ambled into *Miss Maud's Coffee House*, and sat down for a meal. I bided my time for twenty minutes, waiting for the meal to finally be served, whereupon they would be most vulnerable. Timing just wasn't going to get any better, so it was the instant to pounce. Andrew moved into a better position upstairs, and covered the subject from some distance away. He started the camera rolling, ready to capture the event in case he tried to deny the service... or if there was some violence.

I moved forward with the documents, and while there were many people there, it certainly was not overly crowded. I knew anything could happen, and the fact that his family was there was no guarantee that he would stay tame. I decided it would be best to increase the number of witnesses I had available, just in case. I walked up to a young guy working behind the counter, and noted his name tag read David. *'Hi, look I was wondering if you could just watch me for a second'* I inquired politely.

David looked puzzled.

'I have some documents for that guy over there, and I am not sure he will be pleased, so I just wanted to have someone see what happens, just in case' I said nonchalantly, as if this was a fairly normal occurrence.

David seemed mildly concerned about my relaxed attitude, and focused more on my words, replying *'In case of WHAT?'* he said with a quizzical expression, not really sure if he should be wary of me, of what was to happen, or perhaps both.

'Well, I am not really sure to be honest, so I figure if you watch too, then we will both find out', I replied somewhat cryptically, and I walked off towards our guy.

I approached the table and held the package slightly over it. *'Hi, John?'* I asked, and he shot me a glance that suggested it was not worth my while having anything to do with him at all. I paused with material outstretched towards him, waiting for a response. I waited no more than two seconds, while his family stared on in disbelief. Getting no response I gently placed the material on the table, nestling it between the condiments and plates, though there wasn't quite enough room there to be comfortable.

With a half roar he swept his stocky arm across the table, collecting the paperwork, video tapes and some condiment bottles in his sudden motion. I instinctively took a step back and assessed the situation, as a bottle smashed and paperwork floated down. I was trying to work out if he was going to reach up and lunge at me. Fortunately he was hemmed in slightly under the table, so I would have had plenty of notice if this was his intention.

'Those documents are important court documents, and you've been now served. I suggest you read them through' I said, though it was hardly worth the effort. He knew the game was up. As I walked away, I heard his wife asking 'But John, how did they know we were here?', and I pondered this question to myself. It was because we had the experience, because we worked as a team, but mostly, due to the roll of the dice. Investigators can never guarantee success; it's just training and experience that helps you to increase the odds.

CHAPTER 23: WORKING THE ENVIRONMENT

Visibility of the subject is valuable and the surveillance professional is always trying to maximise it. There are many ways to achieve this, such as parking in a good location or finding a vantage point with a clear view. Another way to capitalise on observation time is to actively engage your environment. By approaching people under pretext, you can draw them out and observe their behaviour. You may call them on the phone with a pretext that results in them checking their letterbox, which increases your observation time. Sometimes the simple act of moving a garbage bin or placing a branch across their driveway will give you the valuable seconds you need.

For injury cases this can be classed as *agent provocateur*[66], where they perform actions solely as a result of your 'prompts'. This does require *proof* you have prompted them though which isn't always easy. It's often within the law to do something of this nature, or to 'be' the agent provocateur, however it can taint evidence. A court may discount video evidence of your subject changing their tyre if it's revealed you were the one who let it down. This is an age old PI ploy that is best left alone! It is better to not interact with them at all in order to get the best result in court. A PI could be regarded as an agent provocateur on a theft case if they overly encourage a person to steal something, or in an injury case where they encourage physical actions that may discount the injury claim.

However, these techniques are used by PI's to varying degrees. There are often times where such a prompt is perfectly legitimate. Take this example of identifying the subject. Identifying a subject is never easy, and getting 'good ID' is a

---

[66] Agent provocateur – see page *498*

staple part of any surveillance operation. It is a lot harder than you may imagine as people have this annoying habit of not standing still when you are trying to take their photograph! By managing the scenario you can improve the chances of success, stacking the dice in your favour. The simple act of closing a driveway gate that is normally always open may result in the driver being forced to get out of the car to open the gate, and provide an opportunity to identify or photograph the driver. Essentially, closing their gate has bought you some observation time.

As with all aspects of surveillance, it is a game of probability and chance, so while you can never guarantee a good result, you can always improve your chances, and this is best done by *thinking outside the box*. It would not be the first time that a surveillance professional has called a taxi or pizza to a difficult address in an attempt to lure out a resident. Each scenario is different and requires a different approach, and that challenge is a large part of the appeal for investigators: making the call, finding the key and coming home with a good result, despite the poor odds.

Increasing exposure time

What environmental factors can you change to improve a result? The following points have been used to slightly modify the subject's actions, and therefore increase the 'exposure' or observation time available to video them.

- Place an advertising brochure under a wiper blade, close to the centre of the windscreen. The subject will often lean over to retrieve the item. They may not discover it until they have actually entered the vehicle, thus requiring them to climb out, and then back in again, providing more opportunity to observe their injuries.
- Place a shopping trolley, milk crate or similar obstacle either next to the driver's door, or use it to partially

obstruct the front of the vehicle. This requires them to move the item, and perhaps even bend to pick it up first.

- Place larger denomination shiny coins or some other attractive or unusual item on the ground, clearly in view next to the driver's door. This may tempt the subject to pick up the coins from the ground. Place at least one coin slightly further away, requiring an emu like movement (*bend down, stand up, step slightly then bend down*), to retrieve the last coin. Don't place items too visibly else others may take them instead!

- Place coins *on* the car door sill or wedged in the crack, as they will tumble down when the door opens, making noise and eliciting a brisk response to catch the coins before they roll away.

- Place an empty aluminium can under the rear wheel, driver's side, wedged reasonably tightly under the tyre. On departing, the can will crunch noisily, which can result in the subject stopping the vehicle and getting out to investigate the noise, then climbing in again.

Early warning devices

An investigator may then park further away from the job, and listen rather than watch. This allows more covert or comfortable parking locations, while still maintaining effective observations.

Early warning devices enable investigators to stay further away from the address or even completely out of sight. This greatly reduces the chance of compromise, while increasing the possible positions in which the surveillance vehicle can be parked. If it's not required to have 'eyes on' an address, you can have 'ears on' an address or vehicle, and park your own car well out of sight, in the comfortable shade.

Notification is provided by audio of impending activity well before it is seen, for example an inner front door being opened before a security door is opened. This enables the camera to be up, focused and recording, well before the subject is actually sighted. It results in more video footage, as well as it being of better quality, instead of just a shaky video clip of the back of a persons head getting into a vehicle.

Early warning devices allow more relaxed attentiveness. Operators watch with their ears, not their eyes, which results in less fatigue, but greater attentiveness when actually required. Early warning devices enable greater productivity as the operator can type up reports or conduct other tasks without the need to continually watch. Sounds indicate activity, so the surveillance vehicle can remain out of sight until for example the sound of a lawn mower is heard, at which point it moves in close to capture the activity on video.

Driveway alarms

A wireless driveway alarm is a small device that is designed to be concealed in foliage or trees adjacent to a driveway, or other area through which vehicles or persons may move. These devices detect movement, and silently transmit a signal to a remote receiver. The transmitter is small and camouflaged, and requires very little power. Often these units will run off a nine volt battery for over a year, and some units will transmit more than half a kilometre away. Detection methods can be either metal mass, which detects only vehicle movement, or sensor beam. A sensor beam detector will alert on any movement, including animals and people as well as cars. The receiver will beep to alert any movement, and will also illuminate to show there has been movement detected if you check it later. Some units have multiple channels, so you can set detectors at several locations around a property and detect in which area the movement occurred.

Traditionally these devices are used by people to alert them of imminent arrival of guests, or to protect their property by quietly alerting that movement is occurring on their property. These devices can be placed near a subject's property to act as early warning.

For difficult rural surveillance and some apartment buildings where movement may occur in more than one location, these units can help a PI cover more than one location on his own. A PI may watch the front pedestrian exit of the apartment block, while using a driveway alarm to monitor the rear car park exit. If movement is detected at the rear, the PI can quickly move around to see who has exited the property via this exit which he cannot see from his current location. These units are available in Australia from some electronic shops, and have also been seen in Australia Post outlets. A few websites list these items. An example is www.drivewayalarm.com .

Gate and door alarm

These operate in a similar fashion, where a small transmitter will covertly alert the receiver if there is any movement detected. These transmitters are much smaller, and work off a tiny compass which detects movement by changes in magnetic fields. They can operate for years on a tiny battery, and are designed to be attached to doors and gates.

Where a PI is monitoring the gate on a rural property, or a rear door of a building, these devices are slightly better than a driveway alarm as they are smaller and cheaper, and provide more positive monitoring of movement. A driveway alarm may alert on movement of animals or refuse blowing in the wind, yet a gate alarm will not have such false alerts. One disadvantage is that these units often have a significantly reduced range, such as one hundred metres, requiring the receiver (and hence the PI) to be much closer to the job. These units are available in Australia, but are more common in the USA. One reference to these products is: www.drivewaymonitor.us .

Audio transmitters

Tiny audio transmitters are a very effective surveillance tool, particularly on more difficult operations, or where a subject is aware he is being watched. FM transmitters are available for around fifty dollars from many spy shops[67], and can transmit all day with a range of well over two hundred metres.

Put an audio transmitter near a vehicle for warning of imminent departure. Listen for the sound of the car alarm being deactivated, doors being opened or the engine being started. Early warning devices may also be left near a front door to provide a warning of when it's opened. Listen for the sound of keys in the lock. An 'obstructing' object, such as a box with two bottles inside placed near the door, may make noise on being moved which may also assist in detection. Early warning devices can be placed near garage doors, or near an internal unit door to identify *which* particular unit a person emerged from.

Unlike driveway alarms, FM transmitters are smaller, cheaper, and transmit sound from the sensing location. Driveway alarms will alert on movement, but will not be able to discern between a car moving off, and a person entering the car in the first place. An audio transmitter will 'hear' the sound of a car alarm well before any movement may actually occur. A disadvantage of audio transmitters is that they need more power to operate. Caution needs to be exercised when placing these items to ensure they do not transmit private conversations, as this is against the law. They must also be constantly monitored, where an alarm will remain quiet until there actually 'is' a movement occurrence, and can remain in the detected state with an indicator light. This is handy in case you leave a surveillance job momentarily for some reason (toilet etc).

---

[67] R Tech Electronics 103 Burwood Road CONCORD NSW 97456521
Also: National Spy shop chain: www.ozspy.com.au

The Law: Use of listening devices

These may be lawfully purchased and lawfully used in some areas, provided they don't contravene legislation such as the NSW Listening Devices Act 1984. A baby monitor is an example of a listening device. These items must not be used to record or transmit *private* conversations. This specifically includes the use of video cameras with microphones. There may be situations in some areas where a conversation in a busy café may be legally recorded or transmitted, because it is conducted in a public place where the persons could not reasonably assume their conversation was private. This situation is open to the discretion of the courts, which may then find you guilty of an offence, so it is best not to consider this behaviour. Similarly, the use of these devices placed near a car on a public street may be legal, provided it is used to listen to the sound of the engine (as early warning technique), and not to record any private conversations whatsoever. Some jurisdictions (such as NSW) actually allow *private* persons to apply for a warrant from the court to use a listening device, though this rarely occurs as the majority are issued to law enforcement bodies.

Listening or early warning devices should ONLY be used in non-private places, and never placed in a situation where they may record or hear private conversations. Don't consider they are always illegal as there are several environments where they can be a legitimate, valuable PI tool for movement detection. If in doubt, leave it out.

The case of the paparazzo PI

Key learning points

- Use of early warning devices and the law

- Surveillance industry ethics

Ben McDonald, an associate PI I have worked with for several years was recently 'caught up' in a bugging incident involving the actress Nicole Kidman. I had been doing less and less PI work, but still kept in touch with Ben from time to time. Like many PI's who were faced with a reduction in work due to the general industry changes, he had begun taking on some paparazzi work to supplement his core PI work. Being a paparazzo is similar in many respects to being a PI, and it is common for people to work in both industries from time to time. The paparazzo will stake out his quarry, follow and film them, and generally document their activities. Paparazzi usually try to remain undetected initially, at least to try and get some candid shots of their target, but at some stage their presence will usually become known. Rather than slink away, the 'paps' will stand their ground and continue photographing regardless. In some cases the annoyed response by the target is just the sort of emotion which will sell the photo – similar to the stock standard hand in the camera shot which makes for good current affairs television. While paps usually say they remain discreet and undetected, the reality is not always the case. There is the calling out of personal names or tooting the car horn to get people to turn around and show their face to the camera. A large network of contacts will provide information for a fee to the paps, so the target can never really get away from it all as the cameras 'magically' follow them wherever they go.

Ben is fairly good at his job and through tenacity will get his shot. He was the first to get pictures of Russell Crowe's baby which was achieved only after months of unpaid stakeouts at Woolloomooloo. Whenever I spoke to him he was always waiting for Russell or chasing Nicole, and I knew that neither were particularly fond of him. Russell had a good strategy though – he bought ten tracksuits of the same colour, and would wear this style day in and day out. This meant that the paps couldn't sell the photos as Russell would look stale in the same outfit each time, so Ben and his colleagues often gave up for awhile. There are always two sides to the story of course, and no doubt such personalities benefit from the paps as much as the reverse because publicity is important in their business. It is not unheard of to find some celebrities assisting in providing information about their whereabouts to raise their profile! Other times the 'candid' shots are just blatantly staged.

A similar spin-off occupation for PI's is to provide assistance to TV stations, for news and current affairs, or other shows. Ben often sells video to the stations as a freelance reporter, or investigates stories for them. He 'found' the alleged terrorist Habib recently after following his solicitor for almost two weeks, and subsequently got some photographs and video which were used by the media. I once worked a job for a week in Brisbane, following a young couple each day to document their lifestyle for a reality TV show – not as the primary vision, but to 'validate' them as contestants on a major show. People often lie to get into these shows - for example stating that they are gay to win the role of 'gay' contestant, or overstating their lifestyle to make it sound more interesting for the TV viewers. Reality TV is expensive and so it is worth the cost of hiring a PI to vet these contestants first, or even to obtain information about them which can later be 'revealed' on the show to elicit a reaction. The role of a PI can often be very interesting at times.

I have only ever done one paparazzi job, the subject being a Tasmanian called Mary Donaldson. This was prior to her leaving Australia, when she was still working for the Belle Property group. Several PIs and paparazzi would chase her around Sydney trying to get those elusive shots or information. We followed her for many days, everywhere she went. At the time she was sharing a flat with a few other girls in the Eastern Suburbs and looked to be the most ordinary girl you could imagine. It was hard to believe, but we knew that one day in a year or so we would wake up to find she was the Queen of Denmark – the very same girl who we had just followed home with her shopping, and the one who lived in a normal terrace house like so many other 'normal' people. In actuality, she was never 'normal'.

She was driving a new four wheel drive and had some serious attitude. There was no question of trying to be discreet as she was well aware that we were there, and knew most of us by face already. I could see many people would find it so intrusive or offensive to have such round the clock interest, but Mary never showed the slightest hint of concern. In fact she seemed to treat it almost as a game, and would unashamedly tear off at high speed, leaving us in the media pack scrambling to follow – and she would often make sudden turns to try and throw us off her tail. There were times where I thought back to the circumstances of Princess Diana's death in the car crash – not so much if we may cause Mary to crash but rather that she may cause one of us to crash!

We once followed her to the trendy 'Veranda Bar' in the city. About four cars were on the tail as she left home, and I was the only one who was left at the end! As it was she executed a snappy U-turn on Elizabeth Street in the middle of the CBD at about six p.m. on a weekday. Negotiating the six lanes of peak hour traffic was no mean feat, and I was certain she had waited just long enough for the relatively small gap to close up directly after her so I couldn't follow her. With four cars on the job we soon found her again shortly afterwards in the bar, but I have to hand it to her, she was clearly a spirited match for her active fiancé Prince Frederik.

Seeing Ben's name splashed over the world's media, I had to laugh. I remember talking with him about bugs several years ago. Of course he had no knowledge of the bug placed outside Nicole Kidman's house – so he says – and a PI would never lie. Ben's associates had quite some fun chasing him after that incident, trying to 'pap' one of their own! In this case the bug was placed (by the unknown offender) close to a location where the private conversations of Nicole Kidman's security staff would be likely to be captured. This would clearly contravene the NSW Listening Devices Act. A tree located on the road outside a 'standard' residential driveway would, depending on the circumstances, probably be an acceptable location for an early warning bug to detect the imminent movement of people or vehicles, provided it was not likely to record 'private' conversations. As always however, it must be used carefully, because there is always the risk it MAY record or transmit a conversation, and a judge may later regard that conversation as private. If in doubt, leave it out!

I recognise Ben's skills in this area, and his right to work as a paparazzi photographer, but I've decided that despite the huge money involved, it's not for me. The stars may use paparazzi at times for their own promotion, but on the whole, I think it is rather intrusive. It is one thing to investigate or follow people for breaking the law, but it is another thing to investigate or follow them for the titillation of the media. Several years ago I was doing some casual modelling and TV 'extra' work, and managed to land a role as a stand-in on the movie *Mission Impossible*. I never actually spoke to Tom Cruise, but I did rehearse with him for nearly an hour as he ripped his latex face off inside the mock plane at Fox studios. Nicole Kidman and her children came to visit the set that day and although their own relationship was strained at that time, I got to see first hand how much they both loved their kids. Seeing them close up happily playing with their children really hit home the fact they were very normal people. It's all too easy to think of the stars as the untouchables – so far removed from reality that their very being is just movie folklore and special effects. I could see that such intense and unrelenting scrutiny of every aspect of their lives would be horribly draining on anyone, and the 'stars' are no exception.

CHAPTER 24: INFIDELITY SURVEILLANCE

Sex sells. Infidelity inquiries into cheating partners certainly make for good reading, though it is certainly not the largest area in the industry, which is made up of (more boring, and) predominantly insurance and corporate investigations. There are some PI's who specialise in these domestic inquiries which used to be better known once as *marital* investigations, but we live in changing times and the word 'domestic' now encompasses de-facto relationships and same sex relationships. There are no significant differences in the actual *method* of surveillance for these cases, as the skills used in watching and filming people are effectively the same. Domestic investigations are messy and personal. Clients are often irrational and difficult to deal with. They may not be happy to pay your account if you prove their suspicions, because they often feel they have been 'wronged' by their partner, and now you have the hide to charge them money to find this out? Of course you are running a business, but how could you be so cold? Perhaps in light of their unfortunate personal situation, you could waive or reduce their fee? After all, you didn't really do much work, just hung around in your car and took a few photos!

Cheating lover – indicators

The aim of infidelity surveillance is to highlight instances of intimacy. A good example would be to get photographs of the errant partner having sex with their secret lover, yet this is rarely possible. Fortunately there are a lot of other subtle clues to show that intimacy is present. No one single item proves an affair, but, as a rough guide, the following clues are some of the main ones to look for when considering if a partner is unfaithful. The more clues matching, the stronger the suspicion should be. These points are often best answered by the client themselves, so this section can be used as a guide when discussing a case with them. Sometimes mention of even obscure points may spark some recognition that was not previously there, and the client may then be able to provide new angles to assist your management of the case.

Sexuality

- Subject exhibits new sexual behaviour, including a decreased desire for sex, but perhaps also demonstrating new 'tricks' learned during encounters with others. Occasionally exhibits a greater desire for sex due to being 'awakened' or revitalised by their secret lover.

- Subject is physically unable to maintain an erection after a suspicious period of absence from their lover, as their sexual organs are exhausted from illicit activity.

- Subject has a suspiciously *reduced* amount of ejaculate fluid compared to other times they are with their partner, suggesting they have recently provided their fluid to a third party and have not yet recovered their normal volume.

- Subject has sexual fluid discharge present in their underwear. This applies to men and women, suggesting some sexual excitement occurred during the day, either real or imagined. Not always clear proof of infidelity, but a strong sign if unexpected.

- Subject's genital area smells of sexual activity that is not always present during masturbation – possibly from excretions of an illicit partner.

- Clothing or hairstyle is ruffled on leaving an address

- Sitting close or invading personal space of a suspected lover

- Gesturing in a flirting manner when talking, even on the phone. Women may curl their hair around fingers or flick it back, exposing their neck. Men may arch their shoulders slightly to increase their height and perceived prowess.

- Smell of perfume on clothing, lipstick stains on collar, love bites, freshly brushed teeth

Behaviour

- Subject is highly defensive if asked questions about where they are going, who they are talking to. Subject engenders an atmosphere of *'Don't hassle me'* and gets angry if asked.

- Subject provides more information to partner about movements than necessary or normal, or phones his partner to check where they are: *'Still at work honey? When do you think you will be back?'*

- Renewed interest in their general appearance and personal hygiene. New clothes, new aftershave or perfume, new exercise regime.

- General loss of intimacy and privacy in all areas. Does not discuss their work in detail, locks their car or a drawer in their office, does not readily allow their car to be used by their partner.

- Does not involve partner with work functions or associate with other friends.

- Subject immediately showers on returning home, or has just done so because they were *'at the gym'* again (or perhaps not...).

- Subject very occasionally does their own washing (especially underwear), but particularly following a suspicious absence from their partner. Clothing often retains odour or other evidence of intimate associations, including perfume and make-up.

Telephone

- Subject is very guarded about their telephone, including purchasing pre-paid accounts, re-directing the address or otherwise concealing their phone bills.

- Subject favours their mobile phone to initiate suspicious calls, when the land line may be cheaper. Land line calls can be more easily traced, recorded, and billed.

- Subject does not conduct telephone calls openly, and will often move away from their partner to answer or make a call. Subject may receive a text message and will then move away to make an illicit call.

- Subject is cautious of their mobile phone, which will often be PIN locked, or will routinely delete the call log and text messages.

- Subject is unable to be readily contacted during suspicious time periods, due to excuses such as that they: *'turned their phone off'*, *'ran out of battery'*, *'left the phone in the car'*, *'diverted all their phone lines to voicemail so they could 'finish' their important work uninterrupted'* and so on. Subject may prefer text messages as this enables them to respond in their own time, rather than be 'ambushed' by a voice call and perhaps be forced to make explanations to both their partner and their lover.

Movements

- Subject spends just around an hour at an address then leaves (quite suspicious).

- Subject spends a long time at an address, including overnight. If the subject meets for around an hour, it is even more suspicious as this allows for a quick liaison and a quick shower, and is a common duration for many cheating partners who meet during the day.

- Subject's vehicle parked outside suspect address overnight. There's no need to actually see them entering or leaving the address, as their car tells the story.

- Subject has unexplained appointments or leaves early or works late frequently.

Other

- Subject works freelance or in an occupation that allows them a lot of freedom while on the road such as a salesman, real estate agent or tradesman.

- Subject is private about their computer or internet activities, such as locking email accounts with passwords and not providing them to their partner. Subject situates their computer in a manner that obscures the screen from view, so activities can't be readily observed on the screen. Subject switches screens quickly when their partner approaches.

Focus points

- Focus on the best times for mischief to occur, such as evenings and weekends, or lunch times for the office worker who may have a very flirty lunch with a colleague. Often the client will specify the likely period of activity.

- Focus on the kiss. The actual moment of meeting or departure for any illicit couple is crucial to cover. Usually intimacy is exhibited at these times, such as a kiss in the car before a passenger exits, or a kiss at the door when leaving an address. Often it is necessary to keep a video recording on a loop tape to capture this, or at the very least start recording as you see their car arriving at a potential drop-off point. Capturing a kiss on film is difficult as it is often such a sudden movement that lasts for a brief moment in time. If you wait to be prompted and start looking for your camera when they start to kiss, you will never get results because you will miss the moment every time. It's not hard to observe a kiss through the rear window of a car, as the outlines of the two heads come together. Is the kiss on the lips or the cheek? How long do their lips lock together? A half-second may indicate 'just friends', but a full-second may indicate lovers, and if you don't get it on tape, you won't be able to analyse it later.

- Focus on clothing and hair prior to any suspected activity and again following any meetings. Look for shirts untucked, collars ruffled, ties askew, buttons done or undone, hair tousled or wet from a recent shower. These provide strong intimacy clues, yet are often overlooked unless you zoom in and actively capture this minor detail on tape.

- Focus on facial expressions. Domestic clients want to know exactly how much fun they are having with their lunch date. Are they unusually happy? Flirty? Is there a smudge of lipstick on his face? Is there a love bite? Zoom as far as your camera optics allow, to capture these tell-tale clues.

Working with domestic clients

A domestic client is on the inside. They have ongoing and intimate knowledge of the subject, and access to information and personal areas used by the subject such as their house or car. Some consider a client's role as solely someone who will pay a bill and provide a name, address, and possibly a photograph. Other PI's will delve deeply and look for angles. They will pump the client for information which may not have initially been considered important or useful. They'll devise a scenario based on a full understanding of the case, and will consider using the client as part of the case rather than a person paying bills. Domestic clients are not always rational and must be managed carefully, but they can be encouraged to suggest something to their partner, such as an outing or activity.

For example they may be prompted to say or do something such as *'I am going to my mother's house this Friday night. Would you like to come with me or stay home?'* Assuming the subject chooses not to visit his mother-in-law, it will directly provide him with an opportunity to get up to mischief on this evening. This enables far better targeting of suspicious behaviour, where the evening can be covered by effective surveillance. If the subject is not provided an opportunity, the PI must guess when the opportunity will be taken by the subject. This means it is a less known factor, and may require several evenings of surveillance for anything of interest to occur.

One of the biggest problems in domestic investigation is the unknown nature of the timing of any illicit liaisons. This in itself can quickly sap the limited financial resources of personal clients. There are only so many periods of surveillance that can be afforded, so it is always best to encourage this activity to occur within specific, managed periods. This is unlike insurance surveillance, where you may film a person running across the road (and hence void their claim) with this type of activity occurring at any time. An illicit sexual encounter usually requires two parties, and occurs less frequently than the more mundane activities in life.... like crossing a road. There are many examples of using the client to assist in the investigation, and providing designated opportunities for mischief to occur is only one of many.

350

Domestic client assistance

- Use the client to provide time-specific opportunities for mischief, such as suggesting to their partner that they go somewhere or leave early. Provide ample notice to the subject to enable their better planning of illicit activity, and in order for the PI to cover it well.

- Get access to the subject's vehicle to place tracking devices.

- Get frequent readings of the subject's vehicle odometer. This provides information about the general distance travelled. If a worker travels to work and back each day and this is a round trip of ten kilometres, it would be unusual to see the odometer recording an extra eight kilometres on some days. This is especially true when there has been a suspicious absence or lack of phone contact on a particular day. It may suggest that the subject travels out of the regular route on these days, an additional eight kilometre round trip. If the subject denies any 'extra' travel on these days, their odometer will dispute these claims, and can assist in narrowing down the possible locations of their lover. For example it would not be the home of his ex-girlfriend, if she lives more than a ten kilometre round trip away from his regular route.

- Get access to personal areas to search for information that may be useful for the investigation. This could be either directly associated with the case - such as an unusual phone number on a pad, or indirectly which can be used in later pretexts. Obtaining personal information about the client in any area can provide a good opportunity to approach them on pretext. You may then be able to ring them saying *'This is a follow up call about your vehicles recent transmission repair, is everything working well now? We are just following up on our job management... do you do any long drives or short trips only?'* and so the personal rapport can be cultivated, and the conversation can be steered, according to what information you are trying to obtain.

- Get access to the subject's bedroom, to mount covert recording cameras to record illicit activity that may occur.

- Get access to the home telephone line to attach monitoring equipment such as dial recorders or listening devices (if legal in your area).

- Get access to the subject's computer. Copy the hard drive. Install key logging and remote file management tools.

- Get access to the subject's mobile phone and copy the address book entries, check the text message folders and the recent call lists.

- Get authorisation from the client or encourage them to make changes to their personal phone accounts, such as requesting full local call listing on their home phone bill, so any outgoing local calls can be analysed.

- Get copies of any information about the subject, such as credit card receipts, call records, bank statements, emails etc. Look for contacts, and look for common or unusual locations. Look for activity that occurs during any suspicious periods of absence.

- Get information of the subject's proposed movements from either verbal updates or calendar appointments.

- Check the clothing and materials being taken by the subject on his/her outings.

Suspected sex occurring

If a subject has gone inside an address where you suspect mischief may be occurring, consider if any of the following points are appropriate:

- Walk around the property to see if you can see through the windows if sex or other intimacy is occurring. Often the blinds will be drawn, obscuring the view to the casual observer, however there may be a crack through which a determined PI can see something. It only takes a tiny crack of visibility through the curtains to enable a very good look at the scene. It wouldn't be the first time I've stood for some time on tip-toe next to a bedroom window, straining to hold my video camera high up above the curtain rail with a full view of the activity. You may look like a peeping sex creep, but you will get the evidence this way, as opposed to remaining safely in your car. It is not common for illicit lovers to have wild sex on their front lawn for the benefit of your cameras, so you may need to push some personal space boundaries to get the shot. This is of course partly why a lot of PI's (myself included) do not often take on messy domestic investigations. Even if you do not see anyone working up a sweat, you may see something like a lone shoe lying on the lounge room floor which can easily tell the whole story for you.

- Hear sex. Listen for the sounds of activity. This could be animal grunting and groaning, but could also be an absence of sound which would be normally expected in that environment. You may expect to hear two people chatting normally and only hear silence, which may be suggestive of quiet intimacy.

- Consider ringing the subject on pretext, around the time you feel they may be most intimate. Listen for breathless voices and other background noise, or the fact that they have suddenly switched their mobile off which is just as good a clue.

- If appropriate, slap their car with your palm if possible which will cause any car alarm to start sounding. This may bring them to the porch in a state of undress, or at least bring them to a window to peer out. You can then further assess what is occurring based on the actions that occur, or even which window they appear or how they respond.

- Check the water meter, an easy task at night or in an apartment building. Note the reading and monitor this periodically to detect occupants showering or bathing. Should you detect a significant water usage some time after the subject has entered the address, it may be suggestive of post-coital cleansing. Illicit sexual activity brings a higher need for bathing in order to remove odour evidence, and also as a form of psychological cleansing after the event. It's easier to lie to your partner when you are squeaky clean, but a little harder when you still reek of your last sweaty encounter. When water usage such as this is detected during the middle of the day when showering or bathing is less normal, it may show that there is some reason for needing it. It is also of interest to measure the length of the water use. Is it a short shower (just to clean off the sweat)? Or does it appear to be two separate showers versus one potential 'together' shower which could be of a longer duration. It's not foolproof using water consumption patterns to deduce what may be occurring inside premises, but considering the available options, it's a good clue.

- Switch off the water at the mains. While this technique may arouse some suspicion (unless you are able to turn the water back on without detection later), this will prevent the occupants showering after their sweaty encounters. Cheating lovers will be forced to return home unwashed, carrying the distinctive odour of sexual activity. Alternatively they may be forced to check the water meter in a state of undress or sporting a flushed face and ruffled hair.

- Knock on the front door under a pretext. This is intrusive and does show your face, but can be an excellent method of detecting activity within. No answer to the door knock would be highly suspicious, as would it be if they angrily answered the door in a bathrobe, with mid-coital sweat on their brow and glowing rosy cheeks. While personal interaction may be appropriate to get up close and to see this detail, it could also be best to encourage a third party to do the door knock for you, so they do not see your own face directly. Call a cab to their address which may arrive shortly and honk, or then knock on the door to let the 'passengers' know their cab is here. (Perhaps there was a mistake with the supplied address!) Watch the exchange closely. Does anyone appear at the door? What is their clothing and general demeanour?

- Advise the client to sexually approach the subject immediately on their return home from any suspicious absences. Are they interested in sex? Do they smell of sex or a recent shower?

Managing domestic clients

Unlike all other commercial investigations, infidelity is intensely personal and causes a lot of difficulties in client management. The PI often becomes part investigator, part counsellor as the client speaks out in a very direct manner about their very personal sexual issues and other intimacy problems in their

355

relationships. Often these clients are unable to talk to others due to the nature of the problem, and it is difficult steering them away from discussions about how much of a bastard their husband is, or whether her lover really is still having sex with his wife and will he ever leave her? Love and logic are very different, and emotional clients with personal issues need careful management.

- Charge a retainer up-front, and ensure you are extremely careful in doing any work that has not already been paid for. Clients may refuse to make payments if they are unhappy with the lack of evidence, such as in a nil result or if they are unhappy with the evidence when it shows that their suspicions were right and their partner has been cheating on them. There is also the issue of their 'partner' possibly discovering the payment in the joint account withdrawal, and the excuses and delays that follow. Clients may suddenly realise they can't pay your reasonable fee without alerting suspicion in their partner, or perhaps they may say they have not got full control of the account and could you perhaps wait till after the divorce has gone through? No!

- Be very factual in dealing with them, as they will often become emotional. Ensure that you maintain the relationship on a business level rather than becoming a personal associate.

- Provide clear timeframe guidelines in your discussions with them, as domestic clients will usually be happy to talk about their problems for hours, wasting your valuable time. Clients rarely feel they should have to pay for your 'telephone' consultation, yet it can take a significant amount of time.

- Ensure their expectations of your surveillance are realistic. Many clients hope you will get a clearly identifiable photograph of their partner actually having sex with their secret lover - a 'copulation' photo, which proves their suspicions beyond doubt. If this is not possible, they would at least hope for some compromising photos of them kissing passionately, or some other illicit physical intimacy. The reality is that these images are not easily obtained, and often the only 'evidence' is more subtle, such as visits to an address or clothing or hair ruffled after a person has been inside an address for some time.

- Clients may get back with their partner, despite the evidence. People do not want to accept that they have been cheated on, and will often try hard to mentally readjust the facts before them. A bunch of flowers and a heartfelt apology will often get an errant partner off the hook, as love and logic are very different! Be careful not to make negative comments about their partner who they may well take back. The couple could end up together causing you grief together – the insensitive PI who made those nasty remarks, or was harassing them, and who really didn't prove the infidelity effectively anyway.

- Clients act irrationally and it's common for them to tell their partner they're being followed by a PI. This is used as a psychological weapon, or because they can't help but blurt it out in heated discussion. This is not at all helpful, and makes life difficult. Be sure to ask them not to tell their partner that they have hired you, despite it being obvious.

- Unlike during commercial surveillance operations, you have someone on the 'inside' who can assist you far more than you may initially consider. Use them wisely to provide access to homes and bedrooms for mounting cameras, access to their vehicles for installing tracking systems and for subtly influencing the actions of the suspect partner to assist the investigation. See the section Domestic client assistance on page 351

The case of religious divorce

Key learning points

- Client management

- Vehicle tracking as a surveillance tool

- Covert inspection of premises to determine nature of business

- Work ethics and cultural issues

There was a woman on the phone. Gazala asked about the services I was offering, and I met with her in her home later that day to discuss her issues. She was married to a man who was being very unfaithful. He was a registered medical practitioner, who seemed to have a sexual addiction. His profession made it easy to obtain certain drugs to assist his sexual performance and Gazala had once found him carrying both Viagra, as well as needles with an erection stimulant known as Caverject. Gazala had long suspected him, and several years ago she had hired another PI company to make some inquiries. Gazala had advised them that she suspected her husband was having sex with some of his patients during consultations in his surgery. The company suggested to her that they install covert cameras in the roof of his rooms, in order to see exactly what was going on. Gazala had keys and access to her husband's office, so she was able to organise the camera installation fairly easily. The cameras ran for several days before they reviewed the footage, which was startling.

Gazala's husband Malik was clearly seen in his surgery office, very intimately and gratuitously fondling one patient, and actually having full sexual intercourse with two others on separate occasions. It was even more unusual to see that the last two patients did not appear to be examined in any professional way at all, but rather seemed to enter the surgery knowing what was to take place. This suggested a regular, scheduled liaison. The camera was recording for slightly less than a full week, but evidence was discovered of sexual acts between him and three of his patients. Gazala and the PI agency decided to continue running the camera recording for a longer period, and at the end of a month they had identified and filmed a total of six separate patients where specific sexual activity had actually occurred. In another two cases he was seen to approach patients who appeared to rebuff his advances. In one case he was seen to give the patient a small envelope following the encounter, and in another a small gift, though the other encounters seemed purely consensual. In one case the patient walked into the surgery, performed a sexual act on him and walked out again without any gift exchange or even a single word being spoken.

Gazala continued to talk with me about her lifestyle and culture, which seemed quite removed from my own Australian experience, but I was fascinated as she continued explaining her situation. Her husband's behaviour was not only inappropriate for a married man, but was also against the law for his occupation. The evidence of his activity came as a huge blow to Gazala, and though she long suspected his behaviour, she became very depressed. She had been with him for many years already, and they had several children together. Malik was the breadwinner, and Gazala was unable to earn her own money as she was flat out raising their children and managing their palatial home.

Their strict orthodox culture defined the man as head of the household, with the woman subservient to him. This culture has some benefits to their society, though in cases where the man is doing wrong towards his wife, the culture can be oppressive. Gazala was unable to talk badly about her husband to others. Without clear proof she was unable to take any action, including divorce. Even hiring a PI to investigate her husband's behaviour would be seen by many in her culture as wrong, despite the strong suspicions. She was even required to tell him where she spent the household money, as he would 'authorise' the payments, and this of course meant financial difficulties in paying the investigators accounts. Gazala was a virtual prisoner in her relationship, stifled from speaking out and kept as a slave, cooking, cleaning and producing offspring.

She could not easily take money from him, nor could she leave him. Without proof of his behaviour she was powerless to act, yet obtaining the proof was already difficult. The danger she faced in doing the wrong thing was social annihilation. She would be ostracized and shunned by everyone including friends and her own family. She would be unable to shop, attend worship or do anything without incurring wrath and comment and the dirty looks and sideways glances of others. She would suddenly be very alone, as if she had moved to a totally new country and although she knew the language, she would be forever spurned. For someone as immersed in their culture as Gazala, this would be incredibly difficult, and she would have few options, given that she was not working and had several children to consider.

Gazala had given me much to ponder as she walked off into her kitchen, to make a fresh pot of coffee. There was just so much to learn, such a different way of life and I was struggling to comprehend the difficulty she must be facing. She returned a few moments later with a plate of unusual sweet pastry delights and another steaming coffee. I had declined the offer of cake, but she brought some anyway in a manner that suggested she was comfortable serving others. Although she wore a head scarf and was very modestly attired, I could see that she was very beautiful, with long, dark eyelashes, smooth chocolate eyes and a voice to match. She must have been nearing fifty, but sported an attractive figure. In every respect she was the perfectly polite, demure woman. Since Malik was married to her, it puzzled me that he had cheated on her and I wondered what had driven him to it.

We had briefly discussed her husband's sexuality and the relationship she shared with her husband, as this can sometimes provide valuable clues. I was expecting to hear they were no longer intimate, but Gazala uncomfortably advised that they were, in spite of her strong suspicions. I wondered for a moment why she didn't stop it, until I realised her culture did not permit her this luxury. She was married to her husband and was required to submit to his advances at any time, as this was her lifestyle.

Gazala began explaining about her husband's sexual interests. She had caught him out a long time ago with another woman, though he denied it and she lacked adequate proof. This woman was an Asian girl who Gazala said wasn't particularly attractive. Then there was the issue of the surgery escapade which occurred several years ago, involving several women, predominately Asian, and mostly not particularly well off. Gazala's current suspicion was that he was attending brothels on a regular basis. It was clear that he had an interest in Asian women, but he seemed to prefer the less attractive ones, which came as a surprise to me. Why on earth would he choose unattractive girls when he was wealthy and himself reasonably attractive?

Gazala looked me right in the eye and explained further. Malik liked the power he commanded over women. He revelled in it and the poorer a woman was, or the less attractive, the more power he held over her. It was a drug to him which he enjoyed as much if not more than the physical sensations themselves. 'He can afford the good girls, he could have a white girl so easily because he has a lot of money, and yet he only wants the cheap girls' she said with resigned indifference. I could see she had been living with this problem for years already. 'I mean he does need sex a lot more than normal though, because I even catch him playing in the bathroom sometimes. It is not as if he doesn't get everything from me, but I know what he really likes, it is to own the woman, to make her feel small and he will always belittle her or tell her she is worthless. It's a power trip he is on, and he always seems to need it. I think he is very sick, but what can I do?' she said. 'I think that part of the problem is I don't let him push my mind anymore at home, I mean I don't stop him being with me, but I know how he tries to take the power and I have grown so tired of it that he knows the power game doesn't work on me anymore. I still need to do the right thing by him, but I think he knows I am stronger inside. I don't let it affect me, so he can't bring me down like he used to. This is perhaps part of the reason he goes to other women' she added.

'He sounds like a right creep. But how do you know he is up to mischief now? I mean what signs are there?' I inquired.

'He always prepares. I know he will prepare for each time he will spend with a woman. He acts differently and I see him on his phone. Then the night before he will have tablets and be getting his needle ready. I think he already takes so much and it doesn't work so well, and he needs a lot of help, but that doesn't stop him. So when I see his things I know he is going to do it. He used to keep them at his surgery, but after I caught him out, he doesn't keep anything or do anything there anymore. He hides them here, but of course I can find them. He doesn't even hide them so well, and I wonder if he even cares. It is like he wants to show his power over me, because there is nothing I can do about it, so he needs to rub my face in it I suppose...' her voice trailed off as she looked out of the window. I was trying to read her eyes, but she refused to meet my gaze.

We sat in silence as I pondered the unfortunate situation. When I felt she had composed herself, I continued 'So why can't you just leave him, I mean I guess the video in his surgery was enough proof wasn't it? I mean how can he get out of that? You can't argue with video proof surely?' Gazala looked at me kindly, in a way that implied I still didn't understand the complex nuances of her culture. 'Yes, yes it is true what you said. I did get the proof, but then I got more trouble because I doubted my husband. You don't understand that in my culture we must respect our husband no matter what, so I did a very bad thing by trying to catch him out... (she paused for a moment)... but I did catch him out, badly, so he had to confess to our Mufti for his sins, and I had to apologise for... for catching him out' I began to see what had happened, and the realisation was incredible.

'So, when he confessed he was forgiven?' I asked.

'Yes' she replied.

'But couldn't you just leave him? I mean after what he did to you? Surely you could just divorce him, I mean it was more than just one woman, he was cheating on you with half a dozen!' I replied indignantly.

'You see Chris, even me meeting you now is dangerous for me. If they know I am seeing another investigator it will be very bad for me, very bad. But I have to do something. I can't cope and I have my children and my health to think about. I mean you know he doesn't always use condoms you know, I mean most times in the surgery there were no condoms and then he comes to me and I am unable to say no to him. I am nearly going out of my mind, but here's the thing... I can't divorce him, because I am the woman. He is the only one that can divorce me, and I know he will never do it because he wants the power. I know there is a legal divorce that I can probably get with much trouble, but that means nothing in my culture. I can't escape him unless I get a religious divorce.' she said.

I hadn't heard of the concept of a religious divorce before, so I asked what it was. Gazala continued 'Well, I can only get a religious divorce if the Mufti grants me permission, and that is a very hard thing to do. Of course I caught him badly, but when he confessed, the leader forgave him. That is how it is. The man is always right, even when his is wrong. I have pleaded to my leader for permission, but Malik always tells him how much he wants to keep his family together, and that I am imagining things. My Mufti told me he would grant the divorce but only if I get proof. I mean another proof, because the first time I caught him doesn't matter anymore once he is forgiven. So I need you to help me. I need your help to get my religious divorce, and if I can't get that I don't know how I can go on living because it is so hard to cope.'

Her smooth voice didn't waver, and her eyes were fixed on mine, though I could sense the pain in her voice, the pain of not weeks and months, but of years and decades. The pain of oppression and the pain of injustice. I hoped I could help her escape her life of torture.

I received a photo of Malik, and took down details of his car, his surgery address and other information. Malik was now far more cautious - rarely left his keys lying around, had taken to buying pre-pay mobile phone accounts and hardly ever gave Gazala information about where he was going. Gazala had the presence of mind to keep a set of keys that Malik had lost one day for the car, so she did have access to his car, though it was rarely far from him and he was a light sleeper. We agreed it would be difficult to install a tracking device in his car for these reasons, unless an opportunity presented itself. Gazala said she'd give me a call when she knew her husband was preparing the night before to meet a woman, and I'd follow him the next day.

Several days passed, and then I got a call from Gazala one evening. 'Chris, I think he is going to see someone tomorrow. Could you see what he does?' I agreed, and the following morning I was waiting near the house for Malik to leave for the day. About an hour or two later, Malik emerged from the basement car park of their luxurious apartment building where they occupied the penthouse. I followed his shiny Land Cruiser off down the road for day one of the job. Malik took some of the children to school, and then took the others to another school. He visited his solicitor, before finally having lunch in a Turkish restaurant with several bearded males who seemed to be his associates. He seemed in no particular rush to get back, and did not seem quite ready for mischief, though of course it was impossible to tell. I rang Gazala and told her the unfortunate news. Gazala was not concerned and said that he would possibly go the following day, and for me to finish for the day.

Later that evening Gazala rang to say Malik still had his equipment with him, so she was sure he didn't go anywhere that day, but was now even more likely to go the following day. The next morning I was again waiting for Malik to leave. Thinking about the story, it was all so crazy I was wondering if it was really true. While infidelity suspicions were often true, I'd had several cases in the past that turned out to be over-zealous wives reading too much into their husband's behaviour, or that suspicious activity was in fact not infidelity but something else entirely such as a secret gambling addiction. Still, only time would tell.

The Land Cruiser pulled out of the apartment building and I began the follow. First stop to drop off the children, and then he drove to Croydon where he parked the car and walked off down the main street. I followed behind him, pleased to see he was not particularly attentive, making it was an easy job. I watched as he swung into a doorway, next to a café. As I walked past I saw a set of stairs leading up to the next level. It was the middle of the shopping district and I was curious to know what it was, but there was no signage out the front. As I watched, a male left the same doorway, and several minutes another male left and another entered. Judging by the type of men I was observing, my suspicions grew about the nature of this address. Each one of these men looked just a little creepy. Malik looked quite well dressed compared to this crowd and I pondered Gazala's comments about Malik's sexual preferences. Perhaps this was a really low budget brothel, though it was difficult to tell for certain.

Seeing the windows above covered by screens and heavy curtains, my suspicions deepened, so I returned for my car and parked it directly opposite the doorway. I set up a video camera to record permanently, so that I would record him exiting the doorway. Without a continuous recording I would miss the important shot of him actually leaving the address. It would take him less than a second to walk out the doorway and into the busy street so it would not be enough reaction time to capture his exit. About five minutes later Malik walked out from the doorway and casually wandered off. He'd been inside for nearly forty minutes, and had taken nothing with him inside. I figured it was more important to check what the address was rather than continue following him, so I got out and ventured slowly up the grotty stairs.

As I neared the top of the stairs a buzzer sounded, announcing my presence automatically and causing my heart to skip a beat. About five seconds later a solid looking, steel security door opened at the top of the landing, and an Asian woman appeared. She didn't speak, just reached out and grabbed my hand, pulling me inside in a gentle but assertive manner as she threw me a smile that passed right through me. She was wearing a rather skimpy outfit and I immediately suspected she may be a sex worker. The entire process took just seconds and I was soon standing in a bedroom adjacent to the hallway at the top of the stairs. I turned to speak to her but found she had closed the door and was already half undressed, largely facilitated by the fact that she wasn't wearing much to begin with.

'Oh, look I'm sorry... I... Is there a price list? I mean I was just wondering about the prices really, I wasn't sort of coming here for anything just yet... I mean I need to get some cash from the bank, so perhaps...' I trailed off as I realised her blank stare meant she couldn't understand a word I was saying. She pulled her outfit back up slightly and motioned for me to stay where I was, then she went to fetch another worker, who was only mildly more attractive. I figured the business operated on a process of *'you get who you get'* with the 'workers' physically 'collecting' clients by their hands from the stairs, rather than patrons choosing their own girls. Even then I wondered why anyone would come here at all. *'Sixty five dollar for everything'* she said in a nasally voice that did nothing to enhance her unfortunate appearance. *'You have everything. Sixty five dollar for f...y f...y* (she gesticulated briskly to help me understand her terminology), *and for sucky sucky. Sixty five dollar half hour very good. You want her?'* she inquired, pointing at the other girl who wasn't looking

anywhere in particular, and who appeared indifferent about whether she was selected or not. I got the feeling it was a numbers game, and that I would not really be a special customer if I did decide to partake in this not so appealing opportunity.

'Oh, I see, thank you. I need to get some cash, so I just wanted to check first, but I have to come back. Ok, so sixty five. Thank you' I said and walked off, under the glare of both women. I wondered if it meant my 'girl' had missed her place in the line due to my shenanigans, or perhaps it could be thought that I had taken one look at my selection and just been unable to go through with the business. Regardless I was very much relieved to reach the bottom of those stairs. I burst free into the busy street, filled with Coke signs and baby strollers and everything else that suggested I had returned to the real world after my unexpected foray into a seedy Thai sex house.

I rang Gazala and told her the good news, (or was it bad news? I wasn't sure!), and Gazala seemed quietly pleased.

'I told you, I told you he was going didn't I? Were they very cheap girls? So were they like not so good looking? I mean not because I want him to think I am pretty, but it is just that is what he wants...' she continued, almost musing to herself as it was clear she already knew the answers.

Later that day I provided the video tape of Malik walking out of the building to Gazala, and wished her luck with her Mufti.

Several months later I got another call from Gazala, who said that Malik had told the Mufti he had walked into that building by mistake when he was looking for another solicitor's office, that he had not attended the brothel, and didn't even know what that address was for. Gazala was not impressed that the leader had apparently broken her confidence in telling Malik the specific details, but the bottom line was that the leader had no choice but to believe him. After all my video didn't show the time of him entering the stairway, so it could be easily argued he had just walked in and out in seconds, after realising his mistake. The fact that I would happily swear to him being there for well over half an hour clearly had no weight. After all, I wasn't part of their culture.

Fortunately the Mufti was now slightly suspicious of Malik, though without definite proof he would always take the husband's side, despite the enormous suspicions. He wasn't too hard on Gazala, and forced Malik to renew his vows to his wife. At the time of this particular call, Gazala said she was sure that he had resumed his previous behaviour, and wanted another period of surveillance on him. Malik was now quite aware his wife had been checking on him, and was far more careful in his actions - even his driving. We decided the best option was to install a tracking system into his car. Gazala said he was going overseas for two weeks, alone, and that this would be a good time. So we waited.

Another month later, Gazala rang to advise Malik was going overseas the following week. We made arrangements for her to take his car and meet me so I could install a tracking system[68]. This system would allow me to monitor his movements remotely, and show exactly where he was going. Once the system was installed, we sat and waited for him to return.

Malik did return, and seemed to lead a fairly normal lifestyle, though his movements were very erratic. He would drive around for hours visiting various locations, but not often would they be suspicious, and not often would they be for long enough for any mischief to occur. Since his medical practicing certificate had been suspended by the authorities for his unlawful patient

---

[68] Law relating to covert tracking systems are under review in many jurisdictions or are now being formalised. Some States prohibit their use. Exercise caution when considering these devices.

relationships, he was free to wander wherever he pleased. Occasionally I would identify something suspicious, but Gazala would advise that he had his son with him on that occasion, or that it was the Mufti's house, or some other known address. It was like looking for a needle in a haystack. Tracking a car can be incredibly useful for investigations, though it is far more difficult with such an erratic driver. It wasn't practicable to investigate all of the addresses he visited, and would require door knocking and perhaps another unexpected visit to somewhere resembling one of the seedier parts of Thailand. It was clear that he didn't go back to the Croydon brothel, which is perhaps not surprising as he had been caught there previously.

After several months of tracking his car and weeks of surveillance using several PI's, I identified one address in particular that seemed quite doubtful. We analysed the history, the duration spent there and the time he arrived and deduced that there must be something going on. It seemed he was more likely to go there on a particular day, so we focused our surveillance on this day and this address. Rather than follow him around as I had previously, I decided to move there and wait for him to arrive. Fortunately he did arrive on the very first day I was waiting for him, pulling up in his Land Cruiser with an Asian woman in the passenger seat. The two got out and entered an apartment building nearby. I could see that the woman wasn't particularly ugly, but was certainly Asian, which seemed Malik's preferred nationality. Their laughter was clearly one of distinct familiarity.

It wasn't easy to see into the apartment, so I waited below, and a little over an hour he returned to the car with her. She sat inside for some time, continuing to talk to him, while I recorded the scene on video. It was dark and difficult to get a good shot, but the open passenger door left the interior light on within the vehicle, providing just enough light to see what was happening.

My hand began to tire from holding the camera as they continued talking, but then without warning they kissed and she left the car to return home. We had been working this job for so long and I knew he was up to mischief but it had been so difficult to prove!

Gazala was also pleased and said that she had suspected he had a girlfriend, as a few times she had seem some presents he had bought, which she herself had never received. We conducted further inquiries and discovered that indeed the Asian woman was Malik's girlfriend, who met him several times each month. Gazala requested we continue surveillance for a few more months to ensure her Mufti would be convinced. On a further occasion when she rang, Malik had missed a 'prepared' opportunity to see a woman due to some personal issue, and seemed particularly jumpy, angry and keen to have a liaison. I conducted surveillance on him the following day and tailed him to another seedy brothel in the suburbs, where again there were more Asian sex workers. Knowing Malik still demanded unprotected sex from his wife I felt sad, knowing the dangers she faced at every possibly turn in her life.

After several years and a lot of protracted legal battles, Gazala was finally legally divorced from her husband Malik. The property settlement awarded her half of the very small amount remaining after Malik had either spent, given away or hidden the bulk of his fortune. It was a long, hard battle which he fought heavily at every turn, but in the end Gazala took back control of her own life. The Family Court judge directed in official orders that Malik grant her the additional religious divorce, thus freeing her finally of her marital oppression.

The case of the mistaken itinerary

Key learning points

- Use of wireless cameras

- Loitering excuses / pretext props

Dianne knew something was up when her husband began acting oddly. He was due to go away on a business trip, yet he still had not given her his itinerary despite her asking several times. Eventually he did give it to her, except that it looked suspiciously like it had been manually printed in Excel, and had some spelling mistakes. Shortly after he left for the trip, Dianne rang her husband's travel agency and requested 'another' copy of her husband's itinerary. It was at this point she discovered her husband had made a small mistake. The itinerary he had provided her showed him arriving in Sydney on the eleventh of July, yet the travel agents version of his itinerary (which looked far more professional and had no spelling errors) showed David returning on the ninth of July – two days earlier. Examining the fax in more detail, Dianne discovered yet another discrepancy in the itinerary, which showed her husband checking into the plush Sydney ANA hotel (*now called the Shangri La hotel*). Surely he would return home to his wife once he returned to Sydney, why else would he be staying in a luxury hotel?

Dianne contacted me and I arranged surveillance at both the airport and the hotel on the 'real' arrival date. We watched David as he got off the plane, but he arrived alone, and departed by taxi. At the hotel I made sure I was very close to him when he checked in, as I was trying to overhear his room number. I didn't hear the number, but did manage to follow him up to his room on the 19th floor. As soon as he entered, I was back down at reception, trying to get a room on the same floor. The girl advised me that there were no available rooms on level

19, but there was a lovely room available on either floor 18 or 21. I explained to her it was very important, and that I really needed to be on the 19th floor, for 'sentimental' reasons. She nodded politely at her odd customer as if she was used to strange requests. After some checking of her computer she advised me there would be a room on the 19th available in about an hour if I wanted to wait.

The plush hotel had exits on two streets and two levels, as well as there being many internal bars and restaurants which David may frequent. This made it extremely difficult to observe effectively, and which was why I knew it was imperative to get a room on the same floor.

After checking in to my new room, I discovered it was on the other side of the building to David's. This did make things tricky, as it was not possible to watch his door easily. I set up a wireless camera in a large bag, and left it in the corridor, while I monitored the image from my own room. It was not long before I watched a porter lean down and gaze at the unattended bag with some surprise, and I knew this approach just was not going to work. The lift and corridors of these hotels are spotless and any unattended items draw immediate interest.

I rang my (now) former wife and told her of the situation. She was more than pleased to attend the hotel, and brought our little one-year-old daughter with her. By lunchtime we had spotted two champagne flutes outside David's door, with one sporting rather distinctive red lipstick. This was our first piece of evidence that there was something going on. At this point we had been conducting a lot of walks past his doorway, yet it was very difficult hanging around the corridors without raising suspicion. Then we decided to use our daughter as a 'loitering excuse', and we took turns carrying her sleeping body up and down the corridor for hours without raising suspicion, as it looked like we were rocking her to sleep.

This approach worked, and we finally observed David leaving his room with an attractive blonde girl who was somewhat younger than he was. The pair caught the lift up to the Horizon bar, and I finally managed to get a photo of the two of them together. If I had covered only the street exits of the hotel rather than monitoring the actual lift lobby and corridors on the 19th floor, I would have missed all the action. I hugged my tiny daughter, who had helped solve her first case, though she was only one year old.

As clichéd as it sounds, it turned out that the blonde girl was his secretary. Unfortunately for David, his wife was worth a great deal more than he was and owned their company. David found himself facing divorce as well as the loss of his lavish lifestyle, so the itinerary wasn't his only mistake!

This case was solved by the clever use of an appropriate loitering excuse. Rocking a baby to sleep is an ideal pretext to use in a fancy hotel with multiple exits. I don't usually take my daughter on investigations, but a fancy hotel with mum present was ok. Of course I was lucky because my daughter was the right age, but a surveillance professional would recognise the potential in this approach. In the absence of an actual baby, as I could have bought a large baby doll from a toy shop and a blanket, and wrapped her accordingly. A surveillance 'nobody' would consider this approach stupid, or be too shy to rock a baby doll in public. A surveillance professional, would act assertively and confidently, using the toy prop to maximum advantage, and get the results. Which of the two are you?

PART 3

– ADVANCED SURVEILLANCE –

CHAPTER 25: AGENT COMMUNICATIONS

The work of a PI is often a solitary affair, with the vast majority of cases being conducted by a single agent. Surveillance with multiple agents allows more discreet operations, and reduces the likelihood of a loss of contact, but is also far more expensive. This technique is best used for hard targets who have previously noted or evaded surveillance, or for a job where there is only one good opportunity to capture the event or information such as a home address. If a single medical or other appointment was arranged with a person upon whom you need to conduct surveillance, and there was either no address available, or the address was wrong, following this person home from that one appointment would be a priority.

In this case, the use of multiple agents would be preferable, as a loss of contact would result in an inability to carry on the task, being as the home address is unknown. Mobile phones are a great asset to communications during multiple agent surveillance, however they do have limitations. There is a slight delay prior to making a phone connection. Radios, however, are instant. Surveillance is often time critical, and every second counts, particularly on a vehicle follow, where you need others to respond quickly. Mobile phones cost money to use, and don't easily enable multiple persons to speak or hear at once, whereas radios allows many persons to hear at once. Phones are good for long range communication, but close range and vehicle follows are usually best done with radios. A good alternative are the new, hybrid, push-to-talk phones[69] which act like a radio but use GSM networks, provided there is GSM coverage in the area of operations.

---

[69] www.telstra.com.au/mobile/products/ptt

Radio conventions

Keep transmitting power to the lowest setting if possible. This reduces the number of persons who may overhear the transmission, and increases security. Never refer to specific information over a radio network, unless absolutely necessary. Use veiled speech to convey information. When in a static location, refer to street names by the first initial (in phonetics), rather than the full name. Using full names for an operation that may run for some time in a fixed location is not a good idea, and is asking for any eavesdroppers to identify the exact location, and to possibly compromise the operation. For example, instead of saying *'He has left on foot, heading west on Norman Street'*, a better phrase would be *'West on November Street'*. When on mobile surveillance, the full street names are provided as this reduces confusion, and the actual location is of little interest or connection to the job. If eavesdroppers overheard *'Heading North on Stacy Street'*, they would be unlikely to be able to respond to this in time. Such street name information is time sensitive, so it doesn't matter if it is heard as the information is soon worthless apart from to those on the chase.

When providing a vehicle registration number, there is usually no requirement to transmit the full details. Often the first few letters, together with an accurate description will identify the vehicle to other agents. If a full registration number is provided, eavesdroppers can use this to identify the target under surveillance. For example: *'picked up by a red Subaru wagon, rego: AKW'* as opposed to providing the full registration number: 'AKW 90S'. When referring to people, use the first letter of their name in phonetics, like **C**hris becomes 'Charlie'; **B**en becomes 'Bravo', or use your own code to conceal your identity. Don't chatter too much. This reduces battery power and distracts attention from the observations. It also increases the chance of detection from eavesdroppers.

Radio language glossary

Specialised language and phrases are used during communication between agents, for reasons of speed, clarity or to limit information being transmitted openly. Teams who work together sometimes have their own codes, but the following list is relatively common, and many of these terms are used by government surveillance bodies.

Word	Meaning
1UP	A single agent surveillance operation
2UP	A two agent surveillance operation
ACTION	Something of interest or activity is occurring right now (which should result in some response, such as to record video of the subject). Often used as a command to alert other agents on a job.
BOX	House or building. Used because the term is shorter to say, and uses veiled speech to convey the message. Any person overhearing the conversation may be less likely to realise the *'box'* is a building, hence it may sound less suspicious if conversations are overheard.
BOXED IN	Vehicle is in heavy traffic and unable to move effectively.
BREAK OFF	To intentionally break contact with a subject, or cease operations. *'I think he's heading home now, so break off and meet me at the OP.'*
CHUTE	Road lane, as in *'He's in the centre chute.'*
COPY	Message understood (similar to *'Roger'*). May also be indicated by a single click of the PTT

Word	Meaning
	(talk button), to just crack squelch, particularly by an agent who cannot make too much noise or movement in his location.
COMPROMISE	The target has become aware of the surveillance.
DRIVE PAST	To drive past an address or location, to see what is happening at the time. A drive past will identify which vehicles or persons are on site.
EXPOSURE	The amount of time an agent has been visible, or *exposed* to a target. On long follows, a surveillance vehicle may have had a lot of *exposure*. Too much exposure means you should 'break off', or permit another agent to 'take point' on the follow.
EYEBALL	The surveillance agent who currently has *'eyes on'* the target. Others may be 'out of visual' from the target, but be guided by the *eyeball*.
EYES ON	To see the target visually, as in *'Do you have eyes on the vehicle?'*
FACIAL ID	Good close up, head and shoulders identification image of a target.
FLIPPER	Lane changing indicator. As in *'He has his left flipper on.'*
FOOT PATROL	A walk past an address to see what's happening. Similar to a drive past, but is slower, and enables more detail to be seen without exposing cars.

Word	Meaning
FRESH	Traffic lights, which have just changed. *'fresh reds'* means the lights have only recently switched to red, and will stay red for some time.
GO	Commence a follow. When a target goes 'mobile', this notifies others. To reduce confusion and ensure all agents are aware of this important event, the phrase is often repeated three times, as in *'GO, GO, GO!'*
HOT	A target that is believed to be surveillance aware. *'Careful, he's hot!'*
LOST CONTACT	Agent has lost sight of the target, or cannot continue the follow due to obstructions from other vehicles.
LUP	Lying up place. Commonly used for rural surveillance, meaning the sleeping area. The *LUP* is normally located further away than the OP, and is more secure, and protected from view. An *OP* is selected for visibility of the target, but may be unsuitable for sleeping in. An *LUP* is normally sited out of hearing from the target area.
MOBILE	To start moving. *'He's now mobile.'*
ONE FOR COVER	A single 'sandwich' vehicle is located between the agent and the target. This ensures the target receives less exposure, as the target can only see an unconnected vehicle if he checks his mirror. Cover vehicles are good, but can also result in lost contact if they are too slow.

Word	Meaning
OP	Observation position. Location of a known parking spot that provides good visibility. For operations on foot, a good place to hide. In rural surveillance, an *OP* means the camouflaged hide.
PINGED	Agent has been compromised or *'pinged'*
POLL or POINT	To be the eyeball, or to take the lead in a follow. *'You take point'* means the other agent should manoeuvre into the lead position.
PUT DOWN	To drop off the target at an address
PUT-TO-BED	Continue watching until lights go out in a home, or the occupants have now gone to sleep. Means ensure the target is sleeping at the address, and is not likely to move to another address before the morning. Also means they are unlikely to engage in any other activities.
ROGER	Message understood
ROLLING	Currently recording the activity on videotape. *'I am rolling right now.'* Also used to indicate vehicles are moving *'He's rolling.'*
SPRUNG	Agent has been caught, compromised or *'sprung'*
STALE	Traffic lights which will change shortly. *Stale* reds are lights which will switch green shortly. *Stale* greens will go red shortly.
STAND-BY	Prepare for action. For a take-away, this phrase is often given three times as in *'Stand-*

Word	Meaning
	by, stand-by, stand-by'. Other agents would acknowledge this call with a 'Copy' or 'Roger'.
STATIC	Stationary observation position (as opposed to a mobile vehicle OP)
SWEEP	To search for a vehicle or target. '*I'll sweep the railway car park*' means the agent will check this car park for the target's vehicle.
TAKE-AWAY	Commence a follow when the target 'goes mobile'. A *take-away* is where an agent has identified the departing target, and commenced a follow without detection. A target is '*taken away*' from his home or work by the surveillance agent. '*I lost him on the take-away.*'
TWO FOR COVER	Two 'sandwich' vehicles placed between the agent and the target.

Phonetic alphabet

This is a widely used alphabet in radio communications. The purpose is to ensure there is no confusion when providing important details, like the registration number of a vehicle, or the spelling of a surname. The alphabet words have been selected as relatively unique, with a clear focus on the correct letter being transmitted. **A**lpha, **B**ravo, **C**harlie, **D**elta, **E**cho, **F**oxtrot, **G**olf, **H**otel, **I**ndia, **J**uliet, **K**ilo, **L**ima **M**ike, **N**ovember, **O**scar, **P**apa, **Q**uebec, **R**omeo, **S**ierra, **T**ango, **U**niform, **V**ictor, **W**hisky, **X**-Ray, **Y**ankee, **Z**ulu

CHAPTER 26: WORKING ON MEDICAL APPOINTMENTS

Insurance claimants are required to have medicals, which entails having their injuries assessed and monitored by a nominated doctor or specialist. An agent may be occasionally instructed by the insurance company of the date and time of these appointments, providing an opportunity for surveillance to confirm identification, and to assess the subject's injuries. A medical may be in a city location, which requires use of public transport. This is a prime opportunity to document activity, as it allows for long exposure times, varying grades of terrain such as steep station stairs, and a relatively easy follow for an experienced operator. An amateur will wait for the subject to arrive and announce themselves. A professional will often pick the subject approaching the address, and have good ID of them even before they approach the reception desk. It is not easy picking people, but with experience you can identify subtle cues in behaviour of people as they look for an address, perhaps carrying x-rays or other documents.

In some cases the behaviour of a subject on approach to the medical facility will be unrestricted, as they assume there is nobody watching them. On leaving however, they may be wary, knowing the insurance company could have them followed. This sometimes leads to an amusing change in their gait, as they suddenly exhibit the claimed injury which was strangely not evident on their arrival. This is one reason why the professional will aim to document the approach, not just the departure. Subjects residing in country areas will have a long journey to travel, and will invariably arrive an hour before the appointed time. They will check the address and the actual medical suite, and then go shopping or to lunch, returning at a later time for the appointment. The professional who is waiting for his prey will observe this, pick the subject and perhaps get some time documenting their shopping or lunch activities, well before the medical appointment commences. Experience counts.

Sometimes the home address of the subject is unknown, and is difficult to determine via other means. An arranged medical will provide an opportunity to follow the subject back to a home address, or some other identifiable location, which can assist future operations. Sometimes a medical can have a subject on their toes, while others let their guard down. The professional knows the odds and makes an assessment about how he wants to play the game.

Purpose of arranged medicals

For an investigator, the aim of an arranged medical is:

- **IDENTIFY** the subject visually, and perhaps get a common first name if it is a foreign name which may have been 'westernised'.

- **OBSERVE** the subject outside their usual home environment where they may be normally quite guarded. After leaving a medical, they may feel they are safe from watching eyes, which they usually expect to follow them from their home address. Medical centres are often located in business districts which are most easily reached by public transport, therefore encouraging travel on trains and stairs. If a private vehicle is used, it may need to be parked some distance from the address which requires some walking.

- **LOCATE** the subject's home address accurately. Occasionally a subject will not provide a current home address, or will provide a false one. They may provide a relative's home such as their parents, where if contacted by phone, the parent will always say *'They are not home right now, but I can take a message for you...'*

Action points for arranged medical appointments

There are always many different ways to approach any job, but the following points may be used as a guide to consider:

- Immediately *store the details on a calendar* with a reminder, to ensure you remember the date. Often there is only one bite at the cherry, so if you miss the appointment, you are unlikely to get another opportunity. It's hard to remember one's own appointments, let alone appointments for people you haven't even met!

- If appropriate, contact the medical centre the day *prior* to the appointment, to check it hasn't been changed. Subjects do occasionally change their appointment time with the medical centre, but any changes will very rarely, if ever, be advised to the insurance or investigation company. A poor investigator will charge for about four hours, and report *'The subject failed to attend the medical'* OR, will report they discovered the changed appointment time after conducting the surveillance. A good investigator will just charge for a phone call, and will then conduct the medical surveillance on the new appointment date. Keep the telephone number handy for possible later use on the day of the appointment. Note some doctors may work a round of various centres, and may not have a phone listing in their name at that address. Perhaps they are there only on Mondays, and are listed at their other centre in the telephone book.

- Consider conducting a spot check or even surveillance of the subject's home on the morning of the medical. Identifying a possible vehicle they will later arrive in will enable you to identify them arriving at the appointment. It can also assist you to follow them from there, if you can later find their car in the car park.

- Arrive at the medical centre no later than one hour prior to the medical. Subjects are often early to appointments, particularly when they have not been there before. If the subject is travelling from a long distance away (over an hour's drive), consider arriving at least two hours before the appointed time, to be sure not to miss them.

- Conduct a full site reconnaissance, identifying the exact location of the building, the location of the waiting area, the size of waiting room. Intimate, with just two chairs? A huge fifty-seat general waiting room, serving several doctors at once?

- Identify the location of all exits to the building, including rear and basement, the car park, or the closest car park that may be used by the subject if they drive.

- Identify the location of closest railway stations, bus stops etc, as well as the route from these locations to the centre.

- Identify the exact route the subject will take when arriving or leaving the centre. Identify the best positions to capture this movement. Can you observe the staircase from outside? Can you observe the car park from inside through a window? Are they likely to walk down the ramp? Identify the best position from which to observe the waiting room.

- Consider recording video of all vehicles currently parked in the centre car park if possible. After the subject has arrived, you can eliminate these as potential subject's vehicles, because they were already parked there, or perhaps one of them was the subject's so you already have a good image and plate number on film.

- Some PI's have been known to place a small radio transmitter in the waiting room, to enable them to hear conversations inside, like arriving patients announcing their names to the receptionist. This means they don't need to physically sit in the waiting room but can be discreetly outside watching who enters, yet still be reasonably confident of matching names to faces. This practice has some merit as small waiting rooms mean the subject is likely to get a good look at those already in the room, and some experienced claimants may be immediately wary of others who may be a PI. Caution is suggested however, as there is legislation governing the use of bugs. This is usually relating to private locations or conversations so whether a doctor's waiting room would be considered private is arguable (actually inside the doctor's surgery would definitely be). A simple baby monitor could serve this purpose well, and may not look out of place in waiting rooms that usually cater for children, with assorted toys about the room.

- Consider setting up continuous recording from a second video camera, trained on the entrance. Start this running about fifteen minutes prior to the appointment time. Consider stopping the camera as soon as the subject has been identified, but start it again after about fifteen minutes to assist the subsequent capturing of the subject's departure.

- Unless it is reasonably large, wait outside the waiting room and observe people arriving at the centre. Attempt to identify the subject as they *arrive* at the centre for their medical appointment.

- Getting video evidence of a subject arriving for their appointment is the sign of a professional investigator. Anyone can identify a subject by just waiting inside the waiting room, but this is the lazy way to do it. It also results in significant facial exposure, and provides little or no information about which direction the subject approached the building from.

- Watch for people who fit the description supplied which may be just an age, sex and guessed nationality (from their name). Watch for people arriving at the centre clutching large X-ray envelopes, who are clearly patients coming for a medical appointment.

- Watch for arriving vehicles. Attempt to locate the subject's vehicle if already known or suspected.

- Video all 'potential' subjects arriving at the centre. This will ensure you have ID video of their arrival including the time, when you later identify them correctly.

- When a *potential* subject has entered the centre, consider phoning and inquiring if *they* have arrived for their appointment. Be cautious about giving too much information over the phone at this point. If the subject is right in front of the receptionist at the time of the call, she may inadvertently say something inappropriate such as '*Yes, he has just arrived*' and cause the subject to wonder who is checking up on him. Attempt to wait until the person has actually left the waiting room and is with the doctor before calling to verify if necessary.

- Most medical receptionists will assist investigators in some way, such as providing a description of the subject and their clothing, or even possibly notifying you by phone when they depart. Some even have a formal policy of requesting your licence. Occasionally though, receptionists may subtly let the patient know to watch out for prying eyes. Those that do not fall into either category are often vague and immersed in their work, unable to remember what a subject looked like even though they just spoke to them a minute ago. While it is acceptable to quietly advise the receptionist of your presence and occupation if you wish their assistance, or to allay their concerns over you hanging around for hours without an appointment, it is best to work inconspicuously without their knowledge. Don't be afraid to identify your self if you feel it necessary though.

- When you identify the subject, attempt to get ID footage of them through the window of the waiting room if possible. This is easiest while they are sitting down, possibly filling in a patient form. Often just a crack in the blinds is sufficient to get a good camera angle for ID footage, while they are sitting quietly waiting for the doctor to call them in, if some care is taken.

- When you identify the subject, make a note of his direction of approach. Go back along this route once they have entered the surgery, and identify where they may have come from, perhaps a car park or train station.

- Assess the route for likely locations where you can record them returning after they finish the appointment. Based on the subject direction of approach, or transport method, alcoves, entrance foyers of buildings with glass windows, are worthy of consideration.

- If they are likely to have parked in a small car park, consider recording video of all vehicles parked there. Sweep across the cars one by one, capturing a quick video snap of all cars, ensuring all number plates are easily identified. Should the subject later drive off in a car, you will already have a good picture of it, as well as the exact registration plate. You may not be able to get registration plate details in the excitement of the chase as they leave! It makes it much harder to locate the vehicle later in a sweep if you don't know its exact plate number.

- Consider relocating the surveillance vehicle to a better position, based on the subject's arrival route or method. Return to the vicinity of the waiting room, and stake it out, awaiting the subject's departure.

- If the waiting room is large or you don't feel confident waiting outside, sit inside, close to the entrance door, but facing away from it.   When the subject arrives, immediately leave the room once you have identified them.

- On departure of the subject, consider immediately telephoning the medical centre, and asking if the subject has left. If the receptionist advises the subject has '*Just left*', this will help you accurately identify them if you were perhaps unsure.

CHAPTER 27: DISGUISES

The PI usually works as a single agent, and once they have been recognised they are not able to continue close surveillance very easily. It is important to conceal your identity as much as possible, to remain undetected. While few PI's adopt elaborate disguises, they are sometimes appropriate for very close up work; a door-knock, or a medical appointment for example, where you may be sitting directly opposite the claimant then have to follow them away from this appointment an hour later.

The usual 'disguise' is clothing, whereby the PI will have a range of clothing and accessories to modify their appearance. Subjects rarely notice the details, but will notice broad colours or the difference between shorts and long pants. It is best to have more clothing on in the initial instance, and shed it later on when required. It is faster to remove clothing than to put it on. Another aspect to consider is that any following is hot work, either due to adrenaline pumping or the fact that there is often a lot of running around - either hiding, keeping up, or moving to a good camera position.

- Start jobs with *more* clothing on, such as shorts worn underneath baggy long pants, or a skirt worn under a track suit. You can easily discard these later, when on the run, or when the day heats up.

- Alternate colours. Favour drab or less noticeable colours, but ensure adequate variation between colours such as dark green and brown.

- Alternate styles. Carry a tee-shirt and a polo neck top, or a light long-sleeve jacket.

- Accessories are important. Consider a hat, sun glasses, spectacles but with plain glass lenses (for an innocuous secretary look), a scarf, another bag.

- Wigs are not often used by PI's, though they are sometimes appropriate. It may sound corny or unlikely, but they do work and can be employed easily. Start with the wig on when making a direct close-contact with the subject, and then remove the wig for the follow. Women can make better use of these as they can wear a long wig over short hair, but hair itself is distinctive, so any change will be of benefit. I have experimented with a skin-glue moustache from a costume and prop store which was useful in a few cases, but on the whole, probably more trouble than it's worth.

- Consider buying props while on a follow. If you follow a subject to a lunch date, you may then purchase a cheap hat or other item to provide a disguise for the next leg of the follow when they finish their lunch. This way you didn't need to carry the item in the first place.

- Accessories can be something you are carrying, not necessarily 'clothing' accessories but straight props. You may pick up an empty discarded cardboard box you see outside a shop while following a subject. If they glance at you, they will see a man with a box, which wasn't how they saw you when you started following them earlier. Other props include newspapers, Walkman earphones (good to allay suspicion when listening to conversations on a train or café), an umbrella and many more.

- Consider changing your physical appearance while on a follow. I once followed a business man into the city for a meeting, which I knew was to take over an hour. I needed a hair cut, so I chose to have it while he was in the meeting, so I had a new appearance when I followed him to his next appointment.

- Some props can remove suspicion well, such as glasses with plain lenses to appear less threatening and more of a 'nerd' type personality. They also distinguish facial features well as people look very different without them. A small baby can be a great prop, as it can allow you to wander around or loiter without comment. It is readily seen what you are doing, and a baby is very non-threatening so clearly you can't be there for surveillance. Of course the baby could be just a doll in a blanket.

- Female agents can consider make-up changes. Initially have no make-up and a plain white face (this is less noticeable for close contact such as inside a small medical waiting room), but later in the follow you may put on bright red lipstick quickly, which could be seen at a distance and distinguish them from the 'plainer' girl seen earlier.

- Use your own body to disguise yourself. Cover your face with a hand, as if scratching your nose while sitting directly behind the subject in traffic or when they may look directly at you or walk past. Deny them a good look at your facial features.

- Use the environment to disguise your appearance. Casually look through cover such as parked car windows, or plant leaves in a garden rather than expose your face or body directly.

If you need to make a personal approach to a subject under a pretext, you can sometimes have good results if you give them a dodgy business card. If your inquiries need you to have one off contact with a subject to inquire their identity or some other detail, the card may assist them to accept your pretext. It is easy to get a pile of business cards from an RSL club bucket, restaurant notice board or other business where cards are left for prize draws or other reasons. You can select from the cards to determine which identity may be best to 'assume' for your job, and thus have a professionally printed card to add believability to your story.

Unless there is a good reason to follow up on the business card, most people will just throw it away later, so will never discover it is dodgy. If you need ongoing contact with them though, you should consider the possibility they will follow up on the card and ring the number. Even if they do ring the (dodgy) number listed on the card, there are a lot of people who will just think there is some mistake. Knowing you have assumed an identity means you will always think it would be easy to discover the ruse, yet human nature is more forgiving and accepting of mistakes.

Many years ago I gave a dodgy card to a guy during a pretext, got my information and left. Some time later I had to do some more work on the case, and made another approach. They guy remembered me and quickly said he had called the number and spoken to a guy who said he was the 'REAL' Craig Abbott and that was definitely his card, and he had no recollection of the original meeting. He went on to say that the person he had been speaking to sounded nothing like me.

I could have withered away tail between legs and accepted I had been found out, but instead I took the confident approach and just bluffed my way through the exchange saying *'I can't believe the hide of that guy. We had some difficulties at work and I left that job, but they still take calls on my old line and pretend they are me. I have actually lost a few clients because they made them believe they were talking to me and by the time I found out it was too late. Did he try to get you to come in and see him? Did he try and get your business?'* I asked firing questions rapidly at my target to disorientate him, and make him question his original thoughts about my identity – which were fairly clear at the beginning. By the end of the call he was very much on my side and agreed with me it was a terrible thing to do, to assume someone's identity for commercial gain. He fully accepted me as the real Craig Abbott!

Now onside with me, he was even more willing to provide the additional information I was seeking from him. I never spoke to him again, and often wonder if he ever rang poor Mr Abbott again – either to blast him for his sad 'ruse', or to inquire if what I had been saying was really true. Nevertheless, I was able to submit a comprehensive report which contained all the details the client was requesting – and then some. It could have gone very bad, but due to some quick lateral thinking and confidence I had been able to switch the negative to a positive, and actually use it to my advantage. I have had several similar experiences over the years, such as The case of a favourable compromise, on page 428

CHAPTER 28: UNDERCOVER SURVEILLANCE

Working undercover is both challenging and rewarding. It is a true test of a good PI to infiltrate an organisation, posing as someone they are not, to work alongside the very people they are investigating. It is not easy and it can be very dangerous. Often in corporate jobs there are organised thieves stealing significant amounts of stock. These thieves often make a good profit, so do not appreciate being discovered. It could cost them a lot of money, as well as possibly sending them to jail. The very nature of the undercover agent makes them a vulnerable target. They are often seen as fair game by the offenders, who regard them as something of a 'spy who can be put to death for treason'.

Being undercover is simply an extended pretext, whereby an agent adopts a persona completely, and lives it for a period of time while gathering intelligence from within. An undercover agent can go where management cannot, speaking to staff on a very different level and seeing what really goes on in the factory floor.

- Be very cautious about your own identity. Protect it at every turn. Aim to prevent anyone learning your real name or any other personal details. Assume an identity even to the management of the organisation you are to infiltrate. Some people can't help but talk, particularly about an exciting issue like a real spy working for them in the organisation. Investigation reports can also be accidentally seen by others and may compromise you.

- A good undercover identity story is to say you are from interstate. This is a good reason why you do not have close ties to friends locally, and why you are not involved with local activities. It is much harder for others to check your story if your personal history and former addresses are so far away.

- Consider not using your car to travel to work as it is personally associated with your real identity. Having no car is a good reason to seek lifts from your peers, which can then spark off deeper friendships and help you socially integrate.

- Use your first name. This means you readily respond to it when called, and if recognised by your real friends while on the job they will greet you normally. It is not usually necessary to conceal your first name as it is unimportant. Change or conceal your surname only. In certain investigations you can obtain authorised false ID from government sources, or use your own skills to obfuscate your existing ID in a way that will not give you away, such as changing names or addresses.

- Be cautious about what you carry in to the job. Cleanse your wallet of your real ID and remove pictures of family and all other items. Lock your phone or divert to voicemail while working. Be cautious about any investigation notes or reports you carry with you. Your colleagues may playfully rumble you, and important items may fall out. You may lose them accidentally or they may be stolen from you. If they do suspect you, they may unlawfully apprehend you, and conduct an unauthorised search of your clothing. It would be disastrous for them to find items that may prove you are a plant, or personal information they can use to pressure you to not testify against them.

- Adopt a persona that is very close to your own life. Do not invent a whole new life, but merely modify your own. Stick to subjects and work histories that you are familiar with, and can discuss in great detail. Provide detail to anyone who you talk to, as the more detailed information you provide the less threatening you are to them, and hence the more they will trust you. It doesn't matter if the actual information itself is meaningless or even false, it is the fact that you are comfortable providing information, and the inference is that you would do so for any other subject raised.

- Adopt focus points. Invent or encourage a hobby or other interest that categorises you among them. Cultivate an unusual interest in some sport or player, or a rock band. Plaster images of these focus points on your locker. Mention them in discussions with staff. Allow your generated focus points to define you among your peers. If you bring a lot of donuts to work each day, you will soon be known as the donut guy. If you don't give people focus points they will look for their own within your personality, and you don't want this level of scrutiny. Make it easy, hand them your focus points on a platter, but in a subtle way that suggests it was their idea.

- Quickly learn the persona of the environment and adapt accordingly. Listen to the words and phrases, learn the interests and notice and get a feel for the clothing. Adapt them as your own, if possible, to encourage your integration into the social aspects of the work environment.

- Be lazy. Be rude. Often it is best not to be the perfect worker, but rather just a little of a trouble maker. Someone who tries to get around the time management security systems and leaves work early when they can get away with it. Steal stationery or other items that may engender you with the type of characters you are infiltrating. By exhibiting some small level of theft or an attitude of contempt towards management, you will be showing how closely you are aligned with them. This will cause them to consider you as trustworthy among them, and they will bring you into the fold in order to further their own criminal aims. This is the key to obtaining the real information about what is going on, and may require you to receive some formal 'discipline' from management which is seen by other workers.

- Become unassuming. Wear an Ipod but with the sound turned down. Others may be more comfortable talking about illegal activities if they think you are disinterested or unable to hear them.

- Identify some key players and focus on them personally. Try to become closer friends with them - perhaps suggest a social meeting after work.

- Always look for better opportunities to gather intelligence. Liaise with your investigation controller to suggest changes to rosters or job positions if it associates you better with the problem areas. Actively manage your whole environment, rather than only passively capturing the information you receive.

The case of the dodgy cable guy

Key learning points

- Undercover operations

- Use of pretext to infiltrate criminal networks

- Covert video recording using pinhole cameras

Recently there has been a lot of fraud relating to counterfeit satellite TV decoders, and cable TV smart cards. In Newcastle for example the situation was getting out of hand, and for $100 you could buy a smart card on the black market that would give you free access to all the cable channels, without having to pay a subscription. I was tasked with infiltrating the fraudster's networks and obtaining evidence against them. Armed with some intelligence from the client, I began making approaches to suspects. By working the phones, playing a few pretexts and taking a few punts, I was finally able to get an 'in' and lined up a meeting in a pub with one of our suspects. I was armed with a covert camera housed inside a mobile phone which records live video. This enabled me to record any transaction which took place. Before long I had acquired my first dodgy smart card, with the entire exchange captured on video. I bought a few more and got further 'in' with my supplier and was able to find out more about the overall network. He was not keen to release details, but some carefully steered conversations led to enough intelligence for it to be worth my while. I followed up a few other leads and was able to make some other 'buys' in pubs, car parks and back alleys. We had not made any arrests yet, as we were just working the network and seeing who we could round up. The arrests would take place later.

After a month or so, I had enough information to try for a bigger fish. Up till then I had been buying from the couriers who stole the gear on the streets, but we really wanted to get the guy who was actually producing them or some other key player, well up the chain. Together with the police and the client we had profiled a few likely suspects to work on. One stuck out in particular, though he was reported to be very suspicious and cagey, and a difficult prospect to work if you were trying to get in 'cold' as an outsider. Having done my research homework and with enough experience dealing with the couriers, it was time to go for Mr Big. I chose the best time of day, I chose the best day of the week. I chose my pretext carefully. I only had one shot at it, so it had to be good, my target had to be ready and receptive to providing the information I wanted. I drank a nice hot cup of tea and sat down with the phone. In my mind I rehearsed scenarios, trying to get in character. Every sound I made, every word I said could be responsible for success or failure. Given that the intelligence suggested he was mixed up with some heavy types, the last thing I wanted to do was bungle the call and get his suspicions up, or else he may decide to 'meet' me for a deal, armed with a few beefy blokes to sort me out. Unlike police run operations, a PI frequently works alone and has none of the backup. From reading up on the background intelligence, I knew his penchant for racing horses. I turned on the FM radio to 2KY horse racing, which would act as subtle background noise. It would assist my pretext and put me in character, as well as perhaps putting him just that little bit more at ease. *'A bloke who likes racing has to be a good bloke after all.'*

I made my call using a pre-paid phone card so I could show my caller-ID to him and reduce suspicion. He would not recognise the number, but at least it wouldn't be private, and this would make him just that fraction more at ease. The phone rang. I waited for an answer, trying to honestly believe I was 'Dave', a likable ruffian from Coffs Harbour who was trying to source a better supply of dodgy cards.

'Yeah?' answered the phone gruffly.

'G'day mate, its Dave callin'. I'm from up in Coffs, and I ah... I was told ya might be able ta give us a hand. I was talking to a mate of Johnny's at the track and he said ya might be able to give us a better deal...'

I paused and waited to see how he would respond. I knew it was hugely helpful to drop the name of one of his known associates; else I would be going in totally cold. Despite all the scenario rehearsals I had done, I knew it was now a free-for-all game, and the conversation could go anywhere. I needed to run with it quickly. Any pregnant pauses or hiccups and I would lose the

401

whole opportunity. Mr Big paused for a few seconds, and then replied coldly *'Who told you to call me?'*, as if he was going to be very sure he discovered who I had been talking to before he said anything at all.

'Pete told us to give you a call. He's the ugly one who's always hangin' around the old shed at the track, makin' the place look untidy. He said you was Johnny's mate and ya had a good thing goin'. The guy I've been usin' up here is ok, but his stuff is just crap and he takes bloody ages to deliver...'

I paused, heart racing. I had cast a line and now I was waiting to see if I got a bite. The mention of the old shed would possibly give me some points for recognition as our intelligence indicated this was the general area where Mr Big was usually found on race days.

'I don't know any Pete... unless you mean Johnny's mate Pete who works at the panel beaters?' he replied. It was a game of chess, and I suddenly detected something fishy about his last comment. It was just too easy – he was offering an easy 'in' by suggesting there was a Pete he knew of. I could see that he could possibly checkmate me on my next move. There was just the faintest hint of something in his voice which I couldn't even describe. It was just a feeling, and although my whole body was wanting to shout out *'Yes, that's him, that's Pete...'* I decided to play it safe. It was a quick decision of course, as I had less than a second to think about it – anything more would be a suspiciously pregnant pause. I had to keep the conversation flowing.

'Nah, the Pete I know's never worked a day in his life. (I chuckled). It must be another mate of his' I replied.

'Well, I don't know Pete' he said gruffly, and although he really gave nothing away, I suspected I'd managed to make the right call on the 'phantom' panel beater. Perhaps if I had indicated I

'recognised' Pete's panel beater workplace, Mr Big could have quickly retorted *'There is no bloody panel beaters and there is no Pete you dickhead, now f... off'*. But he didn't, so I was still in the game.

'Will you turn that bloody thing down!' I shouted, not to him, but to myself, trying to talk over the 2KY racing call – which was nearing the end of a race and rising to a crescendo of excitement in the background. I had timed the call to the start of a race to gee up the excitement factor a little, and also to perhaps gain a few points knowing Mr Big was a racing aficionado. It was all about points – each move I made in this verbal game of chess was scored. Each phrase, tone, timing and in fact every single aspect of my call was being scored. Mistakes would lose me points, and clever acting would give me points. I had to win the game this call, because there would be little chance of a rematch. I didn't need to win conclusively, I just had to scrape across the finish line and get him to accept me into the fold just enough to progress to the next step.

I reached over and turned down the volume again, though not quite enough. *'I told you to take that bloody thing to your own room dickhead'* I spat angrily to the imaginary person sitting in the vacant chair beside me. This was a ploy to suggest I was focused elsewhere, rather than trying to infiltrate a criminal network, as well as giving him something else to think about. My angry remarks set me up ready for my next statement – which needed to be delivered with some attitude.

I turned back to Mr Big on the phone and said *'Bloody kids – you tell them a hundred times and they still f... you up... now what was you sayin?'* There was another pause, too long for comfort as I waited for his answer. I hoped I had side-stepped the issue of Pete enough with the distraction about the 'kids', but it was far too early to tell.

'What kind of deal?' he asked coldly, in a way that suggested he hadn't been won over yet, but wanted more information. He had given precious little away so far, and it was clear he was a cautious man. I suddenly realised I had made a mistake, and it could well have cost me the game. I had naively been focused solely on the fraudulent cable TV smart cards, but had not specifically mentioned this in my call. His (very cold) question to me about what *kind* of deal suggested he was personally involved in a wide range of criminal activity. This could well include re-birthing stolen cars, drugs, kiddie porn and goodness knows what else. I had not specified *cards*, meaning Mr Big could well be thinking I meant something else – something much worse than cards, which would be at the 'light' end of his criminal activity. Although I had mentioned a few scant details to suggest I was 'in' somehow, it would be unwise make such a cold approach if I was trying to arrange a drug supplier, and I am sure he would not have taken the bait.

'*Cards man, the cards. I got a guy up here gives me them for fifty bucks a pop, but he always takes ages to deliver – and sometimes they don't bloody work, or they run out after a month. I got heaps of people chasin' me for new cards and I can't even get 'em from him. Ya see me problem? That's why I'm looking around to see what I can get. I reckon he is rippin' me of at fifty a pop, but it's when he don't supply 'em for ages that really stuffs me up. I already got a guy sayin' it's too much bloody trouble these cards and he's just gonna hook up proper and all*' I waited, but there was again a pregnant pause. I strained to hear any background noise which may give me some information to help the case, but there was complete silence.

'*Look mate, if its too much trouble then just leave it – I got a coupla buddies that may be able to help me out. There's a lotta new folk comin' to Coffs and it's getting bigger. There ain't too* many of us selling cards up here, but if I don't get em off you I'm getting them off someone else, so its your call mate...' I said, my voice just tinged with a slight amount of contempt. I needed to push just a little to keep him from thinking, and also to sound like I was about to hang up. After all, I was a busy crook and had work to do.

'Na, look it's OK. I don't like to talk on the phone – but give me your number and I will get Tony to call you' he replied. Bingo! It was yet to be confirmed, but with that statement I was fairly sure I had passed the test and won the game – this round at least. I knew full well my phone number was already on his caller ID, but figured he may well have asked to further gauge my response to giving it out. Perhaps I wasn't clever enough to figure it was being displayed. Some crooks are not very bright. Perhaps I would give some other number. I gave him my pre-paid mobile number and hung up, turned the annoying radio off and sat back into the couch with a sigh. The call hadn't been more than five minutes, but I was already on the verge of sweating, and that wasn't due to my hot tea!

It was several days later when I got the call from Tony. He was similarly cagey, but agreed to meet up with me the next day. I knew the rough area they lived in, and had already chosen a nearby RSL club as the meeting point, saying I came through there for lunch sometimes as I was always on the road for my other job. The following day I arrived at Tony's suburb about midday, though we had arranged to meet up at one p.m.. I wanted to check out an address we had gotten from intelligence, which could be his home – and I also wanted to be very early to 'case the joint' as they say – and have a good look around. I knew I was dealing with some crooks that may play rough, and I could not be sure Mr Big had not been suspicious enough to follow up with his associate Johnny and ask if he knew a Pete. My stated relationship 'link' to Mr Big was two steps removed by the friend of a friend, so it was a little tenuous, but had the advantage of being too much hassle to check easily. I hoped this was the case.

I checked out the RSL and found it to be more than suitable – fairly quiet, with a good view of the car park outside. I drove off to check out Tony's address. It was an unassuming terraced house with a large back yard, though I couldn't help but notice the three satellite dishes mounted on the roof. It looked like a bit of overkill, though it was a good sign I had the right house. Parked outside was a hotted up Holden Monaro with a painted motif of a scantily clad girl holding a medieval sword. I took a quick photo of this, and noted the rego – not that I could forget - 'Scream' which presumably bore some relationship to his personal driving style, or was it his sexual prowess? I wondered about the statistics – how often would he be stopped by police compared to a Ford Laser with a number plate 'ABC-123' Perhaps twice as often? I moved back to the RSL, hid my car and prepared for the meeting, keeping an eye out for any new arrivals.

Shortly after our one p.m. meeting time, I saw the Monaro cruising down the road towards the RSL. I had been keeping a good watch, though I realised this had not been necessary as I could hear the Monaro even before I saw it. I watched it cruise past, then pull up in the car park. My mobile phone rang with Tony saying he was in the car park now, and that it would be best if I came out to see him as he had been banned from the club for life, over an incident that occurred last year. I wandered out to the car park and approached the car. Tony saw me coming and climbed out of his car to meet me. We shook hands and began having a casual chat about several issues such as the club, my work, his car and the game last night. I was sure to comment favourably on his 'sick' paint job, which he appreciated eagerly. Eventually it got down to business. *'So mate... what's the go on the cards?'* he asked me casually – without giving too much away. I began my spiel about having trouble with my supplier up in Coffs, and was looking around for a better deal. Tony nodded at intervals and asked a few questions such as the going street price of the cards, what kind of volume I was talking about and some other issues. At this point I was still cautiously wondering how I was being received – was Tony buying the story? *'Yeah... I know how ya feel'* he replied. He then looked me square in the eye and said *'So how do you know Mr Big?'*

I explained that I had just got a referral from a mate of mine Pete, but before I'd finished my answer to this tricky question I suddenly took great interest in the Monaro again – *'Are those sixteen inch wheels?'* I asked. Tony replied that they were in fact seventeen inch wheels, and I gingerly managed to steer the conversation away from my phantom mate Pete.

Tony seemed to have accepted my story, and soon we were talking about the technical aspects of the cable TV smart card business. The more I expressed interest in Tony's knowledge of the business – the more he seemed to open up. I would ask my questions in a way that suggested I had absolutely no idea of technology, so I wouldn't be regarded by Tony as a threat. The dumber I sounded, the keener Tony seemed to 'put me right' and explain how things worked. It was about this time when he casually mentioned he could supply late release DVD's as well – and I expressed a lot of interest in that too. After chatting in his car for about twenty minutes, he said *'Look Dave, I can show you if you want... me place is not far from here and I got a good setup. Maybe you want to take some gear today?'* he asked.

I thought for a moment. If he did take me back to his house and they were suspicious of me – I could be in real trouble. Alternatively if I had managed to pass the 'Reality acting 101' course, I could get some very good evidence indeed. The answer was clear – I had to trust my performance and give it a shot. There were no warning signs I could detect which may suggest I was in trouble – but you never really know. Soon I was cruising off up the road with my new mate Tony.

When we got inside the house, a large and possibly vicious dog greeted us loudly – though began wagging his tail happily when he saw Tony at the door. We walked in and Tony led me into his 'office', which was enough to take my breath away. It was an Aladdin's cave of computer equipment, piles of blank DVD's, stacks of printed DVD covers of *The Hulk* (which was not due for Australian release for another week) and cable TV smart cards lying around. We chatted some more and soon Tony was at the computer, 'burning' some new cable TV smart cards and explaining the process as he went. I had asked him for two cards to start with, and was currently recording everything he did on my covert video camera. After about ten minutes Tony gave me the two cards I had asked for, and I handed him $140 in cash. We chatted for a bit longer as he explained how he ripped the DVDs for copying using some special software that removed the copy protection. I selected a few titles, and then it was time to go back. Tony dropped me back at the club and I walked in, saying I was waiting for my mate to collect me. The Monaro roared up the hill as I sat in the quiet club, almost unable to believe my luck. Not only had I made a purchase of cards, I had got some pirate DVDs as well, and to top it off I had been able to video the entire process. I checked the tape to make sure it had actually recorded correctly, and then I left the club and drove back to Sydney.

Over the next few weeks I met with Tony several times, having a beer at his house, buying some more gear from him, and chatting about business. He never questioned where I had come from, and I suspected this was partly because I had been referred from Mr Big – even if he did say he didn't know me himself. We got on quite well, but try as I might I could not get him to incriminate Mr Big, or provide an angle I could use to approach him myself. The few times I tried, Tony steered the conversation away again and didn't seem keen to talk. It was clear though, that Tony did some stuff for him, and that he was definitely involved in some way. It was a little annoying, but I was still very happy with what I had got. On one of the visits I had spied a list of names with numbers of cards next to the names, and this was clearly a list of the distributors. I was able to get some good covert images of the list, so we added all the names to our intelligence database. Rather than associating with a lowly distributor, I had forged a relationship with the manufacturer, a level above. It was not the top, but it was good enough.

One of my contacts was a small fruit shop vendor. He was reported selling cards to customers from time to time, so I wandered in and browsed around. After selecting several bags of fruit I approached the counter to pay.

'Actually mate, I was wonderin' – you got any of them cards? Me mate got one ages ago and I'm movin' out so I need me own card?' I asked.

He looked at me a little suspiciously and asked who my mate was. I kept chatting, supplying more red herring[70] information than he could be bothered to hear. It was successful, and soon he was telling me how he always had to be careful, and had to

---

[70] Page 128 has details on the Red Herring pretext technique

vet his card customers carefully. In fact he even said he thought he remembered my (fictional) mate. He said he didn't have any cards right now, but said I should come back in a few days. I left and returned a week later. My dodgy fruiterer said he had still been unable to get the stock, so I said I would return later. The next time I visited, the shop was closed without any notice on the window. I waited an hour, had lunch and returned but it was still closed.

The listed phone number for the shop had been disconnected some time ago, so I couldn't call it. Just as I was leaving after having peered in the windows, a middle aged woman came up and said 'Don't tell me he's not here? Damn. Con is so bloody unreliable!' I decided to work her a little and engaged her in conversation. Before long she told me that she had a TV which Con may want, and since he was not there, perhaps I wanted it? She was moving and needed to get rid of it quickly – though she had no remote control. I could sense she half suspected I was there to meet Con for more than just a bunch of bananas, though she didn't ask directly. I immediately saw through her thinly veiled cover story – she was clearly trying to hock some hot property, and I figured Con was probably the local fence. I said I had a mate who may be able to move it, and that I would need to see him first. I asked her for her number, and she was initially hesitant, but soon gave me a mobile number after I suggested I could always leave a message for her through Con (she didn't seem to want this either). I took the number and included it in the report for submission to the police intelligence database later. I had to laugh – when you get into the criminal world, they are just into everything. It is a parallel universe that many never really see, but it is full of people stealing, hocking, doing drugs, manufacturing fraudulent cards and so on. Each criminal has at least one criminal 'occupation' and while you or I may see the fruit shop, the bad guys see it as the 'fence' shop.

Another week later I tried again – and Con was there, but still had no cards for me. He was clearly annoyed.

'*Look, I will ring the guy right now – he doesn't like people to know who he is, but maybe I can get him to come over today and I can give you the card. Can ya wait a bit?*' he inquired. I said that would be fine. He pulled his mobile phone out of his pocket and cursed.

'*Bloody thing's flat. That's f...ed, and I left me charger at home!*' He looked at me, with a mobile phone in my hand – though of course my handset was not a phone but a concealed video camera in disguise. '*Mate, can I borrow your phone? I can call him right now...*' he said to me.

This sent a shiver down my spine as it was just not something I had anticipated. If he discovered my phone was not a phone but a camera, the game could be up. Con may not appreciate the humour in the situation if he discovered I was working undercover, trying to set him up for a bust. Up till now I had found the whole job extremely amusing and had had trouble not laughing at many stages during my criminal foray. Now was not a funny time.

Con reached over for the phone – not aggressively, but the request was just so natural there could be no reason I would stop him making a call on my phone.

'*Ahhh. Actually me phone's flat as well*' I said quickly, and proceeded to put it back into my pocket. Before Con had time to wonder why I had been carrying a phone with a flat battery around in my hand, I pulled my real mobile phone out of my other pocket. I handed the phone to him saying '*This one's me work phone – you can use this one*'. It was a risk, but the potential in the situation was huge. If Con rang on my phone, I would have the supplier's phone number retained in the handset, and even if he deleted it, the number would be on the bill. It would be a solid lead to the next step up the chain. Con did a very slight double take at the odd situation, then just started dialling on the phone and was soon talking to his supplier.

He then hung up, saying *'Thanks mate – he said he's gonna come round this arvo to drop it off at my place. I guess I will have the shop closed then – but ya can come ta my place and pick it up if ya want?'*

I said this was fine, and Con gave me his home address. I had now had a fair bit of contact with him, and I could see he was very comfortable with me. Later that day I visited Con at home, but yet again the supplier had failed to deliver. I had put too much time into this prospect, and figured it was time to give up. If Con had that much trouble getting fraudulent cards, it was clear he was just not big time, and probably not worth pursuing given the undercover operation was working to a budget. There were plenty of other candidates to chase up – though I did make a point of ensuring that the phone number for Con's supplier was noted in the intelligence.

Finally it was time to 'clean up the town' and make some arrests. Together with a client representative we met with the police and devised a strategy. I placed buy orders with all the suppliers I had been meeting with, asking for a solid quantity of stock. I set up the buys and gave the details to the police. They asked if I thought it was worth a visit to Con, but I said not to bother – it would be hard to get him with any stock, and I preferred not to bust him this round as we wanted to work more on his supplier next time round.

The arrest operation went like clockwork. Although I was not involved personally in the arrests, the police were armed with search warrants and visited each supplier in turn at the arranged time and place, and each time they would be carrying fraudulent smart cards. This, together with the close-up covert video evidence of the cards and cash changing hands made for a very solid case. I had wanted the police to bust Tony before any of the other suppliers, however this just wasn't possible because the police were limited in time and I was not able to line up Tony for a visit at the right time. Still, the later search at Tony's place found everything as I had documented in my report, together with a supply of drugs and stolen property. The client was absolutely astounded when I was able to supply a report containing a sequence of close up video prints showing the offender actually manufacturing the cards in his own home, and then handing them to me in return for a wad of cash. We never managed to bring down Mr Big himself, though we were able to supply some good intelligence to the police which they would use later on. In life, you can run but you can't hide – Big Brother will catch you eventually – it is just a matter of time!

I wasn't required to attend the court cases which all occurred several months later, as every offender had pleaded guilty, and with such watertight surveillance evidence, there was little else they could do. The Daily Telegraph reported the case with photos and described it as an 'elaborate undercover operation' – even though the reality was nothing more than a little homework, a few calls and confidence. I've had no acting training, and wouldn't even consider myself an actor – though on the job, when your life may depend on it – your mind can push you to perform, and thankfully I did well enough to win this game.

CHAPTER 29: RURAL SURVEILLANCE

Most people associate the term 'surveillance' with darkly tinted vehicles and oversized moustaches. Surveillance can also be done on foot, with follows through public transport or buildings. Another of the more difficult modes of surveillance is remote areas or rural surveillance. Here, the professional of the art is still required to carry out their job as usual, yet without many of the resources which are usually taken for granted. Everything is difficult in rural surveillance, and mastering this area shows true dedication to the art.

Finding the right address is often the first nightmare, even for qualified agents. I recall spending an entire day watching the male occupant of Lot 7 in a certain country town, and was pleased to see him being quite active. Unfortunately there were few locations to hide on foot, so I was inside a vehicle. Late in the afternoon I spotted a male walking past, and when he saw my vehicle he immediately began to walk with a very pronounced limp and stare at the car. This struck me as odd, and I began to wonder why. Perhaps he had an injury claim, just like the subject I was watching... who was 'also' claiming for an injured leg. Then I wondered if perhaps this *was* the actual subject, and I had been tailing the wrong guy. Curiosity got the better of me, and after a suitable period I drove off to check things out. It wasn't far down the road when I suddenly saw a sign, and my heart sank. It was a fairly small sign, nailed to a post on a house not far from the one I'd been watching, and on the same road.

The sign said simply '*Lot 7*' and with that everything became clear. While I had arrived very early in the morning, I had not checked out the area properly, and was unaware there were in fact two properties marked Lot 7 on the very same road. Obviously the guy I wanted was residing at the other one, but since he was rather cluey, he picked the tinted vehicle despite it being parked well out of sight of his house. I decided to leave immediately and didn't see him again. There was little point continuing, although at least we were now had a proper photograph of the 'right' Lot 7, as well as a better description. This job occurred early on in my career, but taught me a valuable lesson about identifying properties on rural surveillance. Apart from the very early start and the long drive to get to rural jobs, the next big hurdle is finding the right property.

In NSW, Lot and DP (DP is known as Deposited Plan, which is like a land map of the area) is one method of property identification, property name is another, RMB (Registered Mail Box) is yet another. Newer systems work on the distance in metres from town intersections, with street numbering that may then have #173 and #211 adjacent to each other. For those city folk who take street numbers for granted, the rural environment is another world. To complicate matters, the rural surveillance professional cannot easily knock and ask the locals, because any such contact can quickly be the talk of the town ('a *guy was looking for you Dave, did he find you?*' '*No, what guy?*'). Even if you do ask for directions you may be told to go down that way for about two miles then turn left etc., but of course rural miles are 'different' to city miles, by largely varying factors. And if this was not enough, when you finally get to the right letterbox, you may well find it situated next to half a dozen others, all in a row. Quite convenient for the local postman who already has a large run to cover, but for the surveillance agent who is trying to identify a property based on the numbering on the letterbox sitting out the front, life just isn't that simple.

The answer is in the phrase: *Prior Preparation Prevents Poor Performance.* Time spent in reconnaissance is never wasted, and determining the exact location before attending the address is important. Driving up and down a quiet country road looking for an address is not appropriate, and will often draw attention

415

from locals including suspicion or a desire to help. Neither kind of attention is desirable. The best option is to get the best maps available of the area and study these well. Electronic maps are very good for this, and are readily available from map shops. Government records can also be consulted to see where the property is on a plan drawing, which will show specific layouts[71]. Sometimes it is worth looking at a photograph of the property from aerial photographs. This is often fairly easy to do, and often a stereoscopic image can be viewed for no charge in some government departments. This provides a rich three-dimensional image which can greatly assist any planning, such as where the best location is to site the observation position, or how difficult it is to move around in that area. Three-dimensional images will convey relative contour information, which can show likely obstructions or good locations to observe from. This is far more difficult with paper maps, as the flat contours must be inspected for numeric values to determine elevations.

When there is any confusion about addresses, telephoning local numbers at random will often give you the answers you need. Pick any number at all in any smaller town and the person answering is likely to know the right property, or at least suggest someone who does. This can be invaluable information, knowing before you get there that you are looking for the red brick homestead with the water tower on the left and a yellow picket fence. A few calls to various townsfolk at random can often bring up some surprises.

Let's ring Mr Jones, who we find in the same town.

'Hello, is that Robert?'

'No, it's Pete Jones here, who were you after?'

---

[71] CHAPTER 4: LOCATING PEOPLE / FACTUAL INQUIRIES on page 72

'Oh, sorry, I was after Rob Taylor. Crikey I must have the wrong number, but this was the one Sheryl gave me. I don't suppose you know Rob?'

'Oh yeah, I think he's up on the other side of the hill, but I am not sure where exactly'

'No worries, maybe I will try his work number. Is he still working for the fencing contractors do you know?'

'Nah, not sure sorry mate'

'That's ok. Perhaps I will see him in town sometime. Has he still got the ute?'

'Yes'

'Is that the old blue one?'

'Nah, I think its white actually, but I think he's had it for ages'

Here we have rung a resident at random. By giving more information than we asked for we were able to obtain a lot of information. This is the two for one rule in action. We 'gave' *Sheryl, fencing contractors and ute.* We now know he is on the other side of the 'hill', that he is unlikely to be a fencing contractor, and that he drives a *white* ute. Calling a further resident at random we could almost sound like we know him well, by dropping even just one key piece of information such as Rob's 'white ute' in any conversation, to show familiarity. (*'He must know Rob, because he knows what kind of car he drives!'*) The type of car a subject drives is a critical identifier, especially given the difficulty there is to get good close-up images on rural surveillance. Seeing a person fitting the description *and* driving the right car, we can be far more confident of having the right person.

Another reason that telephone contact may be appropriate prior to doing a job, is to find out of they are still there, or if perhaps they are on holidays. Given that most rural locations are many hours drive away, you want to make sure you are not wasting your time. Unlike going to visit your Aunt Mavis 'in the sticks', you cannot easily call ahead to a surveillance subject directly, and make a firm appointment. Other locals will often be able to assist you in finding this information out and the local post office is a good place to start. Try to call later in the day when the postie is back from his run, as this is the guy you want, not the postmaster himself.

Once you think you have the right property, it is often good to drive the length of the road to get a better feel for it. You could look to see if there are perhaps two properties marked with the same lot number for example, or if there is some other issue you should consider. Note that you also need to balance this with reducing the amount of driving done on the quiet roads, as any movement may be viewed as suspicious by the locals. It is often best to arrive in the late afternoon, so that the property can be identified correctly in the daylight hours. There is nothing worse than struggling to find a rural property in the early dawn, knowing you need to locate it quickly else the residents may leave for the day without you.

Some rural jobs are so delicate, they are nearly impossible to do. I once arrived in the late afternoon to a property, and had a little difficulty finding it. As a result I drove past the right property a little slowly, though not what I would consider suspiciously slowly. Several minutes later I realised it was the right property and returned again, hoping to park on the other side it. I whizzed past much faster this time, and found a quiet location where I stopped to park. I was only intending to go out on foot for a closer look, but shortly after I got out of the car, the subject came roaring out of the gate in his four-wheel drive car and drove past me, right up to where I had parked my surveillance van.

An associate was with me at the time who managed to fend him off, though it was clear the job was blown before it was even started. He was peering into the car looking for cameras and openly said he thought we were investigators. Fortunately there was little to see, so our man returned home in some doubt, though I knew I couldn't use my car on this job again. We had literally driven past once slowly and then again at some speed, several minutes later, but that was enough. With quiet roads and observant farmers, sometimes the briefest glimpse or mistake can spoil the job in seconds, and with any country job it is always a long drive home! He may have been caught by investigators recently, or he may have watched a show on PI's, though the simple fact is that it was probably just the luck of the draw. You get that with surveillance!

Rural surveillance issues

There are many inhibitors to rural surveillance, which is why it is regarded as one of the more difficult forms of investigation. It can require years of experience to get right. Ex-military personnel often conduct this type of surveillance, as they are trained and comfortable in field environments. This surveillance is also frequently carried out by Fisheries Compliance Officers, who hide in rugged coastline and observe abalone poachers. General urban surveillance is difficult enough, but the following list highlights why this area is largely for 'professionals' only.

- Distance and cost to get to rural locations

- Difficulty locating specific rural addresses, including bush navigation

- Difficulty identifying subjects accurately in remote areas

- Visual distance to target. Long stand-off distances require specialised lenses

- Lack of on-street parked vehicles means its difficult to blend in

- Difficulty in following vehicles, with sparse traffic to hide amongst

- Heightened awareness of locals to strangers and unusual vehicles

- Difficult to hide car when moving out on foot, as you can't park too close

- Environmental issues with field deployment. Rain and cameras don't mix well

- Actual distance to target means long walks to deploy in the field

- Communication difficulties. Radios required when there is no phone coverage

- Movement inhibitors. Unable to move easily during day, or at speed when on foot

- Camouflage requires skill and equipment

- Safety issues with lone PI's on an isolated property

- Field environment. Requires carriage of water and rations

- Time issues. Farmers work long days with very early starts

- Animal issues. Aggressive dogs, inquisitive cattle herds. See The case of the inquisitive cow on page 56

- Property sizes. One property can span many kilometres, so action may move away

- Power issues. No vehicle power, so must carry several batteries for cameras

Pre-Surveillance inquiries (Rural)

- Conduct all checks as previously listed for urban areas.

- Contact the subject on a pretext to identify if the address is current. Ensure they are not on holidays or away prior to you actually travelling there.

- Accurately locate address by phone pretext, or by contacting local post office.

- Obtain maps of the area, such as topographical if required.

- Aerial photographs (inspect at Lands Department if appropriate)

- If necessary, contact various local businesses or clubs etc. on pretext, to assist information gathering (e.g. *'he drives an orange ute, he is out fencing with the Johnstone's'*).

Commencing rural stakeouts

You've deciphered the property address, driven for hours to get there, and managed to actually find it. What next?

- Familiarise yourself with the local town area; shops, railway, pubs.

- Physically observe the target property.

- Conduct a drive-past (see page 184).

- Conduct a walk past.

- Conduct a Close Target Reconnaissance (see page 424).

- Assess potential observation position (OP) sites for the vehicle (see page 189).

- If there are no good vehicle OP sites, then:

- - Assess good vehicle hide sites

  - Assess good foot based OP sites

- Enter the OP carefully.

- Pause for a moment and tune into the location. Check if you were seen.

- If vehicle departs early on day one and does not return until late afternoon, the subject is likely working off-site. In this case, day two will have you near the exit in the morning, ready to follow the subject to the work address in your car.

- Two-up operations involve one agent in the vehicle and a field operator. This works better for concealing the vehicle, as well as enabling immediate town follows. The field operator observes the property, and alerts the vehicle agent when there are vehicles departing. This allows the surveillance vehicle to be located well out of sight, but able to be quickly being brought in to conduct a follow when notified.

Camouflage

It's far better to adopt full camouflage clothing, than to have a mismatch such as a hunters' jacket with blue jeans. A professional will dress as a professional, and it is often the little things that give you away. Shiny belt buckles glint in the sun and may be enough to catch their eye as they walk past. The odds are always stacked against you in any case, so make sure all your clothing fits the environment. Full camouflage clothing can also be used for good effect in adopting a pretext as a soldier on operations, as seen in the story The case of a favourable compromise on page 428.

You should consider wearing a full disruptive pattern camouflage uniform, a hat and boots, gloves, watch or wrist covers and a head net or camouflage head wrap. Never apply camouflage cream. Rural surveillance operators often need to change into civilian clothes quickly when moving into town. Camouflage cream is hard to remove quickly from the skin and attracts attention. It is best to use a head net which can be removed instantly, and replaced just as quickly as conditions dictate.

When constructing a camouflage 'hide' or OP, consider using a professional camouflage net. Try to add branches or foliage for better effect, and to break up the outline. Remove foliage for personal space in bushes and to remove noise, or to increase visibility. Always watch for shadows, as a dark 'cave' structure is distinctive when seen from afar. Remember that the sun is constantly moving, so the hide should be continually assessed, and changes made as appropriate.

Covert foot movement

Also known as the ghost walk, this simple technique allows you to move silently through the bush. It involves basic common sense, and a little more awareness.

- Be confident, move smoothly. Faltering movement attracts attention.

- Stride, don't run. Running isn't much faster but is always more visible.

- For stealthy foot movement, adopt the ghost walk. Heels down first to anchor your foot to ground. Roll the outside of your boot slowly from heel to toe, while checking for twig noises. Roll the outside edge of boot towards inside edge, eventually laying it flat. Consider lifting and replacing foot if twig noise exists, or, move noisy items by brushing gently away with a foot or hand.

- Move from cover to cover using shadows or trees, pausing to check your surrounds.

- Preferably move through 'dead' ground which is concealed from view.

- Watch soft earth, especially on tracks as footprints will be noticed.

Close target reconnaissance (CTR)

This technique is where you covertly probe the property to assess it fully. By definition it is close, and requires careful consideration and a heightened sense of awareness. You can be very vulnerable conducting a CTR, but there are a lot of benefits. Sometimes the best observation position is right under their noses, and usually the only way to really find out is to go there and see for yourself.

- Move to general location, best done under the cover of darkness.

- Look for natural lines for concealed movement, such as trees and dead ground.

- Approach the target head-on in a direct line. Don't walk *across* the field of view.

- After observing the target, retreat to cover, then move around the target.

- Conduct another straight 'probe' towards target property.

- Subsequent probes may be deeper and closer if it seems safe to do so.

- Use principals of covert movement.

- Assess ground for observation points, and withdrawal routes.

- Listen and smell, as well as watch.

- Look for tracks on the ground and fur or wear marks on fence posts and other signs.

- Where vehicles are present on site, attempt to get registration numbers.

- If possible approach closely and physically feel registration letters in the darkness.

- If unable to get too close, consider night shot video camera illumination.

- Obtaining a confirmed registration is important, as it enables long-range stand-off. Vehicles can then be confidently picked up later when in town, or if lost.

Second agent

Where the budget affords a second agent, the field operator may be dropped off, and then the second vehicle can withdraw well away and stand by for subsequent action. This method enables dropping field agents much closer to the target than could occur if they used their own transport, while allowing the surveillance vehicle to be taken well away. Any departure from the target address is observed by the field agent, who then notifies the Quick Response Force (QRF) or vehicle. The surveillance vehicle then picks up the follow very cleanly, as contact is established well away from the property.

Vehicle hide

Often a surveillance vehicle is required to be hidden in an area of operations. This is actually quite difficult as unmanned vehicles attract some degree of interest in such environments. A good location can be found on a fire trail, well off the road. Ensure the vehicle is facing the right direction for rapid departure at all times (reverse in). Consider placing a note in the window saying '*John, will be back soon, just went to get another sample – Pete*' or some other note that may allay any suspicion, or prevent theft as it implies there are two males likely to return to the car at any time. Open the glove box and ensure that no documents or other items are visible that may indicate the nature of your business.

Observation points (OPs)

While in an OP, one should ensure it is as comfortable and quiet as possible. On entry, ensure camera is ready and accessible, in case of action while setting up. Advise the second operator of the location (*'Now in OP, 300m south of property'*). Remove all loose twigs and sticks from the immediate OP area. Remove any visual obstructions, such as small branches. Set up a tripod if necessary. Apply camouflage to the hide. Prepare routes of approach or withdrawal, to ensure they are silent, unobstructed and familiar. Commence waiting for action. Listen, watch, smell, and feel.

Periodically check 360° in case of any movement to the rear. Be aware the sun rotates and shadows change. Be prepared to modify camouflage slightly at intervals. If approached, pack up all equipment ready for a speedy departure. Consider withdrawal versus risk of detection. It may be better to remain put and risk the detection as it is surprisingly easy to hide in plain view, or remain undetected provided you remain still and well camouflaged.

Rural inventory

Being prepared means constantly having a mental checklist of necessary items that are taken on operations. They should be in good condition, lightweight and functional. The less stuff you bring the better, because you never know how far you need to walk, or even how far you may need to run!

- Camouflage clothing and boots

- Camouflage pack, netting or 'scrim'

- Camouflage gloves / scarf / head-net / hat

- Food / water

- Small tripod

- Civilian clothes for quick changes (shorts / T-shirt worn underneath)

- Map and compass

- Bush saw for cutting bushes and foliage in OPs

Early starts in rural areas

Capturing movement properly requires arriving before any movement starts, else you may not know if the person you are observing actually came from the address, or is perhaps a worker. Farmers have an annoying habit of rising at the crack of dawn! There are a lot of unknowns in surveillance, so you need to remove any uncertainty where you can, such as being confident that nobody would have already left the property when you start, and anyone that subsequently does leave is an occupant, not just a visitor (i.e. they have stayed the night there). Another issue to consider is movement to observation points. Farmers have years of experience knowing their land and what moves on it, unlike city folk who are far less observant. A farmer may pick you moving from quite a distance because your movement is unlike their cattle, or perhaps notice your boot prints in the soft earth, simply because they know their land and are watchful of the fox prints and so on. The best option is to be well in place before they rise. The sequence of events can also tell more of a story, and seeing a smaller part of the jigsaw may not enable you to solve the whole puzzle. Often there is critical activity that occurs early on in the day. It is a special time, the advent of morning, the rise of the sun, transition from night to day. Gates may be unlocked, feed distributed and blinds thrown open. It is not uncommon to see a flurry of early morning movement, then virtually none during the remainder of the day.

Stay quiet when close to a target

While in motion, the surveillance operator rarely uses the radio to receive and it is best to keep it off lest it blare out at an inopportune moment. An earpiece is better and allows constant contact, though the earpiece wire can be a distraction when moving through thick foliage. There is little need for the vehicle to contact the surveillance agent once the observation position is in place. Contact is far more likely from the agent to the vehicle, as the vehicle enjoys relative safety with the greater distance from the property. Sometimes it is best for the agent on foot to turn down the volume or even switch off a radio while in motion.

The case of a favourable compromise

Key learning points

- Close target reconnaissance / covert foot movement
- Camouflage / hides / observation posts
- Working in teams / agent communications
- Contingency response / convert compromise to advantage
- Preparation and planning
- Surveillance in rural areas

It was a pleasant drive to Muswellbrook, as Bob and I chatted in the car. We had done a map reconnaissance and discovered that this particular property was really quite remote. Situated almost an hour outside of the town itself, the property was located in a dense valley, with the 'driveway' being a winding dirt track nearly eight kilometres long. We had to conduct surveillance on a guy in the property, who had claimed he was nearly totally incapacitated. As always, we wondered and mused about how the job would go, both knowing it may be over before it started, or that it may run longer than expected.

Due to the difficulty and terrain on this job, I had done an extensive inspection of the area, which included viewing stereoscopic aerial photographs of the property in the Department of Lands. Seeing the vegetation overlayed on the rippling landscape helped me to visualise the ground and plan my approach or possible observation points.

We arrived in the early morning, which for rural surveillance means not only before the sun gets up, but before the farmers get up.

*   *   *   *   *   *   *

Finally we rolled up to the turnoff to the property. It took a little searching with the poorly signed roads, but we were finally confident of our position. I unloaded my equipment and donned the final pieces of my camouflage attire, my nets and my gloves. After testing radios, I was ready to depart, dressed from head to foot in military clothing, and carrying a large, heavy army pack.

I began the long walk to the property, while Bob turned around, moved a short distance away from the driveway entrance, and parked up a fire trail. He didn't want to draw attention to the surveillance vehicle, which is always difficult in remote areas. He turned the surveillance vehicle around so it was now facing back in the right direction, ready for a speedy exit.

The night was silent as I crunched up the side of the road, eyes peering into the blackness. I focused on listening between steps, knowing my ears were my strongest sense in the darkness. I glanced at the horizon and saw the faint blue glimmer of dawn rising up. I could see there was still well over an hour until daybreak, which would be plenty of time. I began to descend into the deep valley, which would be hiding from the sun's rays for longer. I was careful to avoid the soft earth for fear of leaving footprints in this remote area. I had considered going cross country, but the additional time taken in navigating and fence jumping was just not worth the potential to remain better concealed. As usual I had made a 'call', and placed my bet. Navigating via roads in hostile areas is contrary to Special Forces doctrine, but with the more limited resources and requirements of commercial surveillance, one must compromise at times.

I sensed the cooler air as I continued my descent. It was welcome relief as I had just begun to sweat with the weight of my large pack, as well as the adrenaline of my infiltration. The mental energy expended in straining to hear the slightest sound, or constantly rehearsing 'what if' scenarios was as draining as the physical exertion. What if a car comes, where will I go? What if a farmer sees me from afar? What if he is very close? What if a dog barks? Each step of my journey required analysis, looking for places to hide, looking for features to navigate by, and looking for potential threats. Movement is a vulnerable state, and I looked forward to finally nestling into my surveillance burrow or hide, safe in the static environment. There, I could quietly listen and watch for danger, as movement itself draws attention, despite the most elaborate camouflage.

A dog barked in the distance, and my heart jumped. It was too far away to startle me, and I knew it was good to keep moving at a controlled smooth pace rather than to be unnerved by it.

Finally I saw a tiny shack in the distance, near the base of the valley, and figured it must be my target. I had moved slightly faster than expected, and was pleased to see that the cover of darkness would still cloak my movement for another half hour at least. It was the perfect time, light just breaking enough to illuminate the inky darkness, but not enough to allow others to see details unless they were close, and this was not something I was planning!

I propped down, and sat the base of my pack on a small mound of earth. The straps creaked slightly with the easing of the weight. I pulled out my topographic map and studied it closely, matching the features around me. The valley was reasonably well defined which made life easier, and my counted paces also confirmed I must be close. Still I had to be sure, as it is always something to worry about, watching the wrong house or the wrong person – with so many unknowns this possibility is all too easy, and can not only waste resources such as time, but also spoil the job. I switched on my radio, saying 'Bravo this is Charlie'. There was a pause, and then Bob responded 'Bravo'.

I continued 'Target now in sight, no vehicles, and no lights. Am moving in closer now.'

Bob replied 'Roger'. I switched off the radio again.

Surveying the landscape, I saw there were bushes at intervals, with a more heavily wooded area located some five hundred metres from the property on either side. Being still too far from the property in the poor light, I decided to venture closer. I found a well defined tree and cached my large pack near the base under some brush. This would allow me more flexibility and speed, as well as reducing my movement outline while so close to the target. I made a steady approach towards the shed, aiming to do so in a straight line. This would make my movement far less noticeable than if I had moved across the field of view.

At each bush I paused briefly and peered through the branches, as is drummed into soldiers in basic training. Why expose yourself and increase movement by looking over or around, when you can gaze comfortably through your concealment? With each bound I could see more and more, though of course this also meant moving closer to the danger as well.

Not only was I looking at the shed, but I needed to assess the likely points of activity. Farmers spend a long time, and cover large distances, on their land, but it is difficult for agents to move easily during daylight hours, to follow and cover the action properly. The trick is to predict the best location early on. I could see no new tracks, or shiny fencing wire – nothing which may suggest a likely place of work. From where I could see though, there were several items nearer the small homestead which were suggestive of ongoing work. There were tools strewn about and a clutter of items that indicated activity of varying degrees. This was a good sign.

I stared at the property for several moments, soaking up the environment carefully. Listening, watching, smelling and feeling. It was not bad, though there was still some foliage partially obstructing the view of the main areas. I could see a winding dirt track snaking its way along the side of the ridge I was on. I wondered if a vehicle movement was likely, or whether any activity would occur solely around the home. It was difficult to tell at this early stage. I could not see a vehicle parked outside, but figured it would probably be around the back, out of sight.

I decided to relocate to the other side of the valley, which would have a better view of both the property and of the dirt track. Walking briskly back to where I had left my pack, I considered my options. I had not surveyed the rear of the property, but it did not look particularly viable as there was not much of a backyard and the rear of the property adjoined the National Park, which was quite dense and difficult to see through. I could probably get quite close to the rear, but this would make life difficult in many ways, particularly if they had a dog. I decided the best observation point would be simply the other side of the valley. I reached my pack and saddled up, figuring there was no requirement for further probes. I moved around the property in a wide circle, among the cover of the dense forested area which was still well away from the homestead. After a while, I chose a suitable line of approach, and again stalked towards the house. There was no sign of the sun, but the light was now bathing the valley in a dull glow. I knew that I was now able to be seen from the house, if they were to look in my direction.

I moved closer to some more bushes, and then on to the next. The field of view improved with each bound, but the coverage became more and more sparse. I propped near the base of a bush and took a load off my back while I soaked in the atmosphere. The dewy scent of the early morning filled my nostrils, mingled with faint manure and fresh country air. Nature was still asleep in this magical moment. I could now see the homestead reasonably easily. There were some more bushes some distance in front which were obstructing my view. If these were gone it would be nearly perfect. There weren't many, in fact only one that would barely conceal me, though a fold in the ground offered a slight improvement. I briefly considered removing the bush entirely, which I had done before. Why put up with visual obstructions when you can remove them and create a cleared 'fire lane' as termed in the military. I did carry a small gardening saw, but this bush was a little too large, and removing it may have alerted a cluey farmer, or result in drag marks across the wet ground.

I realised I had an important decision to make. I could remain where I was, which offered reasonable view, though with some annoying obstructions. I was safe, in that I was concealed and was not isolated. In emergencies I had a covered escape route whereby I could withdraw into the relative safety of the dense forested area at the rear, where I would quickly melt away. I sat for some time, weighing up my options. Being now four hundred metres away, it was a stretch for my camera optics, and I would prefer to be a little closer. The bush was about a hundred metres in front, but it was both small and isolated. Being closer I would probably get much better video, though would have to be slightly more disciplined in my observation position, as it was close enough for me to be heard. Military doctrine cautions against using isolated cover, as it can lead to being hemmed in. Any daylight withdrawal across the open ground will surely be detected if others are nearby.

Curiosity got the better of me. It was a risk, but after consideration I chose better video over better concealment, and began moving steadily to my new, closer position. I took my pack with me, reasoning that I should limit my movements now that I was so close and exposed to the house instead of needing to return for it later if I confirmed the position was good. I pondered my decision.

I reached my new position and kneeled down, surveying the scene. I now had an unobstructed view of the entire property, as well as the dirt track on the far side of the ridge. I hoped any movement on foot would also follow this side of the valley, and be away from the direction of my location. I began to set up my camera on a tripod, and covered it with camouflage, then began adjusting the branches to better conceal my hide. Finally I was happy with my position and began to slightly relax, as much as one can in such an environment. The primitive fight or flight mechanism inside me ensured that my heartbeat stayed slightly faster to ensure I was prepared for the unknown.

'Bravo, this is Charlie' I called.

'Bravo' was the reply.

'Now in the OP at approx three hundred metres. Good visual of property. No vehicles or movement. No lights' I continued. 'Roger' was the reply.

Now the scene was set, so I waited. Nothing happened. Nothing at all. After moving constantly with eyes and ears 'on edge', there was a distinct transition to this new waiting phase. I wriggled slightly, burrowing my hip into the soft earth, and gazed at the homestead, quietly looking for any clues to what may happen.

It was well over an hour before it happened, a sharp crack like a shot, sending my fingers jumping in response. Hairs pricked on the back of my neck and I strained to see anything but there was nothing. A moment later I heard another muffled sound, then the sound of a door slamming. I flicked the switch on my video camera and zoomed in for a closer look, but there was nothing to see. Then the hammering started, slowly at first, but then faster as the worker got into rhythm. I could see nothing but the front of the property, staring back at me, in a stubborn and sullen manner that suggested I had made a bad call. Damn, I should have gone round the back after all. Then the hammering stopped. My finder traced the start button on the video, but there was still nothing to see. I wondered if I should move again, and looked around behind me.

'Oops' I gasped silently. The cover had looked isolated in the darkness of the early dawn, but with the now strong and warming rays of the sun, my position was now looking very exposed.

The warm sun had since come through silently like a swift broom, sweeping away the cobwebs of the night, while I had been preoccupied with staring at the homestead.

I felt vulnerable, like a cockroach caught out in the open, when the light is flicked on. I felt a primitive urge to scurry away, to

435

burrow, to cover myself and hide from predators. I looked back at the safer coverage area that I had considered earlier. It was not that far away, and although it would mean moving in daylight I figured there was nobody out and about yet, so perhaps I still had an opportunity if I moved quickly. That opportunity was soon snatched away.

The sound of a car engine filled the valley with a throbbing sound, and my heart leapt. At least the car meant the movement would probably be along the track, and not through the paddock towards me. A battered green ute emerged from the side of the property, curling around the cluttered area and then stopping directly outside the front door. My video was rolling, and was able to capture the car stopping, and a male climbing out. He began lifting something from the rear of the ute and carrying it to a work bench. Bingo.

I notified Bob of the vehicle's appearance via the radio, and began to describe the scene slightly. Bob sounded mildly annoyed and said 'On the phone, wait out'. I continued to document the scene before me. It was still too hard to get an ID on his face, however his actions were fairly clear as he worked hard, bending, hammering and generally doing what every farmer does on a daily basis. The only difference was that this one had a large insurance claim for his bad back, and given the remote location, he could probably feel safe from prying eyes. Any strange vehicle that dared to venture down the dirt track would be picked miles away. Of course he would not have considered a military approach, with a surveillance agent camouflaged in the bushes! This was the only way to approach such a location.

Eventually he stopped his work and got back into the car. I was very pleased to have seen action so early on in the job, and while I did not know that it was the right guy, he certainly fitted the description supplied. *'Standby, standby, green ute moving now'* I now barked into the radio. There was no response. Assuming Bob had not heard me, I gave the call again, but again there was no response. The vehicle lumbered out and commenced climbing out of the valley. It moved at a steady pace, but I could see it jumping and bouncing along the winding track. Every so often it would put a wheel into a puddle from the recent rains and send a spray of water, signifying the movement. I continued barking into the radio. *'GO, go, go, green ute moving now!'* I shouted loudly under the droning noise of the vehicle engine. I checked my radio set, for the right channel, for the right volume, for anything. I wiggled the antenna and tried again. By now the vehicle was nearly out of sight, and I watched helplessly as it disappeared. I could only hope that Bob had got my message, and it was only his reply I couldn't hear. I knew only too well that failing to get a follow on this vehicle departing so early meant only one thing – a waste of the rest of the day. This movement would probably be the 'off to work' move, and there would be nothing to do on the property while he was gone. It could be worse, I figured, with the warm sun on my face. I tried the radio again, but there was nothing.

'Charlie this is Bravo' sounded the radio in my top pocket.

'Charlie' I replied.

'Sorry, was on the phone. Any further action?' he asked.

I wanted to laugh and cry at the same time. It wasn't that long that he had been away, and I figured he lowered the volume or switched off the radio while talking on the mobile. The chance of missing the action during this short time was probably low. I considered my response slowly, alternating between factual and sarcastic. I decided that a factual answer would probably convey volumes of sarcasm anyway, and replied

'Yes, the green ute left about seven minutes ago'.

There was a pause. It was ever so slightly longer than the pause Bob would normally allow on the radio. I smiled inside.

'What? Has it really gone? Tell me you're kidding!' his alpha male ego replied, though I could detect a subtle degree of concern in his voice.

'Yes, I tried hard to raise you, but there was no reply' I stated. 'Shit, I am going into town' he replied. I could faintly hear his engine whining, despite him being several kilometres away. The dirt track was nearly eight kilometres, but it wound around the valley, so I picked his parking location as about three kilometres away.

Well, that was that. The subject had left, probably for the entire day, which meant I was effectively off duty for several hours. I knew I would have plenty of warning for when he returned, so I was able to relax a little. At least it was not a total loss, as I already had good footage of him working hard, assuming, of course, that it was really him. I looked back at the homestead, peering at the front door as I wondered if there was anyone else home. Perhaps he lived by himself? No sooner had I wondered this than I saw the screen door swing open and a small framed woman came striding out, accompanied by a cattle dog, darting about. I watched the screen door slam shut, the clear sound slightly delayed due to the distance. I got a quick shot of her, to document her identity and time of arrival on the scene, and then lowered my camera. Dogs were not always a good thing, but at least this one was some distance away. At first I thought the woman was going to walk up the track, but then she veered off and began heading up the centre of the valley.

Her new direction began to look closer to my position, with her energetic dog bounding up ahead. I began to feel

438

uncomfortable; wishing I had moved faster to withdraw to the safer location after the vehicle had left earlier. I still had time now, but such a move would be quite risky. Filled with indecision, I made another call, and decided to stick it out. I checked the direction she was going and figured she would come close, but not close enough for me to worry too much, and I could try to melt a little into the folds of the earth! Previous jobs had seen me hiding just metres from people and not being seen, so I felt a degree of confidence, and more so being in my camouflage uniform, but it was the dog I was worried about. There was a small fence between us however, so I quietly packed away my camera and tripod and prepared to lie very still.

The woman got closer, and I could make out her facial features. 'Must be his wife' I thought to myself, wondering if I should have moved earlier. 'She'll go right past' I figured, debating the thought in my mind, as I considered my response to detection. Closer still, then closer, then the dog stopped bounding and stood very still. The woman continued walking. Then I could see the dog looking around slowly. After a while, he took off like a rocket, barking and yapping excitedly. He bounded towards me, almost directly in a straight line. My heart sank as I realised he must have smelled my perspiration. Odour is not so easy to camouflage.

In a few seconds the dog was at the fence, and I glanced back at the woman, who seemed disinterested and kept walking. I sighed with relief, but it was short lived as the dog would not give up. I didn't move, but I could feel that the dog could actually see as well as smell me. For him the game was up! It was now a question of him convincing his mistress. She did not take much convincing, and was soon striding towards me. The fence was only a few metres away, and I hoped she would stop there and move on, though I sensed this was not likely. I had to make another decision. I could run away right now, risking sure detection, but refusing to confront the woman. I did not have much time to think, and soon she was straddling the fence with practiced ease.

My mind racing, I thought very quickly, and... stood up. The response was immediate. The dog fell silent. The woman froze. There was a moment where time stood still, as the three players assessed the new situation. Figuring it was my move, I spoke. '*Hello! Sorry to bother you, I hope I didn't startle you, I am on an Army navigation exercise*' I stated authoritatively. There was no response from either her or the dog, as both stood transfixed, eyes drilling right through me. Pulling a map from my pocket (which elicited a slight twitch in her face) I continued '*See, according to my map I think we are here, but I can't find this ridge line. Have you heard of a mountain called Black Knob?*' She nodded automatically in response to my question, so I continued my dialogue, sensing that the ice had been broken. I explained that I was lost, and that I needed to radio through when I reached my navigation target en route to the mountain. '*Where is it from here?*' I asked, and she pointed behind her house towards the National Park area. '*Yes, I thought that was the right direction. Have you seen any other guys in camouflage around here yet?*' I asked.

She said '*No, no I haven't. How many are there?*'

Her question was a good sign, and she seemed relieved to hear I was perhaps part of a group and not a lone crackpot. I told her there were a few, not many, but that she may see others. I was glad I was in full uniform, as I felt she may not have been so ready to believe me if I had a non-army pack, or perhaps only half camouflage clothing. Looking the part was so important for this particular cover story.

'Look I am sorry to startle you, I won't be that long and I'll be on my way' I continued in a reassuring tone. 'Is this your property?' She replied 'Yes it is, though my husband has just left, which is why I am more worried being on my own'.

BINGO. This was the opening I needed, and I didn't let the opportunity slip away. 'I see. Was that him leaving in the green ute I saw earlier?'

She paused for a brief moment and I thought she wasn't going to tell me, but then she replied 'Yes, that's John, he has gone off to work.'

'What kind of work does he do?' I asked casually, as if it was just a polite thing to say.

'He works at the power station, so he has to leave early because it is almost an hour's drive. There is not much work around here, except on the land' she replied.

I knew I was almost there, and launched into a short explanation of how my uncle worked at a power station before he retired, going into details such as some of the problems he faced as a technician, and how he nearly blacked out half of Goulburn when he wired up a transformer wrongly. I strung the story out while I watched her face intently, then I casually dropped my Trojan question in the most off-hand manner I could muster, with a disinterested look on my face. 'What exactly does he do at the power station?' I asked. This time there was no pause and she replied confidently 'He's a gardener, he does the grounds maintenance'.

Now it was my time to pause. The words hung there in the air, pregnant with expectation. I wondered if I was dreaming. I took a moment to respond. If only this woman realised how hard PI's had to work to get this sort of information. It was pure gold, not only did I know where he worked, but I also knew what he did,

441

and there was even the comforting identification of him by name. In effect, she solved my entire case in the space of ten seconds of conversation. Had I knocked on her door and asked the questions outright, she would never have told me. It was purely the scenario that enabled me to coax the information out of her. By being in such a bizarre situation, I was able to direct a focus well away from her husband's work and possible injury claims, because I was focused on my navigation. Here was the map I waved around. I had filled her head with talk of reporting my position to headquarters, of my uncle's time in Goulburn and other issues that clouded my true purpose. I set up the situation so I was able to throw in the clanger of a question without a second thought, and she answered automatically, with her guard down. It was like taking candy from a baby. I felt a twinge of empathy for her, as it was clear there was not a lot of work around, but that did not give one the right to rort the system, and if her husband was working then he was lying and that was fraud. I tricked the information out of her, but that was the game I needed to play, that was my job as a PI.

I thanked her for her time, and busied myself with my pack, saying I needed to push off shortly. By now she was quite at ease, and said goodbye, walking off without a backward glance. It was a surreal situation. I watched as she disappeared over a slight rise and away. After a few moments, I saddled up and pushed off into the denser bush at the rear of the property, and found a comfortable location to await Bob's return. After a while I moved again, this time much closer to the pick-up point, but still observing the track.

It was nearly an hour and a half when the radio crackled again. 'Charlie this is Bravo' he said with resignation in his voice. I could tell from his tone of voice that he had no success in his search for the green ute, of which we didn't even know the registration number. *'Has he returned yet?'* he added, sounding like he already knew the answer.

I replied *'No, the ute has not returned'* I replied somewhat smugly. I waited for almost a minute for him to stew and fret, savouring what would be my response. Eventually I came through with the news, saying *'So, he hasn't returned, but I have a confirmed ID and know where he works and what he does'*. There was a pause while Bob considered my statement, analysing it for leg pulling.

'Go on' was his cautious reply.

'Yes, I have got all the information we need, so I will be pulling out now' I said.

'You sure?' he asked with keen expectation in his voice.

'Yes. Expect me in thirty minutes' I replied, and began making my way back.

When I arrived, Bob didn't wait for me to unload my equipment into the car, hammering me with questions.

'How the hell did you do it?' he asked. *'Tell me, how'* he fired at me in rapid succession, leaving me no opportunity to respond. We were soon racing towards the power station, as I began changing out of my camouflage clothing. Bob was relieved we had salvaged the job, turning it into a possible failure and into a good success. He goaded me about being sprung, saying I must have been sitting too close to the property, though I knew he was pleased to hear the news and countered with a jibe about him being too comfortable to ever leave his car these days. We managed to get through the relatively weak gate security with a pretext story, and soon located our man working near a shed. We captured well over an hour of video footage then called it a day, knowing we had everything the client could hope for.

I had managed to turn a serious compromise into total success, all within the space of sixty seconds of conversation. Like so many surveillance jobs, the situation can turn on a dime, and nobody can ever be sure where it will take you. An ability to think on your feet, to weigh risk versus reward, and have total confidence in yourself in the face of adversity. That is the signature of the surveillance professional!

PART 4

– AFTER SURVEILLANCE –

CHAPTER 30: SURVEILLANCE REPORTING

Anyone can document what they've seen, yet the professional will write a lot more detail than others. Good surveillance requires lots of detail. The following sentence would be expected from a good agent:

'The male was then seen arriving at the doorway from the southern side of the property with familiarity. He was seen to carry a blue canvas bag in his left hand, and then open the door with keys, using his right hand. He was seen to stoop slightly as if to inspect something on the porch, then proceeded inside and closed the door'.

Many people may need to read the report you prepare, and each is looking for specific detail. The insurance doctor wants to know exactly which *hand* the bag was carried in, and which hand was used to operate the keys. Other surveillance agents who may perhaps run the job again later will be looking for clues as to what is the usual direction of approach. This subtle detail could perhaps dictate where they will park to watch the subject. A company security manager will be seeking details on the type of bag being carried. Was it large enough to conceal the stolen laptops? A suspicious girlfriend will want to know how familiar he was with the property... was he really visiting his friend? Why does he have keys?

Even the fact he 'inspected' something specific may suggest he is at least mildly observant of his surroundings, which may encourage other surveillance agents to park just that much further away to avoid suspicion. A lawyer will be looking for such detail to corroborate the story... *'So you deny visiting the home at that time, and despite the fact there was no video of this event, our agent has specifically identified your blue bag in his report. Do you actually own such a bag Mr Jones? If I put your sister on the stand would she possibly confirm you own such a bag? Of all the bags he could have put in the report you say is false, he chose to write a blue canvas bag... how can you explain that?'*

Surveillance captures the many unknown possibilities of life. Detail is very important, as there is often scant information gathered, so the surveillance professional needs to ensure it is amplified to maximum effect, for the benefit of all who read and then understand not what was seen, but what actually happened. The job of the surveillance professional is to paint a richly detailed picture which can be analysed and dissected. A report is a picture that can be 'zoomed in' to see greater details, one that tells a thousand stories with each scent, each flavour, each feeling, each nuance of exactly how they met? Was there a smile? Who was the dominant party? How did he walk to the door, was she in a hurry, did it appear they were agitated?

The surveillance professional's documentation is so richly detailed, that far from being a simple snapshot, or even a video, his written word brings the scene to life in all its glory, authentic and informative. Along with being a psychologist, a racing car driver, a photographer, an actor and many more occupations, the surveillance professional is an author of the book of life.

Report writing

- Be factual, and highly detailed.

- All times in 24 hour clock. Use 0600 instead of 6 a.m.

- Any movement involving injured limbs, describe in uppercase '... *RIGHT hand'.*

- When describing addresses, list suburbs in all capitals i.e. 'RYDE'.

- Write in the past tense (*'The claimant was observed'*)

447

- Describe actions in a detailed manner that enhances the observed movements, and draws more attention to them: *'The claimant walked briskly to the door'* versus *'The claimant went inside'* or *'The claimant climbed into his car'* versus *The claimant entered his car'*.

- Describe actions in intricate detail, expanding movements into several sections; *'The claimant bent down 90 degrees and took hold of the box using both hands. He was then seen to lift the box up, over his head, and place it on the shelf'* versus *'The claimant put the box on the shelf'*.

- Describe using more than one word to highlight important sections. Rather than just *'weight'*, use *'full body weight'* or *'entire weight'* (*'She was observed standing with her full body weight on her RIGHT ankle for a short period of time'*).

- Draw attention to important things that may be usually implied *'She was then seen to step onto a moving escalator.'* The word 'moving' is implied, however its inclusion draws the readers attention to this important fact, highlighting the 'difficult' action.

Describing people

- Approximate age (25-30 years old)

- Nationality and complexion. Try to describe in detail (Mediterranean appearance, tanned, olive skinned).

- Build (medium, slim, fat, portly, fit, athletic)

- Height (short or tall? Use specific height in centimetres if possible. Use your own height as a frame of reference and work from there to give a more exact figure.)

- Unique features (tattoos, birth marks, piercings)

- Hair colour and style (light brown, shoulder length hair, moustache, beard)

- Clothing (including shoes and accessories: running shoes, dive watch, necklace)

- Gait or stride (walking briskly, ambled, loped, jerky, limping, strode confidently)

- Attitude and awareness (placid, aggressive, sedentary, guarded, unaware)

Describing vehicles

These basic items should be listed whenever a vehicle is first mention in a report. An example is '... a *late model, white Toyota Camry sedan, registration: VLJ 313*'

- Age (early model, late model)

- Colour

- Make (Toyota, Holden, Ford etc.)

- Model (Camry, Commodore, Falcon etc. Include style such as GL / GLX, etc.)

- Type (sedan, wagon, hatch, ute, dual cab, etc.)

- Registration number

The following are extra points to note when conducting a *close inspection* of a vehicle:

Vehicle Exterior

- The registration sticker. Is the vehicle currently registered? When does it expire? (This may indicate financial hardship.)

- Do the registration plates match the sticker? Dodgy subjects have been known to have dodgy vehicles or number plates!

- Is there a resident parking sticker (common in inner city areas)? Exactly what details are listed?

- Any stickers or markings at all (clubs, mechanics, shops etc.)?

- The vehicle dealer's details and location on the plastic numberplate holder. This may indicate a suburb or even allow a possible pretext angle with the dealer or subject.

- How is the vehicle parked? Nose in, reversed in? A requirement to regularly reverse a vehicle may be an issue for a subject's supposed neck injury.

- Where is the vehicle parked? In the driveway, in front of the *left* hand garage door, under the carport, outside the property, parking in front of the other vehicle?

- Take a good photo of the vehicle, front and back corners to show both sides.

- The condition of the tyres. This may assist in showing a general lack of care by the subject. May be of assistance in court as well as providing more information and exhibiting a more professional approach to the investigation.

- Touch the bonnet to see how hot the engine is, which may indicate a recent arrival.

- Exactly what accessories are fitted? Antennas, mufflers?

- Is there a tow bar fitted?

- Type of fuel (petrol, diesel or LPG gas)?

- How clean is the vehicle and what general condition? Mud spray suggests rural use.

- Un-repaired accident damage suggests financial hardship or lack of care.

Vehicle Interior

- Is the vehicle automatic or manual (important with a left arm or left leg injury)?

- Are there any internal stickers, particularly the service sticker normally stuck to the top of the windscreen? What business and location does this vehicle normally get serviced at? This will provide good pretext information to approach either the subject (as their car repairer/dealer) or the car repairer (as the subject).

- The odometer reading. Regularly checking this may reveal how far the car is driving. If checked on successive days may reveal a round trip journey to regular destination, such as to work or college and back. Calculate the approximate distance travelled using the odometer. Divide this difference by two, to get an approximate radius of the regular destination from their home. Review maps to identify likely destinations based on this radius. For a country job, this may clearly identify a nearby town. For suburban jobs, may roughly indicate an area. All the way into the city or just a local six kilometre range?

- Look for any documentation at all which might include names, numbers, companies, time sheets, payslips, business cards, timetables or receipts.

- Look for work boots, uniforms, tools, swimming attire, sports goods, and child-seats.

- Is the vehicle currently locked or unlocked? Is there a steering lock?

- What items are visible in the foot wells, seats, dashboard, or rear parcel tray?

- Get good video documentation of the interior of the vehicle. Start the shot on the exterior; including the number plate to confirm in evidence exactly which vehicle interior you are filming, and then move in to record the internal contents. Try not to get your own face on the reflection in the glass windows, but place the lens right up against the glass, and shield it further using shadows or your hands. Do a practice recording first. It's difficult to get a good focus on internal documents through glass.

- When recording documents or notes, be sure to take it as slowly as you feel you can. Use a steady hand braced with a palm against the glass. Get a good focus, and pan slowly across the document, examining everything. Zoom back out to show the entire document, but the important point is to capture the details such as company names, telephone numbers and dates.

Describing addresses

There are three key areas which should be detailed when describing an address:

1. The exact location and physical structure including all possible access points

2. Any vehicles which appear at or outside the address

3. Any item that may change easily, such as windows, garbage bins and mail boxes

Bins may be moved, mailboxes may be filled or emptied and windows opened or closed. When describing the address for the very first time, a more detailed description is required. Reports are broken into separate days, with all entries preceded by the time of the event using a twenty-four hour clock. It is best to format the entries with a paragraph indent, which clearly separates the time entries. This can be done in Microsoft Word using the CTRL-T indenting command.

Describing buildings

- Building *type and height* (single storey residential home, three storey block of flats)

- Building *construction* (red brick, white weatherboard)

- *Roof* construction (brown tiles, corrugated iron)

- Building *status* (old, modern, well kept, run-down)

- *Security* features (security doors, grilles, intercoms, locks, sensor lighting)

Describing access points

- Gates and doors including the type, such as roller door, security screen

- Driveways, paths, vehicle and pedestrian access

- Is there rear access present?

Describing other items

- Washing lines, pools, garage, sheds and other structures

- Garden status such as well kept or overgrown

- Fences, letterbox, garbage bin

- Pets in the yard

Reporting on arrival

Describe anything which may move or change, such as: Vehicles parked or absent? Was mail seen in the letterbox? Was the garbage bin left out? Was the security door open? Were blinds or windows open or closed? Was there washing out on the line? Was smoke seen rising from the chimney? Were lights on or off?

Report example

0530 We departed our office

0600 We arrived in the vicinity of the claimant's home. The address was found to be located on the south-eastern side of the road, close to the intersection of Duardo Street. The home was found to be a single storey, orange brick house, with a brown tiled roof. Two roller-door garages are located on the left hand side of the house. The front yard appeared reasonably neat, consisting of a small section of mown grass, together with a few landscaped plants that did not appear to have been tended to recently. On arrival, there were blinds observed in all windows. Two vehicles were sighted parked on the driveway in front of the left hand garage door. Directly in front of the left hand garage door, was an older model purple Honda Civic hatchback REGO: **TMD 098**, parked nose-in. Behind this and obstructing the purple car, was a lightweight white dual cab Toyota truck REGO: **SUD 235**. A small brown box trailer was observed to be standing on the left hand side of the property. It was noted the white truck was fitted with a tow-ball, indicating it may possibly be used to tow the box trailer.

0800 A call was placed to Dr David Bernstein Ph 9810 0675, and a female receptionist confirmed the claimant's appointment was still current.

0823 The right hand garage door was seen to open, and a silver Commodore sedan REGO: **AHA 128** was observed driving out. The driver appeared to be a female who matched the description supplied for the subject. **<VIDEO>**

0825 A follow was commenced

0843 The subject's vehicle was lost in heavy traffic, last sighted heading north on Cumberland Highway, WESTMEAD.

0930 We arrived in the vicinity of Suite 12, 2 Beattie St, BALMAIN, where the claimant was due to attend a 1030 medical appointment with Dr David Bernstein, Ph 8250-8220. A search of the area failed to locate the claimant's vehicle parked nearby.

1015 A female fitting the description of the claimant was observed walking into the building, carrying a small bag of shopping and some paperwork. She was observed walking through the building, looking for the surgery. She was then seen walking into the surgery office of Dr Bernstein. **<VIDEO>**

Post surveillance debrief

After completing any major surveillance operation, or after any significant incident has occurred, a post operation debrief is important. This is where each aspect of the operation is discussed and analysed in turn, to identify which situations caused problems, which equipment failed or perhaps worked very well, and what possible training issues have been raised. A surveillance agent may perform poorly due to lack of experience, or perhaps a lack of training. Perhaps the overall procedures were not clearly defined. Was the surveillance plan appropriate? Were resources appropriate for the job? Was the aim of the surveillance clearly defined? Were the actions on events described properly and procedures correctly followed?

The aim of the post surveillance debrief is to identify and resolve all problems as best as can be done, as well as arrange post operation administration details. Who will write the primary observation report? Who will check and store the surveillance equipment for later use?

Ensuring evidence is admissible

Any evidence must be linked to the specific person who obtained it, and the manner in which it was obtained. A video of an injured claimant running will not be admissible as evidence if it is not clear who actually took this section of video. This is particularly important with team jobs or where agents borrow cameras from others to shoot activity. Similarly the specific person who obtained the evidence must be available if required by the court, to prove the evidence. This is where the person must take the stand and assert that this is their tape, and that they recorded that video on that date. Often a video will be accepted as evidence together with just a written statement or report, but in some cases the opposing legal team can have the tape dismissed if the agent is not available to officially 'prove' it. Some general points regarding admissibility of evidence include:

- Relevance. Evidence must be relevant to the case.

- Must not be hearsay. *'He told me he saw him'*. Evidence must be first hand.

- Must not be an opinion. *'I don't think his leg is injured'* stated by a PI who has had no medical training, for example.

- Must be correctly identified. *'This is a video of the subject, which was taken by either Agent 1 or Agent 2.'* The specific source, method of collection and handling must be correctly documented to enable it to be admitted to a court.

- Must not be tainted. Courts may initially admit, but then later dismiss evidence obtained though this entrapment. *See* CHAPTER 32: AGENT PROVOCATEUR on page 498.

Continuity of evidence is an important legal requirement for evidence to be regarded as admissible. The term refers to the handling, processing, access or security of any evidence from the time of collection to the time of presentation to the court. Evidence should be protected and secured at all times to ensure it is original, undisturbed and unaltered. If the evidence is left unsecured, this is a 'break' in the continuity of evidence, and hence it may be inadmissible in court. Video, photographs, statements or any other evidence should be secured by the investigator at all times, and handed to specific, authorised personnel. Ideally, the progress or transferring of the evidence to others should be logged in a register which can prove the continuity in court.

Defining what constitutes admissible evidence is a particularly large and complex area of law. This book doesn't attempt to comprehensively cover this section, other than the basic points as discussed. For further information, readers should peruse the Commonwealth Evidence Act 1995, together with any similar State legislation. Another great reference to evidence admissibility and other legal issues for investigators may be found in the book 'Investigating Made Simple' by Gary Maher[72]

It is also important that you break no laws when collecting evidence, as this can render your evidence inadmissible. This includes video taken while you were trespassing on private land, according to the situation and applicable laws in that area.

Present evidence in court

Court is the ultimate end point of investigations, though cases rarely reach this point. Usually the parties will settle out of court, perhaps with some disclosure of the evidence that has

---

[72] 'Investigating Made Simple' by Gary Maher **ISBN** 0975159429
www.investigatingmadesimple.com

been amassed against them. As an investigator, you are a licensed professional, and should maintain this approach through the court process. The case is not successful until it has been finally settled, and a poor court performance may render your excellent evidence worthless.

- Prepare your evidence. Know your material. Memorise the case facts. Review any photographs or video you may have taken.

- Ensure your equipment and video tapes are ready and working. Test and retest.

- Be very clear about how you conducted the investigation, especially on team jobs. Who did what? Who took what video?

- Dress for the part and wear a suit. Look like a professional and arrive to court early.

- Rehearse the case facts and possible questions you may be asked in your mind.

- Be confident about identity. This can sometimes be difficult, so outline how you know the person in your evidence is the same as the defendant now in court.

- Answer confidently and succinctly. Answer only what was specifically asked, and do not add opinion or elaborate further – even if being questioned by your own legal team. They may want to walk you through the events slowly.

- Do not be drawn into traps. Always look ahead and see where the line of questioning may be going. The other side may wind you up in knots and make the evidence confusing so you contradict yourself, leading to the quality of your evidence being questioned.

- Don't be afraid to admit you don't know or can't recall something. This is legitimate and honest, and is far better than trying to make up details if you are really unsure.

- Court is a whole new world. Be ready to take your place. Remember to bow your head toward the bench whenever you enter or exit the courtroom. Remember to stand and bow your head whenever the magistrate enters or leaves the room. Ensure that your mobile phone is switched off, or is switched to silent mode. Address the magistrate as *'Your Honour'* when speaking to him or her (as appropriate).

- Be respectful of the subject and their legal team, but do not engage them in conversation unless necessary.

The case of questionable evidence

Key learning points

- Court etiquette
- Preparation and rehearsal of equipment and evidence
- Evading legal word traps
- Inappropriate communication with the other party in a case

'Hello?' 'Chris, what are you doing right now?' asked Bob impatiently.

I checked my watch. 'Oh nothing too urgent, just paperwork' I replied.

'Good, because you're needed in court now' he said, sounding slightly frazzled.

'Now?' I asked incredulously. 'Like you mean today here and now, get in my car and drive there right NOW?'

'Yes' he said, pleased with my reply.

He apparently missed the subtle sarcasm and obviously thought I was getting out of my chair with car keys in hand as I was speaking.

'I'm sorry about the short notice and all, mate. The client sent our office a request letter a month ago, but they sent it to my old address by mistake. The case was from a couple of years ago and the old Willoughby address was on the reports back then. You know how difficult it is getting mail from my ex-wife, I only got the letter yesterday and I hadn't even opened the envelope yet. I've just now had a phone call from the solicitors asking why you aren't sitting outside the courtroom this very minute. The case has already started!'

I pondered my options. With such late notice I didn't really need to go if I didn't want to. I hadn't been subpoenaed, so I wasn't really obliged. I wondered if Bob had actually received the request letter earlier but forgotten to tell me, or that it was just another situation where the client wanted the PI to be 'available' for court, without wanting to actually pay anything for him being on court standby. It didn't matter as I didn't have anything urgent on and was more amused than annoyed at being 'asked' so late. I decided to go. Before I could relay this pleasing news to Bob, he was already firing the case details to me down the phone line.

I found a city parking station and lugged my television and video equipment across the road towards the barrister's chambers. In a modern age you'd expect courts to provide facilities for displaying such evidence easily. Unfortunately law is the second oldest profession, and uncomfortable accepting the change of modern video technology. After checking in at the reception, I began to wait. Two hours later I was called to the nearby court, escorted by the barrister's clerk. The steps leading to the courthouse were worn from many years and a hundred thousand weary feet. I passed a barrister leaving the building, his arms full of papers with a solicitor in tow. Black robes trailed him like Dracula's cape as he strode defiantly from the building. A golden wig sat upon his head like a crown. It was clear he was important. Clear to those who knew the law, and clear to those who didn't.

Inside the building my footsteps echoed as we crossed the cold stone floor. Courtroom four was buried deep in the bowels of the ground floor maze. The clerk escorting me suggested I take a seat outside while he alerted the barrister. I sat on a wooden bench near the door and put my equipment on the floor. The door to the court was open wide, inviting members of the public to watch the wheels of the law turn. Seldom is this 'invitation' taken, apart from law students or bored retirees, unless a particularly noteworthy case is being heard. The clerk told me we had a jury on today. Sounds of legal argument wafted through the doorway and echoed around the quiet waiting area. I strained to listen but could never hear more than snippets of the conversations. The clerk re-emerged from the doorway saying *I told the solicitor you have arrived. She'll be out to see you soon*. I tried to listen to the courtroom carefully as his footsteps subsided from the hallway. Soon they were gone.

I got up and looked around. There wasn't much to see, and I noticed there were no pictures on the walls which were stark and bare like the roof of a dentist's surgery. Anything other than stark walls would relieve the tension or boredom for those waiting, but I figured courts were built for justice, not for people. A woman emerged from the door to the courtroom and I recognised her as the subject of my surveillance from a year ago.

An older lady, who glanced at me without recognition was sitting nearby. I watched her, then lost interest, and busied myself with a Sydney Morning Herald I retrieved from my bag. Some time later a court official emerged from the open doorway and beckoned her inside. I was engrossed in my paper for over an hour, and didn't notice another woman standing in front of me, who appeared to be a solicitor.

'Are you Chris Cooper?' she asked tersely.

'Yes' I replied. I noticed she looked slightly frazzled and wondered how the case was going.

She introduced herself briefly. 'I was getting concerned. I'm glad you finally decided to turn up' she said bluntly.

'Well I was only just told about the case this morning...' I began to protest mildly, but she obviously had other things on her mind.

'So I hope you've got your video equipment with you' she said, staring at the oversized bags at my feet.

I felt like saying that my bags contained only several large jumpers, just in case I got cold waiting to go in. 'Yes, it is all in my bags here' I confirmed, and she seemed relieved.

'OK, well it's lucky you haven't been called yet, in fact you may not be called at all today' she said pausing for thought. 'You know the case may run for a few days don't you?' she added.

'I didn't, in fact it was only a few hours ago I was told the case was on at all! I'll be able to attend at least tomorrow and the next day' I replied, quickly reviewing my schedule.

'Good' she said. 'Here's the videotape, I guess I should leave it with you. I'm going out to get a quick coffee then I'll be back. Our barrister is James Banks. I don't expect you to be called for a while yet, but just wait here in case.'

I took the tape from her and recognised my handwriting on the spine. Karen, the solicitor then left, her high heels clicking on the stone floor. She wasn't unattractive, but did look as if she'd had too much red wine at lunch. I settled back to reading my newspaper.

I heard Karen returning well before I saw her. She was cradling a foam coffee cup as she walked, eyes downcast. I glanced from the newspaper and smiled, holding my smile right up to the point where she entered the courtroom, yet not having once made eye contact with her. I shrugged my shoulders at nobody in particular and continued waiting. At three forty five, only fifteen minutes before the court was due to finish, a court officer appeared at the doorway and called loudly in an authoritative voice 'Mr Chris Cooper'. His voice echoed, reverberating through the corridors which made me jump, not expecting to hear my voice called so loudly in such a quiet room. I was the only person in the waiting area, and we looked at each other for a moment. I figured he could have called out in a quieter tone, or perhaps even asked me directly if I was Chris Cooper, though I realised he was just doing his job with gusto, as did many in this strange legal environment. I stood and gathered my bags, walking towards him.

'Mr Chris Cooper?' he asked again, now almost politely. I nodded. 'Follow me please sir' he said, and returned inside. I followed closely behind and didn't expect him to suddenly stop to bow to the judge. It wasn't just a polite nod of his head as he walked, but rather an abrupt stop followed by a distinct and pronounced forward bow. Being unprepared and with mind elsewhere, I almost toppled over his bowing body. I just managed to stop myself in time, though one of my bags swung forward and lightly tapped him on the behind. Fortunately he was already beginning to stand up and wasn't knocked off balance. He glanced at me, not in annoyance being bumped, so much as my obvious lack of courtroom etiquette. I looked up and saw the inside of the courtroom for the first time. All eyes were on the new arrivals, and it was clear that our entrance was not as unobtrusive as I hoped. I dutifully bowed my head slightly at the judge and continued into the room, making a mental note to bow in future. After all, this was the very first time I had been actually called to give evidence.

The officer led me to the front of the courtroom and indicated where I could set up my video. There were quite a few people in the room at the time, with judge, jury and legal teams for both sides, but nobody was speaking. The room was deathly silent, save for the sound of me setting up the video equipment. I was not actually required to take the stand at this point, but rather just operate my video equipment, so I wasn't sworn in by the court. I looked for a power point but couldn't find one in the vicinity.

'Are there any power points nearby?' I asked the officer quietly. He seemed surprised at the request and looked puzzled.

'I don't think so... maybe there's one over the other side' he said and began looking. I suddenly felt personally responsible for the lack of power points in the building. Everyone was looking at me as if to say *'Well you're the video guy, if you needed a power point, you should have brought one with you!'* Luckily, the court officer finally found an outlet hidden underneath a bench. It was a several metres from where I had to set up the screen and I was glad I had packed a decent extension lead. It was frustrating the courtroom wasn't set up for this sort of thing.

I carefully unpacked the portable television set from a large canvas bag and put it on the bench to one side of the courtroom. I angled the set so both the judge and jury could easily see it. The legal teams would have to move around to view it, but I figured that was their problem. I moved as quickly as I could, but the whole process seemed agonisingly slow. With so many people in the room, the silence was deafening and the audience scrutinised every move I made. I uncoiled leads, connected double adaptors and adjusted various items. I lifted the video player from its bag and placed it next to the television, then connected the power and video leads. I checked the connections, turned on the power and inserted the evidence videotape into the machine. Turning to the barrister Mr Banks, I indicated everything was ready.

Mr Banks stood and addressed the judge. *'So your honour, I have taken the court though all of the actions and activities the plaintiff alleges she cannot do. The plaintiff has clearly stated to every question I asked her, that she CANNOT (he raised his voice for emphasis) sweep, clean, hang washing or do any form of domestic chore by herself. I apologise for the length of time I have taken to confirm each of these responses, but trust that the court will appreciate now, after seeing the video that the subject CAN in fact do all of the things she says she cannot, and it will become CLEAR to the court that she has lied to the court and perjured herself under oath. Mr Cooper, if you could now play the tape.'* His voice rose in volume as he neared the end of his speech. It was clear he had been hammering his case all day and had finally brought his defence to an impressive climax.

I felt proud to be a part of something so dramatic. I was but a pawn in the cog of the legal process, but I was a member of the cast none the less. As the barristers and court officials moved so they could see the television properly, I reached across and pressed the play button on the video deck. The machine made a clicking, whirring sound then stopped. The screen remained blank. Everyone stared expectantly at the vacant screen in silence, and it was several seconds before I realised nothing was happening. Glancing at the display, I found the machine had stopped. *'I'm sure the tape was rewound'* I thought, pressing the rewind button just in case. The machine whirred again then stopped. I pressed play again. There was more whirring then silence. I checked the machine, but it had stopped. The hairs on the back of my neck prickled as I realised something wasn't right. I ejected the tape, re-loaded it and tried again and again. I didn't look at the barrister, but I could feel the heat from his gaze burning a hole through my head, as it was patently clear that the machine was most definitely not going to play the vital evidence tape.

I slowly looked up at the assembled audience and announced, to nobody in particular *'Well, there seems to be a problem with the video recorder. It's not working now, but it did this morning!'* The judge glanced at a clock on the wall, which was showing five minutes to four. He said *'I think in light of the time, that we should now break for the day, and recommence tomorrow. Mr Banks, do you think this equipment will be working tomorrow?'*

I was fast learning the court hierarchy was unusual to say the least. As if the barrister had any idea about my video equipment! And why didn't the judge address me directly? Of course that was just not how things operated in this world of court! The barrister turned to me with a scowl, asking exactly the same question but in a slightly different tone of voice. My face flushed as I replied *'Well I won't be able to get this machine repaired by tomorrow, but I can certainly bring in another video machine in to play the tape.'*

The barrister turned back to the judge. *'Yes your honour, I apologise for my witness, but he says he will be able to show us the tape tomorrow.'*

'*All rise*' bellowed the court officer authoritatively, and the judge walked from the room.

Once he was gone, the barrister turned to me and hissed '*So what exactly is your problem?*' I wondered at what point the 'problem' had become my personal one rather than just a technical one. I looked him in the eye and replied as politely as I could '*I think it must have become damaged while it was being moved here. I'll have another working machine here tomorrow though.*'

The barrister rolled his eyes then continued loudly '*Tomorrow? I've spent my entire day building up our case to a climax. I arranged it so you would come in exactly at the time that you did, and now you can't make your equipment work!* He began ruffling his paperwork violently. '*I wanted the jury to go home tonight and sleep, with the memory of that videotape fresh in their minds. The effect just won't be the same first thing in the morning, especially as they will not have had the plaintiff denying everything for the last few hours. Do you understand what I'm saying?*' he spluttered.

I nodded '*Yes, I'm sorry for the disruption, and I apologise for my equipment becoming damaged. It will be working tomorrow though...*' Mr Banks strode away briskly, leaving my words trailing off into the now vacant space.

I felt dejected as I packed up. There wasn't anything I could have done, but it wasn't the point. It didn't work, so it was obviously all my fault. It annoyed me that the equipment was probably damaged as a result of lugging it across town in the first place, which would be more expense in repairs, as well any embarrassment. I allowed myself a short period of self-pity before switching into a c'est-la-vie frame of mind. Such is life! Karen approached me as I coiled some leads. She'd been elsewhere during the embarrassing tape playing attempt and had just walked in, presumably after speaking to the barrister outside. 'So what was the problem?' she asked, looking flustered. I explained and she left muttering something impolite though not quite audible. I finished packing went home.

The next morning I awoke peacefully, sometime after eight. Allowing my mind to wander, I mentally browsed through my daily schedule. COURT! The horror of the previous days' video drama came flooding back, and roused me from my peaceful state. I'd spent most of the night working on another surveillance job, tailing a cleaner around through several Leichhardt businesses as she vacuumed their offices. Finishing after midnight, I hadn't yet prepared for my next day in court, and I wanted to be really sure everything worked this time.

I figured if I dubbed the VHS evidence tape back down to a smaller eight millimetre tape, I wouldn't have to lug another full sized video deck to the court. It would also mean I could use either a camera or my little video Walkman unit as the player, so even if the television set I brought blew up, or there was a power blackout, I could still show the court the footage on the tiny Walkman screen. Technically, the law is vague about dubbing tapes. Only original evidence is permitted, but 'original' evidence in an electronic format is difficult to define. Is the cassette on which the surveillance film was first recorded classed as the original? Or is it the actual footage itself, meaning it can be dubbed onto other tapes provided the investigator can attest to having done the dubbing? Very occasionally it becomes an issue as to which tape is the actual evidence and which as an inadmissible 'copy' (as interpreted by some judges).

I hunted through a box of miniature video tapes that were in my 'spare' box. They'd been recorded on previously, but their contents were no longer needed. Some of them contained old surveillance footage, some contained video of social occasions and some contained programmes taped from television or other sources. Being in the spare box, I could use any of them without worrying about wiping their contents. I selected one at random. One single tape selected from a box of dozens. There was nothing on the spine of the cassette to indicate its contents, which wasn't unusual. Once in the machine, I played it, just to be sure it wasn't anything I wanted to keep. I discovered it was a poor copy of really bad porn video, left by an old flatmate who had given it to me as a laugh. It was more humorous because of how bad it was. The tape was poorly 'simulated' sex scenes rather than explicit ones, with feeble actors whose lip movements didn't match the audio track. I wondered if I should find another tape just in case, but decided time was short. I'd be taping over the porn, and besides, I'd stop the tape playing in court as soon as the surveillance footage finished. What could possibly go wrong?

I started recording over the bad porn, copying the original surveillance footage onto the tape. After sixteen minutes, I stopped the evidence tape player, but left the tiny video Walkman recorder still going to record a blank screen after the surveillance footage. This would finish off the footage cleanly with a black screen, and wipe off any trace of the porn which was originally on that small tape, just in case I forgot to switch it off in time.

It was time to go, so I swigged my coffee and packed everything up. Checking the video Walkman I was using to dub the tapes, I noticed it had run out of battery and had switched off before it had finished wiping over the porn video. This wasn't a problem though, because I knew it had already taped the full sixteen minutes of the surveillance video I needed. I arrived at the courtroom and I plugged in the charger to recharge the battery.

469

'Oh well', I thought, 'I'll be the one showing it, so I'll just have to make especially sure I stop the tape after it finishes showing the surveillance section'. It could be most embarrassing if the tape continued playing past that point. I hurried into the city and made my way into the courtroom. Inside, I spied the barrister striding towards me. Although I was actually part of his team, I wasn't expecting any pleasantries.

'Is it going to work this time?' he asked impatiently, but as I opened my mouth to reply, he disappeared into the courtroom. The solicitor cruised in just before ten o'clock, but didn't give me a second glance. A few minutes later she approached me saying 'The barrister wants you to set up your equipment now, so it will be ready when he wants the tape played. Do you think you will have any MORE problems this time?' At least she was polite enough to wait for my meek reply. I carried my equipment in and began to set up. After I finished, I checked and re-checked everything and fortunately, it all worked. I rewound the tape to the beginning again, and wandered out into the waiting room.

I watched as the plaintiff walked into the courtroom, surrounded by her family and the legal team for the 'other' side. Finally I was called (loudly) by the very same official, as I sat by myself directly outside the courtroom. Perhaps the court official hadn't recognised me from yesterday I wondered, knowing this to be untrue. I gathered up my newspaper and walked into the courtroom, again watched by everybody assembled there, craning their necks to see the star witness enter the courtroom. All I'd done was catch an old woman sweeping when she said she couldn't, so it really seemed like the whole episode was getting out of hand. Still, I had my role to play. The court official had already entered, so I didn't get to see him bow, and totally forgot to do so myself. I remembered the bowing thing as soon as I saw an exasperated look on the barrister's face, and some eye rolling by one of the other court officials. I put my personal bag on one of the rear seats as I walked up to the front, led by my original court official friend.

I stood by the video equipment and looked at Mr Banks. 'Mr Cooper, if you could now play the tape' he said.

Judge Davis, who seemed to be a rather pleasant fellow, said 'Well let's hope it works this time. I must say though that the equipment looks different to the machine we had yesterday.'

He didn't appear to be addressing his comments to anyone in particular, so I decided to voice my feelings about the whole episode, and answer him.

'Well the last unit I brought appears to have been damaged in transit. They're not designed to be manhandled, or moved often'. I was intending to go on and suggest that courtrooms should have such video equipment already in place, but before I'd even started the barrister was jumping back with an annoyed 'Ah now listen here, in this courtroom you will speak only when properly addressed.' I was about to say 'OK' but decided it would be more appropriate to simply mouth the words to him. He turned back to the judge and apologised. Law people can be a little touchy so I discovered.

Judge Davis turned to me directly and asked 'Mr Cooper, are you showing videotape or a film? I was wondering if you think the members of the jury could see the screen better if the lights were turned down?' The judge appeared to be a lovely, but perhaps slightly old fashioned man, and I wondered if he even really understood the concept of a video player.

'Yes, I think it might be better to dim the lights slightly' I answered, pleased to have been addressed directly by the judge this time. I looked smugly at Mr Banks, but he wasn't looking back. The judge nodded at one of the court officials who sprang to life and dimmed the lights. He seemed pleased as well.

I pressed play and the tape sprang to life, leaving me feeling extremely relieved. I looked around for a place to stand, not wanting to obstruct the jury's view. I saw the opposing barrister with a large blank pad in front of him on the desk. He was obviously going to make notes on the film. I moved around, and quietly stood right behind him, looking over his shoulder. He couldn't see me, though he tried to look around twice. I was close behind, and he would have to swivel right around in his chair to see me. I watched as he wrote on his pad, in response to the film. He didn't write much, but things like *'walks (slowly)... sweeps (slowly)... filmed on bus (is that her?)'*. I figured I'd be able to answer better in the witness box if I knew what his questions were first. I wasn't sure how legal it was to read his notes, but I thought it best to remain ignorant, and apologise, rather than ask for permission if I was caught. I suddenly had a sinking feeling that my mobile phone was going to ring, remembering it was still in my bag at the back of the courtroom, and I had forgotten to switch it off. As the tape played, I looked to see if I could go and attend to it, but this would have meant pushing past various people and obstructing the view of the jury. I prayed that it remained silent.

Thankfully it didn't ring, and as soon as the tape finished I was able to stop the machine. If there was still the remainder of the porn video on the tape, it would be well over an hour after the surveillance footage, because the video Walkman had continued wiping over the porn with a black screen for ages before the batteries had gone dead. The barrister said *'Thank you Mr Cooper'* and I walked back to take a seat at the rear of the courtroom.

The case continued. 'Now I put it to you Mrs Jimeous, you said you couldn't do any of those things, and now we see you on a tape sweeping. We see you on the tape catching a bus. We see you on tape hanging out your washing. Mrs Jimeous, you have LIED to this courtroom haven't you! You've lied to me, lied to the jury and lied to this esteemed judge', spat the barrister. Mrs Jimeous stared blankly at the barrister, unemotional and without visible comprehension. A language interpreter then turned to Mrs Jimeous and politely translated what had been said, though without any of the aggressive tone in which it had been originally delivered.

Mrs Jimeous thought for a while, and then said something to the translator, who in turn said to the court 'She says she can't do those things normally, except for that time.' Mr Banks looked furious, apparently not so much that she was still trying to deny she was mobile and could clean her house, but more at the laborious translation process which stripped all emotion and timing from his words. By the time a translated answer was received, the jury would be wondering what the original question was. I could see this was going to be an arduous and time-consuming case.

Mr Banks was continuing with another tirade, when he was suddenly interrupted by the judge saying 'Ahhh Mr Banks, if I could ask you to pause there for a minute, I just want to clarify a point. Now, Mr Cooper is your witness, is he not?'

Mr Banks replied 'Yes your Honour. I'll be calling him later in the proceedings.'

The judge continued 'It's just that I think I can see him at the back of the courtroom, and, as a witness, I think he should remain outside until called, which is, I believe, standard procedure. I am sorry to have to stop you in mid-argument, but I just wanted to be sure we were doing everything by the book as it were.'

Mr Banks glared at me and said 'Mr Cooper, if you could please wait OUTSIDE of this courtroom'. I was clearly losing points left, right and centre, so I scurried quickly outside, forgetting to bow again as I left the courtroom.

Having finished my newspaper, I was staring into space at the blank walls, deep in thought. I noticed a reasonably attractive woman of about thirty-five years old leaving the courtroom. I'd seen her before, and guessed she was the daughter of the plaintiff. She too looked exceedingly bored, and sat down in the waiting area, a respectable distance away. After a long while, she spoke. 'How long do we have to wait here?' I glanced at her, and we soon began talking about how boring the legal system was, what the weather was like outside and other general small talk. After a while she asked me 'Are you the person that was following my mother?'

I contemplated avoiding the question, or denying it outright, but that seemed a little pointless. I had already set up my video player in the courtroom, and been mentioned by the judge as a witness who would be later called. 'Yes... Yes I am' I said. Was she going to insult me? Was she going to get angry? Was she going to ignore me?

She did none of these things, but threw back her head, and let out an uncontrolled burst of laughter. 'Like, did you walk around behind her and take photographs?' she asked with a smile, leaning forward slightly. 'So, you followed my mother around did you? I can't believe that someone followed my mother!' More laughter. I bet there wasn't much excitement though, because she is a very boring person. Her eyes twinkled and I noticed laughter lines at the corners of her mouth. 'I keep trying to get *her to come out and do things, but all she wants to do is stay at home. I think the language problem is big part of it though.'*

I learned that her name was Ruby, and that she was most intrigued at my line of work, and what kind of cases I usually worked on. She asked a lot of questions and listened intently. She began telling me she had a friend who suspected her husband was playing up. She wanted to know what could be done. Without giving specific details away, I told her about a number of cases I'd been involved with, and suggested several things she could do. We didn't discuss her mother's court case other than her expressing amusement that someone had actually taken the time to follow her aging mother around. She did mention it was unfair that her mother was seemingly being prosecuted for performing domestic duties at home. How else could she do them? She couldn't really afford to pay somebody. She wasn't really angry with me, just angry there were so many arguments and accusations in court. I could sympathise with her, but figured she should be entitled to do the chores herself, and should not get paid more for claiming she was unable to do them. Besides, the issue was not whether she was injured, but whether the other side was responsible, and for how much (if any)? It seemed a fairly logical, legal argument but I accepted that I might feel differently if it was my relative on the stand.

Ruby and I talked for hours about a range of subjects. She was interested in the book I was writing, and spent ages reading through my draft manuscripts while waiting for her mother to finish in court. She asked me questions about some of the characters in the stories and made comments. It seemed her English literary skills were much higher than her speaking skills. We also talked about her family and why they'd moved to Australia. She explained that while she could be the best worker at Westpac, she could never be as good as her Australian counterparts.

They didn't have to try as hard, and were forgiven for mistakes more often. She didn't express much hope of promotion, and told of the good jobs and life that she and her husband were forced to leave when they immigrated to Australia. Near the end of the day Mrs Jimeous walked out of the courtroom with her translator. She saw Ruby and I talking, and walked over. I felt uncomfortable until I realised she still had absolutely no idea who I was. She spoke in a foreign language to Ruby, who stood up. 'We have finished for the day. Perhaps I'll see you another day!' she said warmly in her heavily accented English. It was not quite the response I had expected from the opposition, but I waved both her and her mother a friendly goodbye.

The next two days, nothing happened. I arrived, waited, had lunch, and then caught the monorail home late in the afternoons. At least I had plenty of time to work on stories for my book. During this time I dubbed another copy of the evidence tape onto one of the 'Hi8' tapes I had inside the camera. I already had work on this tape from other jobs, but decided I should really have two copies of the vital footage, just in case anything happened to the first one. I've heard stories where the opposing legal team 'bumps' the record button on the video deck accidentally and surreptitiously, during court proceedings and the machine ends up completely wiping the vital evidence. A crafty team could also swap tapes over or hold strong magnets next to it in order to destroy the damning evidence.

By law, the opposition must be permitted to view and handle the evidence, so they will always have a chance to replace the erase tab or otherwise interfere with it. Even though I had already shown the tape to the court, if the tape became damaged then the judge would strike it out. He would instruct the jury to disregard anything they had seen on the tape, or the opposing side could call for a mistrial and we would have to have another court case, beginning all over again. Quite apart from this, it seemed a good idea to have a tape with no possibility of porn left on it. I could have simply rechecked the original copy I had made, but I wanted to have another copy anyway, so that none of this mattered.

On Thursday the solicitor, Karen, approached me. She began talking loudly to me as she approached from a distance, asking 'What did you say to her? What did you tell her was in the film?'

It took me a moment to realise what she was getting at, and that she was referring to my conversation with Ruby.

'Nothing' I said truthfully, 'I didn't discuss the case at all. She asked if I was the investigator who took the photos and that was about it. I did talk to her for a while, but that was about other things which were not connected to the case at all.' I said.

'You told her you were the investigator?' she asked with some disapproval.

'Well yes, she asked me point blank, and I have been in court twice already to show the film, what could I say?' Besides, the judge said...' I continued, but she cut me off.

'OK. But you didn't tell her anything about the contents of the film. Is that right?'

'Yes... Why?'

'It's about to become very important. She's in the dock right now, and her barrister is trying to make her admit that you told her what was on the film,' she said. She seemed relieved, and hurried back to the courtroom.

Ruby approached me as soon as she left the courtroom, saying 'I'm sorry... I didn't want you in trouble. They were asking me these questions about if you showed me the film, or told me things. I didn't want to make trouble for you. I told them I was *mainly talking to you about our family in Serbia, and why we moved to Australia'.*

She seemed upset about her harrowing time in the dock, but was also genuinely concerned that she may have gotten me into trouble. I assured her there would be no problems. How could there be? I was more amused that the daughter of the surveillance subject was concerned that I, the investigator who caught her mother, might get into trouble!

'MR COOPER' shouted my friendly court official, who obviously still did not recognise me, even after three days. I followed him inside, remembering to bow this time. I took the stand.

'Hold the bible in your right hand.' He lowered his voice. *'Do you take the oath or the affirmation?'*

'Oath' I replied.

He began speaking loudly and it seemed to me proudly to the entire courtroom, though I suspected he was really addressing his comments only to me.

'I promise to tell the truth, the whole truth and nothing but the truth. So help me God' I repeated his words and was allowed to sit down.

'State your full name... Do you recall receiving instructions to conduct surveillance?' and so it continues. I finished answering the basic questions, and then we got down to business. Mr Banks took me through the case and what I'd seen of the subject. It was simple question and answer. Despite all of my evidence being clearly visible in the tape, I had to testify about what I had actually seen. Unfortunately I couldn't give a blanket statement that I saw everything as it appears on the tape, because that is not how the law works. I had to say *'Then I saw her sweeping.'*

'How did she sweep?'

'With a left and right motion, at a normal speed.' ('Like on the tape, stupid!') I thought.

'Did you observe her catching a bus?'

The silly thing to me was, the only time I ever saw the subject was through the lens of my camera, so it seemed obvious to me that my verbal testimony was superfluous. After he had finished with my verbal testimony, he asked me to show my surveillance footage to the court again. Compared to some cases I had been involved with, this footage was quite good, being clear and focused, showing the woman performing a range of tasks easily. After the jury had seen the video, I figured we had a pretty open and shut case. I moved to my equipment and played the tape again. This time I was careful to insert the Hi8 copy I'd made, rather than the original one which could still have some porn left on it. I played the tape through, then stopped it and returned to the stand. Mr Banks finished his summing up and sat down. Now it was time for me to be grilled by the other side.

Mr Cooper, your film shows my client stepping on to a bus, does it not?'

'Yes.' I answered

'And you have said you then followed the bus in another vehicle. Is this correct?'

'Yes.'

'Ahhh. I believe your footage then shows my client sitting inside the same bus, clearly filmed from INSIDE the bus. How can you possibly explain you being in two places at once Mr Cooper?' he asked, looking very pleased with himself.

I could see he thought that I had an accomplice who had boarded the bus with the subject and was filming separately to me. If this was true, the video tape evidence may have to be thrown out of court because it would be a compilation tape and I couldn't swear it was my footage, and only my footage. I glanced at Mr Banks, the barrister for our side and could see a look of concern on his face, suggesting he may have now picked up this inconsistency as well. I smiled smugly though, rather glad that this point had been brought up.

'I was following the subject on the bus in my car for a while, and then figured it was probably going to continue into the city. I overtook the bus on a city road, and found a parking spot some distance ahead. I then managed to catch the very same bus by running to the next stop. And it wasn't easy.' I replied.

A murmur went through the courtroom and I could see two members of the jury trying to suppress a smile. It was clear that I'd taken the wind from his sails. Not only had I answered his question without hesitation, but was obviously proud of being a resourceful PI who had completed a rather successful follow under difficult conditions.

On that particular case I had actually had my sister Louise along to help me, I went on to explain. She had caught the bus with the subject, but wasn't filming her and didn't even have a camera. She was curious about what it really was that her brother did at work, and had asked to come along for the ride, just for fun. Fortunately she had picked a case with plenty of action. I smiled as I remembered her surprised face when I boarded the same bus several kilometres later, as she had thought I was still in my car driving behind it! The barrister pressed on regardless.

'And later, you say you observed her apparently catching another bus. Can you explain how this is true because your film does not SHOW my client catching another bus?'

'I saw her run towards the corner and out of sight, and managed to get a few seconds film of her running. I then also ran to the corner, where I saw another government bus. I could see her sitting inside the bus as it drove off.'

'Ahhh, so you didn't catch the same bus, and your car was parked elsewhere. How do you know WHERE my client got off the bus then?' he demanded loudly, trying to intimidate me into making a mistake.

'Well, I looked around and saw a taxi waiting at the traffic lights, so I got in and said FOLLOW THAT BUS' I replied, to further amused murmurs in the courtroom.

One of the jurors stifled a laugh, and the barrister looked at him disapprovingly. The truth was I'd spotted an old Commando mate, Grant West, who was waiting at the lights. Just as well, because there were no cabs in sight. Grant was happy to give both my sister and I a lift, and even helped us with the surveillance for the remainder of the day. It seemed so unlikely for us to have spotted a 'friend' in a car at the lights just when we needed a lift, so I thought it would be easier to say I caught a taxi, which was still sort of true. It was just that our 'driver' was an unlicensed taxi driver, and the car was not quite an official taxi, but more his personal car.

At the time though, I had genuinely intended on approaching someone in the traffic who vaguely looked like they would help. Being reasonably neatly dressed and waving a twenty-dollar note I figured I could possibly beg some assistance from a driver just waiting there, who may be mildly interested in joining in on a PI car chase. I hated to lose contact on a follow, and figured the bus was an easy target provided I could get some wheels quickly. I was not fussed about how I did it. I could have gotten some strange looks or a few refusals, but it was a case of nothing to lose. It was interesting to realise that I would not have seen Grant in the traffic at the lights if I was not looking intently at the drivers to pick a likely assistant to approach.

'I believe you have had a conversation with the plaintiff's daughter outside the courtroom. Is this correct?'

'Yes.'

The judge said 'would you mind standing up Mrs Ristefeas, thank you.'

He turned to me, saying 'Is that the lady whom you are referring to?'

'Yes'.

The judge then said 'For the record, the lady identified by Mr Cooper was Mrs Ruby Ristefeas, the plaintiff's daughter.'

The barrister continued. 'Approximately when was this conversation?'

'Wednesday afternoon' I replied.'

'Who initiated the conversation?' he asked.

I couldn't help but think that none of this would have happened if there had been something more interesting to look at than the walls of the waiting room in the first place. 'I was reading my paper, and she came and sat next to me. She mentioned something about waiting a long time.'

'What did she say to you?'

''I can't remember. Something about how long we had been waiting.'

The judge cut in saying 'You must be more specific Mr Cooper.'

I continued with '*I seem to recall...*' but was immediately stopped by the barrister barking '*WHAT DO YOU RECALL EXACTLY MR COOPER?*'

I blinked, and stated '*She said 'We have been waiting here a long time*', sounding far more confident than I actually was. Who would have thought the words '*I seem to recall*' would be so offensive?

'*What happened then?*'

'*I agreed with her, and continued reading my paper*'

'*And then?*'

'*She said to me: Are you the person that was following my mother?*'

'*What did you reply?*'

'*I couldn't deny it, so I said ' Yes. Yes I am.*'

'*What happened then?*'

'*She burst out laughing... and seemed to find it amusing.*'

'*Did you discuss the contents of the tape with her?*'

'*No.*'

'*What did you discuss with her Mr Cooper?*'

'*Well, about her moving to Australia and about a book I'm writing at the moment*' I said, suddenly thinking that wasn't such a smart thing to say. The last thing I wanted was for the messy unedited manuscript in my bag to be called up as evidence.

'*Mr Cooper sir, I refer to your tape... How long does the tape run for?*'

'*Sixteen minutes*' I replied confidently.

'Sixteen minutes. What is the first action that you record on your tape?'

'The sweeping.'

'And how long is the portion on the tape of the sweeping?'

'I'm not exactly sure.'

'Just estimate. How long do you think it is?'

'About one minute.'

'Right. The next action is the hanging out of the washing. How long did you record that action for?' He was writing down my answers.

'I couldn't say to be exact.'

'But how long would it be?' he asked, rephrasing the question doggedly.

'I really don't know. If I have another look at the tape I could time it', but he cut me off with 'but from your memory, would it be five minutes?' he asked.

I wondered where this was heading, and was just about to say yes, when I realised what he was trying to do. I would give him a series of times for each action I'd filmed, and they wouldn't add up to the total of sixteen minutes. He could then call me a liar, and try to use this to discredit my testimony. More confidently, I told him I didn't know.

'Six minutes?' he asked almost desperately, obviously keen to get any answer he could.

'Sir, I know the total is sixteen minutes, but I don't know the individual times accurately. I could tell you exactly if I watch the tape again though.'

He looked a little dejected. *'Oh... No further questions your honour.'*

While I can't be sure, I thought I saw a slight smile on Mr Banks face, and I wondered if he was pleased with me. Perhaps I finally got something right in this courtroom!

'Any further questions Mr Banks?' asked the judge.

'Yes. Mr Cooper, do you have the tape in your possession?'

'Yes.'

'Can you retrieve it please?'

I explained that the tape was in my bag at the rear of the courtroom. The judge gave me permission to retrieve it, after which I returned to the stand.

'Mr Cooper, could you please hold the tape up for the court to see.'

I complied.

'Are you satisfied that this is the tape you took of the plaintiffs activities?'

'Yes.'

'Your honour, I would like to tender that tape as evidence.' I looked to the judge, a sinking feeling in my stomach, as I realised that my tape was about to disappear. What other surveillance jobs did I have on that same tape? I had assumed that if any tape was actually going to be 'admitted' as evidence, I was going to hand in a VHS copy. Or at the very least the first eight millimetre tape I'd made instead of the second which I'd copied onto the more expensive tape which I was still using on other jobs! Without another word, the court sheriff almost snatched the tape from my hand as I continued looking somewhat dismayed at the judge. I spun my head around to watch, as he carried the tape

to the court secretary, who began writing up some sort of documentation. It was gone. Gone for good, swallowed up by justice. Too bad if I needed it, too bad about the other footage on the remainder of the tape, too bad it was an expensive Hi8 tape worth fifty dollars. It was just gone. I was excused from the court.

The next day, back at the court, I sat typing on my laptop in the waiting room for most of the morning. Mrs Jimeous wandered in with her translator just before ten o'clock. She approached me, obviously wanting to say something. Looking mildly annoyed, she asked me 'But why did you take my photograph?'

Obviously someone had finally explained to her that I had taken the film, and that because it directly contradicted her statements, this was actually bad and may affect the outcome. She wasn't trying to harass by asking me, because it was clear her question was entirely genuine. It seemed she thought I was just someone off the street who had photographed her by accident, or because I had nothing better to do, and that the barrister was very lucky to have found me and my film. The reason why anyone would follow and film an ageing, foreign lady obviously escaped her, but I decided it was a valid question, given her limited knowledge and language. I just shrugged my shoulders, beginning to wonder myself.

After lunch, I watched as all the cast members reassembled on the stage to continue the real life soap opera, which I had been a part of earlier. Since I'd finished my part, I didn't know why I needed to stay, but the barrister had requested it, just in case he wanted to show the video one more time. It was annoying that I wasn't allowed inside the courtroom though, because I would have enjoyed watching the legal sparring. On television, the lawyers argue exciting cases like murder and extortion as if their life depended on it.

Here the barristers were arguing just as passionately as ever, about the rather short, foreign woman who had been caught sweeping her porch. It seemed rather ironic. I figured I might be legally able to sit in on the case now that I had finished giving my evidence, but decided it was not worth the asking Mr Banks or risking a *'let's just see if anyone minds now'* approach.

Later that day I was called into the courtroom to show the film once again. It was a pleasant adjunct to my otherwise dull afternoon. I was handed the tape by the court secretary, and I inserted it into the player. Everyone in the court crowded around the television again, anxious to view the tape, despite the fact they'd all seen it before. Never before has an aging ethnic woman sweeping her porch been such riveting viewing. I was forced to sit over the other side of the courtroom so that I didn't obstruct the view.

There was silence as the tape played. It ran for almost fifteen minutes, when (horror of horrors) my mobile phone began to ring very loudly at the rear of the courtroom. I jumped up and half ran, half strode towards it, watched by two annoyed court officials. The others in the court seemed too engrossed in the show to notice it, though I knew they would if it continued to ring for much longer. Rather than rummage around inside the bag for the offending phone, I simply took the whole bag with me and continued striding out into the waiting room to answer the call. I got off the phone as quickly as I could without being rude, eventually gasping desperately *'I've got to go. I've got to go NOW!'* then hung up and switched it off.

I quickly stepped back into the courtroom, with no time to bow,, but it was too late. The barrister had begun his speech, and the court was back in full swing. The impromptu film show had finished, and the official court process had well and truly resumed. There was no way I could retrieve my equipment. It was annoying not only because I wasn't there as my tape finished playing, but also the fact that I would have lost points by not being inside the courtroom. The barrister could have said something like 'Thank you, Mr Cooper' before launching into another impassioned speech! Since I was already in the courtroom, I took a seat. There was always the hope I could be asked to pack up my equipment and allowed to go home early. Unless, of course, they wanted to see the tape for a fourth time, which I doubted. It really wasn't that good!

I watched, with a sudden sinking feeling in my stomach, as the TV screen flickered occasionally. MY GOD! THE TAPE PLAYER IS STILL GOING and it is the tape with the bad porn at the end! It was like being handcuffed to a steam train that you know will at some stage drive right over a broken bridge and crash down into a river far below. There was no escaping, no way of stopping the train! It was just something that was going to happen eventually, and I was now in serious trouble. I pondered my options. I could simply walk over to the equipment and turn off the television, but would risk certain abuse by both judge and barrister, or apprehension by my friendly court officer.

I could interrupt the court proceeding by calling out 'Excuse me, do you mind if I collect my equipment now?' but I decided on reflection that this wasn't really a viable option. I looked at possibly crawling under the desks and chairs without being seen, and silently pulling the plug from the power point, but I figured the risk of detection and capture was too high. Besides, it would be rather embarrassing if I was caught, and wouldn't do much for my professional witness image.

I was extremely glad I had turned down the sound on the TV, so if it did get to the point I was dreading, at least the sound of grunting and moaning wouldn't disrupt anyone. The screen was facing away from the judge, but was still very visible to the rest of the court and jury, lights dimmed or not. I knew I could count on at least two members of the jury to burst out laughing if soft porn began playing on the screen before the court. Unfortunately I decided, the barristers and judge might not be able to see the funny side of things, and I wondered if I could be held liable for contempt of court proceedings. If only my phone hadn't rung, I'd have been right there to stop the tape playing at the end of the surveillance and none of this would have happened.

Another unlikely option was to anonymously call in a bomb scare and clear the building, but, on balance, this would probably create more problems than it would solve. It was a tough call, but I decided to sit it out and wait. There was always the chance that the porn was fully wiped over, and there was only one way to find out. I felt the sweat building up under my armpits as I watched the case drag on and on, my eyes firmly glued to the flickering screen. After one and a half agonising hours, the screen switched over to a blue background and I heaved a big sigh of relief, knowing that the machine had reached the end of the tape, and that there would be no impromptu porn show in this courtroom today. Whew! Of course I am sure that readers would have preferred a more colourful ending, but I would not want to overly dramatise the truth, which to me was already more than exciting enough!

The next day a particularly droll article appeared in the newspaper about an elderly woman who had an accident and tried to sue for a significant sum of money, but was caught out on video. It was a mundane, almost routine news article, and I wondered why they even bothered to print it. I can't help but wonder what the headline would have been if the courtroom had ended up actually watching the porn show. Thank God they didn't, because, well honestly... it was really, really bad porn!

CHAPTER 31: SURVEILLANCE FEES AND CHARGES

Surveillance is primarily a service industry. Fees are primarily charged as time and kilometres travelled. It is usually a mobile activity, and agents will charge by distance, including from their home or office to a job, as well as for any movement that occurs during the job.

Charging time

Surveillance is charged by time, and usually by the hour. The average surveillance job is around 20 hours which is usually spread over at least three days. Most reputable companies charge a minimum four hours for any job, regardless of the activity that occurs. This is standard for many service industries. As at the average 2006 rates, a PI sub-contractor will charge from $30 to $35 for surveillance. A primary contractor will charge a private client from $50 to $80 per hour, or a corporate client such as an insurance company (who provides a large volume of work) from $45 to $65 per hour. Factual investigation work is charged at a higher rate than surveillance, but surveillance work usually offers more hours than factual, where an interview may only take an hour or two. In some cases a surveillance job is farmed out to another company rather than an individual sub-contractor. In these cases the rate is usually slightly higher than an individual rate, and in return a slightly higher standard of reporting is required. Some surveillance jobs are more important than others, or more sensitive (such as corporate jobs), and require better quality agents to 'make' themselves available for the work. In these cases the rates would usually be either $5 to $10 higher than a standard 'insurance' or domestic surveillance job. The laws of supply and demand apply to PI's, and sometimes a company needs to offer a higher rate for a team job simply to attract agents from other work they may be doing.

Some jobs, such as longer term jobs are charged by the day – where agents are away from home. This includes some rural work where an agent is in the bush for days at a time, or corporate work where an agent may stay in a factory or other premises for an extended period. While this may result in a lower per hour rate, a day rate usually includes the discomfort involved in being away from home and loved ones. An example may be a rural job paying a sub-contractor a flat $300 per day for each day they are working, regardless of the fact they may spend some time sleeping. Even if they are not working, they may be required to be on standby should some event occur and they need to begin work at short notice.

The clock starts for a surveillance job when the agent leaves their home or office, and finishes when the agent returns home. This is kind of like an attendance fee, and while most other industries charge only for time on-the-job, surveillance is charged from door to door. Many agents list travel time to the closest quarter of an hour, with a lot of jobs charged at a standard half hour travel time each way.

Charging kilometres

Surveillance is charged by the kilometre, from door to door. A company may sometimes make a slight margin on kilometres, though it is more common for the company to simply pass on the kilometre charge from the agent to the client. Fuel prices have risen markedly in recent years, but the kilometre rates have not risen much to match them. The average per kilometre rate in 2006 is $0.55 to $0.65.

Very occasionally a company will charge a slightly lower kilometre rate for travel to and from a job, particularly for a remote job. This is because the agent is not actually 'working' as an investigator during their travel time – i.e. travel-time is charged at a slightly lower rate than work time. Some agents and companies charge back any road tolls, though others simply accept these within the existing charges and don't pass them on. It is slightly more common to on-charge tolls.

Charging centres

Charging for travel can result in high expenses for a job which is in a remote location, as agents may spend more time on the road getting to and from a job than doing the work itself. Some of the larger insurance companies have pushed for *charge-out centres* which are regarded as satellite offices for the company. For example, a company may need to advertise Bathurst as a charge-out centre, meaning that any work conducted in the vicinity of Bathurst will be charged out from the centre of Bathurst, despite the reality being possibly that an agent will attend from Sydney to do the job. A charge-out centre is for charging time and kilometres, so any distance charges can only commence from the charge out centre. Obviously the best approach is to have agents scattered around the country, so the closest agent to any job is assigned, which reduces the expense in travel.

The usual approach for travel time is to charge it as per the usual investigation rate of the job. Some insurers have used their influence to push charges down for travel time, which may be charged at a slightly lower rate than job time. An agent may charge $45 per hour for job time, but only $30 per hour for travel time – though this is less common.

While insurance companies and other large corporate entities can and sometimes do define 'regions' and allocate work to the designated company in each region to lower expenses, they dislike dealing with too many companies, and often prefer a unified reporting format, and dealing with one or two companies, who themselves farm work out to other companies – and manage the job as if it were their own.

Charging report fees

Not all companies charge a report preparation fee, though it is fairly usual. This is an administrative charge for any report. Usually, it is a flat fee for a standard report, something like $100, though some companies charge a per-page fee such as a quarter hour charge for each page of the report body itself. A report preparation fee includes typing, formatting, postage and discussion of the report with the client.

Charging video and photograph expenses

These are usually charged at cost. Where video evidence is extensive (over twenty minutes), a dubbing charge is often levied, being the normal hourly rate for each quarter hour of video. Some clients want only the final evidence, which is usually provided on a CD or DVD, though some prefer the older VHS format. Other clients will require the original tape on which the evidence was recorded, perhaps the Mini-DV tape or other on which the footage was recorded from the camera. These formats are usually more expensive than the final DVD, but can be regarded as more 'pure' in terms of evidence, and less likely to be disputed in court. Most judges today will accept a video copy of evidence, provided the continuity of evidence is maintained, and an agent can be produced in court if required to personally attest to the video evidence he recorded. Now that video is more and more commonly recorded electronically to memory rather than media, it is becoming more difficult to determine the 'source' copy of such evidence. The average unit cost for a DVD or VHS evidence tape is about $15 - $20 to the client.

Photographs are usually digital, and embedded directly into reports. While the cost for digital photography is open to some debate, a PI will usually charge a per-photo fee, or a fee for a photo 'page' containing several photographs. Photos include direct photographs taken with a digital still camera, but also video capture images. There is a cost for locating and capturing the appropriate images from within a surveillance tape. A charge of $20 per photo page, or $3 per photo would be a current price average.

Charging expenses

Usually all expenses are on-charged to the client. The most common are video and photographs, but other expenses include accommodation, meals, informant expenses, entry fees to venues and in fact anything at all. Accommodation is usually charged by a sub-contractor back to the company at cost, though a company may on-charge the client at a mark up. It is quite common for an agent to charge a set overnight fee such as $100 to $140 which would include the cost of a hotel, as well as any meals.

Other common expenses are background checks, such as property, credit or company searches. These are usually charged with a small margin, given that the agent must pay the expense well before he receives the money from the client later. Phone calls are not usually charged back to the client, unless they are extensive or have high charges, as do interstate or overseas calls. I occasionally use a bunch of flowers as a delivery pretext[73] to an office location, in order to get inside and talking to workers. The staff members are usually focused on the flowers which will always be large and bright (more than my physical presence), and this is a form of disguise. In this case

---

[73] See Pretext props on page 128

the flowers would constitute a work expense, and be charged back to the client as required.

If a subject enters a restaurant or café, it may be wise to similarly have a light meal or drink there, so these expenses would be on-charged as well. If the subject catches a train, or enters the Easter Show, the ticket expenses are charged back to the client.

Informant expenses are less standard, and relate to the quality or difficulty of the intelligence. Few PI's pay for access to government or other illegal information these days, though it does still occur on larger cases. Years ago this type of expense was commonplace and details would often be obtained for a nominal ten dollar fee, though now they are far more expensive. Paparazzi pay large amounts of expenses to informants, with anything from fifty dollars to several thousand being paid simply for notification that a famous identity is in a particular location, or doing something which would interest the media.

While technically it is not legal to on-charge expenses for fines, this is common in the industry. Where surveillance requires a vehicle to be parked illegally to either get the right shot, or has to be parked for longer than allowed, and a fine ensues – such expenses are usually passed back to the client. I once chased a subject to the airport, where he got out of a taxi and briskly walked off. I was alone, so I just got out of my surveillance car and left it in the highly policed airport drop-off section – then ran after my subject, desperate to identify which flight he was taking, and to see if he met with anyone before he boarded the plane. As I ran from the car, an airport parking official called to me, seeing that I was the sole occupant and driver of the car. *'Hey, you can't park there!'* he yelled with some annoyance, but I had to just ignore him in order to crack the case. As it was I managed to get a good ID, chat to the subject on a pretext before he boarded the plane, and got exactly what was required on the case. When I returned, my car had been booked, and was shortly due to be towed. The sixty-dollar parking ticket was well worth the expense to solve the case, and this charge was readily paid by the client.

Similarly red light camera offences or speeding tickets are also charged back the client, provided it can be shown (to the client) that the offence was in relation to a legitimate pursuit of the subject. Not all clients are willing to pay these expenses, so such terms should be negotiated up front. A client who does not authorise payment of fines in these cases must therefore accept a higher likelihood of an agent losing a subject – should they jump an orange light, etc. Such expenses are not allowed to be charged back, and nor are they able to be classified as a legitimate business expense for taxation - though some PI's would debate this!

Charging terms

Most companies work to a standard thirty day account, though others require payment in seven or fourteen days, though this is less common. Insurance companies and large corporate entities are notoriously late in paying their accounts. Smarter PI companies will levy an overdue percentage, to encourage on-time payment. Sub-contractor PI's are usually paid on thirty day accounts as well, though some of the lower paid PI's or those on full time contracts will get paid weekly. A common PI industry phenomena is the 'I will pay you when I get paid' issue. Some companies only pay their sub-contractor agents after they receive payment from the client. This is very poor form, but unfortunately quite common. I often say 'Would you withhold your electricity payment because your client has not paid you yet?' though this falls on deaf ears. The fact that a sub-contractor has worked a particular job seems to tie their payment to the client's payment. If a company follows this line then I am liable to say *'Well, if I am at the mercy of your clients accounting, I would prefer to invoice them directly'* though this is just not how it works. Clearly the arrangement is fee for service, and a sub-contractor charges a fee to the company they contract to, not the final client. While most work is corporate or insurance, the smaller domestic market has a high degree of cash work.

CHAPTER 32: AGENT PROVOCATEUR

Evidence is likely to be inadmissible in court if the surveillance agent did something to make the claimant 'perform' some action. Letting down the tyres of a vehicle and then filming the claimant changing the tyres for instance, or any similar activity cannot be used. Letting the air out of tyres would be unlawful. There is generally no law against modifying the environment to suit your purposes, provided you do not break any specific laws, such as damage to property. Throwing sticks over somebody's particularly neat lawn will probably result in you later obtaining film of them bending to pick them all up. You probably haven't broken the law by placing a few sticks on their lawn, but your actions have influenced and encouraged theirs, and may result in your video being deemed inadmissible.

An example of courts dismissing a case due to entrapment can be seen in a recent investigation by the NSW Department of Health, which used underage teenagers to buy cigarettes from vendors, and then prosecuted these vendors. A District Court judge dismissed the case against the vendors as they had been 'entrapped' into committing the offence[74]. Judge Peter Berman stated that if the matter had been more serious, it would have justified *higher levels of impropriety,* but criticised the department for 'trawling' for offenders, rather than targeting those who were already under suspicion due to previous complaints.

This is an example of the courts recognising the need for some degree of 'impropriety' when conducting an investigation, which would include providing false information to offenders under pretext, or engaging them in some manner to obtain information that may be later used to prosecute them. As with many aspects of investigations, the actions taken should be appropriate for the circumstances. This may include ensuring there is reasonable

---

[74] *'Using teenagers to buy cigarettes was entrapment'* by Geesche Jacobsen, Sydney Morning Herald 7/5/2005

suspicion involved, as well as being careful not to *overly* influence the actions of others. Some interaction, pretext or influence is acceptable if used in moderation.

It is perfectly acceptable to be an agent provocateur in a large number of cases. These may include an infidelity or a corporate theft case, where you may move a bin in front of their driveway to provoke them to move it later, thus allowing you a better opportunity to identify them by video or photographs. You have influenced their action, which resulted in you being able to take a better photograph, and courts would not dismiss the image evidence or class it as entrapment, because this degree of interaction is generally acceptable.

I had an assignment at Quay West car park several years ago, where there was a high degree of theft from vehicles. We placed a laptop case in full view, on the passenger's seat of the car park manager's vehicle. This vehicle was locked and parked on a lower level where thefts were more common. On the very first night of surveillance, the offender came, observed the laptop case and smashed the window to retrieve it. I arrested (citizens arrest) the offender together with a security guard who was working with me. The offender put up quite a struggle and was clearly not impressed about being caught, but eventually the police arrived and led him away. He was later charged with both the theft of the laptop case and damage to the vehicle, but he pleaded guilty so the case never went before the courts. He didn't have much choice of course, as I had clear video evidence of his actions. If the case had gone to court, he may have pleaded entrapment as we had specifically placed the laptop case (though filled with newspaper) in clear view. It would be extremely unlikely for a court to accept this however, as my actions would not have *overly* influenced the offender's actions. Don't automatically be afraid to manipulate the situation to obtain a better result. However if your evidence may be tainted or dismissed because of how you obtained it, you should consider alternatives.

CHAPTER 33: AGENT SAFETY AND SECURITY

Understanding safety risks

While government agencies may have a cast of thousands, the PI often works alone, and out of the safety and support of co-workers. Like the parking police, his job often entails catching people out at their misdemeanours. Like the parking police, he is not always well received. The surveillance agent's work is often misunderstood and regarded warily by the authorities. Some tend to feel PI's are doing work that should be done by the government. The public often regard the surveillance agent somewhat dubiously, concerned that he may be a paedophile or a terrorist if he is spotted sneaking around with a camera or in a tinted car! The fraudster will often have a more extreme view, the reaction to which can include screaming abuse, smashing cameras and generally making their feelings known rather openly. The plan is to be undetected by them, but this cannot always be avoided and the roll of the dice will occasionally have your heart beating faster as you need to deal with a situation.

Conceal documentation

Many forget how much information their car can give away to others, as a close inspection will often reveal a business card in the centre console, some mail on the front seat, a phone number on a post-it note, a resident parking or club sticker on the window and the list goes on. Leaving surveillance notes on the front seat is a bit of a give-away, yet it is done all too often by the novice PI. This leaves the operator open to detection and hence, leaves them in danger. The best idea is to ensure no information is being given away by your car, even while you are inside. It wouldn't be the first time a nosey claimant has observed the keys sitting in the ignition, and the doors unlocked. Consider what information you are showing.

Defusing a situation if approached out of the safety of the car can often have you thinking on your feet. I was once approached by an aggressive guy who gruffly asked what I was doing following him around. Knowing there would always be a slight amount of uncertainty in his mind, I played on this and began excitedly telling him about my university 'psychology' assignment study on the movement of people, and their general interactions. Pure garbage, but my story held together long enough for me to escape. It wasn't what I was saying, it was more the enthusiasm I projected when asked. If I'd clammed up and said I was doing nothing, I would just be inviting more trouble. He was of a rather stocky build, so I decided to leave him alone after that. I have not always been so lucky.

Camouflage your intentions

Consider leaving misleading information for others to allay concerns. Leaving a baby seat in view is very non-threatening and sends the right message, as opposed to leaving a lens cap visible inside the car which sends the wrong message! Leave out documentation that suggests the driver is involved in a non-threatening occupation - a scrawled note on the dash saying: *'The job is in Smith St, but call Davo to get the number. You will need to bring the generator because we will need to cut the power.'* may at least buy you time if someone comes to inspect the vehicle. They will immediately need to consider the possibility that you are in the area legitimately, and possibly a contractor working nearby. After all, the note does mention Smith Street, and it is unlikely a PI would be using a generator, so you may be able to allay their fears.

Leaving a contact number visible could also assist as they may ring (which would give you their caller-ID) and you or your buddy could talk to them under pretext, saying '*No, of course he is not a PI, he is working on the* (insert as appropriate) *and is probably wasting the bosses time again. Thanks for letting me know. We'll ask him what he is still doing there as he has not rung in yet!*' A surveillance professional will quickly turn the situation around from a possible compromise, and if skilled enough may even be able to use this to GET information, such as '*...look, we have been having a lot of trouble with this guy, so if you see him again, can you let me know? Actually, I would be interested to know when he leaves, can I ring you back to see if he is still there later? What is your number? If I ring around eleven thirty, will you still be there, or are you going to work?*' This approach quickly aligns the focus of both parties, so the suspicious caller quickly feels his views on the car and driver are supported by the person he is speaking to (which may even be yourself), and that both are 'against' this driver.

A 'broken-down' note is a good idea if the vehicle is being left in an unusual location, particularly in rural situations. Consider leaving this note on the windscreen of your car '*Hi Dave, I tried to get the car going but I think it is the spark plugs, not just the fuel, so I don't know how long you will take to get back, but I have gone off myself to get some help. Will be back soon – John 0405 17 445*'. Not only does this note suggest to thieves it is not worth trying to steal, but it suggests the vehicle is there due to mechanical reasons and not for any suspicious reasons.

Lock your vehicle – always

Lock all vehicle doors when on-site, even when inside the car. I know one agent that had his wallet stolen from the front seat while he was hiding in the back. The thief got a big shock when he realised there was somebody inside, but still managed to get away with the wallet! There were two mistakes made with this true story. Doors should be locked and items such as a wallet or cameras need to be out of sight at all times. Always consider the image you project to others. Some discarded fast food wrappers inside the car can be good to project 'nothing worth stealing here'.

The case of the mad mechanic

Key learning points

- Agent safety – Always lock your car
- Why things are seen

I was tasked with surveying this young, Eastern European guy, who had a large claim in. On the first day I lost contact with him on the follow as he drove like an absolute maniac. I didn't really want to do a phone pretext on him, as he looked the type to be too streetwise to safely run a good one, but I gave it a shot. To my surprise he provided me his work address after a short pretext conversation. It was almost too easy, and for a moment I wondered if he was trying an elaborate trap by giving me a dodgy address at which he could then lie in wait... but it did seem plausible that it was correct.

The next day I set up surveillance outside the mechanic shop address in Marrickville which he'd provided me. Before too long I was pleased to see him arriving, and starting to open up the shop. Bingo. There was not a lot of action visible throughout the day, as he was mostly inside the workshop. For a moment I considered booking my car into the shop to get an inside angle of his work, but decided against it. Besides, there was no real need as the mere fact that he was working was a good result. He did look pretty fit though, certainly not lying in bed at home with a bad back like he had claimed!

I was parked in a slightly odd location on the edge of a clearway where there were no other cars nearby, but I figured this would be fine. It was nearly two o'clock in the afternoon, on a blazing hot day, when I decided to get out and buy some cool drinks from the nearby corner shop. It was perhaps a little dangerous to get out while so close to the subject's workshop, but I decided to give it a chance, spurred on by the sweat pouring off my face and the lure of the ice-cream advertising outside the nearby milk bar. I snuck out and walked towards the shop, savouring the cool breeze on my damp sweaty body, and soon I was armed with a bag of cold drinks and ice-cream as I returned to my car. Up until now I hadn't seen any sign of my subject being suspicious at all, and even on my return I didn't notice him, so I felt comfortable diving back into the car and settling down again. I was halfway through my ice-cream when I finally noticed him, standing near the side of the roller door, half in the shadows, staring towards me. I wondered if perhaps he'd seen me leave the car and had waited for my return. Perhaps he saw me approach the car, but noticed that it didn't drive off and that there was no one in the driver's seat. Perhaps he had just noticed the car for the first time. Trying to kid myself it was nothing, I watched as he continued to stare, then suddenly he began striding across the road towards me, as would a man on a mission.

I gobbled the remains of my ice cream quickly to free my hands, a cold headache searing my brain, though this was now the least of my problems. I hurriedly put up the curtains and screens around the glass and waited, knowing what was going to happen next. When he arrived at the car he reached straight for the door handle and nearly ripped it out, then jiggled it madly for a few seconds as he peered inside. I was thankful I'd remembered to lock the door, which was now a subconscious experience. 'Get out of the f...ing car!' he yelled, slamming his broad fist against the window.

He continued yelling and banging, peering in the window, then it went silent. I checked through a peep-hole and saw him walking back to his workshop. Relieved, I figured I would wait another minute before driving off to safety. I suddenly realised I no longer had this opportunity when he returned, this time with two burly mates. Things were not looking good. I picked up my mobile and dialled 000 emergency, and was quickly put through to the police. With the three guys now surrounding my car, I was trapped. '... Hello, is there anyone there?' I heard and realising the police operator was trying to speak to me as I had been distracted and had missed the connection.

'YES, I mean yes' I replied, quickly lowering my voice to a whisper. 'I'm a private investigator, and I'm in my car, and I now have three guys outside who are trying to attack me' I said, wondering if the sound of fists banging on the roof could be heard through the phone.

The operator didn't sound impressed, and said 'well, perhaps you should drive off, why don't you drive off?'

I replied that I couldn't. She then took details of my location and said someone would be there soon. I figured it couldn't take too long since I could almost see Marrickville Police Station from where I was parked.

I felt relieved, knowing the police would be on their way shortly. Peering out again, I could see the three in front of the car, smoking and talking. I suspected their discussion was not really work related or football related, or perhaps anything other than what they were going to do to me when they got me out of the car, or perhaps how they should get me out. I began to wonder how long the glass windows would keep them out. For some reason they continued to talk for a while, then I suddenly realised it was almost ten minutes since I had called the 000 emergency number. I decided to ring again, just to be sure. As I did, the guys came back close to the car, and again I was forced to whisper. While they all peered into the car at different angles, I tried to talk to the operator.

'... yes, I called before. No I haven't driven off, no I can't drive off.... a private investigator... look they are trying to attack me... no they are not inside my car, they are outside... (I heard one of them yelling 'GET THE F... OUT OF THE CAR NOW OR WE WILL SMASH YOUR WINDOW!') ...look I told you they are trying to attack me' I said as loud thumping could be heard on the roof.

I suddenly realised that the entire conversation probably sounded rather odd, and very much like a prank call, complete with my husky whispers and adrenalin-laced, heavy panting. 'LOOK, they are trying to kill me, they are outside NOW, can't you hear them? They are trying to smash the glass,' I half screamed in my quietest whisper, though I quickly sensed the urgent panic in my voice had been finally registered by the operator.

The abuse was getting heavier and louder, and they were rattling the door handles so hard it felt as if they were going to rip off at any minute. I jumped as one of them landed on the front bonnet, sitting there bouncing up and down as he peered into the darkened windscreen. I heard them talking among themselves...

'Well, what can you use? Get the .... from inside... shit just get a bloody brick, look from the garden there... just smash the window!'.

Not good at all. I realised the safety of my vehicle cocoon would be removed in about sixty seconds, and I could only wonder what would happen from there.

Finally the police arrived, pulling up in front of my car in a marked vehicle. Despite this, the men were returning with some implement, and began discussing which window was best to smash. It was almost as if they hadn't seen the very clearly marked police car now parked right next to them. Two police officers got out of the car and walked towards the group, shouting *'Hey... hey put that down... what are you guys doing... get away from the car... no right away... stand over near the fence there'*, and the three guys reluctantly obeyed. Peering out I could see my subject holding something in his hand.

'What are you guys doing here?' inquired the male officer with some authority.

Being close by in the car, I could hear his absurd reply, which was *'I was going to smash the window'*. I couldn't believe my ears, and then he went on. *'...because he is in there, we were going to smash the window to get him out you see, because he is a PI'*. He seemed to think that it was acceptable to vandalise the car, due to my unsavoury occupation. It was as if I had become fair game, and smashing the window or me was a reasonable response. I couldn't believe he was making such brazen admissions to the police. It was a very surreal experience.

The police then realised there was someone inside the car. They had obviously assumed the informant was one of the three males standing round the car, and had not considered that I was still inside. The female officer walked towards the car and called out *'Hello there, can you come out so we can talk to you?'*, and I pushed through the curtains into the front seat, and half rolled out the driver's door, sweat pouring down my face.

'See, I told you, see there he is!' shouted the subject aggressively and stepping forward, as if my mere appearance should somehow spark a lynch mob response. The male officer moved

slightly and held out his arms to stop them, advising them in no uncertain terms that they should remain right where they were.

I explained my situation to the policewoman, who understood. I told her about the investigation, about him claiming to be incapable of any work, yet was running the mechanic shop, and that now I had caught him out working, and he had caught me out working... but that he was less than impressed and was apparently going to do something very violent about it. She noted the facts in her notebook and then let me drive away. I felt such immense relief to escape into the safety of the traffic and away from the drama. It must have been the ice-cream I figured. I was spotted going for my ice-cream. Just when I thought the job was wrapped up, I'd let my guard down and thought it was fine to do a quick walk to the shop nearby.

I could have moved the car instead of walking, but I felt it was best to leave it in position rather than risk moving it again back to the same, slightly unnatural location. I had a choice, either car or foot. I rolled the dice and I made a call. It was a bad call. I should have moved the car. It was very nearly the most expensive ice-cream of my life. Sometimes the watcher becomes the watched, and it wouldn't be the first time a subject has ended up following me after becoming suspicious. It's important to consider this possibility and to take precautions. When leaving a surveillance job, be wary of being followed yourself. A canny subject may not let on they have picked you, but get their mates to then follow you home when you leave the area. Consider having your car registered in a different company name or address to your own for example. You need to consider that any information you let slip about yourself could well come back to bite you later.

Conceal car keys

Ensure the car keys are not in the ignition or are covered from view. It is slightly preferable to cover them in some way, as this leaves them ready for a fast getaway. Where you need to be closer to the target or consider it more likely they may inspect your vehicle, play it safe and leave the ignition vacant, as keys are a giveaway there is someone inside.

Vehicle registration

Consider which address your vehicle is registered to, and what name it is listed, such as your personal name, or your company name. An associate of mine, Michael Rumore, once told me while he was on a job a woman rang his investigation agency, asking why a tinted vehicle registered to him was parked suspiciously in her street. She even asked him who he was investigating. She had obtained the information by contacting the police, and they had provided it to her. Despite this being a serious offence, it still occurs.

Remember you are as open to scrutiny as the subject. Most people have access to the same resources that you do. So having a vehicle registered to 'I Spy for You Pty Ltd' may be asking for trouble, even though your registration details are supposed to be private. Listing the registered address as your private home is usually required by law, but the surveillance professional can trust no one and must take nothing for granted, so ensure your home is secure.

Remember that any parking scheme sticker may lead back to you, particularly when the council operating such scheme may be freer with information than the RTA. In some cases it is not hard to find a vehicle just from knowing the suburb it comes from, provided it is regularly parked on a street. If this is the case, consider a removable sticker in a plastic CD case or other method that allows you to hide these details when required.

Protect your evidence

Never take old footage to a new job if possible. Keep all evidence at home once collected. The surveillance vehicle is vulnerable, and may be trashed or broken into, rendering your vital evidence compromised, or worse, in the hands of an angry thief who may be a suspicious claimant. On departure from a job, ensure that you are not being followed yourself. You don't want to lead others back to your address. When ringing claimants, either switch caller-ID off OR use a safe phone line such as a pre-paid SIM card. Remember you may go mobile on foot in an instant, and will not have time to prepare the vehicle to be parked safely for hours. The best policy is to have everything packed away, with no files or surveillance equipment left strewn around the vehicle unless it is needed at that time. Then, once the job goes mobile on foot, all you need to do is collect your running bag and exit and lock the vehicle.

Communication security

When using two-way radios in non-phone coverage areas, be very cautious if using an open CB channel, as many rural folk will have a radio set and any operation will quickly attract attention. Provided you are vague and speak in veiled speech, and do not mention private details such as road names, registrations, phone numbers and the like, you can use an open channel without much problem. The more laid back and casual, the better. Screaming 'GO, GO, GO, he is leaving now in the red ute, so start the follow!' may draw attention in some circumstances. A better suggestion may be the calmer and direct 'The ute is leaving now, do you want to take it?'

Concealment within vehicles

You should be able to be totally covered when inside the surveillance vehicle. Have curtains, sheets or even a quilt that you can pull over yourself. Often you will have a few seconds notice that somebody is going to check out your car closely, so just throwing a quilt or blanket over yourself and remaining very still for a few minutes may give the impression that there is nobody there. I have been covered inside a tinted car on two separate occasions where I heard the person inspecting say to somebody else *'There is nobody inside there'*. It doesn't take much to hide provided you relax and are at least mildly prepared for a close inspection.

Conceal address details on statements

When providing statements to police, always request they conceal your personal details where appropriate. Common phrases are *ADDRESS: Known to Police, NAME: Known to Detective Smith*. When asked in court to state address details, you can request these be provided to the magistrate or judge in written form, to ensure they are not provided directly to persons you are giving evidence against.

When providing details to police, you should be aware they are not all as helpful as you might expect, due in some part to their lack of experience or knowledge of private investigator activities. Once in Newcastle I was following a lady around and after some time she drove up to the local police station. Soon after this a policeman came out of the station and inspected my car, but did not appear to see me hiding inside. It was clear however, that I had been noticed by the woman. I decided to telephone the station out of professional courtesy, and explain that I was a PI. I asked the officer to not tell my subject, but asked if perhaps he could advise that he had been in contact with the driver of the car, that she had nothing to worry about and the car would not continue following her.

The woman soon came out of the station with a terrified look on her face and was staring at my car as she hid comically behind a telegraph pole before sliding into her car. I then received a return call from the helpful officer who said he had told her exactly who I was, and that I was there to film her in relation to her injury. Talk about discretion!

Proactive safety on mobile surveillance

When on a follow, always give yourself options. When pulling up in traffic, always leave enough room to escape if necessary, rather than stopping too close to the car in front. Be ready for an angry subject to jump out and engage in road/PI rage and give yourself enough room to drive out of danger. This is also the case when parking, as a fast exit is required for a clean start to any follow and also provides room to escape danger. No point trying to do a three point manoeuvre from the tight parking space while the angry subject is ripping off the wiper blades - better to have room to depart quickly!

Legal suppression of details

The RTA has a registration suppression scheme, which makes it difficult to obtain details. This is primarily used for family court judges and undercover police. I have had my details suppressed for many years under this scheme, though have let it lapse now I don't do much surveillance work these days. Police get no details when they look up suppressed registrations, and even RTA workers only get your name and no address. Official inquiries for these records must be made in writing, making it far more difficult to get your details from the system. This is not really necessary in all cases, and the paperwork involved makes life difficult. It must be renewed annually and requires support in writing from senior level police, but may be worthwhile depending on your circumstances. The best approach is to simply have the registered details safe by listing them in names of other entities you may know, and which have little day-to-day contact with you.

Over the last few years I have become aware of at least three instances of surveillance subjects obtaining my personal details via my vehicle registration plates, and I am certainly not the only PI who has had this experience. I made a complaint to the authorities, but it was never satisfactorily explained. On the last occasion I was telephoned directly by the subject who thought he was calling a 'fleet leasing company' which had obviously leased a car to a PI. He told me bluntly that he had got his police mates to check the vehicle registration of a suspicious vehicle which had been following him, and that it was registered to this company. He wanted to know who the vehicle was being leased to, so I told him I would get back to him, but never heard from him again. Perhaps he recognised my voice from my earlier pretext on him, as I certainly recognised his! The ICAC inquiry has stopped the bulk of these illegal record searches, but be aware people can usually always obtain your details if they try hard enough, so take care of personal information.

Make personal information about yourself less easy to obtain. Electoral rolls and phone book entries are a place to start. Facilities exist whereby, in issues of personal safety, electoral roll information can be suppressed and phone numbers kept silent. Ensure the address does not lead directly to you (or you may use an associate's address or a relatives which can enable safety-screening of any suspicious inquiries, while still allowing legitimate contact by authorities). Remember there are many ways someone can get your information, such as video store membership and land ownership. Be aware of all forms of publicly available, personal information.

The case of cheap phone calls

Key learning points

- Liaison with external bodies

- Arresting surveillance suspects

There have also been several cases where I have worked successfully with the police on operations. Once I was doing some contract surveillance for Telstra, looking into phone fraud, and we worked closely with the police in a task force known as 'City Safe' which targets street crime. You would be well surprised at how many ways there are to defraud Telstra using their payphones. There are, for example, half a dozen ways to steal the coins – either from the entry slot or the refund chute! There are ways to make free phone calls using straws or 'wired' phone cards and many more. There was the case of the offender with stolen payphone master keys who would do regular runs up and down the east coast of Australia, emptying out the coin boxes in the middle of the night – we had each run tracked with pins on the map, but he rarely visited the same payphone twice!

Often the payphone offenders would be calling home to Middle Eastern destinations, with some calling the 'pay for phone sex' lines in their own country, as they liked to be titillated in their own language! Goodness knows how much Telstra paid for these calls, which would include the international call leg as well as the 'service' fee – and considering the calls were free, the offenders were in no hurry to get off the line!

Telstra has a legal mandate to maintain a certain proportion of the payphone network operational, and this was in fact more of a problem than the fraud. The offenders were damaging so many payphones that it was well outside the acceptable limits and forced the entity to pay large fines or get senior managers to make embarrassing explanations to the government about the poor service. Telstra technicians were so flat out chasing the offenders that no sooner had they fixed a phone it would be rendered unserviceable again that same day. Next time you see a payphone out of order, give a thought to Telstra and realise it is not always bad management that is responsible! Fortunately Telstra was able to change the security features on the payphones, but it took a very long time to achieve this.

Some enterprising character, who was later caught, had set up his own 1900 pay-per-minute phone service with Telstra, then went around the phone boxes dialling his own 1900 telephone number via the 'free call' method. He would then leave the phone handsets off the hook to keep the line open – at least until somebody else put it back hours later. Telstra was forced to pay him a substantial portion of the five dollars per minute charge he received as a 1900 provider which was amounting to thousands of dollars they never received from the payphones themselves. There is no doubting human ingenuity!

Together with a sizeable team of PI's, we would stake out the CBD payphones and would make arrests with alarming regularity. On one year my colleagues and I arrested about fifty separate offenders, not all of whom were pleased to be caught. We arrested them on the spot, and then held the offenders until the police Task Force came to collect them. One day we arrested one offender and sat him next to the phone. While waiting for police to arrive another offender approached the phone and we caught him as well! Then shortly after than a third offender came by who we had caught a week earlier! He was walking towards our payphone when he saw we had two guys sitting on their hands waiting for collection. He suddenly veered off and decided he didn't need to use the phone after all!

Several of the arrests became a little violent, with one offender pulling a knife and several putting up quite a struggle. Sometimes they would be illegal immigrants who knew the arrest was the first step to a one way trip back home. One of the police teams arrested an offender who had a concealed and loaded pistol. I attended a few court cases over these matters and some cases were reported in the newspapers, though most were just business as usual at the local court.

Throughout the whole operation, the police we worked with were excellent and very supportive. They appreciated our assistance and were pleased the arrests were making their figures look good as well. During 'Operation City Safe Seven' the entire team of PIs and police managed to arrest well over three hundred and fifty offenders over six weeks for a variety of offences such as fraud, drugs, property theft and more. We had a celebratory drink after the whole operation finished, and one of the police agents had some polo shirts manufactured with the NSW Police logo and the impressive operation arrest statistics printed on the back. In all, the police were great to work with. There are always two sides to the story, and there are good cops and bad cops – just as there are the good PIs and bad PIs!

The case of an unhappy caller

Key learning points

- Agent safety

- Agent communication, working in teams

- Present evidence in court

I was working with a huge Fijian guy called Tia. He usually worked for the corrective services in the prison 'emergency response' unit. Whenever there was a prisoner riot, Tia would be called and sort things out. Prisoners would be either intimidated by his size, or would come off second best with this man mountain. Unfortunately the Fijian work ethic is more relaxed compared to my sometimes over zealous attitude to our work. We had a fairly quiet spell and hadn't arrested anyone on that day. I was keen to get someone at least, and had been going flat out as we did the rounds looking for likely suspects to monitor. Tia's motivation was waning, and he decided to get a coffee and relax for a break.

I told Tia I would join him shortly, but wanted to sweep the railway platforms at Town Hall station one last time, so I walked off on my own. Of course this was exactly the time when I needed Tia to back me up. Coming down the platform stairs I spied a male of Mediterranean appearance hunched over the payphone, talking on the phone in a foreign language. Immediately I was suspicious.

Several weeks previously I had compiled a training document for the Telstra surveillance teams, outlining the warning flags which should be considered when assessing potential offenders at payphones. There were a lot of flags to consider, but this guy managed to raise a lot of them. His nationality was the first flag, and the vast majority of our offenders had been of certain foreign nationalities. His behaviour on the phone was suspicious; he was covering the card slot in an unnatural manner. He was on the platform payphone late in the evening, yet there were no trains arriving soon, and no other people on the deserted platform.

I covertly took a short section of video, then swung past closer to him to let him know I was there, and to gauge his reaction to the presence of another person close by. He noticed me immediately, and his body language screamed that he was less than comfortable. He continued his phone call, but kept looking behind several times. I intentionally stood about a metre away from him, slightly invading his personal space on the empty platform. I tried to call Tia, but there was no mobile reception in this underground platform.

The guy finished his call and tried to retrieve his card from the slot without me seeing it. I caught a brief glimpse of a wire attached to the card, and challenged him, saying *'I want to see your card please, I work for Telstra.'*

He mumbled something and tried to shove his card into his jacket pocket, while taking a step away. I reached over and grabbed his arm, pulling away before he could slip the card inside. Suddenly he was struggling and fighting, pushing, punching, and shoving as he reacted like a wild animal. *'You're under arrest'* I shouted several times as we careered over together, crashing down and rolling around the tiled platform floor.

I saw him throw his card onto the train line, and then another card fell from his jacket. He tried to kick this card off the platform as well while we struggled, obviously trying to get rid of the evidence. I cursed myself for not going back for Tia, as I had misjudged the strength of my quarry, or his determination not to get caught. During the melee I was looking for anyone to call out to for assistance, but the platform was deserted. Eventually I had him pinned face down as I sat on top, though he didn't stop and it was all I could do to keep him there. I had a pair of handcuffs in my back pocket, but my jeans were too tight to allow me to grab them while I was in a sitting position. I could only get them out by loosening my grip and leaning forward, but each time I did this he would struggle violently and then nearly escape again. I wished I'd been better prepared, and thought myself lucky that he wasn't armed.

Finally I saw another young male approaching our struggle cautiously, clearly not really certain who was the good guy and who was the crook. Being in plain clothes I guessed it may have looked like I was the aggressor, though by now I had just about managed to tear the cuffs out of my pocket. I called to him for help, and he hurried over and restrained the suspect. Thankful for the assistance, I finally managed to get the cuffs on.

It turned out that the guy who came to help was an off-duty policeman, and together we marched the offender up the stairs towards the Town Hall police station. We must have looked a sight, as the struggle had resulted in torn clothing, ruffled hair and dirt all over our bodies as a result of rolling around on the dirty underground platform. Walking past the Town Hall coffee shop, I spied Tia relaxing with a steaming cappuccino. He looked over at the three of us frog marching along, and gave me a wide grin. He didn't even get out of his chair, as it was clearly all over. Tia had got his break, I had had some excitement, and all in all it was another successful day!

We later searched our prisoner inside the police station and found yet another fraudulent phone card, which made three after we managed to collect the two he had tried to dispose of.

The police then charged him with 'obtaining benefit by deception'.

Many months later the case went to court, with the defendant pleading not guilty. When on the stand in court, I was asked why the defendant had come to my notice. I began by explaining that he was of a particular foreign nationality, but before I could finish there was a ripple through the court and the magistrate stopped me, asking me to clarify my answer. I could see that my comment had been perceived as racist, or at the very least politically incorrect. I apologised for any offence my comments may have caused, but then went on to explain just how many offenders we had arrested in this operation, and that the vast majority had been foreign nationalities. This was in fact one of the very first 'red flags' we looked for when assessing potential suspects. The magistrate accepted my answer, and later found the defendant guilty. On 19th November 2000, the Daily Telegraph printed a small article about the case, together with a photograph of the offender, 'Mr Al-Hlow' – just one of hundreds of offenders successfully prosecuted as the result of our surveillance efforts.

Most cases never reached the court as offenders would plead guilty under the weight of evidence against them, but this was not always the case. The previous year I was casually talking with others on our surveillance team outside the Town Hall police station, when we identified another offender at a nearby phone booth. Perhaps he didn't choose the best place or time to commit his offence. He gave us quite a chase and a violent struggle ensued, though with two undercover police and three private investigators he was a little out-numbered. Despite so many witnesses, he still chose to plead not guilty and so the case went to court, at public expense. Mr Tarrick Abbosh Bene was soon convicted of the offence, as well as a separate one of common assault on me. In addition Mr Bene was ordered to pay me compensation of $3900 for an expensive video camera and clothing that was smashed or torn in the struggle. He paid only $200 in a few small payments over several months, before disappearing and has not paid anything since. I've been too busy to chase this up, but if there are any budding PI's who want experience in locating offenders, feel free to contact me for the details!

These two cases reflect the experience of our surveillance team regarding offender nationalities. It is a sensitive subject, though most investigators seem to agree that the majority of fraud investigations do involve foreign nationality offenders. In the Telstra operation we found over 70% were foreign, though this may have been higher due to the 'type' of offence (fraudulent use of phone services) which may encourage foreigners – who have overseas relatives to talk to.

The National Prison Census[75] 1997 shows that across the entire prison population, Lebanese offenders outnumbered Australians by two to one. Vietnamese outnumber Australians by even more. There are always many factors to consider though. A good related paper is 'Youth, Ethnicity and Crime in Australia' by Jock Collins[76]. A persons race, skin colour or religion should never be used to discriminate against them, but this should be considered statistically when apportioning limited crime fighting resouces. The new NSW "Middle Eastern organised crime squad" is one example of these statistics being employed in practice.

---

[75] 'Ethnicity and Crime', Mukherjee, S. Paper presented to the 3rd National Outlook Symposium on Crime in Australia, Australian Institute of Criminology, Canberra, 23/03/1999
[76] 'Youth, Ethnicity and Crime in Australia' by Jock Collins, Centre for Ethnic and Migration Studies.   25/4/2002 www.ulg.ac.be/cedem/downloads/JCWP.PDF

The case of the panting intruder

Key learning points

- Identification of subject

- Service of legal document under difficult circumstances

- Agent safety

Approaching the front door, I knocked lightly. There was a security peephole in the door through which occupants could view callers. Not that it mattered. I wasn't worried about them seeing me. I was just a messenger and, though I brought bad news, I had nothing to do with the contents of the documents I was carrying. I made no effort to conceal them from view, holding them loosely by my side. A simple messenger, surely they'd understand. The door opened sharply. A man aged about thirty years or more stood squarely, in the now open doorframe. His face was creased and lined, belying his true age. It appeared he'd led a colourful life, and his face didn't disguise this. His hair was unwashed and short; unkempt as if he'd just got out of bed. His nose had a distinctly lopsided bulge. It was flat, almost squashed against a hardened face in typical 'ex-boxer' fashion. He continued holding the doorknob with his left hand, while his right grasped the door jamb. I glanced at his fingers as they slid around the woodwork. He had large, dry fingers with a thickness that suggested a working man. His fingers wrapped around the timber like they were old friends. I noticed his fingernails were grimy and there appeared to be a yellowish stain near his right forefinger. Perhaps he was a long term smoker.

He stared at me for a split second, before uttering a gruff 'Yes?' I looked at his shirt. A business shirt, clean but crumpled. It didn't quite fit the picture, but neither did his house, which was large and well landscaped.

Although I'd traced him here from a previous address and had no way of actually identifying him, I just knew in my bones that I was speaking to the right man.

'Hello Mr Crawley, I have a delivery for you,' I said, offering the paperwork to him. It was a bluff, which is the best approach. When said convincingly, most people don't deny their identity, assuming you already know them somehow. Had I asked, 'Are you Mr Crawley?' the reply would have been 'Why?' and a difficult, time-consuming discussion might have taken place while I tried to ascertain who I was really speaking to. He may have denied he was Mr Crawley, given a false name, or even chosen to remain silent and I would be forced to conduct further investigations. He made no reply at all, merely looking at me and my paperwork. I continued holding the documents out, maintaining a cheerful 'it's just a harmless delivery' expression on my face. 'Take them, take them,' I thought, anxious to get on with my work. His fingers made no move to release their solid grip on the doorframe, and he stood there quietly for a few seconds.

'He doesn't live here mate, I don't know who you're after,' he replied in a monotone drawl.

'Oh, that's odd because it says he lives here,' I said quickly, indicating towards the official-looking documents. This was a lie, but I was hoping to bluff him. He made no move to even look at the documents, but just stood there.

'Well mate, I can tell you he doesn't live here,' he replied. It sounded convincing. I could simply write the code for 'Not known at this address' on the form, and would be paid for the job. It wouldn't be worth my while to pursue things further without a proper investigation budget being authorised, and he did sound convincing, but I wasn't convinced.

'OK, I'll just have to send it back to the office,' I said with resignation in my voice. 'I'll just get your name for the paperwork, to say I've been here,' I continued confidently. I pulled out a small pad from my pocket. 'And you are Mr ...?' I asked, with pen poised.

I heard the voice of a young child laughing somewhere from within the house. After a few seconds of heavy silence, I looked up to see his blank, uncaring expression hadn't changed.

'You don't need my name, and the bloke you want doesn't live here, OK?' he said and began closing the door.

'Can I just...' I began, but the door was closed firmly in my face.

It wasn't often that bluffing failed so completely. 'Damn', I thought. Now I had to waste time checking things further. I was sure it was him, but not sure enough. I may have had to defend my actions later in court, wanted to ensure I was not embarrassed. One side of his house led to an open field, and the area appeared to be a new estate. I walked to a neighbouring house and knocked on the door. An older man answered, and I gave him a reassuring smile.

'G'day mate! I was just wondering if Bob Crawley lives next door, I've got a delivery for him,' I said, motioning to my documents.

He glanced at them, and back to me, saying slowly, 'I really don't know, I'm sorry, they only moved in there a month ago, and they seem to keep to themselves. It's a family there, I know that much but I don't know if the father's called Bob.' He seemed embarrassed that he didn't know his neighbours, but was happy to talk none the less. 'We get a lot of new people moving in here you know. This is a new area. It was only opened up for *subdivision about three years ago, and look at how many houses there are now! I was one of the first to build, I moved from Glenfall because my house was too big.'* I let him ramble on a little longer. He must live by himself, and I felt sorry for the lonely old man.

I soon looked at my watch, cutting him short with *'Oh dear, it really is getting late. I better head back to my office!'* He smiled placidly – a knowing smile from a man that had left the fast life years ago.

'OK then, I hope you can deliver it, I'm sorry I couldn't be of more help,' he said a wistful expression on his face. I knew he didn't want me to go, but I wasn't there for charity.

I looked to the crimson Canberra horizon as I drove off, and watched the street lights flicker on a moment later. It was getting dark, and I only had a few more jobs before I could return to Sydney. I stopped a few streets away to get out a road map, and began looking for a phone booth symbol. I was in luck as there was one nearby, and I was soon parking outside it. My first call was to directory assistance, but unfortunately there were no new listings for Crawley, and none listed for that particular address. I called an associate to see if there was any listing for the house in another name, and it appeared there was. I took note of the name and number, thanked her and hung up. I dialled for the third time. *'It was probably a false name,'* I thought, as the phone began to ring through my handset. It wouldn't be from previous tenants, because it was a new building. Unless it was a friend's house. Unlikely.

'Hello?' answered the voice of a young girl. She sounded about eight or nine years old and I seemed to remember hearing her in the background earlier when speaking to the phantom Mr Crawley.

'Hello there ... I was just wondering if your last name was Crawley. Is that your last name?' I asked in my most soothing tone.

'Yes. Yes, that's my last name ... Jennifer Crawley. What's your name?'

I ignored her question, steamrolling through with, 'Is your dad called Bob, Jennifer?'

'Yes. Do you want me to get him?' she asked innocently.

'Ah ... No that's all right, I'll call back later. Thank you!' I replied. 'Goodbye' she said and hung up. Jumping back into my car I returned to his address, now certain that I'd been speaking to him all along. Children can be so blissfully ignorant sometimes!

I cruised along slowly. There was nobody outside his house, and I wondered if my call to Jennifer had alerted her father. I parked five or six houses away from the Crawley residence, just in case. His squashed nose, thick hands and aggressive attitude were still fresh in my mind. I didn't want trouble, and preferred that he didn't have a chance to attack the car, or see my registration plate number. Dusk had fallen and I noticed the council hadn't finished installing the street lights yet on this street, perhaps because it was a new estate.

Walking to the front door I tripped over a small tricycle in the pathway, hitting it with my shin and sending it skidding a metre or so, rusty wheels screeching loudly through the quiet evening. I stopped and waited while the pain in my shin grew warmly. Ouch. I remembered noticing the tricycle there when I'd left earlier. Why did I forget it? Perhaps I was preoccupied. I looked expectantly at the windows. Light shone through curtains, illuminating the garden outside with an unnatural brightness. I waited, but there was no response. More carefully this time, I walked towards the front door and stood listening to the sounds of family conversation inside. *'No time like the present,'* I thought, rapping loudly on the solid wooden door.

No sooner had I knocked when the voices fell silent. I listened to the sound of work boots clomping loudly towards me on a polished wooden floor. I waited, not unlike I imagined Jack (of The Beanstalk fame) would wait for the nasty giant. The door swung open, and bright light slapped me in the face. I squinted at the silhouette of Bob Crawley as he filled the doorframe.

'Yes, what is it this time? I told you he doesn't live here,' he said roughly. I could tell he was genuinely surprised to see me, and was glad my call to his daughter had been a clean pretext. At this point, I intended to dump the documents on him, regardless of any thoughts he may have about the matter.

'Ah, yes. I called my office, and they said there was no problem after all. Apparently this is the right place, and I was just told to leave the documents with you,' I said dismissively. I was wearing a barely noticeable grin on my face, and was having difficulty in stopping it from spreading. I thrust the documents towards him, but he leapt back from them as if physical contact would somehow seal his fate. The power of paperwork! He scowled at me as he slammed the door violently. I paused for a moment, allowing myself a full and uninhibited smile. 'OK, have it your way!' I thought.

Kneeling down slightly, I saw a sliver of light shining underneath the front door; I carefully edged the documents into the opening. I tapped them, sending the paperwork slithering into the house and turned away, happy I'd sorted out this difficult job. It gives one a certain sense of satisfaction to be able to complete the harder jobs, and I was feeling rather smug as I continued down the dark pathway.

CRASH! I spun around in response to the noise, finding the front door had been thrown violently open, hitting the other side of the house. The dark figure of Bob Crawley charged at me through the brightness like a locomotive from a tunnel. He had a determined scowl on his face, and it didn't take me long to decide I didn't want to be caught. I turned and ran, body straining to accelerate as fast as it possibly could. I knew he wasn't far behind, and he had the advantage of momentum as well. I hit the road and turned right.

My legs began pounding the pavement like pistons, as I ran for my life. It was dark and I strained my eyes to check the path ahead was clear; thinking that to trip now would be fatal. I stole a glance behind, and saw he was close, but wasn't gaining ground. 'Where can I go?' I thought, glancing about as I ran. There was nowhere. The streetlights didn't work, and I was nearing the last of a row of houses. Across the road was an open field, and soon there would be open fields on each side. This wasn't good as there would be no witnesses to my drama, nobody to hear my screams. I cursed myself for gorging some fast food only half an hour ago, my stomach still heavy and sluggish. He surprised me with his speed as he didn't look like an Olympic sprinter. Why wasn't anybody else around? Why were there no cars driving past. Isn't there anybody in this whole street to run to? I wondered frantically.

I ran past a well-lit, open, but empty garage, deciding it would be my only hope. I didn't want to continue running into the dark wilderness, and this house was almost at the end of the row. I turned sharply and ran back towards the garage. I saw the look on his face, one of grim determination. He wasn't surprised to see me turn and run towards him, but he didn't alter his speed either. I thundered down the concrete driveway into the empty garage, and saw a ten-speed pushbike leaning against the rear wall.

I wasn't scared of facing him (much!), but was going to do everything I possibly could to avoid it. I intended to pick up a bike and hurl it towards his advancing body in an attempt to entangle him in a mass of spokes and cogs. Just as I was lining up to grab the bike, I saw an internal doorway. With seconds to spare, I grabbed the handle, flung it open, leapt inside and pulled the door sharply closed behind me. It had a tiny twist lock on the interior of the handle, and I tried to twist it quickly. In my haste, I fumbled on the first attempt, but tried again and secured it. Just as the lock turned, there was an enormous thump as the Crawley monster slammed into the other side.

The handle began twisting and rattling frantically as he tried to get through. The door was flimsy and hollow. I knew it wouldn't hold out for long. Lungs heaving, I spun around inside the tiny laundry. I saw a bucket of washing powder and thought about throwing the powder into his eyes if he broke through the door. I noticed another door out of the laundry. Without a moment's hesitation, I launched myself through this new door, leaving the loud, angry, banging noises behind me. I slammed it closed and looked for the lock, but there was none. I spun around to search for further escape routes or other weapons, quite unprepared for the sight that greeted my eyes.

Before me I could see a family at home in their living room. A mother was stirring dinner on the stove, a son halfway through raiding the fridge and a daughter spread-eagled over the carpet, talking to a girlfriend on the phone. A father sat comfortably on the couch watching television, while two pimply youths, stood by the dining-room table. In union, as if it was a well-rehearsed movement, their heads turned towards me, eyes looking directly into mine. Nobody spoke. I stood, heaving and panting from my sprint and the excitement. I tried to say, '*I'm terribly sorry for bursting in on you like this*'. What actually came out of my mouth was something more like, '*I Ahahah rry ... bus ahaha busti ... ting ahahah hisssahahah.*' I couldn't get a word to make sense due to my rapid panting. I tried again but my heaving chest failed me. I gave up, realising my panting garble might be more alarming than my actual presence. I stood there heaving while I got my breath back, trying hard to offer a smile to the startled occupants.

They sat motionless and watched. The room was silent, save for my heavy breathing, and the sound of the television. Nobody screamed, nobody moved. Oddly, none of them seemed the slightest bit concerned, as if they were calmly waiting for me to catch my breath, so I could explain what I was actually doing in the middle of their living room. It took a while. I gulped the air hungrily, making hand gestures to the effect that I would explain everything just as soon as I physically could. The daughter on the phone began saying, '*...Yes, I'm still here, Cheryl, but you just won't believe what has happened. There's this guy who has just burst into our living room...*' Their eyes drilled right through me. Not in a malicious way but more as an audience watches a performer, waiting for his next act. After my dramatic entrance, there just had to be more.

'*I'm sorry,*' I said, thankful that I'd finally said something that could be understood. I paused as I took another few deep breaths. '*I was being ... I was ...*' I heaved.

'*Take your time, mate ... get your breath back first,*' said the father gently from the sofa. He made no move to get up. I took a few more breaths, and the mother began stirring the pot again. Life was getting back to normal in this household.

'I was being chased, I'm a process server, and I just served some court documents on ... (I took a breath) ... on one of your neighbours.'

'That's fine mate, no worries, you're safe now. Would you like me to ring the police?' he asked, slowly rising from his chair.

'No, it's all right. I think he may still be outside though,' I replied. 'I'll go and have a look. Would you like a smoke?' he asked politely.

'No thanks,' I heaved at his inappropriate offer. I wondered why they didn't think my presence was odd, and I decided that Canberra must be a little different to the rest of the country.

'How about a cup of tea?' asked the mother kindly. 'I've just put the kettle on if you want one.'

'I ... ah ... OK,' I replied gratefully.

'I'll check if he is still outside,' said the father, leaving the room.

'So what exactly was it that you gave to him then?' quizzed the mother.

I explained what it was, and why it might have upset him. The documents related to a tax fraud that had recently been exposed. The government had allowed tax deductions for those investing in the horseracing industry. To take advantage of the various tax incentives, an enterprising con man devised a scheme where people could 'invest' large amounts of money to obtain a 'share' of various expensive racehorses. This investment would then be claimed as a tax deduction. The group induced a large number of well-paid people from various groups such as solicitors, who had each agreed to outlay anything from a hundred thousand dollars to over a million dollars in some cases.

After the first year of operation, it was revealed that the horses in the scheme were nearly worthless, and many people lost money.

Mr Crawley had actually borrowed a huge sum of money to take part in the scheme, and was now faced with paying off a large loan for something he'd never receive. It wasn't surprising he was annoyed. Apart from suddenly becoming seriously out of pocket, there were even doubts about the legality of the scheme, and it was suggested that the tax deductions themselves were not legal either. I didn't go into detail, but explained to her that he was being faced with a large bill for nothing, due to a fraud. She seemed to understand. Soon I was cradling a comforting cup of tea.

Her husband returned shortly to report that their angry neighbour was still lurking outside.

'I'm just going to go and talk to him,' he said. I admired his courage, noting that he wasn't a well-built muscle man, looking more like the puny desk jockey. I stood partly behind a curtain near the door, and watched as he approached Bob Crawley. They spoke briefly then separated, the father returning inside.

'He wasn't real happy, but I think he'll leave you alone now,' he said. 'He seems very emotional at the moment. I haven't seen him before, but I know which house he lives in. His kids ride their bikes around this street after school. You can stay here as long as you like, it's no trouble at all,' he said comfortingly. I gulped another mouthful of hot tea, which burned my throat.

'No, thanks anyway, but I must get going,' I replied. I took another sip of the steaming tea, wincing slightly. 'Do you think he's still out there?' I inquired.

'No ... no I don't, but I'll walk you to your car if you want,' he said. I finished most of my tea, and thanked his wife profusely.

Feeling silly, I waved goodbye to the rest of the household saying, 'Sorry if I ... startled you all,' then followed the father to the front door. I let him walk out first then followed close behind.

We arrived at my car, and again I was glad I'd parked it a short distance from the job. A quick check revealed all windscreen wipers in order, and no dents in any panels. I hopped into the driver's seat and started the engine. Winding down the window I called out, *'Thanks again,'* meaning it far more than I could ever make it sound. The father nodded knowingly, a slight smile on his face as I pulled out, accelerating into the night.

CHAPTER 34: TRAINING COURSES

Skills and training formalised

In the last few years, as part of the national vocational and education training system, investigation training has become more formalised across Australia, as the skill requirements or competencies have become identified in National Training Packages for different industries[77]. These industries range from Asset Security, Public Safety and Local Government where there are identified compliance and investigation roles to industries such as Seafood (Fisheries compliance) and Mercantile Agents, where investigations and surveillance are a specialization.

There are now a number of nationally recognized qualifications in investigation and surveillance, like the Certificate III in Investigative Services (PRS30303) in the Asset Security Training Package. This Certificate is now a prerequisite for Investigator licensing in all states of Australia.

The section at the end of this chapter shows how different parts of the book relate to these qualifications. One of the positive developments in training is the recognition that many people learn skills informally, through the hard experiential school of knocks. Under the new training system, training providers are required to recognize what skills students already have so they do not have to relearn what they can already do. This is known as Recognition of Prior Learning (RPL), and means students with experience in the area need only complete part of a course, to get the whole qualification.

Finding a good course provider

There have been several 'dodgy' PI courses over the years, so it is important to ensure you are getting nationally recognised

---

[77] www.training.com.au

training and qualifications through a reputable provider. You can check registered training organisations (RTOs) against the national register[77]. Ask around and check the quality of the training before you part with your money. Due to the eagerness of some who have been strongly influenced by James Bond movies, a market niche has evolved providing some courses of dubious content and at exorbitant prices. Some naive trainees have found themselves paying excessively to be trained in real PI situations, unrealistically centred on the airport and limos, or the odd chartered helicopter flight. Far removed from the average working environment, such courses are light on content and heavy on entertainment.

Charles Sturt University[78] runs a very good, but not widely known, investigators course. Although largely designed for government investigators such as police and Australian Customs Services (ACS), it does have very good instructors who provide comprehensive training in the industry, mainly aimed at the factual side of investigation. It is live-in, tertiary-level training conducted at the Goulburn Police Academy.

TAFE Plus[79] at Meadowbank, NSW runs a detailed Investigative Services Certificate III course. Participants of this course develop detailed knowledge and skills in planning and conducting investigations both factual and surveillance investigations. The course also provides access to the latest investigative techniques, equipment and invaluable *practical* surveillance exercises. These include hands on experience in areas such as document examination, debugging and camera specialist equipment. The National Investigation and Research Training Centre (NIRTC)[80] is a good investigator training establishment, located in NSW. They offer a range of courses, including practical hands-on experience.

---

[78] Charles Sturt University www.csu.edu.au
[79] TAFE Plus Ph(02) 9942-3695 www.tafensw.edu.au
[80]National Investigation & Research Training Centre www.nirtc.com.au

Another valuable PI training school is *The Australian School of Security and Investigations*[81] run by Adrian Holt. This school conducts courses all over Australia, as well as occasionally running courses overseas. This is an excellent training organisation, which provides comprehensive training over both investigations and security courses. They also have an online facility for students to train in a home environment.

The Australian Security Academy[82] is run by Mike Evans, and is highly recommended. Based in Queensland, they run PI courses all over Australia, and provide training to several government departments. For general PI training information and resources, the best Australian PI website would have to be www.investigateway.com. Michael Hessenthaler has put together an extremely informative site with many excellent PI resources. Michael has also written a great book titled *All You Ever Wanted To Know, And All You Should Know About Private Investigation*, among others. Aimed primarily towards the factual side of the investigation industry, it makes an ideal companion to *Behind the Private Eye*, which concentrates on physical surveillance. Another great companion book to this one is *Investigations Made Simple*[83] by Garry Maher, which is one of few Australian investigator resources.

The *Investigator's Guide*[84] is also another good training book which covers general investigation topics, though more on factual areas than surveillance.

Two excellent international PI websites are www.nettrace.com.au and www.pimall.com, which have a range of resources and links to PI's in other countries.

---

[81] Australian School of Security & Investigations www.trainingschool.com.au
[82] Australian Security Academy www.australiansecurityacademy.com.au
[83] Investigating Made Simple www.investigatingmadesimple.com **ISBN** 0975159429
[84] *The Investigator's Guide* by Ashley Keith **ISBN** 0731671716

Private investigator licensing

Current licensing legislation and administrative bodies are listed below. The Commonwealth Mutual Recognition Act 1992 - Section 17 also provides interstate recognition for some licence holders in several states[85].

NEW SOUTH WALES – Commercial Agents and Private Inquiry Agents Act 2004. Licences are administered by NSW Police. Applicants need Certificate III in Investigative Services and have no criminal record. Prior to July 2005, NSW PI licences were issued by local courts.[86]

QUEENSLAND – Security Providers Act (1993). Licenses are administered by the Office of Fair Trading (QLD)[87] Applicants need Certificate III in Investigative Services.

VICTORIA – Private Agency Act (1966), though this legislation is being amended due to the introduction of the (separate) Private Security Act 2004. Licenses are administrated by the Private Agents Registry, Victorian Police[88]. Applicants need Certificate III in Investigative Services.

SOUTH AUSTRALIA – Security and Investigation Agents Act (1995). Licenses are administered by the Office of Consumer and Business Affairs[89] Applicants must complete Certificate III in Investigative Services.

---

85 www.ocba.sa.gov.au/licensing/security/09_interstate.html
86 www.lawlink.nsw.gov.au/lc.nsf/pages/ca_pial
87 www.fairtrading.qld.gov.au
88 www.police.vic.gov.au/document/VP1080.pdf
89 www.ocba.sa.gov.au/licensing/security

WESTERN AUSTRALIA – Security & Related Activities (Control) Act (1996) Licences are administered by the Commercial Agents Branch, Western Australian Police Service[90]. There are no educational prerequisites (yet) to obtain licences, but applicants must not have a criminal record.

AUSTRALIAN CAPITAL TERRITORY – There are no license requirements yet, but this will change soon with new legislation. Clients may require ACT PI's to hold a NSW licence though. Associated legislation recently released is the Security Industry Act 2003[91] though this doesn't cover investigator licences.

NORTHERN TERRITORY – Commercial and Private Agents Licensing Act 1979. Licences are administered by the Consumer Affairs Office.[92] Applicants must be at least 18 years old and not bankrupt.

TASMANIA – Security and Investigations Agents Act 2002. Licenses are administered by the Magistrates Court of Tasmania[93]. Applicants must pass a criminal record check and complete a minimum Certificate II in Investigations within 12 months of licence issue.

---

[90] www.police.wa.gov.au/Services/CommercialAgents.asp?InquiryAgentLicence
[91] www.fairtrading.act.gov.au/Sectors/security.htm
[92] www.nt.gov.au/justice/graphpages/cba/licences/commercial.shtml
[93] www.consumer.tas.gov.au/business_affairs/security_agents

CONCLUSION

The surveillance professional is a photographic spy, working deep under cover. Alone and without support, he can only use his wit and skill to get results within a difficult operating environment. The surveillance professional has few friends, as it is often a lonely occupation, where you spend solitary hours just watching and waiting. You are a coiled spring that never sleeps, waiting for a few precious seconds of activity that can be caught on tape, but only if you are ready.

I've been a PI since 1988. Now with a lovely family, I figure there is more to life than unpredictable working hours and very early morning starts. It's a tough business, and sometimes best done by the young or single. I now work more as an industry speaker and training consultant, rather than sweating it out doing surveillance, but still take on occasional jobs as it keeps my mind sharp trying to second guess the other side.

Few realise the massive national benefit of the PI's work - keeping fraud in check. I guess the surveillance professional is sometimes too good at remaining hidden from public view, and with it being such a niche industry, nobody really knows what goes on in our world.

This book may allow others to really see a little of what happens and why. It may in some tiny way, show surveillance professionals doing a lot more for society than the shadowy PI images give them credit. The general trend is that privacy is to be protected at any costs, and this includes high insurance premiums, though few would ever make the association between absolute protection of privacy and the insurance premiums they pay each year. Hollywood has long depicted the profession as something it is not, and few really know the inside story on the surveillance professional. It is a lot less 'Hollywood' and a lot more psychology, a lot more probability, a lot more patience, and a lot more difficult. Replace the Hollywood image with one of a sweaty agent in the back of the car, waiting for hours, knowing he may return with nothing to show for his day's work. Replace the image of the fast-paced PI lifestyle with a week spent getting only thirty seconds of video evidence.

The life of a surveillance professional has a flavour that few will ever taste. It's never easy, but for those who have enjoyed the sweet nectar of success, pitting your wits against others when all the odds are stacked against you, succeeding and winning the game, climbing the mountain for no other reason than because it is there, for having the confidence in yourself to succeed. That, to me, is life itself. It's now time for a new generation of PI's to continue this challenge, this crazy, unpredictable journey, this important community service of being a Private Investigator.

© **Chris Cooper**

About the Author

Chris Cooper began working is security from 1987 and was soon locating debtors and delivering court papers as a process server. By 1989 he had started his own PI business, and also passed selection for the Australian Special Forces Reserves. For the next thirteen years Chris worked as both a Commando and a private investigator. He completed several investigator training courses with both NSW TAFE and Charles Sturt University. Having secretly followed and photographed hundreds of people throughout his career as a PI, Chris has a wealth of experience which he now shares with readers in this book.

Chris has worked on large factual investigations like the Kangaroo Rock disaster at Manly (91 injured). He worked as team leader on many large surveillance operations, including some requiring the arrest of many offenders. He has conducted inquiries and subsequent raids to recover counterfeit stock. He has been undercover on covert operations under the guise of occupations ranging from factory worker to 'qualified' X-Ray technician. He has infiltrated criminal networks distributing counterfeit goods and pirate pay-TV services, resulting in arrests and subsequent convictions. He has been a live-in armed bodyguard to several clients. He has worked on a remote goldmine in the Philippines in a heavily occupied terrorist area, narrowly avoiding a kidnapping attempt.

In 1999 Chris was posted overseas to Bougainville with the Army, where he personally devised and instigated "*Clean-up Bougainville Day*" which was approved by the Defence Force. It brought the Australian Army and several warring factions such as the BRA together for a community orientated activity day.

On a personal level Chris has experienced life in many areas, including a qualified BridgeClimb tour leader, personally manufacturing the torches for the 2004 Greek Olympics, working as a model and stand-in actor on films such as Mission Impossible, among other unusual occupations. Author photographs are available at www.neomatrix.com.au/books .

Chris is experienced in all aspects of surveillance. Although still involved in the industry as a speaker and consultant, he is now conducting government funded research and development into a new positioning and tracking technology. Chris lives in Sydney with his wife Alison and two children.

RELEVANT TRAINING PACKAGES & QUALIFICATIONS

The following tables indicate how specific parts of the book relate to units of competence from a number of national Qualifications in the Asset Security, Public Safety, Public Sector, Seafood Industry and Financial Services Training Packages:

PRS03 Asset security
PRS30303 Certificate III in Investigative Services

Core Units:	Page reference
PRSIS311A Work effectively in the investigative services industry	3, 349, 456, 498, 498, 498, 500, 534
PRSIS301A Determine method of investigation	13, 47, 72, 116, 148
PRSIS302A Compile investigative report	13, 72, 446, 447, 490
PRSIS303A Provide quality investigative services to clients	176, 349, 351, 355
PRSIS304A Conduct surveillance	13, 47, 72, 116, 148, 177, 178, 179, 189 , 421, 445, 446, 447, 456, 490
PRSIS305A Organise and operate a surveillance vehicle	159, 159, 160, 172, 178, 184, 264
PRSIS306A Gather information by factual investigation	72, 177, 178, 179, 179, 184, 187, 189 , 421, 446, 447, 456, 490
PRSIS307A Conduct interviews and take statements	116, 446
PRSSO302A Maintain a safe workplace and environment	500
PRSSO306A Maintain effective workplace relationships	376, 349, 355, 421
PRSSO307A Manage own work performance and development	29, 172, 200
PRSSO311A Prepare & present evidence in court	446, 447, 456

Electives:	
PRSIS308A Operate information gathering equipment	148, 151, 154, 159, 179, 184, 187
PRSIS310A Use and maintain operational equipment	148, 159, 334, 376, 426
PRSSO315A Store and protect information	72, 108, 116, 421, 456, 498
PRSSO221A Contribute to investigative activities	13, 148, 447, 490

PSP04 Public sector

PSPREG414A Conduct surveillance	177, 177, 178, 178, 179, 179, 189 , 189 , 421, 421, 445, 446, 447, 490
PUAPOL028A Manage investigation information processes	72, 108, 116, 177, 421
SRSOGP012A Carry out an investigation	72, 177

PSP30204 Certificate III in Government (Border Protection)
PSP40204 Certificate IV in Government (Border Protection)

PSPBORD301A Conduct patrols	47, 421, 428
PSPREG414A Conduct surveillance	177, 178, 179, 189, 421

PUA00 Public safety

PUAESU001A Plan an electronic surveillance operation	72, 148, 376
PUAESU002A Execute an electronic surveillance operation	148, 376
PUAPSU001A Conduct surveillance of subject(s)	177, 178, 179, 189, 421
PUAPSU002A Plan a surveillance operation	177, 178, 179, 189 , 421
PUAPSU003A Provide surveillance evidence and documentation	445, 446, 446, 447, 490
PUAPSU004A Communicate in a surveillance environment	376, 377, 378, 425
PUAPSU005A Perform physical foot surveillance	175, 240
PUAPSU006A Perform physical mobile surveillance	175, 264
PUAPSU007A Take covert surveillance photographs & video imagery	148, 151, 154, 179, 184, 187

SFI04 Seafood industry

SFI30404 Certificate III Seafood Industry (Fisheries Compliance)
Functional area: Compliance operations Specialist Units:

PUALAW003A Give evidence in a judicial or quasi-judicial setting	446, 447, 456
PUAPOL004A Gather, collate and record information	72, 177, 178, 179, 179, 184, 187, 189 , 421, 446, 447, 456, 490
PUAPOL005A Use and maintain operational equipment	148, 159, 376, 376, 377, 378
PUAPOL006A Facilitate effective communication in the workplace	376, 377, 378, 425
PUAPOL009A Assist in the judicial process	446, 447, 456
PUAPOL010A Perform administrative duties	116, 446, 175-176, 426, 445-446, 455-456
PUAPOL011A Manage own professional performance	29, 172, 200

SFI40404 Certificate IV in Seafood Industry (Fisheries Compliance)
Functional area: Surveillance

SFICOMP402B Plan the surveillance operation	13, 72, 176, 177-179, 184, 189, 421, 424
SFICOMP403B Operate and maintain surveillance equipment	148, 159, 376, 376, 377, 378
SFICOMP404B Operate an observation post	179, 189
SFICOMP405B Perform post-surveillance duties	175, 176, 426, 445, 446, 455, 456
SFICOMP406B Perform mobile surveillance	233, 235, 175, 264, 177, 421, 178, 179, 189 , 189, 190, 270,

FNS04 Financial services

FNS30404 Certificate III in Financial Services (Mercantile Agents)
Sectoral Core unit:

FNSMERC304A Locate subjects	72, 104
FNSMERC303A Serve legal process	522, 327

www.ingramcontent.com/pod-product-compliance
Lightning Source LLC
Chambersburg PA
CBHW070925100726
47908CB00001B/102